The Scott-Dunlap Ring

By George La Fountaine

TWO-MINUTE WARNING
FLASHPOINT
THE SCOTT-DUNLAP RING

The Scott-Dunlap Ring

George La Fountaine

Coward, McCann & Geoghegan, Inc.
New York

Copyright © 1978 by George La Fountaine

All rights reserved. This book, or parts thereof, may not be
reproduced in any form without permission in writing from the
publisher. Published on the same day in Canada by Longman Canada
Limited, Toronto.

SBN: 698-10871-X

Library of Congress Cataloging in Publication Data

La Fountaine, George.
    The Scott-Dunlap Ring.

    1.   Scott, Bob, 1849–1882—Fiction.   2.   Dunlap,
Jim, 1844–1928—Fiction.   I.   Title.
PZ4.L1678Sc   [PS3562.A312]   813'.5'4   77-20112

Printed in the United States of America

Acknowledgments

I wish to thank the following for their time and energy in the researching of *The Scott-Dunlap Ring*: Bette Barker, New Jersey State Library, Trenton, New Jersey; Jacqueline Bicket, Watseka Public Library, Watseka, Illinois; Mrs. Marion B. Cook, Waterford Public Library, Waterford, New York; Margaret E. Craft, Wyoming Historical and Geological Society, Wilkes-Barre, Pennsylvania; C. A. Davis and Sal Apablasa, Southern California Safe Company, Montebello, California; Mrs. Joan Dye, Quincy Public Library, Quincy, Illinois; Ralph Eckley, Monmouth College, Monmouth, Illinois; Charles A. Isetts, Ohio Historical Society, Columbus, Ohio; Oscar R. Guilbaut, Rockville Public Library, Rockville, Connecticut; Sarah K. Rugen, Troy Public Library, Troy, New York; Mrs. Martha Squires, Chemung County Historical Society, Elmira, New York; Marion Taub, Saratoga Springs Public Library, Saratoga Springs, New York; Mark Harris, Louisville Free Public Library, Louisville, Kentucky; Elizabeth Hildebrand, Peoria Public Library, Peoria, Illinois; Michelle Hudson, Department of Archives and History, Jackson, Mississippi; Irma and Bill King, Lee County Genealogical Society, Keokuk, Iowa; Mrs. Dorothy Lacomis, Pittston Memorial Library, Pittston, Pennsylvania; Linda Larson, Kenton County Public Library, Covington, Kentucky; Charles A. McCarthy, Journalist, Pittston, Pennsylvania; Bruce McSheehy, Connecticut State Library, Hartford, Connecticut; Cathy Moore, Carnegie Public Library, Clarksdale, Mississippi; Phyllis Morse, Steele Memorial Library, Elmira, New York; Vernon H. Nelson,

Moravian Church Archives, Bethlehem, Pennsylvania; New York Historical Society, New York, New York; Dawn M. Tybur, Albany Institute of History, Albany, New York.

Especially helpful were those dear friends to whom I turned time and time again: Stanley Greenberg, Forbes Library, Northampton, Massachusetts; Ruth Reuter, Warsaw Free Public Library, Warsaw, Illinois; Robert Colwell, Los Angeles Public Library, Los Angeles, California; Ruth Richards, Osterhout Free Library, Wilkes-Barre, Pennsylvania.

For my mother, Milly Verna,
who taught me how to laugh.

The Scott-Dunlap Ring

Chapter One

The old man with the silver imperial goatee stood in the small dark space between the millinery shop and the bakery, hypnotized by the gold-leaf lettering that occupied most of the window just across the street. Beyond the lettering a small gas lamp had been left burning near the safe, its lively flame beckoning seductively.

A chill March wind screamed between the buildings, almost bowling him over with its force. He raised a hand to steady the derby on his head. With the other he massaged the chilled skin of his lower leg. But his eyes, narrowed to tiny slits, never left the flame beyond the gold lettering.

The aching leg relieved somewhat, he steadied himself with the gold-topped cane. The sound of melting snow sliding from the roof was interrupted by the clopping of a horse's dull hooves. A gray mare steamed across his view, drawing an empty wagon home, its headless master dozing in a high-collared coat. Leaning into the shadows, he waited for the intruders to pass his sanctuary.

When the street became silent save for the wind, he withdrew his pocket watch. Shucking it from inside the warm vest with great difficulty, he moved out under the streetlamp. The watch

9

*was snapped closed and returned to its nest, as he noted with sat-
isfaction that he had been there over two hours. The years had
taught him patience, but all his senses were beginning to stir with
a great excitement.*

He returned to the dark shadows and his careful vigil.

Jim Dunlap had been thinking of Bridget Hickey since he had
first heard of the great fire three days before. As soon as the Chicago,
Rock Island and Pacific pulled into the yard, on the outskirts of the
ruined city, he hurried through his brakeman chores, pulling the coupling pins on all the cars before joining the crew on their breathless
journey into what had once been Chicago.

Familiar landmarks were gone. Four square miles of rubble made it
impossible to take a bearing. There was no way of telling what street
you were on, or even guessing what had been there before. The hundred thousand homeless were camped out on soot-covered lots, in
lean-tos salvaged from the debris.

The Rock Island crew disbanded on a corner they thought might be
Randolph, moving off uncertainly in the direction that might have
been toward home.

Strange charcoaled people appeared in Dunlap's path begging
coins and water. Dark-skinned children tugged at his clothes long after his pockets were emptied. Others sprang up before him, searching
his face as if he were someone they knew. He left them dazed and
disappointed.

A few temporary structures had already been erected on Clark
Street, a part of the fifty-nine hundred such buildings that would be
hastily thrown up in the first week following the fire.

A crudely lettered shingle attached with twine announced that the
Clark Street Saloon was doing business as usual beneath a huge canvas covering. Dunlap eased the wooden door aside and found himself
confronting several dozen soot-smudged men seated on makeshift
boxes, playing faro.

He drew only a brief glance from the players until a woman's voice
cried, "Jimmieeee!" Bridget Hickey dodged a rye barrel, circled two
roof supports and crashed into his arms. He spun her twice around
the room, the players smiling appreciatively.

"Oh, Jimmy, I was *so* worried about you!"

"I hurried faster than a man has a right to travel," he said into her auburn hair as he held her off the ground.

"The depots were all destroyed," she said. "I thought they might not let you back into the city."

"We came into the freight terminals outside of town."

She held him at arm's length, looking him over carefully. "Then you're all right?"

"I'm fine," he assured her, "and you look beautiful." He couldn't tell her that she smelled of smoke or that the once carefully arranged hair was awry and looked as if it might tumble to her shoulders at any moment.

She led him to an isolated corner. "It was terrible, Jimmy. There was no time to do anything. I could only save a few things . . . my clothes are all gone. The house where I lived is ashes. Kibbie took me to the lake where we spent the night."

Dunlap stiffened at the mention of her policeman suitor. "Then he's still around."

"He's been very good to me, Jimmy. While you were gone he took care of me," she said defensively.

"I see." He dropped her hand gently, letting the slim fingers slip from his grasp. He hadn't told her of their violent rivalry, had never mentioned the numerous times the Clark Street patrolman had had him arrested or beaten. He doubted she even suspected that his long periods of absence were arranged by the jealous patrolman and his friends.

"He's on duty today," she warned. "He's been by twice already."

"I can take care of myself," he boasted, taking her hands and drawing her into the lamplight of the gloomy tent saloon. "You're still the most beautiful girl in Chicago, Bridget Hickey—what's left of it, that is." He gave her a gentle tug and she came forward willingly. He kissed her hard, wishing he had been thoughtful enough to bring something for her to wear, a new dress or a Paris hat. He felt the full figure beneath his fingers. Then her eyes went wide and his head exploded.

Patrolman Kibbie had found them like that, alone in the corner, arms wrapped around each other. The younger man, the trespasser, had his back to Kibbie. Anger and jealousy carried the burly patrolman swiftly across the tent, the shot-filled stick a toy in his hands as he dropped Dunlap with a single blow.

Falling helplessly, Dunlap could hear Bridget scream. Wildly swinging kerosene lamps and angry voices crowded his head. Small charges went off in his skull, and for the brief instant when he hung suspended over the planked floor, he was back in Gettysburg with the 61st Ohio Volunteers. He heard the screams and shots, the cannon exploding near-by, the whistling of the balls, then nothing.

Someone jerked him roughly erect, but his legs were too fluid to support him. He thought he'd been shot again and tried to tell his companion it was difficult to travel when wounded.

Kibbie dragged him out to the ruins of Clark Street. One hand held him up to the October sunset, the other buried itself in Dunlap's middle, collapsing him completely. Jerking him taut, the patrolman sent a well-aimed fist into Jim's face.

Dunlap was unable to protect himself; his arms refused to respond. Someone kept urging him to fight, but he was powerless. Kibbie battered the limp, bloody face.

Dunlap woke as he was being unceremoniously loaded into an old phaeton. Several men with shields on their chests labored over his inert form.

"I told you never to show your face on my beat again, Jimmy Dunlap. You've been warned for the last time." The angry face boomed close and he could smell cheese. "I'll kill you, boy, if you ever turn up on Clark Street again."

Later he was bounced upright, and several patrolmen held him before someone who asked, "Complaint?"

"A toyer. Nabbed him with an eye tethered to the jeweler's shack on Clark Street."

"The Jew's place," someone added. "Up to no good, this one!"

"Looting?"

"Burglary be more like it."

"What happened to his face?"

"Put up a stiff one, he did."

"The bugger!" another offered.

The judge had little compassion. "Four previous offenses. This is very serious, Mister Dunlap. Two thirty-day sentences already this year. Perhaps sixty days' laboring in the toils may give you sufficient time to contemplate your future."

A sharp rap signaled the end of his case. Dunlap was led from the box and his vacancy quickly filled by another.

Released in time for the holidays only to find that his brakeman's job had been filled in his absence, Dunlap joined the bread lines. With thousands ahead of him, he patiently waited. His body had healed, his face no longer bore Kibbie's signature, yet he had gone two days without food, and it was common knowledge no one could survive longer than three days without sustenance. Years later a man named Dr. Tanner would prove to the world that he could fast for forty days, but in Chicago as the new year of 1872 blew in off Lake Michigan, three days was the outside estimate.

A looter hanged the night before from a lamp post swung in the breeze. The leather toe of the man's boot struck the post a hollow thump, but most gave it only a glance, for many looters had been stretched in the months following the great fire.

Dunlap's preoccupation was with finding work. He'd applied at several construction sites but had been turned away. Masons were doing a brisk business even in the dead of winter, but for the inexperienced there was nothing. Teachers and merchants labored under the weight of blocks of marble and stone, happy to have any employment. Salt added to the mortar allowed the workmen to lay stone and brick throughout the bitter winter. There was an army of manpower to choose from, and wages were pitifully low.

A carriage drew aside to allow a herd of cattle to bellow their way to market. "Jim! Jim Dunlap!" a voice cried. "Here, Jim!"

Dunlap saw a hand waving from the carriage window—Dave Raggio, his former landlord. "Over here!" he beckoned. Dunlap looked down the long file of men. There were four thousand still ahead of him; behind, the bread line stretched out of sight. Would he lose his place?

"It's all right," Raggio urged.

With a shrug Dunlap threaded his way out into the black dust raised by the cattle.

Raggio was a thin, nervous, rodent-like little man. "I heard the beak gave you two months this time."

"Aye," Dunlap shrugged good-naturedly.

"Two months," Raggio repeated to the man beside him in the carriage, who leaned out into the gray twilight and gave Dunlap a careful assessment. The passenger was a brute of a man, older than Raggio, with short, iron-gray hair and a large scar that ran from ear to chin, taking a wide hook at the corner of the mouth.

"Tom here just did five years," Raggio explained, bobbing his head between the two men. "Now *that's* something, Jim."

"Aye," Dunlap agreed.

The scar tugged the mouth open to reveal several missing teeth. Tom gave Dunlap his best attempt at a friendly smile. "Beats the picture frame," he grinned, thumbing the man dangling from the lamp post.

"That it does," Dunlap laughed.

Dust from the cattle enveloped them, depositing a fine layer of black on their clothing.

"Damn!" Raggio cursed, brushing at the sleeves of his gray coat. "If it's food you're wanting, Jim Dunlap," Raggio slapped the last particles free, "I've got a new place on Desplaines, just across the river. Cost me a fortune. Food prices are terrible, but it's there if you want a place."

Dunlap stuffed his hands deep into the pockets of his threadbare cloth coat. "I've no money, Dave—no prospects either. You wouldn't be able to make any profit from the likes of me."

"You've better times ahead," Tom Reilly prophesied. "You could do worse than taking Raggio's offer."

"I can't pay my way."

"You've always played square with me, Jim," Raggio grinned agreeably. "Brought me good customers," Raggio explained to his passenger. "Some of them are my best friends now."

That had been true, Dunlap thought. His travels with the Rock Island Line had brought him into contact with many Chicago-bound sharpers and gamblers. It was an easy matter to steer them to Raggio's boardinghouse. Once there, they met others of their kind—the city's cleverest gamblers, confidence men and thieves. Raggio provided

them with contacts, funds and alibis and for these favors was rewarded handsomely.

"You've got a heart-and-a-half, boy, and if it's work you're needing, who knows more people than Dave Raggio!"

Tom Reilly shook his bull head in the direction of the bread line.
"Is this more to your liking?"

"*That's* the most persuasive argument I've heard in months!" Dunlap laughed aloud.

The Desplaines boardinghouse was a large, sprawling brick mansion that had seen loftier days. Men flashing gold watches and pearl
stickpins paid little attention to Dunlap as he mounted the stairs to his
room. There were no clothes to unpack, no personal belongings save
what he wore on his back and carried in his pockets. Kitchen servants
filled a tub from boiling pots, and he had his first bath in months.
Reilly provided a razor, and Dave Raggio miraculously produced a
wardrobe left behind by a former tenant who had no doubt just beat
the law to the railway depot.

The cloth waistcoat with satin-faced lapels and the striped trousers
were a near fit. The waistcoat was a little tight through the shoulders
and the trousers reached the ground, but a kindly kitchen maid
rectified that.

Following a hearty lunch of beefsteak, boiled potatoes and steam-
ing cabbage, Dave Raggio and "Scarface" Tom Reilly took Dunlap
into an empty card room. Raggio worried his teeth with a solid gold
toothpick. "I understand your problem. You can't win against the
coppers, Jimmy boy. When they don't have the palm out, it's the back
of their hand! What's an honest man to do?"

"I'll find something soon and pay you back. You have my word on
it."

"Everybody knows Dunlap's word is sterling," Raggio told Tom
Reilly.

"How old might you be, then, Jim?" Tom asked.

"Twenty-seven."

"A young man of twenty-seven should be be thinking of his future."

"How many times that copper arrest you for nothing?" Raggio
asked. "How many?"

"Five . . ."

"And what has it got you?" Dave demanded, pressing in close. "You've lost your job! Been branded a common criminal! Who'll have you? You can't walk Clark Street without that fat copper thinkin' yer out to steal his girl! You've been marked for nothing!"

Reilly nodded. "That's the truth, boy."

"If it was me, now," Dave continued, "mind you, I'm jes saying, *if* it was me, I'd start thinkin' of Jim Dunlap. Start to find me some new friends. If it was me, I'd be saying to meself, 'Why should I take the blame and not share in the rewards!' You follow my thinkin'?"

Dunlap nodded soberly.

"There's always someone on the lookout for a levelheaded, square fellow, Jim," Reilly offered.

"I don't know what use I'd be . . ."

Reilly scoffed at this. "You've plenty of talents, lad! Dave told me you were a fine soldier!"

"Wounded even!" Dave announced.

"You never ran when the going got rough?"

"I never ran," Dunlap said firmly.

"When things got a little close you stood your ground."

"Aye," Dunlap said, "that I did."

"That's all that's asked," Reilly grinned.

Raggio struck a stick match to the twisted end of the cigarette that hung from Dunlap's lip. "Somebody is always needed to keep an eye open, somebody who won't dash for cover when things get sticky."

"Somebody who won't leave his friends in the lurch to save his own neck." Tom nudged Jim for his attention. "Dave says that you're a fellow who can be trusted, Jim."

Dunlap blew the smoke aside as he studied the two men studying him. He knew exactly where they were leading him, and though he didn't know the precise nature of the proposition, he knew it would be tempting.

"There's a good bit of change around for the right man," Reilly added, "but he has to move now."

"How much change?" Jim asked.

Reilly's eyes twinkled, he smiled his slow smile. "Two thousand dollars."

"Two thousand?" Dunlap blinked rapidly.

"How many years would you have to work on the Rock Island to make *that* kind of money, Jim?" Dave asked.

"Two thousand!" Dunlap shook his head, the pale blue eyes roving the room.

"A man can live pretty damn well on two thousand . . . a new wardrobe, pocket money—"

"Two thousand dollars!"

"A trip now and then."

Dunlap smiled warmly. "Your new man has just spent half of it."

It was a relatively simple assignment. All that was required was that he station himself outside the railway office and keep a sharp eye. Each time the night watchman moved toward the building, Jim gave the small window a single tap, warning the men inside to "hold the work." After the watchman had rattled the doorknob and was satisfied all was well inside, Jim waited until the guard moved from sight, then gave the window two loud taps, "Resume work." He had been given instructions for one last signal that thankfully was never required— three taps indicating "clear out as fast as possible."

Whenever the coast was clear, Jim would peek inside to watch the operation. Black gossamer hung over the front windows, while in the rear men with sledges sweated over the railway safe. It was impossible for him to see exactly what it was they were doing, but outside, it sounded to Jim like an army of blacksmiths worrying a large anvil into smithereens. Yet despite the racket, there were no curious shades raised in homes nearby, no questioning lamps lit. Jim could not understand why the commotion was not heard clear across town.

The night was ominously still—the sort of night every soldier on patrol dreaded. The moon was full, the air still. Every sound carried for miles. Every moving figure could be easily seen. Yet the hour before dawn found Jim easing a four-in-hand drag to the rear door where large cloth bags of tools were hurriedly loaded along with the prize. Dressed in a livery driver's uniform, Jim urged the four horses into a steady trot. The rented team was back in Chicago before the railway office opened for business, and everyone agreed he had done an ex-

cellent job. For the dozen signals given, for the arrangements with the
rented livery, he was paid $2,100.

It was Jim Dunlap's first trip to New York since the war. Fashionably dressed, he rode in the Pullman dining car, mingling with the
new rich of the industrial boom that was sweeping the country. The
Bessemer process had made steel an economical product, and several
hundred thousand tons were going into rails. Refrigeration had just
been developed, and Gustavus Swift was shipping dressed beef East
from Chicago in cold cars. Charles Pillsbury had brought the European chilled rolling process to the mills, and his company was shipping
thousands of tons of the new snowy white flour to be used in bread.
The discovery of oil provided jobs, built cities along the rail routes,
and gave birth to wooden tank cars, then pipelines. Oil created a need
for more rail, whose mileage in the few short years since the war had
doubled. A thirty-three-year-old man named John D. Rockefeller had
just formed the Standard Oil Company of Ohio. George Westinghouse
had improved his patented air brakes, inventing a new automatic air
brake for stopping trains. Alexander Bell was experimenting with a
dead man's ear to discover the means of transmitting sound.

Dunlap was swept east amid the heady excitement of growth,
wealth and progress. He rode with money in his pocket for the first
time in his life, listening to the new millionaires, laughing at their inside tales as if he'd been privy to this sort of information all his life.

George White had a small office over Meriam's Brevoort stables at
114 Clinton Place. The smell of horse, hay and tack pervaded the tiny
enclosure. Charles Meriam, White's business partner, moved in and
out frequently, forcing White to speak in a low soft voice.

Dunlap knew little about White. But all the information garnered
from Tom Reilly indicated that White was one of the best in the business.

According to Tom, White had been a successful businessman who
one unfortunate day had rented a livery to Mark Shinburn, a noted

bankie. Shinburn had been linked to a robbery and the team traced to White, resulting in White's conviction for bank robbery. After serving his sentence White had become Shinburn's partner, but their alliance had ended a few years earlier. To all appearances White was now the partner in a small respectable livery in New York City.

"I know Tom Reilly well, Mr. Dunlap. A square fellow if ever there was one. Unfortunately, he is so identifiable by now—the scar you understand—that, sadly, it makes it impossible for anyone to use him."

"He's just been released from Joliet and he's sorely in need of employment."

White sighed helplessly. "He'll be back inside soon, I'm sure of it. A pity to be sure—the waste of an excellent man."

"I was to tell you hello and mention that I yacked for him on a railway job." Dunlap laughed in embarrassment. "Those magic words were to open doors for me."

"'Yacked,' Mr. Dunlap, is a term used by the hoi polloi. I would advise you to eliminate Tom's quaint phrases from your vocabulary as soon as possible."

"Aye," Dunlap stammered.

"You might add 'aye' to that list, Mr. Dunlap. A gentleman should not resort to the language of a ragabash. Appearances, Mr. Dunlap, are the secret in this trade. Manners and appearances—those are the magic words that open doors."

"I'll heed your advice, Mr. White."

"Now, this venture of yours, was it your first?"

"Aye—I mean, yes, sir."

"A railway safe?"

"Yes, but I'm afraid the methods used left me with a very bad impression."

"In what way, Mr. Dunlap?" White was an older man with intense, watchful eyes.

"It bothered me the way the safe was broken," Dunlap explained. "Surely there must be a more civilized means of cracking a safe than simply smashing it to pieces with hammers!"

White smiled thoughtfully. "A noisy adventure, I'd wager."

"Not just noisy, Mr. White. Loud, tedious and risky."

"There are *always* risks, Dunlap, regardless of the methods employed. Never, ever, underestimate the risks. Each member of the group is dependent on the other. A moment of panic, someone leaves his post, and chains or leg irons are the reward. There is always risk."

White swiveled the chair to the desk, apparently absorbed in his papers. From far below a horse neighed, another answered, and soon a chorus of whinnies echoed throughout the stable.

"What assets do you offer, Mr. Dunlap?"

"I know a great deal about horses . . . explosives . . . I can handle both." White turned back and inspected Dunlap closely. "I expect nothing except your absolute loyalty. Disobey any of my rules, regardless of how foolish they may seem, and we will fall out immediately."

"Yes, sir."

"I do have something . . . an assignment in upstate New York. The man I send should be well dressed and of obvious means so as not to arouse suspicion. Do you think you can fill the part, Mr. Dunlap?"

"Yes, sir. I might very easily pass as a successful horse trader."

"Good. I think you might well be convincing. You will in no way be obligated to me beyond this one job. Is that clear?"

"Yes, sir."

"The planning is all. I will tell you what to look for and what to expect. I will teach you another way to turn off a bank. If the dangers exceed the rewards, then this too must be noted. I do not expect slanted reports. Without careful planning, without that special wisdom that tells us when to turn away from a lost cause, we face disaster. There are the Tom Reillys of the world and the Mark Shinburns. The laborers and the planners. A prison cell awaits the one, riches the other."

"I understand."

"Good." The desk drawer yielded two hundred dollars which White pressed into Dunlap's hand. "You'll need a good tailor and expense money." A business card with a quickly scrawled address was handed him. "Have him fit you out in a manner suitable to a successful trader."

"Yes, sir."

White smiled wistfully. "The great adventure, Mr. Dunlap, the great adventure."

The telegram delivered to the Meriam's Brevoort Stables in mid-August stated simply, "The horses await your inspection." It was signed "James Barton."

Two days later, George White arrived at the Delavan House in Albany. Seated in Dunlap's room, a dozen drawings before him, White said, pleasantly surprised, "You've done an excellent job!"

"Thank you," Dunlap chuckled modestly. "The drawings are accurate to four inches either way."

"Splendid. What about the watchman?"

"They have none. There's a burglar alarm over the door. It's a telegraphic alarm that works off batteries. It signals a small bell in the cashier's quarters upstairs and another in the bank's counting room. If the bank is closed, we won't have to worry about the one in the counting room."

"Anyone live in the bank?"

Dunlap drew aside the floor plan and directed White's attention to the drawing of the bank's second floor. He indicated the various rooms as he spoke. "The cashier and his family. There are two teen-aged daughters, Mary and Sarah, who sleep here, opposite the parent's sleeping quarters. There's a boy, about thirteen, he sleeps here. Down these stairs there's a servant girl, Ann Driscoll. Her quarters are clearly marked. The stairs are marked leading to the front door. The furniture in each room is drawn and the distance to the exits calculated. It's all there," he said confidently.

"Yes, I can see that. You've been very precise."

"The vault is on a separate diagram. Do you have a plan for how we turn it off?"

"No." White shuffled the drawings. "I'll have to study these first and double-check your floor plans. One can't be too careful."

"Of course," Jim acknowledged.

White slid the papers away and took up his glass of Old Crow. He sipped it, appraising Dunlap quietly. "You have a talent for this. You've nailed down the times and routines of all concerned and even some who may or may not be indirectly connected with the bank. These show a lot of thought. How did you get the inside of the cashier's apartment down so accurately?"

"Once their habits were established, it was a simple matter to gain entry while they were at church," Dunlap grinned, lighting a cigar. "I took the measurements required and planned an entry if needed. I wanted to have a copy of the door key to give you, but Mr. Van Hovenberg, the cashier, carries it with him at all times. So I did the next best thing. I made certain easy access was available through one of the windows. I've taken care to see the latch doesn't fit properly. We wouldn't want to find the window locked if we decided to use it."

"Very wise."

"You'll find train schedules there for Albany, Troy, Schenectady and Pittsfield. I wasn't sure what plans you might want to make for a hasty departure, so I included steamer schedules as well."

"Excellent!"

Dunlap blew a cloud of smoke at the ceiling. "What's the next step?"

"I think it's time for you to return to New York. I'll have no further need of you until everything's ready. If what you've shown me proves to be as you say, I should say . . . a month, weather permitting."

"What sort of weather did you have in mind?"

"Weather that will drive decent men indoors. I think you'll find that our sort of work requires our laboring in the most treacherous conditions. It would be nice to have a warm moonlit night to work by, but that is also the worst time possible. Villagers take moonlit strolls, young lovers chance late meetings. No . . . rain, sleet and snow are our allies. They require the windows to be shut, the curtains drawn. The fire crackling can mask an army marching by in song. The wind can drown out the sound of a steam engine, if need be. That, Jim, is *our* kind of weather. It may be another month yet."

Dunlap nodded wisely, rolling the cigar about between his fingers, inhaling the aroma of the rich tobacco.

"The clothes have done wonders for you," White laughed. "You look like a merchant prince."

Dunlap bowed his head graciously. "I was hoping you'd noticed the fruits of your investment."

"Well spent, I should say!" White roared, hefting the whiskey glass in toast. "Here's to a substantial return!"

The driving rain pelted the small courtyard of St. George's Episcopal Church in Schenectady. It gathered between the grave markers, leaving ankle-deep pools. There was just a small stone marking her grave. "Ellen Dunlap. Died August 22, 1852."

Dunlap stood alone in the courtyard, remembering the day as if it were only a month before, but twenty years had passed since they gathered there. His brother Andrew had stood solemnly on his left, while his sisters, Rebecca and little Ellen, had clung desperately to their ailing father. It would be weeks before he and little Ellen realized that she was gone forever.

Now from beneath the sealskin coat Jim drew two bundles of dried flowers. He held them close to his face, beneath the wide-brimmed hat to protect them from the downpour. Then he stooped to place one against the gravestone.

The hat was shifted to his chest and held over the remaining blossoms as he waited for a prayer or inspiration. When none was forthcoming, he said softly, "I should have come back sooner, but I couldn't. I couldn't bear to come here again. I didn't want to blame you for what happened, but I had to blame somebody. Nothing was ever the same after you died. We all did our best, but it just wasn't the same. I'm sorry."

The rain ripped across his face. He placed the hat on the damp, dark locks and tucked the flowers to his coat. The tiny offering against the marker sagged noticeably in the drenching rain. He shrugged helplessly before moving across the yard to his father's grave. Less than a year after his mother's death, they had assembled one last time to say goodbye to John Dunlap. "Died July 15, 1853," the stone reported.

Jim placed the remaining flowers against the marker. Rain poured off the gray slate roof of St. George's and down the limestone walls, leaving dark stains along the engulfing ivy. He glanced toward the church as he tried to find something appropriate to say. *What promise we must have had,* he thought. *Marriage, children, baptisms, a long line of Dunlaps to carry on what promised to be a blossoming, successful family.* Then, when he was seven, the unexpected death of his mother. Before the adjustment could be made, his father's funeral. Suddenly, the family was no more.

It had taken twenty years to return to the gravesite. Lean bitter years before Jim could make this last pilgrimage and put it from his mind forever. Now he stood hatless in the rain, unable to summon the words to explain his long absence. The rain ran down his face and deep beneath the collar. He placed the hat on his head, pulling the brim low over pale blue eyes. Thunder rolled and growled in disappointment. His boots sloshed through the water to the waiting carriage. He headed the animal toward the Mohawk River, past the shipyard where he had labored between crops when there was still a chance of holding farm and family together, before it all became impossible.

He crossed the Mohawk and checked the horse for a brief glance back at Schenectady, gray, dark and forbidding. Lightning flashed in the distance, and the accompanying thunderclap had the horse tugging insistently at the reins. He gave the animal its head and sent the carriage bowling toward Waterford, only a dozen miles distant, but a lifetime removed from the soggy graveyard of his youth.

Traffic on the Mohawk and Hudson Canal had been halted by the high winds and driving rain. Waterford villagers huddled warmly in their beds, secure against the first signs of approaching winter.

Jim Dunlap had reached the outskirts of town heading his team toward the home of cashier Van Hovenberg. He encountered no travelers or late-night villagers. It had been exactly as White had predicted.

The horses were tied downwind of a barn, beneath a large painted sign touting "Rising Sun shoe polish." He gave each one a reassuring caress, careful to see they were out of the wind-driven rain. A struck match, hidden between cupped fingers, allowed him to read his pocket watch. Right on time. The match dropped hissing to the mud. Hands inventoried the essentials,—the knife, the dry matches, the heavy Savage Navy revolver with the figure-eight trigger guard stuck in his waistband, the putty knife and cloth mask. Satisfied, Jim threw back the tarp at the rear of the wagon and brought out four bull's-eye lanterns. Each had been carefully checked for fuel before loading. The rest of the tools were covered again as he waited.

In only a few moments White appeared, walking casually. He lifted the tarp and Dunlap silently passed him a lantern.

Pete Curley, a local resident of some notoriety whose previous indiscretion at the Jennings Brothers Jewelry store in Waterford had hastened a quick retirement to the city of Troy, was the first to join them. Dunlap disliked Curley on sight.

George Leslie, a dapper Greek with formidable qualifications in the art of "turning off banks," arrived and took a lantern from Dunlap, cursing the rain under his breath in his native tongue.

White led off the procession toward the Saratoga County Bank. On the corner of Broad and Second streets, Ira Kingsland, a last-minute addition and an old friend of White's, showed himself momentarily, then stepped back into the shadows.

Jimmy Hope and Ned Lyons joined them as they passed the home of Doctor Heartt. Together they moved to the northeast corner of Broad Street and their two-story target.

The six assembled on the east side of the structure. They waited a full five minutes before Ira Kingsland arrived to tell them "All's well." Silently masks were pulled on, cloth sacks with eyeholes and a mouth opening. White nodded his first signal and Dunlap passed his lantern to Jimmy Hope. Leslie gave Dunlap a boost to the second story window, where the putty knife slipped the latch.

Curley took up a position next to Leslie, and Dunlap stepped from Leslie's hands to Curley's shoulder. In a few seconds he slid through the opening. Fishtailing into the house, Dunlap moved swiftly to the stairs. Treading the outside of each step, he unlocked the rear entrance. Each man moved quickly inside and the lanterns were struck.

Dunlap carried the lantern as he led Curley to the servant girl's quarters. Above him, Jim could hear the others moving into the cashier's bedroom.

Lamplight played on the sleeping figure. Curley placed the cold thick barrel of a Freeman Percussion Army revolver against Ann Driscoll's forehead, the icy weapon waking her immediately. Clapping a hand over her mouth, he hissed, "I'll kill you in a second if you make nary a sound!"

The girl struggled out of warm sleep, the cold barrel and wet hand following every evasive action. It took her a moment to realize it was not a dream.

"Not a sound or you die!" Curly warned her.

Dunlap's heart beat wildly in his chest. The fear that something was about to go wrong suddenly seized him. Their plans had already been compromised by two unforeseen events. Shortly before the bank closed for the weekend, and under White's watchful eye, a Mr. Pruyn had removed some seventy thousand dollars to the Trust Bank in New York City. Despite this reversal, it was decided to follow through with their plans.

"Where do the others sleep?" Curley demanded, ignoring White's rule on no unnecessary talking. The floor plans of the house had been mastered, and Dunlap thought there was no reason for Curley to question the poor girl.

"Mr. Van Hovenberg's brother is with us for the night," she whimpered defensively.

This had been the other surprise. Mr. Van Hovenberg's brother had indeed arrived for the weekend. "We have enough men to handle the brother as well." White had decided, "We will proceed as planned." But only hours before the robbery was to occur, while Dunlap was riding back from the cemetery in Schenectady, the brother happily had left for the station and boarded a train south.

"You're lyin'!" Curley grunted, the revolver pressing her head deep into the pillow. "He's gone!"

Ann Driscoll began to cry.

"Enough!" Dunlap warned. Raging with anger, he had his own Savage revolver pointed at Curley's head. "Don't bully the girl."

It was impossible to see the expression behind the mask, but Curley set his pistol aside and proceeded to handcuff the girl. They hurried her up the stairs to the cashier's bedroom. Dunlap saw that Van Hovenberg's bedroom door had been broken and the wall lamps lit. Ned Lyon held a large, cumbersome Wesson and Leavitt revolver against Mrs. Van Hovenberg's temple while Jimmy Hope had the cashier by the throat.

"Follow instructions," White ordered from the corner, "and no one will be hurt."

The cashier made one last, futile attempt to disengage Hope. Leslie jumped to Jimmy Hope's aid, flinging himself on the bed where he forced the cashier to stare down the ominous barrel of a large revolver.

What a horrible way to awaken, Dunlap thought as Van Hovenberg collapsed against the pillow.

"Number six! Number two!" White barked. Immediately Kingsland and Leslie moved to the girls' bedroom.

"Please don't hurt the children!" the cashier's wife screamed.

The woman's cry cut Dunlap deeply. When no one responded, he said soothingly, "They won't be hurt. I give you my word."

"Number three!" White snapped and Curley released his hold on the Driscoll girl and moved to the boy's bedroom.

Sarah, the youngest daughter, was led in first, clearly terrified. She saw the masked men. "Do you mean to hurt us?"

"Not if you behave yourself," White answered.

Mary, the eldest, was just entering the room when the Van Hovenberg boy slipped from between the men and jumped into his father's bed. Pete Curley advanced on the crying child with a large skinning knife. "I'll cut your throat for you if you're not quiet!"

Dunlap was about to move against Curley when the boy fell to whimpering and the father embraced him reassuringly.

"Number two!"

Leslie came forward and lifted the boy gently from his father. "It's all right, boy. No one's going to hurt you." The boy was led wide-eyed and weeping into a closet. Though Leslie talked softly to quiet him, the whimpering continued. The women broke down now and began to weep, too, and the sound tore Dunlap's heart. He had not prepared himself for the sobbing of women and children.

"Take us to the banking room!" White ordered the cashier. Before the man had a chance to move, Curley had him by the arm and had dragged him to the floor.

"Be quick about it, man!" Curley threatened, the wicked knife against Van Hovenberg's throat.

"Don't kill him, please!" his wife screamed.

Dunlap moved the servant into the vacancy on the bed. He tore linen for gags and told Mrs. Hovenberg, "He won't be hurt."

"But he must obey our orders!" White shouted angrily.

The cashier was forced from the bedroom while Dunlap finished tying and gagging the women. Leslie and Lyons were left on guard in the bedroom as Dunlap joined the others.

The cashier was led trembling to the vault door. White cocked his pistol, pressing it to the man's head. "No tricks," he warned. "Just open the vault."

Dunlap's next assignment was the front window. He breathed easier when he saw the street was still empty, the rain discouraging any traffic. He checked his pocket watch—twenty minutes past one. Above his head was mounted the Submarine Telegraph Burglar Alarm. With the cashier captive, it had been neutralized, its only capability to warn of a forced front-door entry.

"Kill the bastard if he don't open it right away!" Curley raged.

The cashier protested weakly, "I can't work with my hands cuffed." White removed the bracelets and Van Hovenberg rubbed his wrists for as long as possible. Kingsland cocked his pistol, ending any hope the cashier might have had of delaying for miraculous rescue.

"Open it!"

The desolate man gave the group one last look, his Dutch pride crumpling before their weapons. One set of numbers were set on the dial, a second set spun shakily into position. Van Hovenberg faltered, his hand unsteady, as White prodded him with the revolver. A third and fourth row of tumblers were aligned. White reached across and threw the bolt. There was an audible sigh from the men as the doors opened and rows of tin security boxes came into view. Kingsland threw open his oilskin coat and undid a sash cord from around his waist, freeing two small, glazed bags. Jimmy Hope followed suit, dropping two more to the banking-room floor.

White replaced the handcuffs, and Van Hovenberg was forced to watch the looting of his trust. Forty tin boxes were thrown to the floor, and the bonds and securities swiftly removed. Jimmy Hope worked feverishly to crack several cast-iron boxes that had resisted his repeated attacks.

"We'll take those with us, number five," White ordered, holding the cashier at bay with his pistol. Hope nodded gratefully and stuffed them into the glazed bags.

"Number seven!" Dunlap turned from the window and saw White motion him outside, the sign to bring the horses. He left the bull's-eye lantern on the banking-room floor and walked quickly out the rear entrance. The rain was beginning to slow as he hugged the building and pulled the mask free. The cold air shocked his damp perspiring face. Moving casually to the team, he climbed into the seat and drove slowly to the rear of the bank.

According to White's plan, the cashier would by now be back upstairs with his family and tied securely in his daughters' room.

Pete Curley came out first with two of the filled bags. Jimmy Hope followed. Masks were pulled free and Dunlap could see that each one was as sweated as he had been.

"The rain's slowin'," Hope grunted as he climbed aboard.

"The worse for us," Curley offered.

White was the last to leave. He closed the door silently behind him and gave the men a broad grin as the mask was pulled clear. Dunlap sent the horses off as hammers and tools were counted and bagged, hats pulled into place.

The first wagon was tethered to a tree, an enclosed one-horse brougham. Jimmy Hope and Ned Lyons dismounted and took one of the glazed swag bags. White passed them a key as the pair boarded and headed for Cohoes.

A short distance later, George Leslie and Ira Kingsland boarded yet another wagon, a closed village cart, and with bag and key set off in the direction of Mechanicsville.

George White and Pete Curley were taken to the Rensselaer and Saratoga Railroad line and left without a word, carrying their bag and key. Alone, Dunlap headed for the canal and Albany. The tools and masks were tossed far out into the Mohawk where they sank from sight.

Dunlap hadn't reached Albany when Sarah Van Hovenberg struggled free of her bonds and released her father, who ran into the street firing his pistol to wake the citizens of Waterford.

Jim spent three idle days in Albany reading the local account of what the *Troy Daily Times* called "The Daring Bank Robbery," comparing it to "the audacity of Claude Duval," claiming that it "even outrivals the freaks of that distinguished genius."

The *Troy Press* published a warning to other banks, listing Waterford's loss at $11,600 in cash and an undisclosed amount in securities and bonds belonging to private citizens. They hinted the loss might well climb above the $500,000 mark.

A $10,000 reward was posted the day Dunlap left by train for the city Washington Irving described as Gotham.

"Percentages and expenses deducted, Jim, your share comes to thirty thousand. Of course you may not realize that amount in cash."

Dunlap stopped dead in the courtyard, but White walked ahead slowly. Above them towered the seven-story stonework of the Park Avenue Hotel, one of the fire-resistant structures currently in vogue. White's spacious room opened into the interior courtyard where Dunlap stood in shock.

"What's the matter, Jim, your newfound wealth sapped your speech?"

"I just never dreamed . . . "

"Dreams are for fools, Jim. The doer acts and makes his dreams reality."

Dunlap sat on the iron bench and opened the leather valise. He lifted his share of Chicago, Cincinnati and Louisville first mortgage railroad bonds. "I wouldn't know how to sell these. Perhaps I can leave them with you. I would pay you a fee to exchange them for cash."

"That could be arranged."

Dunlap removed the packet of cash inside and stuffed it into his coat pocket.

"Don't you want to count it?" White asked, mildly amused.

"I trust you, White. I've learned a lot from you, good and bad. The most important lesson was that you can be trusted."

"What else have you learned?" White laughed.

"That giving each man a locked bag while the key went off with another was very smart. There could be no question of anyone being cheated."

"And the bad?"

Dunlap hesitated. He liked White and didn't want to damage their relationship, but the robbery had given him a great deal to brood about.

"The holding of the cashier and his family was not for me—crying women, hysterical children. I'll never do it again. I can safely say that the banking industry hasn't seen the last of me. But never—ever—will I employ the methods you used in Waterford."

"It is disagreeable," White agreed sadly. "I won't argue the point. But without terror, the cashier may stall or risk even bolder action. Terror, I'm sorry to say, is absolutely necessary. The target must know that to resist may cost him or his loved ones their lives."

"For you that works!" Dunlap explained haltingly. "For me, it's too risky. Something could so easily have gone wrong! A hysterical woman! A madman like Curley, and it could easily have ended in murder, and that's not to my taste."

White laced his hands over his vest, the small gray head tipped up to the patch of blue above. "We work with what we have, Jim. Until a better method is developed, the cashier will remain a target."

"It's unfortunate . . . "

"Equally unfortunate is that Pete Curley's been arrested in Hudson. I don't know if he'll talk. A good attorney may buy his silence, but one can never be sure."

"I disliked the man the moment I met him," Dunlap snapped.

White gave Dunlap a forced smile. "Part of the ragabash necessary to our line of work, Mr. Dunlap."

"You're quite right, Mr. White."

George hefted the leather valise. "What plans have you?"

The studied disinterest prompted Dunlap to ask, "Do you have something in mind?"

"Yes . . . " He rose slowly and with the suitcase in both hands walked toward his apartment. "It's not a bank job, I assure you. It's more in the nature of a favor. I need two men, unknown to this city and the New Jersey police, to perform a personal commission for me. You would do very nicely. Have you someone you trust and whose face isn't known?"

"Not in New York," Jim shrugged. "I was planning on returning to Chicago and straightening out my affairs before a permanent move east. But that will mean a delay . . . "

"A delay of a few weeks won't alter the situation. These friends in need aren't going anywhere. Perhaps you'll find this other party in Chicago and telegraph your reply. Of course it cannot be our friend Tom Reilly or any of the Chicago sharpers. One sight of them and our ploy would be doomed. I must advise you that there may be little if any money in it for you. As I said, it's a personal favor."

"I'll wire you as soon as I reach Chicago."

"I'd be most grateful, Mr. Dunlap."

Dunlap caused quite a stir on the return trip to Chicago. Fashionably dressed, tipping generously, an expensive cigar between his fingers, a stack of the latest papers nearby, he was obviously someone, the passengers decided, just who they could not be sure.

The men decided he was scanning the papers for the latest stock quotations, while the women were sure he must be a gambler or some other exotic operator. Had they been able to see what it was he followed so religiously, they might have been surprised, for he was totally absorbed in accounts of the Waterford robbery.

Clues had been frustratingly few. The maid, Ann Driscoll, was now suspect. A nearby resident, Doctor Heartt, had his son questioned and under suspicion as it seemed he had once passed a check with his father's name forged upon it. Innocent citizens of Waterford, whose only offense had been an indiscretion sometime in their youth, were immediately suspect and brought before the frustrated city detectives.

The *Daily Saratogan* listed "500,000 reasons to never forget!" The *New York Herald* ran an advertisement requesting holders of certain bonds, taken from Waterford, to contact a New York stockbroker whose name was listed. "No questions will be asked." Yet the *Saratogan* promised, "There will be no rest for the wicked." The two conflicting statements had Dunlap roaring, much to the puzzlement of those around him.

The *Greenwich Journal*, breathing easier that one of its own institutions had not been robbed, listed in great detail and with diagrams the new security precautions taken by their own Washington County National Bank. Seeing how much easier they had made his job, Dunlap chuckled to himself and tore the item from the *Journal* for later reference.

The *Troy Press* announced a general meeting of the Waterford citizenry, at which time, the *Press* declared, the nine robbers would appear. How the paper had come by the figure "nine," or concluded that they would foolishly expose themselves to a general meeting of angry stockholders, was unclear.

"York!" the conductor announced weaving through the car, "York!"

The rented carriage took him to the Emmitsburg road, where he drove the last ten miles north to Gettysburg. On his last arrival—as a soldier some nine years before—the villagers had cheered wildly, a young girl had thrust a thick slice of bread into his hand and the apple butter had stuck to his fingers. This time there was no fanfare, no cool water to drink, just the horse and the creaking wagon. He left the wagon outside the Lutheran Church where he'd been taken on that July 1 when the battered troops had arrived to the crowd's cheers. The pews were empty now, though bloodstains still soiled the floor. The aisle where the surgeons had separated shattered limbs from living bodies was smaller than he remembered, the room itself silent and peaceful as he thought it could never be again.

Tell-tale gouges lingered on the buildings, as he walked to the site that had almost claimed his arm and life. The stone walls were not the same; someone had stacked them neatly back the way they had been that first day.

Looking down into the valley, he could hear the fife and drum of the Iron Brigade, white gaiters and black slouch hats moving in time to "The Campbells are Coming." But the valley was empty now. The long gray lines that had stretched a mile wide and a mile deep had vanished. The roar of the cannon and the screams of horses and dying men had given way to the quiet of a cool autumnal evening, nothing at all like the oppressive heat of those July afternoons without water or shade.

There had been over 450 casualties on that first day in Dunlap's brigade alone. But they were nothing like the losses suffered by the grays on their last march to the Union breastworks. They had advanced a steady march at right shoulder arms, banners waving as the artillery punched gaping holes in their ranks. Closing the holes in tight as the thirty-minute onslaught continued unwavering. The finest of Virginia, Tennessee and North Carolina moving relentlessly forward, ignoring fallen comrades in a panorama that took Dunlap's breath away. Never again would he see such a spectacle. Many of his Dutch comrades wept openly at the bravery shown by the enemy. By the time the remnants of their lines reached the Union position, Dunlap too was weeping. Loading and firing as fast as his arm would allow, he helped stop the doomed march across the deadly valley. But as he stood here nine years later, the words "war" and "glory" seemed distant and hollow indeed. As an eighteen-year-old corporal, he had witnessed the most heroic sacrifice known to determined men. Bull Run, Chancellorsville, Lookout Mountain, Mission Ridge and Kenesaw Mountain had made the rest of his life seem humdrum. Two years before, George Pickett, the rebel leader who led the charge at Gettysburg, was discovered selling insurance, and doing very badly at that. Dunlap had read the newspaper item with interest, for his own life was going awry. He had tried to settle down to civilian life—tried valiantly to play out his life according to the rules. But pressures and routines stifled him, and until he met George White, he felt his life had been merely a marking off of time. Standing on the hill, a sizable roll of bills in his pocket, he felt for the first time in ten years that he could let go of the past and look forward to the future.

The drum and fife were silent, the fields below offered up wheat, not bodies. The air was still, he was now free to go ahead.

The carriage jerked to a stop in front of a dark gray snowdrift on Desplaines Avenue. The driver hurried to open the door and unload the baggage, mindful of a worthwhile tip. The weighted silver cane emerged first, then an elegant young man stepped carefully from the carriage. Patent leather shoes with tan spats gingerly sought a secure footing. The chamois gloves pressed a bill into the driver's hand, and the man bowed and scraped his way through the drift, depositing the luggage on the steps of the brick mansion.

"Well I'll be a toad eater!" Reilly shouted as he brushed past the driver and caught Dunlap picking his way through the charcoal-colored snowdrift. "I was beginning to worry about you, Jim!"

"Where have you been, lad?" Raggio called from the stairs.

"Seeing the country," Dunlap called up the stairs.

"We were sure you were pinched," Tom said.

"Things have never been better," Dunlap laughed. Once inside, he pressed a bill on each man. "That's for looking out for things while I was gone."

Raggio pocketed the money without looking at it. Reilly, however, was genuinely embarrassed. He gave Dunlap a sad look. "There's nothing I've done worth this . . ."

Sensing that Tom was about to return his bill, Raggio scurried off to the parlor, leaving the two men at the foot of the stairs.

Dunlap placed a hand on Tom's shoulder. "You're a good friend, Tom, and it's you alone I have to thank for my good fortune."

Reilly scratched at the scar and shrugged his broad shoulders in discomfort as he ruffled the bill. "I've done nothing."

Dunlap slapped the heavy arm dismissing the gift forever. "George White sends you his best."

"Fine man," Tom said.

Dropping his voice, Dunlap whispered, "I have to return to New York. I've promised George I'd do a favor for him."

Tom's eyes widened. "You and George going to be working together?" he asked, obviously impressed. "He's a big man, Jim! You couldn't be doing no finer than working with George White! No, sir!"

"I'm just doing a single favor for the man. I can't truly say that we'll be working together again." He didn't want to reveal his plans. Heeding George's advice, he knew Tom could never be part of them.

"Have you learned anything?"

"Yes," Dunlap laughed. "I've learned the world is full of us crooks. And if what George tells me is right, New York's finest citizens are the biggest of the lot!"

"So you'll be leaving right away?"

"In a day or so. I want to pay my debt to Dave for the clothes and board. I have to write a certain young lady and tell her goodbye forever. I also have to find somebody to take back to New York with me;

that's where you come in. I need somebody unknown . . . smart . . . a pleasant face . . . somebody who could pass for a man of means. Can you help, Tom?"

Tom sent a hand to Dunlap's cheek, the grin slid around the face.

"You don't move, now," he said, backing into the parlor. He returned a minute later, dragging a tall, dark-haired young man in an ill-fitting suit. He was several inches taller than Dunlap, standing a full six feet.

"We was in Joliet together," Reilly grinned, shoving his friend a step closer. "Bob, this is me friend, Jim Dunlap." Hurrying to Dunlap's side, he added, "Jim, this is Hustlin' Bob Scott."

Reilly thumbed the expensive jacket on Dunlap's chest. "Jim's going to be somebody to reckon with, you wait and see."

Turning back to Scott, Tom said, "We call him Hustlin' 'cause he's smart as a fox, Jim. . . . Jim was a soldier, too. The ah . . . the ah . . ."

"The 61st Ohio," Dunlap stated. "Eleventh Corps."

Scott looked him over carefully. "That's a colored outfit, ain't it?"

Try as he might, Dunlap could not hold back the smile.

Scott shrugged in dismay. "You don't look colored."

"Cool as you please, ain't he, Jim?" Tom fretted nervously. "Doesn't have a nerve in his body, this one. Bob was just thirteen when he joined the army."

"What outfit were you in?" Dunlap asked.

"The blue one with the stripe down the leg."

Dunlap grinned in amusement, then slowly shook his head. "I thought for a minute you might have been wearing gray."

"Jim," Tom pressed, inserting himself between the two. "I gave you my advice once and you took it. Now I'm telling you one more thing that'll change yer life. This boy and you would be better than White and Shinburn, you mark my words! You boys will make ol' Charley Adams hisself sit up and take notice! You boys are *born* bankies, and I'm tellin' you, Jim, you couldn't find a better man in a dozen states than Bob Scott here!"

Dunlap continued to stare at the boy who looked like he had grown through his clothes.

"Just try him!" Tom urged. "You'll never do better than this boy, and I'm a good judge of men, you know that to be true, Jim."

Tom suddenly whirled on Scott. "You'd do well to say somethin' to show the man you've still got yer tongue!"

Scott shrugged indifferently. "I've never been to New York and ol' Tom here's always steered me right. A square fellow he is. If Tom says it's so , then it must be. I'll go with you to New York."

"You can't go to New York looking like that," Dunlap responded carefully.

"I won't," Scott grinned. "I figure you can afford to stake me to some new clothes. Get me one of them canes like you got."

"Hush, boy," Reilly snorted, elbowing him.

"Whoever called you Hustlin' saw that you were aptly named," Dunlap said, laughing.

"Nobody calls me that except Tom here and a few of his friends. Everybody else calls me Bob."

The hand was offered and Dunlap took it. "Jim Dunlap."

Reilly cemented the handshake with his own two meaty palms. "You boys are gonna do jes fine. I can tell."

Chapter Two

The old man with the silver imperial goatee examined the watch. It had been three hours and still no one stirred. The gold leaf lettering announced it was Pate's Bank, but he had no way of knowing if Pate employed a night watchman. It was after nine; the night was becoming too cold to prolong the vigil.

Tucking the gold-crested cane under his armpit, he pulled the glove from his right hand. Frozen fingers picked their way through the raglan coat pocket until the two small wedges were found. Each was three-quarters of an inch long and a quarter inch wide, tapering to a needle point. The smooth hickory wedges were slipped into the gold band about his finger, tightly binding the skin and gold ring.

Stepping from the shadows, he gave a casual glance in both directions before moving down the boardwalk opposite his target. Upon reaching the corner, he crossed the frozen thoroughfare, approaching the bank from the far end of the street. To all appearances he was just an elderly stroller out for an evening walk, well dressed, silver moustache and short goatee shining in the streetlights as he inspected the shop windows, carefully checking for movements in the reflections in the glass.

Pate's Bank and dry goods were housed in the same large premises. On one side was the counter with its shelves and dry goods; on the other, a cashier's window and a lone Hall safe. He knew there were two entrances that would have to be checked.

At the front door, the elderly stroller lost his glove. Discovering it immediately, he bent to one knee, the gloved hand snatching up its fallen comrade while the right hand slipped one of the tiny wedges free of the ring. A slight awkward stagger upon rising and the hickory wedge was jammed into the minute gap between door and jamb. He straightened with great difficulty—in fact his leg ached painfully from the exercise—and continued his late night saunter past the bank.

Turning the darkened corner to Court Street, the officer saw a well-dressed figure pointing drunkenly with his cane. The policeman stopped to observe the man weaving in the light of a shop window. Clearly intoxicated. The figure pointed to a spot ahead with his cane, the tip circling warily as he desperately tried to propel himself toward his goal. Several uncertain steps led him far astray. The cane was raised and sighted and a new destination plotted.

The officer approached slowly, amused at the drunk's antics. He came to the side of the tall, elegant young man, saw the cane lifted to indicate the next hazy cobblestone and caught the figure as the legs splayed and the drunk fell heavily into the patrolman's arms.

"Had a bit much to drink, I daresay." The dead weight was eased to the street, the hat falling back to reveal dark hair and a young, boyishly handsome face. The patrolman shook his head. "It's a bitter lesson I'll be teaching you, me boyo."

The drunk was taken to the Hudson County Jail in Hoboken, New Jersey, and detained for the night.

"Blessed Lord," the drunk mumbled as the turnkey shot the bolt home.

"You've gotten yourself into a fine mess, my young friend," the turnkey chastened. "Your family would be badly disappointed in you if they could see you now."

"Blessed Lord," the man mumbled drunkenly before falling off to a loud snoring.

As was his custom, Chief Donovan of the Hoboken Police Department made his rounds early the next morning, checking each cell personally to see the fruits of a night's work. He noted with satisfaction that the three most celebrated guests in some time were present and accounted for. Dago Frank, alias Frank Denning, occupied the cell closest to the turnkey's office. Frank was leaning against the bars when the chief went by. Neither man spoke, though Dago Frank ventured the semblance of a smile. The chief maintained his gruff exterior as he passed to the next cell. Bill Proctor sat on the cot, his feet to the floor, yawning his unshaven face to the ceiling. The third cell was occupied by Moses "Mose" Vogel.

"Good morning, sir!" Vogel called cheerfully through the bars.

"Morning," the chief replied tersely.

The fourth cell held a new occupant, and the chief stopped before the bars as the prisoner dropped the hands from his face and raised bloodshoot eyes to the visitor.

"Well?" the chief asked sternly, "what brought you to our hotel?"

"Too much of a good thing, I'm afraid."

"What's your name?"

"Alexander . . . William Alexander. At least it was last night." The young man dug into his pocket frantically and pulled a large wad of bills free. He sighed with relief and stuffed them back in his pocket, but not before the chief witnessed the size of the roll.

"Where does your family live?"

"Far from sight and hearing, I hope."

"Intoxication your only crime?" the chief asked suspiciously.

"As far as I can remember."

"Has this ever happened before?"

"Oh, no sir!" Alexander smiled quickly and in obvious pain. "It was just a celebration. It got frightfully out of hand, I'm afraid."

"A man in your position has no business in this place, Mr. Alexander." After a moment's thought, the chief decided, "I'll speak to the judge, but I hope you've learned your lesson!"

"That I have!" Alexander cried. "I can assure you, sir, you've seen the last of me!"

The chief dropped his voice and whispered, "I'll try to have you home in time for lunch."

"That would be most kind!" Alexander smiled warmly. "I'll be glad to be away from these desperate characters. Worst looking lot I've seen in some time."

"Three of the most notorious bank robbers in the country," Donovan said distastefully. "You've read of the attempt to holdup the Jersey City National?"

"Just three or four weeks ago?" Alexander asked in horror.

"That's the one!" the chief sneered. "Stopped them just a few feet short of the safe. Tried to tunnel into the vault, they did. They'll be tried shortly, and a long prison sentence will be their punishment, I guarantee you that!"

"Well!" Alexander seemed deeply impressed.

"Now you can see the folly of excess, when it makes you spend the night with such disreputable companions."

"That I do!" Alexander vowed. "That I do!"

The chief touched his braid-trimmed cap in salute and, with hands laced behind his back, gave each of the bankies a surly look as he left.

When the entrance to the cell had been cleared, the area quiet, Alexander went to the bars separating himself from Mose Vogel. The bankie drifted over to join him.

"Bank burglars?" Alexander asked.

Vogel smiled, yellow-stained teeth partially hidden in a long, black, unkempt moustache. "The worst kind."

"I never would have guessed it."

Vogel feigned sadness. "Thank heaven me sainted mother ain't here to see it."

Alexander removed several bills from his pocket and passed them through the bars. "That's for Dago."

Vogel passed them to Proctor and the money went from the second cell to Dago Frank. By this time another set of bills was on its way to Proctor. When each man had been given the exact same amount of money, Alexander said, "Next time *I'll* bring the tools."

"When will that be?"

"Tomorrow possibly, or the day after."

"Who's working with you?"

"You don't know him," Alexander answered.

"Does he work for George White?"

"Sort of."

"What's your name?" Vogel asked.

"Bob Scott."

"I'm in your debt, Mr. Scott."

"It'll be collected, you can rest assured of that."

True to his word, Chief Donovan spoke with the judge and William Alexander was freed in time for lunch. It was therefore a surprise to the Court Street patrolman to see the same drunken figure lurching up the darkened street later that evening. A wagon was sent for and once again William Alexander was lodged in the Hudson County Jail.

The following morning the unsympathetic judge surprised the prisoner with a thirty-day sentence. But the good chief came to his rescue and kept the contrite Alexander at the Hudson County facility with the other "ten-day" men.

The following day a sparkling brougham pulled to the curb and a well-dressed young man swept into the chief's office.

"I'm looking for a Will Alexander," Dunlap said.

Impressed by the diamond stickpin, the chief rose from behind his desk. "There is an inmate named Alexander here, but most unfortunately for him, his reservation is for thirty days."

"Damn!" Dunlap cursed. "But surely there must be some way to secure his release?"

"I'm afraid not, sir."

"I'd be willing to pay any fine—"

"That would not be possible."

"One hundred dollars!"

The chief shook his head. "I'm afraid not."

"Two hundred!"

"I'm sorry," the chief insisted.

"Damn! This Alexander was to marry my sister last week! For some unknown reason he failed to put in an appearance at the church. The poor girl's frantic! Surely there must be *something* that could be done to relieve a young girl's broken heart?"

"I would suggest, Mr.—"

"Barton, James Barton."

"I would suggest, Mr. Barton," Donovan explained reluctantly, "that you return to your sister and tell her, as gently as possible, of course, that the young man is unavoidably detained for thirty days. I'm sure that once he's released, with proper supervision, he may be led to the altar. That is, providing there's not a bottle between him and the church. He has a serious problem, I'm afraid." The chief held a thumb to his mouth and threw back his head.

"I see."

"You may visit as often as you like. I would not advise you to bring the young lady, however."

"Of course."

"Perhaps you could say he was ill—it's a small enough lie. You'll think of something, I'm sure."

"Yes." Dunlap paced the room nervously. "I'm sure I'll think of something. May I see my future brother-in-law?"

"Of course! I'll give you a pass that will admit you anytime."

"Thank you," Dunlap mumbled glumly. "You've been most kind."

The turnkey admitted him to the cell area. Dunlap went down the rows of iron cages until he found Scott. A quick look to insure they were not being watched and Dunlap raised his coat and backed to the bars.

Scott removed the hammer from the rear of Jim's waistband, while Dunlap held the coat skirt to his shoulders.

"If I had known this was going to cost me thirty days!" Scott hissed furiously as he passed the hammer to Mose Vogel, who sent it down to Bill Proctor, who in turn slipped it to Dago Frank.

"How was *I* to know?" Dunlap insisted, as two steel chisels were pulled free behind him. The coat was dropped and one leg was raised to the bars.

"You *knew!*" Scott whispered through clenched teeth as he pulled a cement bit from Dunlap's pant leg.

"I didn't know! How was I to know?" Dunlap offered Scott the other leg, and a large three-eighths-inch metal bit was removed from the ties about the calf.

"After five years in Joliet, this is not my idea of doing someone a favor!"

"I'll make it up to you!" Dunlap shook his trouser legs into position and adjusted his coat.

"Is that all there is?" Scott fumed.

"That's all I could bring this time. They can start with that and next visit I'll bring a brace for the drills. White's making a model that comes apart. Tell them it'll take a few more days."

"Thirty days . . ."

Dunlap leaned close to the cell and whispered from the corner of his mouth, "Do me a favor, find out all you can about how they tunneled into the Jersey City bank?"

"Is that all?" Scott bellowed. "You sure you wouldn't like me to smuggle you some food?"

Dunlap smiled broadly as he flicked a speck of imaginary dust from his lapel. "No, I've got plenty to eat. Just find out what you can about the bank job."

"Don't wait up for me."

Dunlap tipped his hat and jauntily sauntered past the prisoners to the turnkey's office, where he rattled the bars for attention.

Scott dropped heavily to the bunk as Vogel, Proctor and Dago Frank hid the tools. Vogel reached through the cell and laid a hand on Bob's arm. "It's going smoothly."

"Peachy," Scott frowned.

"So that's your partner?"

"That's him, the one leaving for a warm room and a fine meal."

"Looks like a real gentleman—not that you don't, of course. What's your line?"

"Same as yours."

"Banks?"

"That's it," Scott said confidently. "As soon as this caper's finished, we're going into banking in a big way."

Vogel nodded in appreciation. "You boys must do all right, judging by the duds."

"It's all right for openers," Scott grinned, "but Jim and I have some big plans, as soon as I'm out of here, of course."

"May I be of some help, sir?"

"I hope so. My name is James Barton. I deal in horses and live-

stock near Abilene, Texas, and my company has seen fit to send me to
your factory here in Troy just so that I might see what sort of vaults
and safes you have to offer."

The Dutchman beamed. "I'm sure we can provide a most satisfactory arrangement to protect your investments."

"I must warn you ahead of time," Dunlap cautioned, "I've seen
several other companies. I've spoken with Hall, Marvin and the Herring people. I must be absolutely sure of the construction before I decide which safe is best suited to my needs."

"I assure you, sir, that the Lillie safes and vaults are among the
best in the world."

"Perhaps," Dunlap said casually, "but that is exactly what each of
the others has told me. If you're prepared to prove that, I'll let my
eyes be the judge."

"Certainly!" the salesman approved. "If you would be so kind as to
accompany me to the workroom, you will see our secret process—
chilled iron being poured, the works being secured by the latest Lillie
combination lock."

What Dunlap saw was a patented wire casing over which molten
metal was poured. The impeccably attired Dutchman boasted, "The
special wire frame and hot metal pouring prevents the doors from being broken by sledging or wedging."

"I'm afraid I don't understand," Dunlap said above the din.

The Dutchman led him to a quiet corner of the shop. "It's very simple, really. Cracksmen are notorious for hammering the doors to ruin
and breaking down the casing until entry is made. Another favorite
trick is to drive tiny metal wedges into the corners and peel the skin
back, allowing room to insert explosives."

"Are you telling me a Lillie safe cannot be either hammered or
wedged?"

"*That* is correct," the Dutchman gloated. "It's impossible to bust
our Lillie safe. The secret's in the wire frame," he explained. "It
holds the iron together. Even though a strong explosive charge is set
off, the wire frame will keep the doors intact. It also provides one additional safeguard. The wire is soft, while the chilled iron is extremely hard. If a drill bit was invented to withstand the pressure required
to wear through the chilled iron, it would strike the soft wire and bind
instantly, shattering itself in the attempt."

"Very commendable," Dunlap said, secretly stunned. He had thought the trip would reveal the weakness in the Lillie safe. Instead, he found a formidable box with no apparent flaws at all.

"An exclusive Lillie patent," the man puffed securely. The aquiline nose was sent about the room, sighted the next lesson and was off down the aisle.

Dunlap hurried to catch up. "You mean a Lillie safe cannot be drilled, hammered or wedged?"

"Absolutely not!"

"You've tried to drill the finished product?" he asked in disbelief.

"Every safe we manufacture is tested with a drill before it's sold."

"Incredible," Dunlap mumbled.

"Yes, isn't it!"

The salesman led him to a finished model. An artist was hand painting the name of the firm for which it was intended. Before Dunlap stood his gleaming black adversary, 6½ feet high, 4½ feet wide. It dwarfed the artist, who backed discreetly out of the area.

The Dutchman read the tag, adjusted the combination and offered Dunlap the chrome handle. Jim took it in his hands, hesitated, then threw the bolt clear. With a great effort, he opened both doors.

"Two and a half inches of impregnable metal with a fireproof filler to prevent fire damage. Each door poured in one piece with the patented safety wire inside."

The opening of the outer doors revealed yet another smaller set that closed off the upper two-thirds of the enclosure. These, too, were fitted with a Lillie combination lock. Below that, a two-foot-high burglar box was built across the front with a third combination lock.

"Incredible," Dunlap repeated in shock. He had never seen such a safe in his life.

The salesman dropped to one knee, read the combination from the card he palmed and dialed the numbers on the double doors. They opened to reveal the inside of the safe and the double row of safety boxes. The third combination was set and the burglar box unlocked.

Dunlap whistled, impressed. "It staggers the imagination."

"Soundly constructed, wouldn't you say, Mr. Barton?"

Dunlap could only nod his reply.

"Drillproof, fireproof and unbreakable. The best Lillie has to offer.

Combine this with a Lillie vault and I can guarantee you a fortress free of worry."

The doors were closed, the handles flung home, the painter stepped forward to continue his lettering. Dunlap stared at the container and wondered if such an invention could indeed have an Achilles heel. Three doors, three combinations. Blowing the outer doors, if that was at all possible, would only provide access to the safe's inner workings. It was a challenge that could require years of mastering. He envisioned tunneling into a vault and confronting the 6½-foot-high Lillie safe with its triple combination and shuddered.

The salesman had his arm and Dunlap saw the mouth moving, but the words refused to register. "I beg your pardon," he said, shaking the safe from his thoughts.

"I was saying, since you know a great deal about horses, I was hoping I could entreat you to give me a bit of advice."

"Most certainly."

"I have a mare, a fine animal, but she has one great fault. On various occasions she limps."

The salesman was steering him toward the vault material as Dunlap asked, "Limps?"

"Yes. She does it for no apparent reason. Sunday, on the way to service, she limped. Yet on the way home from church she was perfectly sound. I've taken her everywhere! The veterinarian is baffled. There is just no medical reason for the limp! What should I do?"

"Find a day on which she doesn't limp—"

"Yes?"

"Then sell her," he smiled.

The prisoner William Alexander was freed at the end of his thirty-day sentence. A few days after his release, it was discovered that the three "bankies," as the chief called them, had almost completed a hole through the cell wall. Someone had mysteriously supplied them with all the necessary tools, including a sizable cache of dynamite. Unfortunately, for the bankies, the escape tunnel was disclosed by a young pickpocket who replaced Alexander in the cell. The message was immediately relayed to the chief, and Dago Frank, Bill Proctor

and Mose Vogel were tried and found guilty of attempting to rob the
Jersey City National Bank. Fifteen years imprisonment guaranteed
Chief Donovan they'd face sterner quarters.

New York's answer to traffic congestion was an elevated railway
that ran from the tip of Manhattan to Thirteenth Street. Traveling
above Ninth Avenue, it ran past stores already flooded with ready-
made suits, the product of a Staten Island man's invention of the me-
chanical cloth cutter earlier that same year. Suits could be had for
fifteen dollars, and the railway was doing so well that another was
planned for Sixth Avenue.

At the Fifth Avenue Hotel, the men responsible for the attempted
break were dining on Maine lobster and Coney Island clams. Dunlap
and Scott were present, as were George White and Dave Cummings,
the leader of the ill-fated attempt on the Jersey City National.

Davey Cummings was just twenty-four, but a seasoned bankie
nonetheless. He had been a waiter on the passenger ships of the upper Mississippi. Then one day someone realized that on each ship that
Little Davey Cummings served a robbery had been perpetrated. He
was arrested, and a considerable amount of stolen property was found
in his quarters. By his seventeenth birthday his face was well known
to St. Louis police, and he fled to New York.

The flyweight 130-pound bankie told the trio, "I really appreciate
what you tried to do. Especially you, Bob, as you did your share the
hard way."

"I'd rather not talk about it," Scott bristled.

"Still, I'm in your debt."

"We tried," White sighed, dabbing at his moustache with his napkin.

"How come you didn't get pinched with the rest of them?" Dunlap
asked.

"I was outside when the old lady called the police. I just had time
to step into the shadows, and they went right by me."

"Davey piped the job," White explained.

"And not a very good job I did at that," Davey admitted. "Me here
having supper with the swells while my friends dine on prison ra-

tions." Davey downed a clam with a sorrowful shake of his head. "Good men, too."

"What was the plan?" Dunlap ventured.

"To take it from above. We rented quarters over the bank, presented a reasonable front while we dug down into the vault by night. Figured if we could get inside, we could work on the safe without being seen from the street."

"An excellent idea," Dunlap said.

"Once inside, I figured we could take our time to work on the strong box and safe. The landlady must have heard us digging—the old harridan went for the coppers. I was outside taking a break when they arrived. I had no time to warn anyone! You know the rest."

"Unfortunate," White offered.

"Damn her!" Dave countered. "It was an expensive job, too. We lost all our tools—everything's gone! Worse yet . . . I've nothing left to cover the cost of doing another."

Scott asked quietly, "Do you have another bank in mind?"

"I had a couple piped, but the Jersey City one was the closest and easiest." Cummings chewed slowly, his fork in one hand, the knife in the other. He looked at first Scott then Dunlap. "You planning on turning off a bank or two yerselves?"

Before Dunlap could answer, Scott leaned in close and whispered, "Jim and I have been talking about putting together our own group. You know, a solid, dependable organization, each man skilled in his own line."

Dunlap found himself looking from Scott to White. The older man smiled paternally, sanctioning the meeting. "There were no definite plans made!" he wanted to tell White. "It was just something we discussed!" Here was Scott now, babbling about the gang as if it had been with them for months.

"We're putting together the finest gang money can buy." Scott couldn't conceal his enthusiasm.

"Ring," White corrected.

"Ring?" Scott asked.

"Ring," White counseled. "When the ruffians of the street gather together to rob the people, it's called a gang. When gentlemen set forth to rob the people, it's a ring. For example, the Tweed Ring, the

Erie Ring, the Press Ring, the Canal Ring—all did very well at lining their pockets. If you're interested in just a few paltry dollars, then a gang would suit you very nicely. But if you intend to rob people of large sums, over an indefinite period of time, I would definitely suggest a ring."

Scott rapped the table with his fist. "Then by God that's what we'll have, a ring! Jim's for a ring and so am I!"

"What about tools and financing?" Davey asked suspiciously.

Scott dismissed this with a snort and to Dunlap's complete surprise stated, "Jim here has all the money we need! We'll buy whatever tools we need or have them specially made! Jim's been traveling around the country studying safes and locks, and there's nothing he doesn't know about 'em. Explosives? Jim knows all there is to know about explosives! George here can help us with anything we don't know. What we need, Dave is a few more dependable men like yourself. Men throughly experienced in all forms of robbery."

"Tools cost a bundle," Cummings said doubtfully.

Scott roared and slapped Dunlap's hand. "Money's no object to making money! Right, Jim?"

Dunlap hid the laugh behind the napkin. Scott knew they were short on cash. Until the bonds and securities of the Waterford job were compromised, there was very little cash at all. He dropped the napkin, gave Hustlin' Bob a resigned "Of course money's no object!"

"See! Now, Davey, you tell me how much those tools are going to cost us?"

"I dunno, fine English hooks and braces could go as high as three hundred . . . "

"I know a German on Hester Street," White said, "John Steurer, a fine machinist and locksmith. Fair prices, too, fifteen dollars for a sectional jimmy, jackscrews, wedges, chisels, anything that's needed can be had for a reasonable price."

"Excellent!" Scott crowed. "Whatever is needed, Jim and I will get!"

"You'll need a good hide man," Cummings offered, "and I think I'm about the best there is. I can peel the hide off any safe you can name—Diebold, Lillie, Herring, Hall, Marvin—I busted them all. Explosives are my weakness."

"With Jim here we have that area taken care of," Scott boasted. "Jim worked with explosives under the direction of the army itself!"

Dunlap placed a calming hand on Scott's arm. He had never blown a safe. He had no idea of the amount of powder necessary to blow heavy doors free of inch-thick iron bolts.

But Scott was unstoppable. "If Dave here doesn't sound like just the man we're looking for, Jim, then I don't know who does!"

It was all moving too fast for Dunlap. He turned to his mentor, George White. The older man shrugged. "I'm too old for this. A few more jobs and my financial worries will have taken care of themselves. Don't count on me."

"Then it's settled!" Scott said quickly, relieved White had taken himself out of the group, though for the life of him he couldn't understand why Jim wanted the man in the first place. "Dave, you're the first man in the new Scott-Dunlap Ring."

"Scott-Dunlap," Jim choked in surprise. "It's my money! I think the least we could do is to make it the Dunlap-Scott gang."

"Of course, Jim," Scott laughed with Cummings, "Dunlap-Scott it is!"

White signaled the waiter for a bottle of bourbon to celebrate New York's newest criminal ring.

Following the toasts to long life and financial success, Dunlap asked Cummings, "Davey, you mentioned Lillie safes. I've just returned from Troy and the Lillie factory. From what I understand, the damn things are impregnable!"

"I don't know about the new ones," Davey replied, "but the old ones peeled real easy like."

"Jim's right," White intervened. "The new ones are extremely difficult. However, let me just say that as soon as we leave here, I'll show you something of interest about Lillie safes. Is that fair enough?"

White directed a hansom to Broadway, and they climbed from the carriage in front of the showroom window of the Herring safe company. Bellies full of good food, heads light with bourbon, they jostled each other as White fought for their attention. "Gentlemen," White announced, "a Lillie safe."

In the window sat a safe, its doors twisted open, the strong box blown free. "The impregnable Lillie. One piece casing, chilled iron on a wire frame. Is this the Lillie you saw, Jim?"

"Different size," he said in wonder, "but I'll be damned if it's not the same type!"

"This safe came from Olean, New York. Herring bought it to replace it with one of their own. The undrillable, unbreakable Lillie. It took a wonderful old man named Langdon Moore to question Lillie's claim that the surface was so hard any drill made would slip from its skin without even leaving an impression. Moore drilled the outer doors in forty-five minutes. Two hours after he entered the bank, he'd opened both the safe and strongbox and was on his way back to the city. That, gentlemen, is a Lillie safe."

The following morning, as Dunlap dressed before the mirror in their room at the Grand Central Hotel, Scott asked, "Where you off to with that diamond stickpin and smelling like money?"

"The Herring showroom. I have to have a closer look at that safe Langdon Moore busted."

Scott laughed aloud. "You think you can duplicate that feat?"

"I hope so!" He turned to Scott for final inspection, the square jaw set stubbornly. "I'm going to go wherever there's someone who makes safes and locks. I'm not coming back until I learn what makes them work."

"You could be gone for years," Scott chuckled. Coming forward in long johns, he adjusted Dunlap's tie and stickpin. He tugged the coat and vest into position, a thin, fashionable cigar held between even, white teeth. Leaning away from the smoke, he observed, "There! You look like a proper swell!"

"I may be gone a few days. You have money in the drawer—the room. If there's anything you need, see George White."

"I'll be all right." He flicked a speck of dust from Dunlap's shoulder and winked in appreciation, clicking his tongue admiringly. "You look smart, Jim. You could fool the bishop himself."

Dunlap turned back to the mirror. A careful examination and he decided Bob Scott was right. "We'll be getting you some clothes, too, Bob, some real clothes. That bishop's gonna have to be fooled by both of us if we're going to have a ring of our own."

Scott asked in surprise, "Then you're not put out by what I said to Davey Cummings?"

"Nope." Jim grinned into the looking glass. "Been lying awake thinking about it all night long. It's a good idea. A *damn* good idea! Why should we work for someone else? But you were right—it's going to take money! And a lot of work and good planning on our part. We don't want any mistakes. I just traded my railroad clothes for this fine tailoring and I'm not eager to exchange them again for prison gray."

"Oh, I agree, Jim!" Scott shouted, on the tips of bare toes with excitement. "I couldn't agree more!"

"But we're gonna need us some money," Dunlap said worriedly, "real big money!"

"Leave that to me!" Scott boasted. "You worry about the safes and let me worry about the stake. I'm gonna show you ol' Hustlin' Bob in action!"

"All right," Jim agreed. "I'll be responsible for the safes, if you'll get us the money for the tools."

"Agreed . . . partner!" Scott stuck his hand forward and Dunlap took it, pumping warmly.

"And about Hoboken," Dunlap frowned.

"I hope that's the last dirty trick you pull on me."

"I swear it," Dunlap smiled.

"I'll do my share, Jim, I promise!"

"And I'll do mine."

Dunlap selected the ebony cane from the rack. He buffed the silver handle against his jacket as he made his way to the door. Raising the walking stick, he touched it to the brim of his top hat. "So long, partner."

Scott touched his forehead in a military salute as Dunlap went out, then he fell back on the sofa in elation. For the first time in his life, he felt he had a future worthy of consideration. A veteran of the great war at sixteen, he saw before him a bleak and dismal prospect. Home was just a way station between destinations. His mother remarried; his new father had destroyed what little bond existed. "Goin' Home" were just words to throw out to comrades one would never see again. The disappointment was that the war had ended so abruptly.

It was common knowledge the large industrial cities held all the promise a young man could want. But within the year, Scott was destitute. A hand at the confidence game netted him five years in prison. It was there he earned the nickname Hustlin' Bob Scott from his fellow inmates. His glib tongue and quick wit were rewarded with extra portions and light duties.

A close examination of the Lillie safe revealed Langdon Moore's technique. The man had drilled through the lock casing and filled the hole with powder. The inside doors had been removed by knocking the combination spindle free and charging the opening with explosives. The burglar box across the bottom had been drilled in exactly the same position as the outer doors, and powder freed it of its mounts. It was all so simple Dunlap visibly sighed with relief.

"This certainly is a strong argument against purchasing a Lillie safe," he told the salesman.

"We thought our customers would like to see the type of safe offered by one of our competitors," the salesman smirked.

"Hardly competition," Dunlap observed as the salesman led him to one of Herring's finest models.

Dunlap's tour of safes and locks ended in Stamford, Connecticut, at the Yale and Towne Lock Company, where he met the incredible Yale combination lock. A wire to Scott, and his partner was waiting for him in Boston.

"Did you learn anything?" Scott asked aboard the *Narragansett* steamship returning them to New York.

"I learned that the key is made first, the lock afterward," he laughed. "I've seen the best of Marvin, and Briggs and Huntington in Rochester. I think we can beat them. Moore attacked them in the one place they're vulnerable—the lock. I see no reason why we can't do the same. But the Yale combination lock is by far the best piece of work ever, with over a hundred million different possible combinations that would require eighty-three years, working twenty-four hours a day, to try them all. The only safe I've seen that really could be a problem is Herring's. They've never had one opened."

"Then we don't try for a Herring." Scott grinned as he gazed out at
the ice-bound Atlantic shores, the white rocks of New England marking the frozen boundary.

"Any news of Davey Cummings?" Jim asked.

"He's on to two banks, one in Elmira and another in Louisville.
He's found us the best pipe in the business, a fellow named Billy
Connors. Billy's gone to meet him in Louisville."

"Sounds good. How about yourself? Did Hustlin' Bob come up with
a scheme to finance this venture?"

Scott ignored the taunt. He rubbed a clear spot in the cabin window
and continued peering outside. "I said I'd take care of everything,
didn't I? You've a tremendous lack of faith, Jim. A weakness in all
you Scots." He rolled his eyes to the ceiling. "How could I have
teamed up with someone whose only ambition was to sit in front of a
train and go whoo-whoo!" He pulled an imaginary whistle cord several
times then dropped his hand in disgust. "A dreadful lack of ambition
and confidence. It'll be your undoing, Jim, mark my words."

Dunlap wasn't fooled by Scott's bravado. "Let me see. . . . This
scheme of yours requires a dozen men and twenty fast horses, right?"

"Now where would we get a dozen men?" Scott asked, faking annoyance. "God knows we've little enough to finance the rental of a
dozen fast horses!"

"Then what do we need?"

"Nothing." Scott shrugged. "You said you would do your share,
and I said I'd do mine. I can do it myself. If you'd like to have a carriage standing by in case a speedy exit is required, you may if you
like. Otherwise, I can handle it myself."

"No you don't!" Dunlap cried. "I want a ringside seat to whatever
plan you have."

"All right!" Scott answered, throwing up his hands in surrender.

Dunlap walked to the far corner of the cabin and eyed him skeptically. "Why don't I trust you?" he asked himself aloud. "Why is it
that I get this feeling you're hustling me?"

"It's that suspicious Scots nature of yours," Bob explained.

"No no, no no, that's not it at all!"

Scott pulled a harmonica from his jacket and blew it free of lint.

"When do we do this?" Dunlap demanded.

"Friday," Scott replied, stretching out on the horsehair lounge where he began a slow, mournful rendition of "Dixie."

"This Friday?" Dunlap asked in surprise.

Scott nodded as he played on. Dunlap wanted to question him further, but Scott had dismissed him completely, and Jim was forced to pace before the frosted windows and wonder what it was that Scott had up his sleeve.

Dunlap sat in a fast, light phaeton rented from George White, eagerly listening to Scott's instructions.

"You just keep abreast of me and when I signal you, a tip of the hat in acknowledgement will do nicely."

"That's all?"

"That's all."

"You sure?"

Scott looked at him evenly. "Would it help you to write it out?"

"No . . . just tip my hat?"

"Tip the hat. Touch the brim, whatever you like, just so long as you look a little stern," Scott said impatiently.

"I got it."

Scott blew a blast of steam from his mouth and clapped Dunlap on the back as he went off to his position.

A snow crew was working the far side of the street, shovelers throwing up drifts to the rear of a wagon. The laborers took a breather against their shovels as an empty wagon was moved up into place.

Scott had stationed himself against the corner of the building, where a quick glance through the window every few minutes told Dunlap that all was going well.

Inside, everything was proceeding nicely. At the appointed moment a little man rose from his desk and went to an inside closet. A respectable hat was placed firmly on thinning hair. Tailored gloves were adjusted, cane and black bag snatched up.

Outside, Scott watched carefully, adjusting the front of his coat as the man left the savings bank. The target moved briskly up the street, passing Scott's position. Bob gave the man a twenty pace lead, then followed behind. A quick smile to the puzzled Dunlap. It took a moment before Dunlap realized they were moving away from him, and he urged the horse to a slow walk. Scott nodded in appreciation, urging Dunlap to close the gap.

The little man with the black bag led them several blocks before turning into a deposit bank, with Scott and the carriage trailing behind. Scott took up a position thirty feet from the door, as Dunlap spied the patrolman emerging from a shop just a few doors away. He wanted to warn Scott and tried whistling, but his lips were near frozen. The uniformed officer rolled confidently down the street, moving up on Scott's position at an alarming rate. Dunlap tried clearing his throat, but no sound emerged into the raspy dryness of the winter air.

The two were almost abreast of each other when Scott saw the officer. Instead of hurrying away, Scott actually signaled the patrolman over. Dunlap saw Scott's arm go around the man's shoulder as they huddled conspiratorially. The officer nodded several times, then moved off a step to glance in Dunlap's direction. It took Jim a long moment before he remembered his duty and touched a quivering hand to the brim of his hat. The officer nodded in agreement to something and moved cautiously to the corner of the deposit bank.

The small man with the cane emerged into the street, gave a cursory glance in both directions before returning in the direction of the savings bank. As he passed Scott, Bob grabbed the man's arm, signaling the officer.

The frightened messenger turned to face the tall stranger as the policeman seized his free arm. "I'm detective La Fave," Scott announced, flashing a badge briefly under the man's nose, "from headquarters, and you, sir, are under arrest!"

The messenger cried, "But there must be some mistake!"

"That is correct, my friend," Scott announced, "and you've made it."

The policeman was placing handcuffs on the startled man's hands as Scott broke the clasp on the bag. Several people gathered to watch the criminal protest his innocence. A packet of bills was shown the

officer as Scott broadcast, "You see!" The interior of the bag was
flashed and the policeman happily noted the contents.

"You scoundrel!" the patrolman added, squeezing the handcuffs
down tight until the messenger cried out in pain.

An elderly woman shrieked, "Thief!" the point of her umbrella
stabbing the man about the chest and ribs.

"Take him to the station house!" Scott commanded. "I will take the
bag to Superintendent Kennedy, and we shall meet at the station!"

"But I *work* for the bank!" the man protested to anyone who would
listen.

"Some bank officer you are!" a passerby screamed in anger.

"Consider it done!" the patrolman saluted, visions of impending
promotion dancing in his head. Chin thrust forward, he roughly
shoved the messenger through the gathering crowd.

"This is all a mistake!" the messenger wailed.

"Villain!" another shouted. Several others took the man's arm and
assisted the officer in hustling the robber to the station house. Scott
climbed into the carriage, placed the bag on his lap and smiled as
man and mob buzzed angrily up the street.

Dunlap set the horse to a quick trot and demanded, "What was that
all about?"

"The man was a renowned counterfeiter. I showed the officer my
badge and told him I'd been working on the case for months and
asked that he assist me in making the arrest. Convinced it would look
good on his record, the poor fellow was only too glad to oblige. As you
probably noticed, the bag was full of money, and the patrolman was
already convinced it was counterfeit. The rest was relatively simple."

"My God!" Dunlap cried, sending the phaeton around a slow-mov-
ing coal wagon. "How much is in there?"

Scott tipped his hat to several passing females as he casually replied, "Enough to get us going. About thirty thousand, I would say."

Scott was at the window of Dunlap's room; below him on Broadway
the crowd hurried about their errands. "I wish it were spring, Jim," he
said wistfully over his shoulder as Dunlap counted the bills out onto a
marble-topped dressing table. "I want to see young ladies in parasols

and the latest Paris creations. Everyone is so bundled against the winter it's impossible to tell whether they're fifteen or fifty!"

Dunlap threw the last bundle down and said softly, "Forty-five thousand dollars."

"Where are the blue-stocking ladies I've heard so much about?

"Did you hear what I said?" Dunlap asked, crossing to Scott at the window sill.

"Uh huh," Scott mumbled, the strong chin cupped in his hand as he gazed down on the street below.

"You're a wonder, you are," Dunlap sighed, thinking that Reilly had been right. Bob Scott was the coolest man he'd ever known. Dunlap knew he had never met anyone like him, and there had been many brave men in his life.

Scott stroked the dark moustache raised during his thirty days in the Hoboken hostelry that added several years to his youthful appearance.

"Don't you miss the ladies, Jim? Don't you miss that Bridget Hickey of yours?"

Dunlap moved the bills into tidy little bundles. "I see ol' Tom's told you about her. Yes, I miss her. But I was never what you would call a ladies' man. It's hard to go callin' when there's a hole in your boot big enough to allow your foot to escape. It's hard to go callin' with hands rough as plowshares and nails dark with railroad grease and soot. I never had more coin in my pocket than would buy my next meal or five cents worth of cigarette papers. Not 'till I met Tom Reilly did I have a penny to squander."

"And not 'till I met you, Jim," Scott said against the pane, "had I a penny, either. Now look at me!" he announced, turning into the room. "Silk ties, braid tucked twenty-dollar shirts, and me having to think twice about which end of the cane touches the ground!"

Scott swaggered to the mirror, fingering the fine silk tie about his neck. "My mother swore that the only thing I'd ever wear around my throat would be a rope. 'Scragged to the gallows,' she warned me. I ran away to join the war when I was thirteen. That didn't set well with her. Then when I was sent off at seventeen, she was sure of it. Now, thanks to you, I'm a gentleman! But I've missed five good years of my life, Jim. I don't intend to spend any more time inside cold stone walls. I'm going to learn to speak properly . . . and dress properly. I'm going to be a real gentleman, Jim, you can count on that."

Dunlap grinned. "You're beginning to look the part."

"I feel it, too, Jim! I feel it!"

Scott shrugged quickly into the dark sack coat and adjusted the shawl collar. He drew the material tight across the broad shoulders, then tucked an errant hair into place on his moustache. He tapped a black felt hat to his head and plucked a piece of lint from its ribbon.

"I'm going to do my share, Jim! You'll see that my word's golden!" He squeezed into chamois gloves and struck a pose with his gold-crowned walking stick. He carefully inspected himself in the mirror from patent leather shoes to the fashionable hat atop his jet black hair.

"Hurry, Jim!" he suddenly shouted. "The ladies have been kept waiting for five long years! They won't wait forever!"

Dunlap chuckled, "I have to visit the machinist. We have to order the tools for Louisville."

"That can wait, man! He'll still be there tomorrow! There are ladies at Shang Draper's who have been kept waiting for years! Must we disappoint them for even a moment longer?"

After a moment's hesitation, Dunlap hurriedly smoothed the vest. He drew the jacket from the bed as Bob Scott counted quickly through the money.

"A thousand should do us tonight, Jim, what do you say?"

"A thousand?" Dunlap choked.

"We'll need money for cards, man! There'll be cards of fortune awaiting our nimble fingers! Hurry, man, hurry!"

In the short period of time that Mr. K. W. Smith had been entrusted with the Louisville office, as agent for the Mutual Life Insurance Company of Newark, New Jersey, he had built up a reputable clientele and just three months before had been dutifully rewarded by the home office with a sizable Christmas bonus.

Smith danced out of his topcoat that protected him against the brisk March morning and had just settled at his desk when a sharp knock signaled an early client.

A tall, stylishly dressed young man entered wearing a short, dark goatee and moustache, introduced himself as Hill and, shucking expensive gloves, began enumerating his insurance needs.

Smith jotted down the information as rapidly as it was given, while the young man paced the room. Smith could tell a large policy was in the offing and he ignored the nervous shrug of the man's shoulders, as the visitor moved restlessly from one wall to the other then back again, stopping only momentarily for Smith to catch up with the figures.

"The employees of the Fall City Tobacco Bank just below you gave me your name," Hill concluded.

Smith brightened considerably. "I'm glad they think so highly of me."

"I do have one reservation," Hill shrugged again, setting the broad shoulders into place in what Smith was now convinced was a tic. "My family has to be sure that a far-reaching company in New Jersey can provide us with proper representation in Louisville as well as St. Louis."

"I'm sure I can put those worries to rest, Mr. Hill."

"I hope so." Hill frowned, checking his pocket watch briefly. "I'm late for another appointment, Mr. Smith. I've just purchased twenty-five hundred head of beef, and I must be there to make the down payment. If you will excuse me, we will conclude this at another time."

"Of course."

"Tomorrow, perhaps." Hill smiled in a businesslike fashion before breezing out the door and down the stairs to Main Street.

Smith waved goodbye and added a slight bow. He gave the visitor just a moment's thought before the policy figures settled home. The pacing and nervous shrug were discounted as he began adding the figures to what he was sure was an impressive new account.

The Great Eastern Menagerie, Museum and Circus arrived one week later in Louisville, Kentucky, setting up their single-ring tent on the corner of East and Chestnut streets. Unlike P. T. Barnum, who had just introduced the second ring to circus fans, Eastern had not yet been caught up in the new fad.

The sky was clear, and the citizenry was promised a spectacular weekend. But by Saturday evening, a wind rose that sent the canvas beating over the heads of the sell-out crowd, causing a minor disturbance at first between the spectators and the animals. The winds gathered force. "La Petite Anna," the tiny female equestrienne, was having a difficult time with her mounts, but the audience responded with enthusiasm to the added handicaps, cheering wildly each time she dismounted.

High against the billowing canvas, the Miaco brothers drew the breath from the crowd as they darted from bar to bar, unperturbed by the rising gale.

A few blocks away, Phil Lottech, the proprietor of the St. Charles Hotel, prepared to turn in for the evening. A gust of wind rattled his window, an insistent reminder to draw the shades. Lottech saw an empty barrel rolling down the street. He hoped the hotel roof wouldn't be damaged by the high winds. A man stepped from the shadow of the Fall City Tobacco Bank directly across the street. Ducking into the wind, he took up a position directly beneath Lottech's window. The proprietor felt a momentary twinge of remorse for those poor individuals forced out on this ungodly night. Then he drew the shade against the elements.

Below the window Billy Connors huddled protectively against the hotel. A tall silk hat jammed firmly on his head, several layers of clothing about his portly frame, a string attached to his wrist, Billy was prepared for the long, cold evening.

If the proprietor's eyes had been what they had as a youth, he would have seen the string. He would have been alarmed to realize that it ran from below his window, across the street and up the stairway to the second floor of the building. He would not, however, have been able to see that from there it continued down the hall, through the door of the Mutual Life Insurance Company, past the desk of agent Smith, where it disappeared down a hole cut in the floor and into the vault of the bank below. The string ended its long journey firmly fixed to the wrist of Bob Scott.

A massive steel frame bolted to the floor in front of the safe would give Davey Cummings the opportunity to prove his claim of being one of the best "peelers" in the business. The inch-thick upright frame, properly braced, had allowed a feedscrew drill to bore a hole in the upper corner of the four-foot Diebold Borhmann safe. Davey removed the drill and attached a threaded hook into the safe front that slipped through a slot in the frame where Dunlap and Scott applied a gigantic threaded nut. Tightening the nut drew the hook tightly into the safe. The leverage exerted thousands of pounds of pressure, demanding that something give. In a few seconds, the sweating trio was rewarded with a loud crack, as the safe door surrendered its precarious grip on the upper corner, allowing ample room for the placement of explosives.

At Scott's feet lay the combination dial, broken from the safe door with a few powerful swings of a sledgehammer. To the right stood a second, smaller safe, as yet unassaulted.

There were now two openings for powder. The frame was removed, as Dunlap made a paper funnel. Six ounces of Harvey and Curtis ducking powder was poured in. Three heads watched it drain slowly into the upper corner of the safe. Four more ounces were sent into the gaping dial wound, a paper fuse attached.

"You think that's enough?" Dunlap asked.

"I've never blown a door before," Cummings explained.

A glance to Scott brought Dunlap an undecided shrug.

"The army taught me about explosives," Dunlap mumbled, "but they said nothing about breaking bolts on safes."

The fuses were set just as the long black beard of George Mason dropped through the hole in the floor. "I have the wagon ready; you want I should load anything?"

"Not yet," Cummings said. "We need some blankets, though!"

Large horse blankets tumbled through the opening, and they were quickly packed around the safe to muffle the explosion.

The seams were puttied, the fuses set, there seemed nothing left for Dunlap to do but touch the match. "Everybody upstairs," he ordered.

George Mason pulled Scott up first, together they pulled Davey Cummings into the insurance office, then the three heads reappeared at the hole to watch Dunlap finish the task.

Mason had a wild excitement in his intense blue eyes. Having burgled his first bank at twenty, he was by far the most experienced of the group. At thirty-five he boasted a dozen turn-offs with men like Langdon Moore, Jimmy Hope and Ned Lyons. And now, his excitement was so great that his laugh through clenched teeth was a low, sensual moan.

"I'm ready!" Dunlap called up. Scott took up the slack in the string. He gave it a hearty tug, asking Billy Connors outside if all was clear to blow the safe.

Connors had crossed back to the Fall City Tobacco Bank, winding the billowing string about his wrist as he did so. The wind made it impossible for him to operate from the best vantage point; he would have to be near the end of the sring where the wind wouldn't pull at it constantly. He felt the signal and checked his watch to see just how much time was left before Varilla, the watchman, would be making his rounds. He decided there was plenty of time yet. The street was clear. He gave the go ahead with two sharp tugs.

Dunlap had spent over a month working daily with the German Steurer in the Hester Street basement. He had practiced setting up the heavy frame until the watchful machinist was satisfied Jim could do it alone in a darkened vault. All that was left was to touch the match.

Scott called down, "All right, Jim!"

Dunlap closed his eyes and took a deep breath. A wooden match was struck and held for a second to insure its proper burning. A nervous glance to the hole showed him his companions were waiting with dangling arms to pull him quickly from the vault.

The match was touched to the paper fuse. The flame jumped quickly from the match and raced the paper into the blankets. Even before Dunlap turned to the hole, he knew the fuse was burning far too rapidly.

Scott waited at the hole, his arms hanging far into the banking room. When Dunlap turned to him, Bob saw the wide eyes, the fright and confusion in Jim's face. Dunlap took two steps to the offered arms. He extended his own in the air, felt the reassuring slap of hands on his wrists as his friends lifted him from the ground. The explosion caught him a foot off the floor. The tremendous roar blew him from Bob's grasp, sent him tumbling in the air to bounce off some solid object.

White plaster dust enveloped the vault and rolled up the hole into the Smith office. Scott woke to find himself almost in the hallway. He choked his way back to the hole on hands and knees. "Jim!" he called frantically. "Jim! Are you all right, man?"

Outside, the raging winds carried the sound away with a fortunate howl that began just a split second before the explosion. Its force nearly bowled Billy off his feet, and he would not have heard the detonation at all had he not been properly alert to it. He checked the windows of the St. Charles Hotel as he regained his balance. All was quiet.

That same gust broke the center pole of the circus tent and created a momentary panic. Luckily, it snapped just ten feet from the top, where the rigging could hold it in place, allowing Charles Lowry to complete his daring hurdles and distract the crowd.

"Jim!" Scott screamed into the dust-filled hole, waving the air about like a madman. He wasn't sure if he heard a moan or groan, his ears were ringing so. The string was thrown aside as Bob eased himself down through the narrow hole in the floor. He stumbled over Dunlap huddled in the corner, covered completely by a fine white powder.

Dunlap remembered the surgeon probing his arm for the minié ball. The opium pill had eased the pain until the surgeon's finger moved deep inside his shoulder. He saw him remove bits of material from the wound, the scalpel gripped between his teeth, ready to amputate the arm when the ball was found. Dunlap woke in a fury, swinging his way free of the hands that gripped him.

"Jim!"

"Huh?" he cried, backing as far away as possible, scooting across the floor to put a safe distance between himself and the surgeon with the crippling scalpel.

"Jim! Are you all right!"

Dunlap was breathing rapidly as he managed to open one eye. Scott's white-powdered face materialized from the white gauze that hung about the room.

Scott tipped the head up with his fingers. "You all right?"

Dunlap shook his head once, then again before anything made sense. "Damn paper fuses . . . "

Cummings jumped into the whiteness and hit the floor heavily. "It's open! By God, it's open!"

Scott hugged Dunlap with abandon. "We did it, Jim! We did it!"

Dunlap had to be helped to his feet and shown the doors hanging askew. Scott slapped him on the back several times as Jim stared dizzily at his handiwork. The Diebold Borhmann's bolts had been blown free and the casing twisted and warped beyond repair. Above them, Mason gleefully moaned his insane laugh as Cummings punched Dunlap about the back.

Jim was close to collapse. The strain and uncertainty had been overpowering; now he wanted to sit on the floor and recreate every step taken so he might never forget it. It had been a long week's work on the entrance to the vault. It had been a long month of study with the German machinist. *It had all been worthwhile.*

Billy Connors dried his nose on the edge of his glove. At the appointed hour, the watchman appeared on Main Street. Billy gave the warning signal on the string, received a reply and took refuge in a dark doorway.

Varilla went to the front door of the bank, shook it to his satisfaction, placed his muffled face against the glass and peered inside. A lone lamp burning near the vault enabled him to see that all was quiet inside. He gave the area a quick glance, then resumed his route down Main Street. Connors gave the man five minutes more before tugging an all clear.

Billy had no idea of the ring's progress. There had been no second explosion, nor had he been asked for permission to detonate a second charge. There was also the question of the two men, Dunlap and Scott. He thought them inexperienced and young. Likable though they seemed, turning off banks was a business fraught with danger, and one could easily be killed trying to flee an angry town whose citizens had just been robbed. People didn't take too kindly to having their life's work stolen. He liked them both immensely, but Scott appeared heedless of the dangers. Billy thought the tall young man either crazy or immature. Dunlap, on the other hand, was cool, receptive to suggestions, and showed a willingness to adapt. Scott was not so easy to convince. Scott was a gambler, Billy thought, and a high roller at that. Perhaps the combination was a good one. There was no way of knowing. These things took time to decide, and it was hopeless to try and reason it out with the wind driving an icy spike into your eardrum.

The exuberant circus crowd filled the streets with patrons bent double into the wind, forcing Billy to signal a halt to the work inside the vault. It was to be a delay of more than an hour before the crowd had cleared. During this time, Mason was stationed near the rear stairs, a large pistol in his pocket to interrupt anyone surprising the men at the hole. He had been lurking in the shadows, deep eyes burning, hair wild, and a maniacal grin half-hidden in the foot-long beard. Connors had been almost upon him when Mason said, "Billy?"

"Aaah!" Connors screamed, delighting Mason no end.

"I was just makin' sure it was you, Billy," Mason chuckled.

Connors backed away from the man, throwing a "Damn you, George!" back into the darkness. He was still shaken when he gathered the string to signal the men back to work. He had known Mason for six years before he grew that enormous, evil-looking beard. He knew it was meant to conceal a six-inch scar on Mason's cheek, but it gave the man a truly terrifying aspect.

At six in the morning, Lottech, the proprietor of the St. Charles Hotel, raised his shade on the debris scattered about Main Street. The wind had filled every available nook with leaves and branches. A large limb lay in the street between the hotel and the bank. Across the street, a man with auburn whiskers and a light moustache was blowing on gloved fingers. Lottech turned back to his room, picked up a collar to complete his toilette, and the man was gone.

Promptly at the usual hour the bank clerk, Henry Sauer, opened the front doors of the Tobacco Bank for business. He noted the rubble outside and made a mental note to see it was cleared before the bank's patrons arrived. He removed his hat and coat, withdrew the key to the teller's drawer from a vest pocket. He unlocked the drawer, concluding the first part of his morning ritual.

Charles Brent, a junior clerk, was next on the scene, and Sauer issued orders to have the front swept and a fire stoked in the stove to take the chill off the morning's depositors.

The next order of business was for Sauer to open both sets of vault doors. He dialed the combination while Brent stoked the fire, talking excitedly of the circus and the high winds that almost canceled the evening's entertainment. In his inspired reenactment of the night's events, he did not see that Sauer was having a difficult time with the vault handle.

Puzzled, Sauer cleared the tumblers, slowly reset each of the numbers on the combination dial and threw his weight behind the handle. It refused to budge. Twice more he tried the four numbers, painstakingly placing each one under the arrow, spinning slowly to the next number, only to have the handle defy him.

Brent returned with a bucket filled with coal, saw the clerk's trouble and lent his assistance. For the better part of an hour the two tugged and dialed, yanked and sweated over the massive doors.

The officers of the bank were called. "There's either something wrong with the combination or the bolt mechanism's jammed," one of them decided. Locksmith Charley Sneed and his foreman Ellis were sent for and ordered to "bring all the necessary tools for entrance into the vault."

After several hours of drilling, Sneed and Ellis managed to bore a large hole near the combination dial. A pry bar was inserted, and the two attempted to force the main bolt from its moorings. It was three in the afternoon before they succeeded. As several dozen spectators watched, crowding the tiny bank, Sneed forced the vault door open. A simple pine wedge, several inches long, fell at his feet.

"What is it?" someone asked anyone in a position to see.

"A piece of wood."

"A piece of wood?"

"A piece of wood."

Sneed had it in his hands. He rolled it about for the director's inspection. "It must have been driven in behind the large iron lock bolt," he commented with authority, much to the chagrin of the bank officers, who now exchanged worried looks, suspecting the worst, for there was yet another set of doors between them and the two inside safes.

On the opening of the inner doors, the bank officers confronted a scene to justify their alarm. The doors of the large iron safe hung open, tools littered the floor, horse blankets lay bundled in the corner, and empty safe deposit boxes were scattered on the floor. The smaller safe did not appear to have been touched. But directly over their heads was a large, covered hole.

The officers stared at the ceiling in bewilderment. A twenty-four-by-fifteen-inch hole had been cut through a one-inch-thick sheet of chilled iron. Above that, two feet of masonry and brick had somehow been removed. But beyond that, the hole was dark, and they could see no more.

Sauer led the silent gathering outside and up the stairway to Smith's office. The agent was surprised to see thirty men crowd into his tiny quarters, and rose in confusion. The men glared at the agent, the carpet covering the floor, the desk, his papers. Without a word, the cavalcade did an about face and thundered down the stairs. Smith listened to their retreat, scratching his head in bewilderment, and sat back down.

In the vault, the gathering stared sullenly up into hole. There was a second stampede up the stairs. Smith heard them coming and backed from his desk in alarm.

"There's a hole here!" someone insisted.

"What?" the agent cried.

"There's a hole here!"

"Where?" Smith choked, certain they were all crazy.

Then the carpet near his desk began to rise and Sauer's head appeared.

"Daring as well as skill marks it as one of the boldest robberies ever perpetrated." the *Louisville Courier-Journal* stated, "and but for a fortunate mistake of the burglars would have resulted in a tremendous haul for the daring and successful operators. But they made a great mistake in passing up the small safe, and for all their troubles they secured only a few thousand dollars. It bears the footprint in every step of its progress of the PROFESSIONAL BURGLAR, and it must have been done by the most skillful and versatile of that class as no precaution seems to have been neglected even to muffled tools and the smothered sound of the explosion."

By the time New York's newest burglary ring reached Columbus, Ohio, the Tobacco Bank's revised losses had climbed to $100,000.

Upon reaching Pittsburg, they learned that another audit had sent the figure escalating to $300,000, and the bank officers admitted, "The figure was still climbing."

Sneed, the locksmith, marveled for the *Courier-Journal*, "The burglars had drilled 190 holes in the iron ceiling to gain entry," estimating a week's work for their successful operation.

Later the paper admitted, "The fact that they did it is beyond dispute, and their success stamps them as men of genius in their time."

Kentucky courts found that the robbery posed a new dilemma. Private parties having notes due the bank, yet secured by collateral such as stocks and bonds which were now among the missing funds, questioned the bank's liability. The bank insisted they could not be held responsible; the bank's patrons thought otherwise. The matter was left to the courts of Kentucky. Suddenly banks across the country were nervously watching the outcome of the litigation.

"How does it feel?" White asked.

Jim held the cut-glass container to his lips, smiled serenely across to White as he indicated the red and gilt opulence of Delmonico's.

"Exquisite," he giggled drunkenly.

"Where's Scott?"

"Well . . . Robert met a young lady on the train and is hotly pursuing her to some remote village in Pennsylvania. He says he and Billy are going to look at a bank. But I know better."

"And George Mason? Did he work out all right?"

"George was excellent! A little strange, maybe, but excellent."

"He's had a number of years running with old Jimmy Hope and Ned Lyons. He's one of the best."

"And Davey Cummings was everything you said he'd be. And Billy Connors, well, ol' Billy stood his ground though a cyclone raged around us. A cool one, he is."

"Billy's piped for the best of them. When he tells you the layout of a bank, you can be sure it's so. He's become something of a celebrity at Red Leary's saloon. That four-leaf clover birthmark on his cheek is considered an omen of true good fortune. I wouldn't be a bit surprised if he isn't in great demand when he returns from wherever Bob's taken him."

"He's certainly brought us good fortune," Jim acknowledged. "But I had a two-fold purpose in seeing you. First, I want to thank you for all your help. We never would have turned off Kentucky if you hadn't come up with the team we needed."

White spun the end of his gray moustache attentively. "You're very welcome, my boy. Amd what was the other item on your mind?"

"I need more information," he apologized. "Davey Cummings led me to believe there were certain men within the police department who might be of great service to Scott and me, if we were willing to pay the price. I think Davey mentioned 'a share.'"

"The Bank Ring," White conceded, "as we call them. But they are very expensive," he warned.

"The question remains, can Scott and I operate out of New York City if we don't strike some sort of bargain with this Bank Ring?" Possibly it was the liquor muddling Jim's thoughts, but it seemed to him that each day brought forth yet a new "ring" of graft, corruption and outright larceny. The Tweed Ring had been easy to understand—a city government bilking the treasury for millions under various guises. Then there had been the Erie Ring which he'd never truly understood. The Canal Ring, a group of businessmen, had something to do with the finagling of canal moneys. The Whiskey Ring, the Tammany Ring, which he wasn't sure wasn't part of the Tweed Ring, the Press Ring, the Indian Ring—now the Bank Ring. If the Bank Ring consisted of policemen, and the Tammany and Tweed rings were made up of politicians, and the Erie and Canal rings were businessmen, and the Whiskey and Indian rings were government officials, who was there left to steal from?

"It will be very unlikely that they'll let you operate for long," White cautioned. "I'm sure the Louisville police are here in this city right now, meeting with our own police, trying desperately to find a clue to their robbery. You and Scott might operate for a while untouched, but for any length of time—impossible."

"Who are they?" Jim demanded.

"Let's just say they are the top detectives. Captain Irving heads the group, and you can't go any higher than that." White smiled reluctantly. "It's something you'll have to do eventually, Jim. My advice to you is the sooner the better."

"You pay them a share?"

"Of course."

"What will this service cost us?"

"Twenty percent. Right off the top."

Dunlap whistled softly. "That's what you would do?"

"That is what I would do," White regretfully advised. "These men have connections everywhere. I wouldn't be a bit surprised if they already know you were involved in the Louisville turn-off. My guess is they'll give you a little time just to see how smart you are. If you wait too long, it will be too late."

Dunlap forced a grin. "If that's how it is, that's how it is," he said helplessly.

"Make no mistake, Jim," White warned in a low voice. "You'll have to be wary. What reward has Louisville offered?"

"Fifty thousand."

"A tempting enough sum. You in turn will offer them their 20 percent to keep hands off. What is the figure at 20 percent?"

"A little over sixty thousand."

"On the one hand, we have fifty thousand that will not have to be split with anyone. On the other, you're offering them sixty thousand that will have to be split among a dozen different detectives. Do you understand my meaning?"

Dunlap nodded thoughtfully. "I see what you're saying . . . "

"I could handle this for you, but it would be best if you met them yourself."

"I'll be careful."

"Good!" White said. "They can be valuable allies. They can send the Louisville police to Canada and Europe chasing decoys. So you must not underestimate their value! The men I deal with have been loyal to me; they warn me when an out-of-town sheriff is nosing around. For this I reward them amply."

"A definite advantage."

"Keep them informed of your plans. Not too far ahead, but certainly informed. Myself, I see they are paid immediately upon my return to the city. I don't cheat them on their share but offer it willingly. They've done all right by me over the years. When you stop and think that while there was but one bank robbed ten years ago, now there are dozens turned off every year, they stand to make a great deal of money as protectors of the citizens of New York. It's a very lucrative job to be sure."

The shield was stamped "New York City Detective Bureau." The man who palmed it said thickly, "Radford."

"Jim Dunlap."

The detective kept Dunlap half-stooped to the table as he surveyed the prominent and professional in the lobby of the Grand Central Hotel. The man appeared to be scenting the room.

Dunlap finally slid back into his seat as Radford glanced disdainfully around one more time. When the man took the seat, he gave Dunlap a leisurely examination and clearly found him wanting, too.

A large envelope lay on the table, and Jim slid it toward the man. "I think this is for you. I know you will see it gets to the right people."

Radford drew back his hands. "What's in it?"

"Second mortgage bonds valued at a thousand dollars each. Twenty percent of the cash and securities from Louisville's Tobacco Bank. Sixty-three thousand dollars in all."

The detective was obviously unimpressed.

"I think that makes us even," Dunlap added.

"You do, huh?" Radford sneered.

Dunlap showed a smile. "I do."

"What about the bank messenger?" Radford snapped. "You think we're local boys with hayseed in our ears? You owe us for that one, too!"

Radford was very well informed, Dunlap decided. "Yes" he fumbled, "the bank messenger."

"Scott's little trick makes it another nine thousand," Radford shot back, turning his back on Dunlap as he studied the other patrons.

"You'll have to trust me for another day or so."

Radford spun back to the envelope; he seemed undecided.

Dunlap took the opportunity to say, "The reward's only fifty thousand. You lock Scott and me up and there'll be no more envelopes—none at all. We plan to do a lot of busines with you. I took the liberty to see that Captain Irving received a note this morning, informing him that I was meeting with you and passing over sixty thousand to be di-

vided up. So if you're entertaining any thought of going for the reward, you'll have to explain it to Irving and the rest of the boys. I
doubt they'll be too happy with you."

Radford's fingers crept to the envelope. He hefted it mentally as it
balanced on his hand. A resigned shrug and the envelope inched into
the vest until it was lost from sight.

"You'll let me know when the Louisville authorities arrive?"

"They're already here," Radford grumbled. "The captain's giving
them the runaround. We knew who it was that done the job. We knew
it was you and Davey Cummings and Billy Connors. Mason was the
one who drove the wagon and handled the tools, am I right?"

"Absolutely," Dunlap admitted.

"We were giving you just a few more days to see how smart you
were."

Dunlap laughed. "I like to think I'm above average."

"Maybe you are," Radford relented. "So what do you have going?"

"We're looking at a couple of banks out of town."

Radford asked quickly, "Anything in New York?"

"Not at the moment."

Radford tapped his chest. "When you do a job in town, you let me
know. Most of them have a Holmes alarm that's hooked up to the station house. You give the word and I'll see it don't work that night. I
can also arrange to have a beat cop on patrol who's an all right guy."

"That's comforting to know," Dunlap grinned.

Radford tapped the bulging vest. "I'll see that this is taken care
of."

"And I'll tell my friends to breathe easier?"

"Get the nine thousand!" Radford shot back, "*then* you can
breathe!"

"Consider it done."

"And your friends have no cause for worry—they have the best
money can buy."

"We'll see," Dunlap said cautiously. He knew all about men like
Radford. All his life he'd known them—all swagger and small substance.

"Pinkerton's won't bother you none, either," Radford assured him.
The detective chinned his collar into position, rubbed his nose and
was gone.

Dunlap laughed sarcastically. He had just paid a man over sixty thousand dollars, and the man hadn't even been courteous enough to mumble a "thank you." He deliberated a moment about Pinkerton's, wondering why the railroad detective agency should bother him. *What do they have to do with us?* he thought. He made a mental note to see George White and ask him about Pinkerton's, and what Radford had meant when he'd said, "Pinkerton's won't bother you none."

There were 200,000 Germans in New York by the early spring of '73. Thousands of beer halls and rathskellers had sprung up to accommodate their taste in music and beer. The Bowery sported two of the finest, the German Winter Garden and, just across the street, the most prominent of all, the Atlantic Garden.

White reserved a rear table directly beneath a multi-globed chandelier and across from the orchestra playing a succession of Strauss waltzes from its balcony perch to the noisy appreciation of the crowd. A barrel vault ceiling, lavishly ornamented with gilt and plasterwork, ran the center of the great hall, and a half dozen enormous chandeliers lit the entire room.

White ordered huge steins of dark German beer, nibbling at assorted cheeses, his hands dancing across the table in time with the orchestra's three-quarter beat.

Eyes twinkling, he informed Dunlap that it was he and he alone who had christened the detectives "the Bank Ring." The ring consisted of James Irving, head of the detective bureau, John Jourdan, captain of the sixth precinct, and several inspectors right below them. A dozen or more detectives were linked to this chain of corruption, and the patrolmen below them White couldn't begin to number. He admitted that ten years of contributing to their cause had gained him tremendous political clout. Several hundred thousand dollars had made him an important stockholder in departmental procedure. When a vacancy occurred at the head of the bureau upon John Young's resignation for refusing to split a $17,500 reward for Mark Shinburn's capture, it was White who met with Boss Tweed to suggest that Irving be given the post to stabilize a shaky department. Tweed had accepted his recommendation, and Jimmy Irving became head of the Bank Ring.

White told Dunlap there were only two types of duty for a lowly patrolman—"Goatsville," or cold rocky fields for the honest, and "snap" for those on the warm under-belly of corruption. "It's a snap" meant for good duty.

"Radford said something about the Pinkertons," Dunlap pressed above the music. "What do railroad detectives have to do with me?"

White looked at him in surprise. He popped a radish into his mouth and chewed it slowly, washing it down with a deep draft of beer. The foam was wiped carefully from the gray moustache. "Where have you been, Jimmy? They're no longer railroad detectives! They work for the banks as well!"

"They do?" he shrugged, unimpressed. He raised the beer stein in toast. "Then we'll just stay away from them!" he laughed.

They detrained at the depot in Philadelphia amid a crush of travelers hurrying off to other trains and waiting friends. A porter struggled with their luggage as Billy Connors and Bob Scott made their way toward the interior of the depot. Suddenly they were stopped in their tracks by the terrified cries of a child. Hundreds of heads turned at the commotion.

Two porters were down on their hands and knees at the platform's edge, peering beneath a huffing engine, while a young girl nearby sobbed uncontrollably. Each fresh blast of scalding steam had the porters dodging.

"What's the commotion?" Scott asked a porter.

"The little girl's pet, sir. Its basket tumbled from our cart and fell beneath the engine."

"Well, retrieve it, man!" he ordered. "The child's hysterical!"

The porter held the empty basket aloft. "The cat's loose, sir, lost in the steam somewhere."

"Snowball!" the child wailed.

If the elder sister hadn't taken that moment to cry, "Poor puss!" Scott might never have noticed her. She was in her teens with flyaway curls and large luminous violet eyes swimming with tears. Cornflowers atop a yellow straw bonnet framed the perfect face. For several moments, Scott stared in numbed admiration.

"My God," he whispered to Billy, "that's the most beautiful girl I've ever seen."

"C'mon, Bob, we're goin' to miss the train to Pittsburgh!" Billy tugged vainly at Scott's arm.

Bob shrugged him away as the girl turned her pleading, tear-filled gaze upon him. She drew the younger girl closer while the burly rail-road men shouted instructions to the engineer. She seemed to single him out for support.

Removing his silk top hat, Scott covered the distance between them quickly, and offered, "Perhaps I could be of some help?"

The youngest howled her response, while the elder sister said simply, "Oh, please, sir, please."

"It would be my pleasure," he said firmly. He thrust the silk hat into Billy's surprised hand, then shrugged the MacFarlon cape from his shoulders. Offering a slight bow as he backed to the tracks, he drew the cape over his head and ducked past the porters and crew beneath the engine. Snatching the empty wicker basket, he elbowed his way between coal car and engine. Hooded by the cape, dragging the basket, he made his way between the massive, spoked wheels to a spot directly under the engineer's controls.

The Baldwin engine blew off jets of steam, making visibility all but impossible. Continuing on his belly between the bull-head rails and timber sleepers, he paused directly beneath the fiery boiler. Peering from inside the hood, he found the object of everyone's concern.

Snowball was little more than a kitten, huddled into a terror-stricken ball, basted in heavy engine oil and floured with coal dust. It crouched against the bolt holding the rail to the wooden ties. The intense heat, the crackling of the furnace above, the hissing of the safety valves made the kitten's pitiful cries inaudible.

Squirming forward, Scott nabbed a handful of wet fur. One hand flipped the basket open, and the protesting kitten was placed safely inside.

There was a hearty round of applause from passengers and crew alike as he emerged between the wheels, the basket offered before him. Hands whisked it away to the golden-haired sisters, as Billy Connors and the porters worked to draw Scott from the searing steam. The soiled basket safely within the grasp of the weeping child, her sister rushed to embrace him. Scott waved her away with sooty palms, and she blushed at her uncontrolled outburst. Stepping back uncertainly she cried, "Oh, look at your clothes! They're ruined!"

"It's nothing," he said lightly, tremendously pleased with himself.

"How can we ever thank you?" she asked excitedly, cheeks flushing as she started to brush his clothing then as quickly withdrew her hand to her mouth.

Scott smiled his boyish grin. *He was certainly a mess,* he thought, trousers and sleeves dripping oil, smudges marring nose and chin. *What a way to meet the most beautiful girl in the world.*

"Perhaps you could tell me your name?"

"My name is Mary Wood," she apologized, "and this is my sister Amelia."

"Robert Scott," he said, bowing slightly from the waist.

She answered with a proper curtsy, sending her eyes to the platform. When she rose, she smiled so brilliantly it took his breath away. "My . . . " he said somewhat stunned. "My . . . "

"I've very pleased to meet you, sir," she said demurely.

"My goodness . . . " he sighed.

Armed with books on locks, in a small rented stable not far from the shop of the machinist Steurer, Jim Dunlap began to equip the wooden structure as a workshop. Several small safes were purchased, their locks carefully studied. He learned that a padlock was originally designed as a lock for a basket. He littered a makeshift workbench with every type of lock made—Yale and Towne, Chubb, Bramah, Lips, Cotterill, Hobbs, Andrews, Perkins, Sargent, and the safe locks of Lillie, Herring, Hall, Marvin, Diebolt, and one of the new Holmes electric time locks.

The Holmes promised the end to White's modus operandi. No longer would a terrified cashier and his family be able to open a safe in the wee small hours that was timed to open later. White viewed the lock with distress. "It's the end of an era," he said woefully. Then with a profound sigh he whispered, "It was bound to happen. . . . Who can blame them? I still have a few more years before the locks find a wide market. Maybe by then I'll retire." He shook his head in disappointment and regret.

The Yale combination lock caught White's eye. He held it aloft for Dunlap's attention. "What do you think of it?"

"The damn thing seems impregnable," Jim replied. "If there's a flaw in it, I can't find it!"

White shucked his coat, a gleam of amusement in his eyes. He locked the Yale into the vise, tossed several tools aside until he found a particular wrench. A hammer was held ready. The wrench was carefully attached to the combination knob. Tapping lightly while rotating the wrench, White wore the threads off the brass screw holding the spindle to the works.

George slipped the spindle free, exposing the inner workings. He fashioned a similar spindle in size, but hollow. The White replacement was put into place, a thin rod inserted down the hollow spindle, and with a single tap, George White punched the cogs free. The old combination knob was placed on the lock and removed from the vise.

"Open it," George insisted. Dunlap pulled the iron bow, and the lock came open.

"Lock it and open it again."

Dunlap found he could lock and open it at will.

White rolled the cuffs into position, gathered up his coat and smiled securely. "The trouble with you, Jim, you believe every lock is impregnable. I remember you said the same about the Lillie safe."

"I know so damn little about this business!" Jim confessed ashamedly. "You and Davey Cummings and George Mason are so much more experienced. That's why I hired this shop, to try and catch up."

"You know, Jim, there's no such thing as impregnable," George said. "Strike that word forever from your vocabulary! People like you and me and the others decide what is or isn't impregnable! Nobody else! Our talents create an industry! There are people all over the world, huddling together just as we are, a handful of locks at their disposal. Only they're trying to figure a way to prevent what we just did to that old Yale combination. The safe companies have brilliant young men analyzing your method of cracking that safe in Louisville.

They're bound and determined it will never happen to one of their boxes! But it will!" he said eagerly. "We'll beat them at their own game! They'll design them bigger and better and we'll bust them open on some dark weekend and back they'll go to their little workshops!"

White held the coat for Dunlap to assist him into it. "You're a lot like me, Jim. The opening of the box is everything. What's inside is just the gravy."

Dunlap grinned at the dapper little man with the silk hat. "I think you may have something there."

"Of course I do!" White chuckled.

Dunlap gathered his coat and allowed White to lead him from the rented stable. They strolled down Hester Street, two successful businessmen at odds with the wooden shanties around them.

"I'm reminded of a story," White began. "There were these two lock companies in England, Chubb and Bramah—companies of the finest reputation, their locks known the world over. Though they were competitors, they both prided themselves on the fact that no one had ever picked their locks. A truly outstanding record, for you know the English have the finest cracksmen in the world! No matter. . . . Twenty years ago, the International Industrial Exhibition opened in London. Among the wares displayed, the world famous Chubb lock, and over in the other corner, the Bramah. Both featured huge signs offering rewards to anyone who could pick their locks. There was an American there, Alfred C. Hobbs, who asked the Bramah salesman if he might try their lock. Well, our American friend removed his coat, and much to the salesman's dismay, picked the finest lock Bramah had to offer. Gathering his coat, Hobbs moved over to the Chubb display where he repeated the feat before an astonished crowd. Jim, in twenty minutes an unknown American had ruined two lock companies! He collected a reward that had been standing for over forty years!"

"Incredible!" Jim said. "Whatever happened to him?"

"You have one of his locks in there, the Hobbs. But I would have given anything! Anything, to have been there!"

"I haven't had much chance to work with the Hobbs. It must be a fine lock."

"I can pick it," White puffed proudly. "I can pick the finest Hobbs can come up with."

Jim couldn't help noticing White's jaunty air—that of a man of boundless self-esteem. "Maybe you could teach me about the Chubb?" Dunlap asked respectfully.

White slapped Dunlap resoundingly on the back. "Of course, my boy! All in due time! Where shall we have lunch? I'm starved!"

Their carriage arrived at the Walnut Street Theatre just moments before the curtain went up on *Rip Van Winkle*. The Wood sisters, Robert Scott, Billy Connors, and a matronly chaperone, Mrs. Adams, slipped into their seats just as the house lights dimmed and the curtain rose on the village of Falling Waters.

Seated between the Wood sisters, Scott felt Amelia's chubby hand grasp his tightly in excitement. Seconds later, Mary's warm fingers crept cautiously into his palm.

Rip Van Winkle entered with a child on his back, surrounded by a swarm of playful children hanging from his coat. There was warm applause from the audience as Scott whispered to Mary, "That's Joseph Jefferson."

"That's Joseph Jefferson," he repeated to Amelia, "a very famous actor."

"Robert?" Mary whispered, tipping her head until the long blond curls were against his cheek.

"Yes?" he said, keeping an eye on Jefferson, who had scattered the children and sent them off.

"Did you by chance tell my sister Amelia that you loved me?"

Scott avoided her eyes and swallowed noisily as Rip Van Winkle called offstage for his dog, Schneider. "I think so," he mumbled.

"I see. . . . And did you tell your friend Mr. Connors that you thought me the most beautiful girl you'd ever seen and that nothing would do until you had me for your wife?"

Scott nodded uncomfortably. "I might have."

"And did you beg Mrs. Adams to accompany us here tonight, just so you could be intoxicated by the pleasure of my company?"

Nervously he replied, "Those could have been my words . . . yes."

"Who else knows of this?"

"I don't think there was anyone else."

"Oh," she said softly. "Did you not tell Mrs. Coopersmith at the school that you intended to ask my father for my hand as soon as classes were completed?"

"Mrs. Coopersmith?"

"Mrs. Coopersmith, from the Moravian Seminary for young ladies, who would be very upset if she knew you had taken me to the theatre."

"Oh, *that* Mrs. Coopersmith . . . "

"Yes, that Mrs. Coopersmith," she hushed him.

"Yes," he faltered, "I think I did mention it to her."

"Who else might know this?" she whispered.

"Who else?" He thought a moment. "No one else," he said with finality.

"Did you plan on telling me? Ever?"

"Of course!" he said, louder than he intended, sending annoyed heads twisting in his direction.

"I do love you," he whispered.

"At last!"

"No, I do! Truly!"

"Are you asking me to marry you?" she asked, eyes on the actors, giving little attention to the shaken Scott.

"Of course!"

"Then please ask properly," she hissed. "It is my turn to know."

Turning in his seat until his moustache was against the golden curls, he whispered, "I love you, dear Mary. I've been able to do nothing, think of nothing else but you since that first moment we met. I would be a ruined man should you deny me. Please marry me and put my suffering to an end."

"That's better," she smiled, nestling her head on his shoulder.

"Please say yes!" he insisted.

"A girl needs time to consider the proper course of action."

"How much time?" he demanded, drawing a "ssshhh" from outraged patrons.

"Time."

"Does that mean no?" he asked hesitantly.

"Does it appear that I've refused you?"

"Yes . . . no . . . I don't know!"

"Time is the proper way of saying yes."

"Dear girl!" he exclaimed, faint with relief. "You've made me the happiest man in the world!" He drew her hands to his mouth, kissing the fragrant fingers first of one hand, then the other, only to find that one of the hands belonged to Amelia, who was staring up at him in surprise.

Passengers from Pennsylvania were required to take the ferry to New York. The crew was busy securing the lines when Dunlap arrived. Wagons and carriages waited for passengers or transport, and Jim had to shoulder his way through the crowd.

The cable had been dated May 15, yesterday, and had arrived only minutes before the steamer was due in port. The cable promised Dunlap a surprise, and Jim thought he could guess what it might be—a bank in Pennsylvania or New Jersey, since the telegram had been sent from Jersey City.

The gangway had almost emptied, and Dunlap hadn't seen either Bob Scott or Billy Connors. He reread the wire until he was certain he was meeting the right ferry. A tall dark head with a tan hat appeared above the stragglers, and Dunlap waved. They were almost upon each other before the passengers in front parted to reveal Scott with his arm around the waist of a young girl. He could not think of her as a woman, for she was obviously still in her teens. Velvet jacket, long crimson skirt snuggled to a tiny waist were ushered before him. Dunlap didn't know what to say. Behind them came Billy Connors with an immense amount of luggage.

Scott stood a full foot taller than the lovely blonde, and he had to bend at the waist for the introduction. "Mary, this is my dear friend James Dunlap. Jim," he said straightening, "this is my wife, Mary."

Blue velvet ribbon caught by the breeze flitted about a cascade of golden curls. Sparkling violet eyes dipped demurely as a tiny voice whispered to the pier, "It's very nice to meet you."

Chapter Three

The old man with the silver imperial goatee wandered the
Wellington, Illinois, dark streets for the better part of an hour.
The March winds raised havoc at the intersections, blowing his
coat about, tumbling the derby from his head. It led him a merry
chase until he cornered it between rain barrels and speared it with
his cane. Brushed clean, it was pulled firmly over the white hair
and tapped into place.

He made a circuitous approach to the side door of Pate's Bank.
When he was certain no one was about, he slipped the second
wedge from his ring and stabbed it between the door and the
jamb. He now had both entrances covered and could return to his
hotel quarters and rest until morning.

He was exhausted by the time he undressed and slipped beneath the quilt. His legs ached and the bitter cold had made his
eyes water. Only his head protruded from the covers. Gradually
he warmed and the gasping left him. He was much too old for
these nighttime excursions. They were better left to younger men
than he.

He was five miles north of Watseka, Illinois. An easy journey
to the train. He anticipated few problems, should he follow

*through with it. He still had not made up his mind. The challenge
at the moment was just to see if it was feasible. He would make up
his mind later about the rest.*

*The wind rattled his window, but he smiled warmly now the
covers were about him. His last waking thoughts were of the Hall
safe waiting there against the wall. He knew the type well. Knew
exactly that there would be two doors—outer and inner—that
would have to be blown. The prize inside? No one ever knew for
sure, but he reckoned there might be several thousand dollars. A
paltry sum to be sure, he thought, sighing wearily, closing his
eyes to the unfamiliar room with its ironed sheets and smell of
wallpaper paste.*

The Scotts purchased a new home on Washington Square. Bob and
Mary spent the summer browsing about New York buying furniture
for Mary, a pair of horses for Bob. Jim alternated his days with Bob
and Mary, seeing the sights of New York and Coney Island, negotiating a cash settlement for the return of the Fall City Tobacco Bank se-
curites. This last arrangement was dangerous, and Jim covered his
tracks by bargaining through discreet brokers and lawyers, still uncertain as to the extent of the protection to be expected from the Bank
Ring. Had he been more attentive to the burglary business, he might
have noted two events of that summer which might have made him not
a little apprehensive.

The first was on Wall Street when a man named Robert Gleason in-
vaded the district with forged bonds. In a short period of time, Gleason had milked the investment community of a million dollars. Trusting to the protection of the Bank Ring, Gleason paid his percentage.
He had hardly begun to enjoy the rewards of his labor when men
swooped down on his home and arrested him. Identifying themselves
as Pinkerton agents from the recently opened New York office, they
hustled Gleason off to jail. Having one of their dues-paying members
snatched from under their very noses staggered the Bank Ring. Pinkerton agents provided the evidence necessary for conviction, and Irving and his men found their hands completely tied.

A further test of the detectives' powers occurred just a short time

later when Bank of England forger George Macdonnell boarded the
liner *Thuringia,* sailing from Britain with a million and a half of the
bank's funds.

Worried their money might be lost forever once it reached New
York and mindful of the way New York police harbored criminals, the
Bank of England wired ahead to Pinkerton's for assistance.

Fearing the bank might do just that, Macdonnell sent his own wire
to Captain James Irving and the Bank Ring, pleading with them to
save him from possible arrest.

Twenty percent of a million and a half dollars was a great deal of
money, and Irving lost no time. He set to sea with a few men to intercept the liner and take Macdonnell as *his* prisoner. Once at sea however, Irving found that a second craft with Robert Pinkerton aboard
had embarked to intercept Irving's own interception. The boilers of
both vessels were tested when they spied each other at sea. Irving
cursed Pinkerton's and their craft, offering vast sums to the skipper to
either beat Pinkerton's or blow the boilers in the attempt. It was the
determined Irving who boarded first. Macdonnell became his prisoner
and several thousand dollars was immediately passed to the head of
the Bank Ring as a show of faith. The smiling prisoner was paraded
past the angry young Bob Pinkerton and hustled aboard the police
boat. In all the excitement, Macdonnell left the money in a suitcase
on board the *Thuringia.* The prisoner was taken off to the Ludlow
Street Jail while the suitcase was stored at Customs. It didn't take
either side very long to realize the money was missing. Pinkerton had
the suitcase watched by detectives while Irving considered the problem. A woman was ordered up, and as the "wife" of George Macdonnell, she was sent to Customs for the case. Pinkerton's arrested her
and the money, depriving poor George and the ring of its rightful
spoils.

Jim Dunlap heard none of this, bored by inactivity and Mary's
questions regarding decor and color of fabric swatches, none of which
he had ever heard of, colors like Seine Silt and London Smoke or Suppressed Sighs. He fled to Connecticut for the month of August.

When he returned at the end of the month, Scott informed him,
"I'm broke."

"How much do you need?" Jim asked in the foyer of the newly decorated home.

"I haven't paid the servants this week, and I promised Mary a new carriage for the promenade on Sunday," Scott announced nonchalantly.

A quick calculation by Dunlap revealed that Bob had gone through forty thousand dollars since April. He shook his head worriedly. "How much do you need?"

"Five thousand would last me the month," Scott smiled.

"Five thousand!" Jim exploded. "I still haven't negotiated the railroad bonds!"

"You'll get it, Jim," he said coolly, placing an arm over Dunlap's shoulder in genuine affection. "I'm not worried."

"I would be!"

"Things will work out," Scott laughed as he walked Dunlap into the walnut-walled den. He led Jim to the bar and poured him a bourbon. "I can't tell you how my life has changed, Jim. She's changing my whole life!"

"I can see that." Jim thought of the vast sum already spent. "And she loves you, Jim. It's always, Mr. Dunlap this or Mr. Dunlap that! She's been asking for two weeks when you'd return. This supper tonight was her idea! She's marvelous, Jim, I can't tell you how she's transformed my life!"

"You've told me!"

"You'll come for dinner tonight? Mary has a sister she wants you to meet—"

"No sisters!" Dunlap declared. "I'll bring one of my own girls! One other matter—the sooner she gets over calling me Mr. Dunlap the better I'll like it."

"That's what they taught her at the Moravian school. She's a lady, Jim! And very young at that. Patience is well rewarded," Bob advised. "Mary taught me that."

Mary swept into the dining room with a black lace mantelet over a stunning blue silk gown, and the women present gasped with envy.

"She's beautiful," Jim's companion whispered.

"Not half as beautiful as you," he hastened, for his companion was the dark side of the coin. Where Mary had golden curls, Linda Knight had luxurious raven tresses swept up in an elaborate twist atop her head. Doe-eyed and vivacious, she was the only other beauty in the room besides Mary. Davey Cummings had brought his plain wife, while Billy Connors' wife was a plump young girl much too heavy for Dunlap's taste.

"Is this something new?" Billy asked, addressing himself to the ring on Mary's finger.

"Bob surprised me with it just today," she said. "It came from Tiffany's on Union Square. Don't you love it?"

"It looks very—expensive," Cummings offered to no one in particular.

Scott took his wife's hand. "Beauty should wear beauty."

Across the candle-lit table, Billy silently passed Dunlap the cost of the ring by holding four fingers against his birthmark. Dunlap dropped his head in acknowledgement, for Billy Connors was also concerned about Scott's extravagance.

"Did I tell you about my proposal?" Scott asked them.

"Robert!" Mary cried in embarrassment.

"I asked her, 'May I have you for my wife?' And do you know her reply?"

"Let me guess." Dunlap ventured. "She said 'yes.' "

"Oh, Jim!" Scott roared. "You're so naive about women! She said, 'I will not have you, but you may have me!' "

The Scotts laughed at this while the others smiled politely.

Mary insisted, "Our guests don't want to hear such things!"

"Of course they do!" Scott said. "Oh, Mary, do you love me still?"

Billy cleared his throat as everyone turned to their plates. Dunlap mumbled, "The stiller the better."

The newlyweds tossed verbal caresses down the length of the table for the remainder of the meal until the men retired to the den, while an Irish servant poured drinks and cigars were passed. "You know, Jim," Scott said philosophically, puffing his cigar to life, "and this is for your ears, too, my friends. A pair of pretty eyes is the best mirror to shave by."

Dunlap winked at Connors. "Especially if they're the same color," he teased.

"I can't begin to tell you what she's meant to my life, Jim."

"I'm beginning to get the idea," Dunlap groaned.

It was impossible to annoy Scott. He ignored each taunt, eloquent as a preacher on his text. "You know, Jim, a man should have a wife while he's young and can still enjoy life."

Dunlap rolled his eyes. "I think I'll wait for one a little older. I've never been fond of schoolgirls." For it was common knowledge Mary had been a student at the Moravian Seminary in Bethlehem, Pennsylvania, and that it was from this school that Scott had stolen her away. Connors insisted she had never finished, while Scott told Jim she had indeed graduated. Jim was sure the correct answer was that Bob had whisked her away immediately upon graduation.

Dunlap studiously inspected the lit end of his cigar. "I imagine they'll forward her grades here to New York."

This had Billy in convulsions and Davey choking on his cigar.

"Someday, Jim," Bob said without malice, "you'll find yourself head over heels in love, and it will be my turn to laugh up my sleeve."

Dunlap tried to control his laughter. "No offense intended . . . but we really came here to talk business. Winter's almost upon us and we should be getting back to work."

Billy Connors took that as a signal to lay out some drawings on the library table.

"I've been thinking of buying her a piano," Scott said absently. "I thought I'd make room for it in the corner there—maybe have this room redone as a music room."

Dunlap was bent at the drawings as he asked, "What does a piano cost?"

"I saw one on Broadway at the U.S. Piano Company. It was a hand-carved beauty for only seven hundred."

"Let's figure out a way to earn seven hundred before you buy it."

"You ought to hear her sing 'Molly Darling.' She has the voice of an angel! Damn! If we only had a piano, I'd have her sing for us this very moment!"

"It's a shame, all right," Jim mumbled, trying to get Scott to take an interest in Billy's plans.

"I want to give her the best. I owe it to her to improve myself to the best of my ability. I've even been thinking of going back to school and getting a diploma. Of course she thinks I'm well educated, a college graduate even."

Dunlap ignored Scott and asked Connors, "What do we have that's worthwhile?"

"I came across several in Pennsylvania. There's a small one in Pittston, another in Wilkes-Barre, and Wellsboro . . . "

"George Leslie's piped that one," Cummings stopped him. "He's been after it for a long time. But if Leslie doesn't turn it off soon, George Mason will. He's been talking about emptying it as soon as he thinks Leslie's passed it over."

"There's a good one in Pittsburgh." Billy shuffled through the plans and pulled the East Liberty Bank drawings to the top.

"I'd like something closer," Bob complained. "I hate to leave Mary for too long."

"There's the Long Island Savings in Brooklyn," Davey suggested.

"Elmira," Billy added.

"I'm all for either one of those," Scott stated.

"Wait a minute!" Dunlap stopped them, "just because it's close doesn't mean a thing! I would rather see us go out of town and get something worthwhile than choose a bank because it's close and probably empty!"

"The East Liberty is loaded with federal revenues," Billy countered.

"Where is it located?" Scott asked.

"Pittsburgh. There are two there, the East Liberty and the Mechanics Savings."

"I'm for that," Davey voted.

Dunlap added, "It's all right with me."

"Pittsburgh," Billy decided.

"Elmira!" Scott cried to no avail.

Dunlap and Scott were to enter the East Liberty Bank together. They would strike up a conversation with the cashier while Cummings and Connors took a quick look at the position of the vault and the all-important ceiling inside.

"Let me be Barton this time?" Scott begged.

Dunlap agreed, placing the diamond stickpin in plain view for the casher's appraisal.

They strolled the two blocks to the East Liberty Bank, Scott and Dunlap in front, followed a block to the rear by Billy Connors and Davey Cummings.

They were not prepared for the locked door barring their way. Dunlap shook it twice. "Is it a holiday?"

Scott pointed to a large sign in the adjoining window. "Closed by order of the United States Court."

"I'll be damned!" Scott shouted.

There was a smaller notice posted in the corner of the window. "There will be a three months' notice on withdrawing sums over three hundred dollars. Institution in bankruptcy."

"If that don't beat all."

"Damn!"

"Gentlemen," Jim sighed, "I'd like to take this moment to switch my vote to the Mechanics Bank instead."

"Mechanics . . "

"Mechanics."

"Elmira!" Scott insisted.

Even though he was outvoted, Scott demanded a vote for Elmira. People were giving them strange looks, moving into the street to avoid them.

"How many for Elmira?" Scott demanded, holding his hand aloft. He made a big show of searching for hands, but his was the only one raised.

"Shall we leave them a notice of our own?" Davey asked as they filed away from the bank.

"I can't *wait* three months!" Scott announced, reluctantly joining the group moving off in the direction of the Mechanics Savings Bank.

The Mechanics Savings Bank was also "Closed by order of the United States Court."

"This is ridiculous!" Dunlap shouted to the barred door.

"What the hell is going on?" Scott wanted to know. He caught the arm of a silver-whiskered man passing by. "I beg your pardon, sir, but I've just returned from the West only to find this . . . very confusing notice posted on my bank. Do you have any idea what's going on in there?"

The man shook off Scott's hand. "The banks are broke!" he cried angrily. "The country's going downhill fast! It's ruin for a decent businessman!"

"Broke?" Dunlap whispered.

"The whole country's going broke!" the man explained.

"Broke?"

"The country's ruined! Bankrupt!"

"Broke . . . " Dunlap repeated numbly.

"Bankruptcy is the order of the day! This is what happens to fools who elect an army general to run the country!"

"I'll be damned!" Scott whistled.

The old man was nodding rapidly to the group. "And there's no relief in sight! I urged my friends to vote Greeley into office. Oh no! Not Greeley! I told them Grant would make them rue the day!"

The four stood thunderstruck as the old man spun about them flailing the air with his cane, driving off the ills of society. "There's a run on all the banks! Everywhere! Ruination is upon us! Go back west or wherever you came from! Go home! Go home!"

Cummings stepped nimbly aside as the old man rushed away, stopping momentarily to give the building a resounding lick with his gnarled walking stick. Pedestrians gave him a wide berth as he cursed his way through traffic.

"My God," Dunlap sagged visibly.

"How can this be? We just got started!" Scott demanded of someone, anyone.

"I heard there was a little trouble," Connors shrugged, "but I never took it to mean this."

"What'll we do?" Scott asked Dunlap. "We just got started!"

"What a time to become bankies!" Dunlap recovered, chuckling at the whole idea of robbing banks at a time when they were apparently collapsing all around them.

"I vote with Bob on Elmira," Cummings grumbled.

"Elmira," Billy sighed.

Dunlap asked slowly, "Will it be any different in Elmira?"

"It can't be worse?" Scott offered.

"Elmira," Jim agreed, barely suppressing a laugh at the notion of their breaking into abandoned banks from coast to coast.

There were many Newtowns in the State of New York during the early 1800s. Assemblyman Emmanuel Coryell was designated to meet with the local residents of one of the Newtowns and select an appropriate name for the growing communtiy. A meeting was called at the Teall Tavern on Water Street. Nathan Teall's young daughter, an adventurous miss, joined the proceedings atop the assemblyman's lap. As names were bandied about she proceeded to doze off, remaining there until her mother called "Elmira." *A fitting name for a growing community,* the assemblyman thought. Others agreed, and in 1828, Newtown, New York, became Elmira.

The number of banks in the state had doubled in the eight years since the Civil War. But in New York City, the Market, Bowery Savings and Bowling Green banks closed amid circumstances bordering on scandalous. The bank panic was on. Cities across the eastern United States saw a run on their treasuries. The Eighth National failed, The Guardian, National Savings, the Ocean, Stuyvesant, Third Avenue Savings, Union Square, all crumpled into bankruptcy or receivership, and these were just the banks in and around the metropolitan New York City area.

Other communities fared no better. In Elmira, however, trust in the banking officials, a solid economy, stable leadership under a firm administration prevented chaos. Instead, they were ripe for another sort of assault—burglary. Those with designs on the bank arrived on the Number Twelve of the Erie Railroad. It was late at night when they detrained at the town straddling the Chemung River. Scott and Dunlap were the first pair to enter the depot. To the rear of the Number Twelve, two others, Connors and Cummings, stepped onto the platform. To all intents and purposes, they were total strangers.

They arrived in pairs at the Hotel Rathbun, registered under fictitious names and retired to their rooms. To Dunlap's intense relief, he learned that the bank was still doing a thriving business.

When Dunlap entered the Second National the following morning, Scott was already engaging the cashier in conversation. "I'm terrified that something will happen to my money! Our firm's account has been frozen in Pittsburgh. How can my company be sure their funds won't suffer the same fate here?"

"We are a very large bank," the clerk offered politely.

"So was the East Liberty Bank! But they too have gone under!"

The clerk's voice dropped low. "You have my assurance that we are a substantial establishment."

"The Mechanics Bank was substantial, too," Dunlap said. "I'm afraid we'll need more positive assurance before we can do business here," he told Scott.

Scott agreed somewhat ruefully and made as if to leave. The clerk whispered carefully, "I can assure you gentlemen that any firm that has $6,000,000 in bonds and $200,000 in greenbacks, as we do, is a sound firm to be sure."

"Six million . . . " Dunlap said carefully, trying to keep the excitement from his voice.

"This is a United States government depository," the clerk said confidentially. "Sound business principles are well rewarded."

Scott appeared convinced. He turned to Dunlap. "Well, shall we wire our firm and tell them we've finally found a reliable bank?"

Dunlap was not so easily convinced. "That they're still in business is admirable. But you know me, Charles, cautious as ever. I still can't be sure the monies here are secure. It would be a dreadful calamity if we urged our firm to deposit half a million in company accounts, only to find that some scoundrel walked out with our money in the dead of night."

The clerk went to the end of the counter and beckoned them toward the vault. "Six years old," he boasted. "Several tons of mortar and stone, most of the stones as big as that desk. Each one must weigh several hundred pounds at least. Beneath that, several layers of steel and railroad iron." He held his fingers wide apart for emphasis.

"Each layer that thick. Believe me, gentlemen, an army of workmen, undisturbed for weeks, would be confounded trying to reach the inside of that vault."

"But what about the outside?" Dunlap persisted. "A clerk like yourself, and you must pardon me for saying this, but a young man sometimes finds himself in debt . . . the combination of access and need is a tempting one for most men."

"Impossible!" the clerk assured them. "Only two men can open that safe. Each keeps the other honest, as the combination is frequently changed. Make no mistake about us, your company could never find a sounder, safer home."

"Well?" Scott asked his partner. "What do you think?"

"He's convinced me."

"Good!" the clerk beamed.

"The transfer will take several weeks, of course," Scott explained.

"I understand."

Dunlap added, "I can guarantee you our business, you can be sure of that."

"I'm just pleased that I could be of service." The clerk bowed graciously.

Gray felt hats perched atop their heads, they caned their way out into bright fall sunlight.

"Beautiful." Scott whispered.

"He was so convincing I think we should give him our business whether he wants it or not," Dunlap laughed.

Billy Connors was first to leave the Rathbun Hotel. He slipped out the rear door and waited in the darkness for the others. Without a word, the three followed Billy to the Second National Bank. The portly bankie led them past the bank and to the steps of the YMCA where they climbed the dark stairwell to the second landing. At the outer doors, Cummings picked the lock in a matter of minutes. Once inside, Connors lit a bulls-eye lantern and paced off the room. His pacing led them to a locked wooden barricade. "The top of the vault is in there."

Cummings fingered the lock and shook his head. "It's a Yale improved, I can't pick it."

Dunlap held it to the light and admitted it was beyond his means to open.

"We'll break it down!" Scott stated. "It's only wood."

"We can't break it!" Dunlap cursed. "Someone will know we've been here."

"Jim's right," Dave offered. "We have to be able to get in and out at will, otherwise it's no good."

"You're sure the vault is inside that room?" Dunlap asked.

Billy nodded reluctantly. "I'm positive."

"Then we either have to be able to pick this, or we need a key," Scott decided.

The four stood looking at the simple lock barring them from the vault roof. The lantern light played over its metallic surface.

"We have to find the key," Dunlap admitted. "Somebody must have it. Billy, you and Dave get on that first thing in the morning. We have to get inside that room or we might as well go home."

"Six million is worth the effort," Scott said quietly.

Everyone was in agreement, the key had to be found.

The key to the Yale improved lock traveled about on the person of Dr. Ira Hart, the man in charge of the YMCA. As accurately as Billy or Dave could guess from their daily positions in the Y's reading room, it never left the good doctor's person.

Dunlap set up a plan whereby Billy and Dave would "bump" the man and, in so doing, lift the key from his clothing. But Billy returned to the hotel empty-handed.

"If Molly Matches were here, he'd have got it," Billy cursed longing for the presence of the pickpocket John Larney, who as a young boy had often disguised himself as a very young girl and worked the crowds to the tune of several thousand dollars a day.

"The key has to be somewhere on him," Dunlap insisted.

"Maybe I should try and bump him," Davey offered.

"That's no good," Scott sighed. "We can't go bumping the man about town trying to find the key. We'll tip our hand completely!"

"He has to sleep sometime," Davey muttered.

"That's it!" Dunlap shouted.

"Of course!" Bob agreed, laughing with relief. "He has to sleep sometime, doesn't he!"

The white clapboard house on East Church Street was dark. Billy Connors took up position at the front of number 306, and Davey Cummings the rear. Armed with only a bulls-eye lantern, Scott and Dunlap slipped the window latch and crept inside. They eased past the manservant's quarters into the Hart bedroom. On hands and knees, they crawled the carpet to the sleeping doctor and his wife. The doctor's clothes were discovered and his pants carefully searched to no avail. The tweed coat and vest were missing and finally tracked to the closet. A thorough search failed to uncover the elusive key.

"You sure he was wearing the tweed today?" Scott whispered.

"Billy stayed with him all night and said he was wearing the tweed jacket and vest at supper time."

"Damn!"

They worked their way back across the carpet to the nightstand. Bob slipped the noisy drawer free from the marble-topped stand. A light was sent inside but still the key eluded them. Dr. Hart and his wife snored, undisturbed.

Dunlap felt for a hook on the rear of the cabinet, signaling Scott a moment later that there was nothing. Scott pointed to the opposite side of the bed and Dunlap nodded, following the light on his hands and knees. He had gone a foot when he thought of the underside of the bed. He sent his hand exploring the frame while Scott waited patiently at the foot of the bed. Finding nothing, he searched the darkness beneath the bed. He reached into a container, felt an icy liquid and closed his eyes.

"What is it?" Scott hurried back.

Dunlap drew his hand from beneath the hanging covers, and shook it vigorously. "Bedpan."

Scott made a sour face that gave way to a smile. As Dunlap urgently wiped his hand on the carpet, Scott began to laugh.

"That's not funny," Dunlap hissed.

Scott had his hand clapped over his mouth and the lantern was shaking with his suppressed laughter, splashing its beam around bed and walls.

"Shoes!" Dunlap whispered frantically, searching both the doctor's and wife's footwear.

They explored every surface they encountered—still the key eluded them. They searched under the lamp, among the fireplace tools, in the drawers and dressers. Scott even slid a hand under the doctor's pillow, cautiously feeling with his fingers for something that wasn't there.

After what seemed hours, they sat back on their haunches in frustration. Scott shrugged wearily and pointed to the closet again. Dunlap shook his head violently. Scott thumbed the outside, and Dunlap reluctantly agreed.

"Did you find it?" Billy rushed them.

"It's nowhere to be found."

"So what do we do?" Davey asked.

Dunlap limped off on his sore leg, the others hurrying to catch up. "We go home to New York!" he snapped. "That's what we do! Until we can find someone who can pick a Yale improved, we're finished here!"

"Where's the lantern?" Davey asked suddenly.

Scott looked at Dunlap's empty hands, then at his own. "Damn!"

Dunlap shrugged it angrily away. "The doctor's just been given a souvenir of our visit."

When Doctor Hart woke in the morning he was surprised to find the drawers ajar on dressers and nightstand. The shoes placed so carefully beneath the bed now stood on their ankles in the center of the rug. Without frightening his wife, he searched the house carefully, discovering a lantern still burning upright on the carpet. Other than the addition of the lantern, nothing was missing. He shaved and dressed for work, sitting on the edge of the bed to pull on his shoes. That done, he flipped the edge of the carpet back, picked up the key hidden there every night and placed it in his vest pocket. He was still bewildered when he left for breakfast a few minutes later.

* * *

The four members of the Scott-Dunlap Ring returned to New York as charges were being pressed against Captain Irving and Detective Farley by the Bank of England. The three-week trial resulted in a dismissal of charges, but the forger Macdonnell was convicted by the persistent Pinkerton's.

October promised a cold, long winter ahead. Still it did not keep Mary from pressuring them into a trip to Washington Park. Dunlap brought Linda Knight, the raven-haired beauty from Shang Draper's saloon, to keep Mary company on her excursion into the park. Four hundred and twenty five sparrow cages had been hung there for the protection of the birds, and Mary was determined to count each one. Linda Knight seemed a perfect partner for Mary's outing. Awed by the simplest things, Linda loved the excitement of discovery.

A simple trinket from Dunlap brought tears to her eyes. He would have the pleasant task of holding her in his arms for a long period of time until she calmed enough to thank him. Trusting to a fault, she worried Dunlap, who wondered how she could possibly avoid becoming one of Shang's upstairs girls. Right now she was just a barmaid, popular to the point of being an attraction, for she somehow managed to find the warm side of the hardest knave present. It was no secret that the clientele of Draper's was about the worst lot in the city.

Dunlap had armed himself with a stack of newspapers from Brentano's, determined to see that he never be caught as uninformed again as he had been in Pittsburgh. He vowed to begin each day with a search of the *Herald* and *Times* to see what effect the news would have on him and his business. With dozens of banks folding everywhere, only the knowledgeable among them might survive. The situation had become so sticky that the *Times* listed the banks still in business. The panic had begun with the collapse of Jay Cooke's Philadelphia Banking and Brokerage firm. Credit structures were folding across the nation, forcing the closing of the New York Stock Exchange for ten days. Thousands of firms were approaching bankruptcy. Before it was over, the mortality rate would climb to 5,000 businesses leaving some three million unemployed.

Each day saw dozens of banks in trouble. Faltering institutions often found that their ledgers failed to tally with the cash and securities on hand. Hundreds of bank presidents and treasurers set out during the night for parts unknown. "Defalcation" and "bankruptcy" were so common the papers relegated them to the back pages.

"What do you find so captivating about the news?" Scott demanded.

"Mainly that half the banks we're lining up to rob are either broke or rapidly approaching it. There were nine closures last week in New England alone!"

Scott shifted on the park bench, stretching long legs far out in front of him. "Elmira's solvent," he grinned boyishly. His face darkened quickly. "Dave Cummings came to see me this morning. He can't wait any longer. He has a friend in New Orleans who has something lined up. I wished him the best of luck."

"He was a good man," Dunlap said glumly. Nothing had gone according to plan. The banks were folding just when they needed one. The best member of the group had already departed. Scott was deeply in debt and rapidly diminishing Dunlap's own savings. *We couldn't have picked a worse time to enter the banking business,* he thought. To make matters desperate, the *Times* was predicting that the depression might last another ten years.

Scott asked, "Have you seen Billy Connors?"

"He's working on something," Dunlap mumbled, his head buried in the paper searching frantically for a hint of good news from any quarter. "He met a fellow who knows someone who knows someone."

"Does this someone know how to open a Yale lock?"

"He didn't say, but he seemed excited. For the life of me, I can't begin to guess what it is he has up his sleeve."

Dunlap dropped the paper. "Jimmy Hope was arrested in Delaware," he said to the trees.

"I don't know him."

"Jimmy Hope. . . . I wonder if George saw this?"

"It can't happen to us," Scott announced. "You have to rob something to be arrested. Isn't that still the law?"

"I think so."

"Well then," Scott announced to the park, *"we're* safe."

"My God!" Dunlap announced excitedly. "They settled!"

"Who settled?"

"The Waterford Bank people!" he shouted, as he read aloud from the upstate *Troy Press*. "Immediately after the acquittal of Pete Curley—he was one of the boys George used in Waterford. He was arrested later—the only one who was. 'The bank committee, whose lukewarmness in the trial had been too obvious, went to New York City on an errand they dare not lisp to a single soul out of the posted trio. Stealthily, as the thieves beat the bank on that eventful night, did these respectable men prowl about the metropolis, visiting strange haunts and dealing with hard characters that shunned the light—' "

"We don't shun the light," Scott said defensively. "They must be talking about George White and his friends."

" '—until at length their purpose was realized and the surrender of the bonds for a certain sum was agreed upon. The place and hour having been specified, this worthy triumvirate of the banking profession was on hand. With that vast sum within their clutch, they dreaded lest the other unreliable parties to the bargain would back out and again defeat them. But the burglars kept their covenant, and ere long a rickety hack rolled up to the door, drawn by a skeleton of a horse arrayed in patched and rotten harness, and managed by a Jehu whose livery would have shamed the beggars of Berlin—' " Dunlap was laughing so hard it was impossible to read further. Scott threw back his head and roared with delight.

" 'From its appearance not even a clairvoyant would have dreamed of the treasure it bore. The servants of Justice were as blind as their mistress, and so a big ragpicker's bag was removed from the carriage—' "

"Sure sounds like George White to me!"

"God knows who they're talking about!" Dunlap replied, faint with laughter. He let the newspaper fall to his lap. "There's an excellent lesson here, Bob. George held back the securities, forcing the bank people into a situation where they were powerless to convict without the bonds in their possession. For they had no idea whether they would ever see them again. It's a good example for us. If we hold the securities in a safe place against capture, we could use them to barter for our freedom. Should we ever be caught."

"Bite your tongue, you beggar!"

"Should we be caught and sentenced, the securities would be lost to them forever. They're as crooked as we are!"

"If something doesn't happen soon," Scott said soberly, "there may be no next time. I haven't a cent, Jim. My creditors are pressing me to the wall. They hounded Mary all the while we were gone."

"What about the five thousand I gave you just before we left?"

"Gone," Scott said, feigning contrition.

"You're totally irresponsible!"

"Love is the great magician, James. I cannot refuse her a thing."

"Can you afford to present her to debtors' court?" Dunlap asked.

"I would never refuse you, either, Jim. That's my nature and the single flaw in an otherwise flawless character. I cannot refuse anyone anything. My mother saw it in me at an early age. The rewards of my first robbery were spent on her. It wasn't until I was in prison that she realized I was totally incorrigible. I'm sorry, Jim, truly I am."

Dunlap realized the truth of the admission. "I'll get you some money now the Waterford thing is settled."

"Another five thousand would do me nicely," Scott laughed, doubling the original amount he'd planned to ask for.

"Oh, Jim!" Linda cried, racing across the park. "You should have seen them! There were *thousands* of them, of every color and size imaginable!"

Mary was right behind her, and Scott caught his wife and spun her about the lawn. Linda, caught up in her great excitement, cheeks flushed, dark eyes sparkling, lost control of her words and hopped in place, arms waving until Jim stilled her by drawing her close. "There were thousands, Jim," she said against his coat.

"We'll come back and see them again."

"Oh could we? Could we? But we must bring food next time."

"Of course." He waltzed her about on the path, the wind catching at the newspapers, turning the pages in a slapping frency.

"Mary?" she called. "We must remember food next time!" When she realized that everyone was watching her, she quieted, suddenly embarrassed. "It was a beautiful day. ˙. . . "

Alone with him in the carriage she whispered, "I make you ashamed of me."

"Absolutely not!" he laughed, settling the blanket around her legs.

"I do," she insisted. "Bob thinks me funny."

"*I* think you funny," he replied warmly, kissing her forehead as the horses danced nervously into traffic.

"Mary's a real lady, with fine schooling—she thinks I'm funny, too, I can tell."

"I think you're beautiful."

"Oh do you, Jim?" Her hands pulled nervously at the front of his waistcoat. She snuggled against his sleeve, praying that one of her friends might see her in such an elegant carriage with such a handsome man.

"I would do anything for you, Jim . . . " she said softly.

"I know," he smiled, genuinely touched by her confession. The tugging of the harness drew his attention to the street, and he began to think about Elmira.

They were on the outskirts of the large crowd at Brooklyn's Capitoline Grounds, Mary, Linda and Mrs. Connors eager to see the exhibits promised, the men behind them talking in whispers.

"His name's William Edson," Billy explained. "He works for the Herring Safe Company. John Barry put me on to him. Barry met him at Ryan's stables."

"What does Barry know about this?" Dunlap asked.

"I had to tell him everything," Billy apologized, "but John's a square fellow. Both he and Ryan can be trusted. I told Barry I was looking for someone who could open a Yale improved. He suggested Edson."

Scott asked worriedly, "Then he knows about Elmira?"

Billy nodded. "But he wants in! I had to promise to take him with us. He's a square fellow, Jim, really!"

"How many others know about Elmira?" Dunlap frowned.

"If those boulders are as big as you said, we'll need all the help we can get!" Billy said defensively.

The crowd jostled them forward. Dunlap held Linda's arm securely to keep her from being swept away. Scott had already been pushed forward with Mary while Billy's wife was lost somewhere far ahead.

"So tell me about this Edson."

"He works for the Herring Safe Company and he's in deep to Ryan for stabling his horses. Barry also says Edson lost a large sum of money at Jerome Park last month. Barry thought he was ripe for picking so he asked for my go-ahead. I told him, 'Why not?' It was set up by Barry and Ryan, set up so's I could hear everything. Ryan tells this Edson, 'I wouldn't be worried about money if I was you, not with all those bank connections of yours.' But this Edson is very casual and doesn't get the point. Now Barry isn't one to tread lightly, so he comes right out with it. 'I know a lot of people who would pay a great deal of money to know what you know.' 'What sort of information?' Edson asks them. 'For one thing,' Barry says, 'how a Yale improved can be picked.' 'Impossible!' Edson laughs. Then Barry says, 'I know some people who would pay a goodly sum to know how to open one at will.' 'There is a way,' Edson tells them. So immediately I keen on the whole conversation. But this Edson's a slippery fellow. He won't say what it is, except that he knows a way."

Dunlap demanded angrily, "So where do we stand with the man?"

"I'm going to meet with him, and I have to know what I can offer."

"I'll have to ask Bob."

The crowd milled around a large sign proclaiming, THE IMMENSE AEROSTAT! 200 FEET HIGH! THE LARGEST EVER CONSTRUCTED! Other exhibits were listed below the artist's drawing of the Aerostat. "Chicago! *The smallest boat ever built to cross the ocean! For the First Time! The Paper Boat* Donaldson!"

"I can't see it!" Mary complained as she stood on tiptoes staring up into the sky.

"Patience, love," Bob Scott counseled.

"Suppose it doesn't fly today?" Linda cried worriedly.

"There is a breeze," Dunlap observed.

"They're probably waiting for the wind to die down," Bob added, as he joined the multitude peering up into an empty, cobalt blue autumn sky.

"What I was thinking," Billy continued, "if this Edson works for a safe company, he could be a tremendous help to us. We might even think about offering him a full partnership, a full share divided equally."

"It would depend on what he has to offer," Dunlap said over his shoulder, eyes locked on the vacant arena overhead.

Fifty rods in front of them, out of sight except for those very fortunate few in front, lay several tons of canvas and rope. Forty male volunteers stood by holding a limp rope, in case they were needed, as they most certainly would be should the winds relent and allow the young man in tights to become airborne. A huge fire pit was stoked and ready, and everybody waited for some sign to proceed from the nervous, pacing aviator.

Those to the rear had to content themselves with a barren piece of sky. Heads turned skyward, afraid to look at those beside them for fear of missing whatever was about to happen. They rose on tiptoe with each murmur of the crowd for a better view of the cloudless heavens.

"I've never seen an aerostat!" Linda cried excitedly.

"You may not see one today," Dunlap shuffled impatiently.

Mary called, "Could it really be two hundred feet high, Mr. Dunlap?"

"We may never know, my dear."

"We have to see it, Robert! We just *have* to!"

For a long hour the crowd waited with necks craned while an angry young man in flying silks hurried about in tight circles, cursing the gusts that blew in off the Atlantic. Then a rumble of disappointment signaled a thinning of the crowd.

Dunlap asked the group, "Shall we?"

Linda was beside herself with dismay. Mary stamped the ground in frustration.

"There'll be a run on linament tonight," Scott laughed as he tugged Mary toward the other exhibits.

"But I didn't *see* anything!" she balked.

"You saw several delightful birds and a cumulus cloud, as I remember," Scott teased.

"That's not funny at all!"

"Perhaps the paper boat will be more exciting," Dunlap announced.

"I thought you didn't want to see the paper boat," Linda challenged.

Scott hurriedly explained to her, "He's a very skeptical man who does not believe men can sail in paper boats."

"Oh, I believe they can sail in them," Dunlap snorted, "the question is, how far?"

Linda tried to draw him along quickly. "But they also have the smallest boat ever built to cross the ocean!"

"But it hasn't *crossed* the ocean!" Jim observed sweetly, "and until it does, we'll never know if it is the smallest, will we?"

"It must be true!" Mary insisted.

"It must. It must." Linda took up Mary's cry.

Dunlap removed his silk hat as the ladies dragged them along. "This hat could be the smallest vessel to cross the ocean!" he cried for all to hear. "As long as I don't try it, I may say anything I please!"

The ladies joined forces against him while Scott laughed at Jim's inevitable surrender. They somehow lost Billy and his wife in the crush of people.

"I shall stop being contrary this very instant!" Dunlap yielded as they went to the paper boat exhibit.

Ailing New Yorkers could buy magnetic clothing—sheets, pillows, cushion seats, vests, hats and neckties. For the ladies, there were even magnetic corsets and brassieres. All were guaranteed to cure paralysis, inflammatory rheumatism, asthma, inflammation of the lungs, varicose veins, bleeding of the lungs and congestion of the kidneys.

Grocery clerk Charles Ehrig might well have benefited from these garments. Suffering from delirium tremens, a diagnosis volunteered by his East Fourteenth Street employer, Charles ignored the magnetic clothing cure in favor of massive dosages of Paris Green. He had been on the medicine for one full day and had stopped on Houston Street to take another treatment, when he collapsed in a faint and died before help could be summoned.

The curious crowd paid little attention to the person who climbed the steps to the Connors dwelling. A short, stocky man, forty-six years of age, he beat the knocker twice, glanced curiously at the clerk lying in the center of the gawking throng and waited nervously for admittance.

Once inside, his cocky confidence reappeared. He shook Billy's hand with an air of professional courtesy. A second man was present, younger, an inch taller than himself, the beginning of a dark beard on his face, looking remarkably like President Grant, Edson thought.

"This is my friend Jim Dunlap. Jim, this is William Edson, the gentleman from the Herring Safe Company."

Dunlap smiled pleasantly. "Pleased to make your acquaintance."

Edson wondered what part Dunlap played in the matter of the Yale lock as he declined a cup of coffee and accepted tea instead.

The three men measured each other silently until Mrs. Connors arrived with liquid refreshments. She tactfully retreated with the tray, closing all doors firmly behind her.

The men sipped politely as Billy broached the subject of the meeting.

"I've been telling my friend Jim here that you've been a salesman for Herring Company for a few years and do a great deal of traveling."

"That is correct," Edson acknowledged.

"And how is business?" Dunlap asked.

"Dreadful."

"I imagine this run of the bank thing has hurt your sales?"

"Ruined would be the appropriate word. Have you seen the list of bank foreclosures in the *Times*?"

"Yes I have."

"I was in Concord, Connecticut, just last week to make a sale, and while I was there, the treasurer was arrested for embezzlement! Right before my eyes!"

"Horrible," Dunlap offered sympathetically.

"Here they were trying to close the bank while I was there trying to sell them a safe!"

"I take it then that your commissions have sadly fallen off?"

"Plummeted would be the appropriate word."

"Then it would be correct to assume you would not be above earning a few extra dollars, if the opportunity presented itself?"

"I would be willing to listen to any . . . agreeable offer," Edson smiled.

"I won't beat about the bush, Mr. Edson," Dunlap stated, proceeding even though he already knew he disliked the man, and that Edson viewed them with a haughty disdain. "I'm in the banking business, too. A few friends and I work the banks from the inside, to be precise. Right now, we have need for a man who can open a Yale lock."

"As I've told Mr. Connors," Edson said firmly, "that is almost impossible."

"I know that, but you also mentioned there might be a way that this same end could be accomplished."

"There is."

"As the employee of a highly reputable safe company, you have access to many banks that might be of interest to me and my friends. We would pay highly for any information you might give us."

Edson twisted the handle on the china cup, spinning it slowly in the saucer. "What might this information pay?"

"It would depend on your involvement—a totally cooperative attitude, valuable assistance in certain areas—we might even go a full share."

Edson nodded thoughtfully. "Are you asking me to join your group?"

"In a sense, yes. You would not have to participate actively beyond picking certain banks you feel are ripe, shall we say, for a midnight visit."

"I see." Edson grinned broadly, "A full share?"

"Yes."

"You would blast the safe I picked out, and we would share in the rewards?"

"Exactly."

The grin turned into a chuckle, and Edson asked them, "You must forgive my candor. I know my line of work. How do I know that you gentlemen are qualified in yours?"

Dunlap tried to hide his annoyance. He rubbed the scruffy beard he and Scott had agreed to grow as camouflage for their winter's work. "The Herring Company tried to sell a new safe at the Fall City Tobacco Bank in Louisville, Kentucky. The former model was a Diebold Borhmann that yielded three hundred thousand in cash and securities. I have the list of securities taken if you would like to review it."

Edson tried to hide his surprise, but not before Dunlap saw that he had scored heavily. "You ripped the corner and powdered the lock," Edson sniffed distastefully. "Very archaic."

"You know a better way?"

"The Herring company has a new invention, for I'm sure by now you realize that we are in the same business."

"Of course," Dunlap lied, for he had no idea what Edson was talking about.

"On occasion, even our own tumblers stick, bolts fail to do their bidding and we must be prepared to open our own safes in much the same manner as yourselves. This new invention makes our work quite simple. No ripping or drilling is required, just the use of a simple tool and the door is free."

Dunlap tried to hide his eagerness. He downed a gulp of coffee and asked, as casually as possible, "What sort of tool is this?"

"A vacuum pump. It sucks the air from the safe and doing so, draws in the explosive. A very simple affair, but unique and effective."

Dunlap's breath caught in his chest, and he forced the hands to still the chattering of the cup. "Could you provide us with this pump?"

"For a fee, yes."

Dunlap eased back into the horsehide sofa. He gave Edson a long, questioning look. "How would the sum of ten thousand dollars sound, for each time we used the pump?"

It was Edson's turn to tremble. He fought to still his eagerness. His salary with Herring had dropped from two thousand four hundred to a mere two thousand a year, less than forty dollars a week. The young man with the steel blue eyes and seemingly patient inattention was offering him five times his yearly salary.

"You must now forgive my candor," Dunlap continued before Edson had a chance to respond. "I know you lost a small sum at Prospect Park and Jerome. I also know you bet heavily on a trotter that went lame at Deerfoot Park. There is a sizable bill at Ryan's stables. You once lived in Minneapolis to avoid a lawsuit here in New York. You're plagued with bills. I would think that ten thousand dollars per use might do you very well at this point in your life." Dunlap smiled victoriously.

Edson tapped nervously at the saucer, wondering for the life of him how they knew so much about him and why he couldn't bring himself to utter a simple "Yes."

"You have serious doubts?"

Edson shook his head quickly. "No. I find the sum mentioned—very adequate. I will provide the pump and the names of those banks I feel inadequately protected. And you in turn will pay me ten thousand each time the pump is used."

"*Successfully* used," Dunlap amended. "We have plans to use it twice a year. Seldom more. Always in winter or inclement weather. There may be a few failures, for one reason or another. In that period of time, you should be free of your debts."

Edson stammered nervously. "That sounds most agreeable."

"Now, I must return to the subject of the Yale improved lock. What plans might you have for opening one?"

"Billy said it must be a technique that will allow the lock to open and close at will?"

"We will need to be able to lock or open it every night for a week or two. It is imperative no one knows the lock is being used outside normal business hours."

"Where is this lock?"

"Upstate. Elmira."

"Ah, out of town. I will need an excuse to be there."

"I'll get you there if you have a plan," Dunlap vowed.

"I have a plan," the salesman secretly chuckled.

It had been almost a thousand years since the first all-metal locks appeared in England, and since that time they had undergone radical changes. There had been adjustable tumbler locks, adjustable key combinations. Keys with teeth, keys without teeth. Locks with their inner workings in plain sight and locks with the works completely hidden. There were locks that ejected the false key, locks with detector plates that snapped shut across the opening to prevent picking. Keyholes had been moved from the center to the right, to the left, and back to center. Each was a short-lived improvement over its predecessor. When the mechanics failed to frighten off the determined burglar, the names were changed in hope this might turn them away. There was the "Infallible," the "Magic Bank Lock," the "Double Treasury Bank Lock," the "Lips Protector," the "Patent Climax-Detector," the "Monitor," the "Grasshopper," the "Double Dial."

Doctor Hart, the proprieter of the Elmira YMCA, knew little of locks, but what he did know was that his Yale improved failed to accept his key and was thoroughly jammed. He was on his hands and knees, preoccupied with the cursed lock, when someone volunteered that there was a lock expert at the Rathbun Hotel.

"I will get him for you, if you'd like," the tall, bearded stranger offered.

The doctor grunted in approval, certain something was jammed inside the lock.

Within minutes, the bearded stranger who had been lounging in the reading room returned with a short, thickset man who said he was William Edson of the world-renowned Herring Safe Company.

The doctor was mindful of his manners now help had arrived. He peered over Edson's shoulder as the lock was being inspected.

"Key!" Edson called.

Hart passed it and watched as the expert tried several times to insert it.

"I'll need a few tools and complete privacy with the lock. Professional ethics, you understand. I can't have anyone see what I'm about to do."

The doctor agreed swiftly and left the locksmith alone, never bothering to wonder why he couldn't see what was being done to his own lock.

In a matter of ten minutes, Edson rose to his feet, dusted his trousers and handed the key to Hart. "You may try it if you like."

Hart opened and locked the Yale several times. "It worked perfectly!" he laughed in relief. "What was wrong with it?"

"The stump was stuck in the gating bending the pin key."

"Ah!" the doctor nodded wisely. "What do I owe you?"

"Nothing," Edson said expansively. "My good deed for the day."

The doctor thanked him profusely and waved a cheery goodbye as Edson negotiated the stairs. The doctor looked for the bearded stranger to offer him his gratitude, but the man was nowhere about.

Edson made straight for the depot, where his bags awaited him. His duty performed, there was nothing left to keep him in Elmira.

Dunlap and Scott were waiting at the corner of Water Street. Edson stopped for only a moment to slip them the oiled silk package.

"You did very well," Scott praised him, as Dunlap slid the black wax impressions free.

"I made two molds," Edson whispered, "just to be safe."

Dunlap sighed in delight. "We'll have the keys made right away."

Edson tipped his felt hat, bid them a quick "good day" and hurried off to the Erie train. Billy Connors joined them to take the oiled silk, and Scott warned him, "Guard it with your life."

Billy rushed off, calling, "I'll have the keys as soon as possible!" His chubby figure boarded the same train as Edson, just before the engineer pulled out of the station.

"Whoo whooo," Scott called. "Make you homesick?"

"Not really," Dunlap smiled. Scott made the sound whenever they passed a train. It was a friendly jab at Dunlap's former occupation, and Scott would never let him forget it.

The station was empty; the engine could be heard in the distance pulling its load back to New York City. They left slowly for Water Street, their biggest hurdle behind them.

"It went pretty well," Scott observed.

"Edson may turn out to be all right, after all."

"Do you like him?"

"No," Dunlap laughed, "I really don't."

"Neither do I."

"But it was clever to plug the lock with paper. It gave us the impression we needed of the key."

"Do we have to like him?"

"I don't know."

"I mean," Scott shrugged, "I don't like you, but I work with you."

Dunlap was shocked. "You don't like me?"

Scott continued unperturbed by the damage of his remark. "It's just personal," he explained. When he turned and saw the crushed look on Jim's face, he began to laugh. "I was just sporting!"

"Sure!" Dunlap shouted, still unconvinced.

"Whoo whoo!" Scott tugged the make-believe whistle, laughing easily at Jim's discomfort.

* * *

At Baldwin and Third streets, in a house rented just a few blocks from Elmira's Second National Bank, an elderly woman swept the steps clean, an aged shawl over her shoulders against the weather. She beat the broom against the porch and tottered indoors. Billy Connors gave her a brief glance as he read the daily newspapers.

"Get your damn feet off the furniture!" she barked.

"Sorry, Sophie," Billy apologized, dropping his feet quickly to the floor.

She made her way past the card game in progress, threw open a kitchen cupboard and selected a Kentucky whiskey. A half water glass was poured to warm her body, and she downed it in two long pulls. The neighbors would have been shocked to learn that the elderly, gray-haired woman who so carefully tended her home was instead an elderly shoplifter from Baltimore named Sophie Elkins, mother of Sophie Lyons, mother-in-law of Ned Lyons, one of the Waterford bankies. Both Sophie's daughter and son-in-law were escaped prisoners, wanted throughout the United States.

Sophie shook some warmth to her limbs, scrubbing her arms with her hands as she idled into the parlor to watch the game in progress. She stopped at Red Leary's chair and looked at the cards hidden in large cupped hands. Her daughter and Kate Leary, Red's wife, were old friends, and it pleased her that the Fort Hamilton saloon keeper had decided to join the ring in Elmira.

"You lookin' at my hand?" Red roared.

"Is that yer hand?" Sophie countered, moving to Eddie Goodie's chair. "Hell, a pair of jokers would beat what you've got!"

"Damn you, Sophie!"

Eddie Goodie was the driver for the turn-off. A butcher cart thief by trade, twenty-four years old, sporting red whiskers and moustache, he was the youngest in the group. Eddie made a good living in New York stealing the loaded delivery carts of butchers as they transacted their business. Many a butcher heard his wagon pull away with the expensive carcasses of hog and beef disappearing down an alley. They always gave chase, long, bloodied aprons flying. But Eddie was never caught.

He held the cards in both hands, sleeves rolled up to reveal tattooed arms. Prematurely bald in front, he had gray eyes and red hair that gave him a startling appearance.

The pot belonged to John Barry, much to the disgruntled surprise of the players. A thirty-eight-year-old steel cutter by trade, Barry had been promised a spot with the ring since his discovery of William Edson. His moon face beamed with delight as he raked in his winnings.

Big Jim Burns shook his head in disgust. It had been his misfortune to lose every pot of the day. He checked the dwindling coins as Sophie moved beside his chair.

"Oh, Sophie!" he cried. "What are we doing here! The world's ripe for pickins and I sit here feedin' all my hard-earned money to the likes of John Barry!"

Sophie slapped the broad back. "I've yet to see an Irish beggar that could win at cards!"

"Don't leave!" Barry pleaded with the two-hundred-pound Boston giant. "I need those coins you've got there!"

Burns winked at Sophie as he cried in anguish, "I'm gettin' good an' tired of throwin' me hard-earned money into yer pocket, Mr. Barry!"

"Let's up the ante!" Barry suggested. Red Leary's stern glance made him quickly withdraw the motion.

"Bring us a bottle, love!" Burns called to Sophie.

"Yer arse!" she snapped. "I'm not yer nigger!"

"The tongue of an angel," Burns sighed, as he inspected the new cards.

In the chair near the fire, James Greer dozed the day away. A small-time pickpocket from New York, he had been recruited at the last minute by Billy Connors.

In a bedroom upstairs, the last two members of the eight-man, one-woman team slept until nightfall.

The house had been rented to John Barry on November 10 for twenty dollars a month. None of the neighbors ever saw anyone except Barry and "his mother" about. Under cover of darkness, they slipped from the house one by one and made their way to the room above the bank. The key was fitted to the Yale lock and the cut-away flooring uncovered.

Two nights had been spent in chiseling the bricks free of mortar. The material taken up was placed in wicker baskets and taken to the adjoining roof of the opera house. The brick removed, they found a small air space, and beneath that more masonry and the harder substance, stone.

The clerk had not lied. The stones before them *were* massive and weighed several hundred pounds apiece.

"Cripes!" Big Jim Burns exclaimed. "This could take us a month!"

"And we don't even know what's below that!" Leary complained.

The stones had surfaced slowly. Hours of chiseling and chipping mortar free revealed a stone tip. Over a long night, the digging spread in all directions as they tried to uncover the edges of the boulder. It soon became apparent what had happened: they had tunneled into the apex of a half dozen carriage-sized boulders. In order to dig one free, they had first to remove another. In order to free the other, two desk-sized boulders had to be detached from their cement grip.

The small hole of twenty-four inches had grown to some five feet in width.

"Cripes!" Big Jim swore each time a new boulder barred their way.

Lifting the stone out of a hole below foot level was no easy chore. Six of them would crowd around the foe and inch fingers down into the rough cement walls. A tipping or lifting before all were ready would shift the weight onto unsuspecting fingers, and cries of agony filled the YMCA.

"My fingers!"

"Who's lifting?"

"Set it down!"

"Aaaah!"

"I was just trying to get a grip!"

"My bloody fingers are killing me!"

"You tore my nail off!"

A boulder free of the hole, the two giants, Leary and Burns, would stagger under the load to the opera house roof.

The lookouts were changed each hour. Dusty coveralls were set aside and the close quarters exchanged for clean fresh air, but in no time the cold December night chilled the sweat of the body, and, long before the hour was up, the watch found himself wishing he were back in the hole and its relative warmth.

At 3:30 in the morning a signal was given and the tools were packed into the hole. The area was swept free of dust, the wooden flooring carefully replaced. One at a time the team filed out to Lake Street and on to the house at Baldwin Street. They collapsed from exhaustion, each wondering if any progress had been made.

It took a week to break through the stone breastwork. Several tons of stone, brick and mortar had been carefully stored on the roof of the Lyceum Opera House. This removed, a network of railroad iron faced them. Three days were required to free the end of the railroad bars and spring them aside. A plate of chilled steel, reinforced with iron braces, lay beneath. The jackscrew was brought up and set in the hole. Extensive bracing was required before the first quarter-inch hole could be drilled. Turning at 100 revolutions per minute, they bored the first hole.

Scott was in the corner playing his harmonica when the drill went through. He stopped midway through "The other side of Jordan," as Dunlap put an eye to the hole.

"I think that's it!" Dunlap told them excitedly.

Red Leary fell into the corner of the hole, sweat beading his face from the exertion of turning the feed screw drill. "Do we finish drilling tonight?"

"We can't," Dunlap cautioned. "Once we start, we have to be able to go all the way into the safe. It's not something we can leave."

"How would it look," Scott explained, "if we drilled a half dozen holes then left for the day? Don't you think the bank people would think something's a little odd?"

Connors wasn't totally convinced they had drilled into the vault. "It might just be another air pocket!"

"Did you see the safe?" Scott asked.

Dunlap admitted he hadn't. "It's too dark down there!"

"I think we should drill another of yer holes," Big Jim Burns decided.

"You should drill it!" Leary bellowed.

"I'll drill it!" Burns shot back. The big Irishman began throwing the braces aside, muscling the huge jack brace into a new position, the men giving him a wide berth.

Scott launched "Dixie" on the harmonica, racing the tempo as Burns cursed and kicked the brace into place.

The second quarter-inch hole was drilled by Burns himself, and when the drill went through, he toppled over from exertion.

"It's still too dark to tell," Dunlap said at the hole. He called for a piece of twine and fed several feet of it down into the darkness. It was bounced up and down repeatedly, and Dunlap shouted, "We're through into the vault."

Scott passed a lump of colored clay, and Jim filled the two holes with the soft gray substance. Billy Connors had taken it into the bank on an earlier visit and guaranteed them that the color matched perfectly with the interior of the vault. The clay inserted, they were assured that no premature dust would filter down through the holes on cleanup, plus, there was less chance of the pilot holes being detected.

The entry into the vault and the busting of the safe were set for the evening of December 6, as the bank would be closed the following day.

The Langdon mansion was the scene of a small Thursday night dinner that included two guests, the Reverend Thomas K. Beecher, and Daniel Pratt of the Second National Bank. The Langdons were among Elmira's first families. Less than four years before, a young writer named Samuel Clemens had married young Olivia Langdon in a ceremony performed by the Reverend Beecher in the Langdon library. Samuel "Mark Twain" Clemens had fallen in love with a picture of Olivia shown him by her brother Charley. An invitation to call in Elmira was quickly accepted, and Clemens married, becoming one of the city's most illustrious summer residents.

The dinner party was in aid of two of the city's latest projects. The first concerned the Reverend Beecher, who was distressed over the many delays in the building of his new Park Church. The second involved the host, Langdon, who was worried lest the surprise study be-

ing constructed for Clemens at the Quarry farm, just 2½ miles outside town, might not be ready in time for the author's visit.

Daniel Pratt's presence at the dinner was expected, as his bank
handled the monies for both projects.

Thomas Beecher was the next to the youngest of Lyman Beecher's
children. An avid abolitionist, he was destined to build what was possibly the first institutional church in America. His older brother,
Henry Ward Beecher, the Plymouth minister of Brooklyn, had been
equally fired by the evils of slavery and actually auctioned women and
children from his pulpit to demonstrate the monstrous practice of selling human beings. Their sister Harriet gave the world *Uncle Tom's
Cabin.*

But the table talk that night focused on the church and Clemens'
study. The following morning, a Friday, a check was to be issued to
cover delivery of material to the Park Church construction site. Pratt
intended to make that the first order of business in the morning. Toy-
ing with his dessert, the pastor's anxiety directed at him, Daniel Pratt
decided to make a late trip to the bank that very evening and ensure
the check would be at the construction site even before the bank
opened in the morning. He would not want to be the one responsible
for yet another disappointment to the good reverend.

At the house on the corner of Third and Baldwin, there was also a
change of plans. On visiting the bank that afternoon, Billy Connors
had noticed that the two holes in the ceiling were not completely filled
with putty. In fact they were easily visible from the vault entrance.
Why no one in the bank had spotted them was a mystery. With two
more banking days before the planned entry, one of the clerks was
sure to put an end to their scheme. It was decided to enter the vault
that very evening.

James Greer was to take the evening watch in the YMCA's reading
room, to make sure the hollowed flooring was not discovered. John
Barry was to take up position outside and notify the members of the
group when the library above had cleared of occupants.

At eight that night Barry drifted into the reading room, scanned the
material offered and saw Greer's all-clear signal. He returned a brief
dip of his head and sauntered down the stairs. Carroll and Lake
streets were filled with carriages and buggies due to a performance at

the opera house. Knowing there was still time before the Y would be clear, he went to Hemingway's and ordered a drink from bartender George Dewitt. He did not know Daniel Pratt, or he might have been alarmed to see the bank's proprietor arrive in the closed carriage. But he simply figured the man to be a late arrival at the Lyceum and ordered another drink.

Dressed in coveralls, to all outward appearances a mechanic, Barry left Hemingway's, walked past the bank, never dreaming someone might be inside, and took up his position at the foot of the opera house stairs. Barry lit a cigar, stuffed his hands deep into his pockets, dreaming of the money that would soon be his and the presents he would lavish on his wife as soon as he returned to New York City.

Daniel Pratt had opened the vault, thrown back the large doors and gone immediately to the safe. He went to one knee, dialed the combination and eased back the bolts. He rose as the heavy safe door swung open and brushed the white dust from his pants. He was about to remove the Park account, searching in the dim light from outside the vault, one hand still absently brushing the striped trousers clean of dust, when he realized there was no reason for him to have chalk dust on his pants. Bending to the floor, he pressed his fingers into the substance and brought it into the light. Rubbing the fingers convinced him it was fine plaster. Puzzled, he glanced around the vault, trying to locate the source of the plaster, when his eyes went to the ceiling and the two tiny half moon shadows thrown from the gaslight in the banking room. He saw two tiny quarter-inch craters he had never noticed before.

In a moment of alarm, born of years of suspicion, he left the Park account and locked the safe. It seemed farfetched to believe the holes in the vault and the YMCA directly above it might somehow be connected, but Pratt had to see for himself.

Barry might have seen Pratt leave the bank had not a man entered the landing at the top of the stairs. Barry looked up at the man lighting his pipe, reasoned he had left the performance for a breath of fresh air and turned away, missing Pratt's exit up the stairs to the YMCA.

James Greer saw the banker, but, not knowing Daniel Pratt, he assumed the man was searching for someone and dismissed it.

Pratt saw a dozen men in the reading room and thought nothing was unusual, though the beating within his breast continued its silent alarm. Down the steps he raced, confusion taking control now, uncertain his cynicism might not be ill-founded. He saw a man in a mechanic's coveralls smoking a cigar at the foot of the entrance to the opera house. Both men gave each other a wary appraisal.

Barry realized it was just someone leaving the YMCA and turned away, busying his mouth with the cigar, ignoring the man above him who puffed on the pipe and the man at the stairs of the Y.

The man with the pipe was Michael Kennedy, an off-duty policeman, who had left the minstrel show for a quick smoke. He had opened the door to the landing and saw below him a man in coveralls smoking a cigar. He might have discounted Barry except that he wondered why a man would stand in a doorway and peek out first in one direction and then another. Kennedy watched for several minutes. He did not see the banker Pratt walk uncertainly away, nor did he see the YMCA empty for the night, or James Greer give a signal to Barry that he was off to rouse the ring to work.

Kennedy watched Barry for almost ten minutes, certain the man's suspicious actions were involved in some unexplained criminal act. Moving silently down the stairs, he grabbed a fistfull of coverall and stated those dread words: "You're under arrest!"

Scott and Dunlap were waiting for Greer, their tools wrapped in the *Daily Gazette*. A sleepy Red Leary carried the last tool they would need in the venture, the Edson air pump. Big Jim Burns toted several pounds of Laflin and Rand gunpowder, an extra fine ffffg granulation that would draw well into the recesses of the safe. Scott carried the putty to caulk the seams. Dunlap checked their quarters, making sure there was nothing left behind to incriminate them. Sophie Elkins had returned to New York late that night. They would leave for the city as soon as the robbery was over.

Both he and Scott had grown sizable beards. Eddie Goodie, busy harnessing two wagons to be used for the escape, had dyed his own hair black. Burns and Leary had no concern, as neither man had been seen outdoors by anyone in town. The apprehension of criminals was still in its infancy. Verbal descriptions were wired across the country, and, more often than not, two eyewitness descriptions often totally disagreed. There were no rogues galleries or police photos. Fingerprinting was unheard of. It was a simple matter to grow a moustache before a burglary and shave it off after.

They were glad to leave the house, having been virtual prisoners since the tenth of November. Twenty-four days of nightly digging and shunning the sunlight. Twenty-four days of hard work and topsy turvey schedules. The night was day and day night. Breakfast was supper and poor at that. Each of them was eager to be done with it and home with his family as soon as possible.

They arrived at Carroll and Lake streets just as Barry was being led up to a group of men occupying the front of the bank. There was no disguising the fact that Barry had handcuffs on his wrists or that the bank's interior was too well lit.

They took to the shadows just as Pratt was asking, "What's your name?"

"Henry Myers," Barry replied, using the name under which he'd rented the house from Bob Hylen. No one would ever connect Henry Myers with John Barry, since there were no cross-filing of names or indexes. None of the police departments ever exchanged information.

"What do you know about this?" Kennedy demanded, obviously pointing to the vault inside.

"It's over!" Dunlap whispered, fighting the nausea that claimed him.

"Barry's been arrested."

Disbelief quickly gave way to fantasies of flight. The tools were hidden in nearby lumber piles as escape became the order of the night.

Goodie was still hitching the teams when the men bounded out of the darkness. Fumbling hands hurried the chore, and the two wagons raced off. Leary, Greer, Goodie and Burns went east toward Binghamton, while Dunlap, Scott and Connors whipped the wagon south toward Bradford, Pennsylvania, hoping to board a train in the next state undetected.

The traffic at the Pennsylvania depot was minimal, though Connors saw several men casually inspecting the passengers.

"Detectives!" Scott warned from the nearby bush.

"We'll have to break up!" Dunlap whispered. "They'll be looking for a group of men!"

"Everyone take a different car. Let's not sit together in the same damn one!" Scott admonished.

They remained hidden until the train arrived and then slipped to the platform, purchased tickets and moved off in various directions.

Dunlap wandered into a second coach where he found a young mother and her bright eight-year old lad. When the detectives came into the car, the boy was at Dunlap's knee absorbed in a vanishing coin trick, and they passed the family by focusing their attention on a sleeping figure two rows to the rear.

Further back in the car, a harmonica trembled into the old slave song "Many Thousan' Gone." Dunlap knew Scott had somehow ended up in the same car. The detectives gave the soloist a brief glance, then turned back to the sleeping figure. The felt hat was raised from the eyes, and Dunlap saw the clover birthmark of Billy Connors. The burly detective kept the hat in his fist as Billy blinked awake full of appropriate surprise.

They had him on his feet in the aisle, coat wide open as hands searched for anything to tie the small man to Elmira. Connors showed panic when he glanced Dunlap's way. Though nothing incriminating had been found on Connors, a hunch had one of the detectives whispering to the other. Connors knew he was doomed, bank officials would recognize him as having been in the bank on various occasions, certainly suspicious behavior now the holes had been discovered.

Suddenly the harmonica stopped breathing, and Scott was in the aisle. He whipped the watch from Billy's vest and flashed the gold case at the startled detectives. "This is mine!" he insisted. "Thief!" he shrieked, striking at Billy with the palm of his hand.

"Hold on now!" the first man recovered, pushing Scott aside.

"He stole my watch!"

"I did no such thing!"

"For the last two days I've been watching him changing seats, and when I woke a moment ago, my watch was missing!"

"That's my watch!" Connors argued.

"Open it!" Scott pressed the two sleuths. "You'll find an inscription from my wife. 'To Billy with all my love.' On the back is my wife's name!"

Connors hung his head as the engraving condemned him. The watch was passed back to Scott. "You have a bit of explaining to do," Billy was advised by the detective, a sure grip on his arm deciding the matter.

"Would you accompany us, sir? We'll put this scoundrel under lock and key."

Scott appeared undecided. Somewhat hesitantly he said, "I don't want to press charges against him. I'm in a hurry to get home. The watch is all I care about."

"It's your lucky day," the man surrendered, shoving Connors back into his seat, disgusted with Scott for failing to do his citizen's duty.

"We'd better not see you on this line again!" Connors was warned, a huge, menacing fist shown for emphasis.

The detectives were at the window when the train pulled out. They followed Billy with eyes hard and unforgiving, walking along with the car to the end of the platform.

A spirited "Dixie" broke out on the harmonica.

Chapter Four

The old man with the silver imperial goatee emerged from the hotel at daybreak. Dressed in a clean gray bowler and Chesterfield, gold-crested cane leading the way, he stepped onto the boardwalk fresh and energetic. A cocky jaunt about town led him to the rear of Pate's Bank. The tiny hickory wedge was still in place. He grinned.

He made the far street without detection, an incongruous sight, black leather shoes topped with gray spats, stepping carefully around frozen mudholes capped with ice. Once on the boardwalk, he fit right into place.

He approached the front of the bank slowly, checking window wares along the way, watching the city come to life as sleepy horses led creaking wagons into town. The small hickory chip was still in the jamb, and he was now certain no one had entered the bank through either entrance anytime during the night. There was no need to gather the wooden detectors, they would fall harmlessly unnoticed when the doors were open for business.

The stroll led him a block further, then he crossed the street, an early morning shopper interested in the community's merchan-

dise. There was nothing left to do this morning but await the arrival of the clerk, or Pate himself, if there was such a person, opening the bank for business.

This he did from the far side of the street, patrolling the shop windows until promptly at eight when a young man inserted a key to the front door and went inside. He watched the whole procedure in the reflection of the window, his back to the street, a pocket watch in his hand. He snapped the gold case shut contentedly, assured that he would find the young man's routine precise each day. He smiled to himself and went off to breakfast.

New York City's budget for 1874 totaled $1,000,000 for street cleaning alone, and the city was worried the figure might climb to $1,333,000. This to rid the city of its daily accumulation of manure, ash, garbage and winter snow.

It required the contractor to scrape and sweep each street two times a week, with the exception of Broadway, which was to be cleaned every night. Snow was plowed to the side while men followed with shovels, throwing it into piles. Behind them came another brigade that tossed it into wagons to be drawn away, leaving the streets clean for the morning's carriages. But the fifteen-degree nights caused ice to form between the stones, and the roads were perilous until the morning sun sweated them free.

Opposite the Fifth Avenue Hotel was a single patch of experimental paving. City engineers watched it closely to see if New York streets might endure if paved in that substance known as asphalt. Arguments abounded about the merit of asphalt versus concrete, or stone block paving, the traditional street covering.

At best, winter provided a few jobs. The frozen Hudson offered employment for eight thousand men at $1.75 a day. Thirteen hundred boys would be hired at $.75 to $1.25 a day for cutting the Hudson into blocks nine inches thick. Until the season ended, the Hudson alone would yield 1.4 million tons of ice, requiring 580 horses and 41 steam engines to cut and store its valuable cargo.

Those not fortunate enough to find employment during the holiday season that led them into the new year would spend their days seeking food or a pail of coal to enable their families to make it through the deadly winter nights.

The prosperous citizens, called Society since 1870, bought and spent with abandon, forcing the A.T. Stewart Company to send out twenty express wagons to deliver 20,000 packages in the three days before Christmas. The affluent minority had summer to look forward to, with a new game called tennis just introduced at the Staten Island Cricket and Baseball Club. While the poor assembled in Tompkins Square, those of means roistered in Central Park. Designed by Frederick Law Olmstead in 1858, it suited their winter needs quite nicely. An eight-horse team pulled large rollers through the park, packing the snow for their sleighs. The nabobs took advantage of this gesture to have their rigs polished up and trot them through the park. Even those outsiders to society could not resist the parade. Thousands of Albany Swells slid in through the Broadway, Fifth, Sixth, Seventh and Eighth Avenue entrances, their large, graceful curves sliding on runners drawn by spirited horses.

The more sporting of the group rode in Portland Cutters, pulled by trotters that champed impatiently at the five-mile-per-hour speed limit set within the park, eager for the headier pace of Harlem Lane or St. Nicholas Avenue.

Scott and Dunlap rode Bob's Portland Cutter, with Scott's new trotter Knox in harness. Puffing at the nostrils, mouthing the bit in frosty expectation, Knox coughed past the frozen lake where Mary and Linda Knight skated the ice.

Dunlap waved to the girls, though he wasn't sure he'd been seen. "I've settled with Barry. I settled six thousand on him for his silence and provided him with a fairly competent attorney for the trial."

Scott gritted his teeth and slapped Knox past a slow Albany Swell filled with children. "That's a lot of money."

"His family has to be provided for. The authorities have him dead to rights. They've tied him into the house and the tools. They even found Edson's pump hidden in the lumber pile."

"Does Edson know we've lost the pump?"

"I don't dare tell him," Dunlap sighed, expelling a cloud of white vapor.

"The lawyer can't get him off?"

"They found all the tools in the hole upstairs. There's a bartender who saw him having a drink just before the YMCA closed. They'll have him in Auburn Prison, I'm afraid."

"How are we going to pay Edson the ten thousand we owe him?"

"We can't, not just yet. Barry wants an auger. He thinks he can drill through the ceiling of his cell and make it to the roof. One of us will have to go back there and slip him the tools."

"They might recognize us even with the beards gone. It would be better if it was a girl."

"Maybe Red Leary or Shang Draper can lend us one. She could hide the drill in her skirt."

"I'm short of funds, too," Scott stated. "I'm on the fence again."

"Bob," Jim wheezed, pulling the blanket tight to his chest, "you're always on the fence. I never saw anyone go through money like you! You tell me you're on the fence, I give you money. What do you do with it? You buy a couple of horses!"

"Not just horses, Jim! Matched bays!"

"Then you tell me you're on the fence again and headed straight for debtors' prison. Another five thousand and you buy a piano, a sewing machine—"

"Not just a sewing machine! It was a Willcox and Gibbs that Mary wanted because it had an automatic tension control!"

"A refrigerator—"

"An Ice King!" Bob corrected.

"What is it this time?" Dunlap shouted as Bob reined Knox at the restaurant at the north end of the park. "A summer place?"

Scott refused to be drawn. He tied off the horse, threw his arm around Dunlap and guided him toward the eatery. "It's time you settled down, Jim. You should marry Linda and start a family."

"I can't afford to fund two households!" Dunlap glowered.

"That's cruel, Jim. There's a mean streak in you! Here I was going to let you take Knox around the park, and you come back at me like I was some sort of hired hand. Whenever I mention marriage, you bristle. You're just afraid of it, admit it!"

"I'm reminded of St. Paul, who said, 'those who marry, do well. But those who don't, do better.'"

"Coward!"

* * *

What had once been a Sauk Indian village between steep bluffs and the rambling Mississippi grew into one of the largest towns in Illinois—Quincy. It boasted two banks on Hampshire Street, the Ricker National and the First National.

Situated on the northeast corner of Fourth Street, the First National began in 1857 as the Quincy Savings and Insurance Company. It was to become the Quincy Savings before its name and location were changed to the First National, headquartered in a three-story brick structure, with large, arched windows. It was the selected United States depository and home of the Internal Revenue Department's eighth district. Government funds for pension payments were stored in its vault.

Davey Cummings, fresh from a successful robbery in Macon, Georgia, had long been a champion of the Quincy bank, and the ring needed little encouragement to proceed. Leasing offices in the Walker Building, just two doors east of the *Whig* newspaper, Cummings opened a patent office. He had no clients, but few poeple understood what transpired in a patent office anyway.

The First National's vault stood only six feet high, set under a tenfoot ceiling. The second floor directly above the bank was leased to the Quincy, Missouri and Pacific Railroads. The vault ceiling fell directly in the hallway. Inside the vault were two safes.

"We have to face the fact that the area between the hall floor and the top of the vault is probably four feet of solid stone and brick," Dunlap warned them.

"And boiler plate," Scott added.

Cummings added a few coals to the patent office stove. Two men occupied both chairs of the sparsely furnished facility, forcing three others to sit on the carpet next to the stove. The ring had shrunk somewhat. Leary, Draper, Greer and Goodie were disgruntled with the Elmira fiasco and had stayed in New York. George Mason, Billy Connors and Davey Cummings rounded out the group.

"It means a lot of work," Dunlap said softly. "The floor will have to be taken up in the hallway each night, and the area will have to be swept clean so the railroad people using the hall suspect nothing."

Billy explained, "There's the police station house in the next block—that means there'll be a lot of foot traffic."

"But there's no watchman!" Mason added, black eyes gleaming from the darkly bearded face. The growth reached his shirtfront and the glow from the mica windows sparkled in his eyes. "It's because it's so close to the station house that it's best for us!" he giggled.

"George's right," Dunlap agreed. "They feel safe, so they won't be looking for us."

"We left out one person," Scott threw out.

"Who?"

"The kid who works at the Reiss Saloon sleeps in the basement directly below the vault."

Mason whipped out a long, thick-bladed Bowie knife. "He'll be no problem!"

"Not until we blow the safe do we have to worry about him." Dunlap lay on the floor on one elbow. He slowly pushed the knife from in front of his face.

"Let's do it!" Scott decided eagerly. "I have a good feeling about this one!"

Davey asked Dunlap, "Did Bob have the same feeling about Elmira?"

Dunlap closed his eyes and nodded. "He'd already spent the money."

"Count me out!" Davey whooped.

"Me, too!" Mason eased.

"See what you're doing?" Dunlap told Scott. "You're giving us a bad name."

They toiled each night in coveralls and linen dusters. Sweat stained their clothing and mortar dust clung to the dampness, turning them chalk white.

Before daybreak they would clean the area, drag their weary frames to the patent office and collapse on the carpet. They were forbidden to leave the quarters, and each time Davey ventured out with a market basket, the talk turned to what Cummings might manage for food. Breakfast, lunch and dinner came in a wicker basket. In order to keep from arousing suspicion, Cummings purchased Dupee hams, oysters, large gentian and winesap apples. Being February, there were few fresh vegetables available that didn't need cooking of some kind.

Each time the basket was uncovered, the group would groan in unison.

"I refuse to eat another piece of ham!"

"This is a Pomroy ham!"

"A ham is a ham!"

"I won't eat it!"

"Apples give me the runs!"

"I need a piece of meat!" Mason insisted.

"Corn!"

"Potatoes, dripping with butter!"

"I need meat!"

Somehow Mason managed to find a large cut of beef. He stoked the fire and lay it atop the stove. The smell drove them wild, though none of them would admit they wanted a taste. Mason guarded it with his drawn knife, using the tip to lift the meat and peek beneath. He retreated to the corner as the others eyed him enviously. He held the steak skewered on the Bowie and tore at it, stripping large greasy hunks away. He ripped viciously at his prize, while the others watched, glumly chewing on tough, cold ham.

The meat had been cooked without benefit of pan and the stove top held a large grease spot the exact size of the steak. It was the only clean surface on a rusty, speckled top. The group speculated that the stove had been outside for some time prior to installation, and Scott guessed the white speckles to be bird droppings. Mason ignored them, gorging his steak, groaning in rapture with each noisy bite.

That night at the hole, just minutes after his first shift with the mallet and chisel, Mason stopped cold. He gave the men a startled look, grunted in disbelief and bolted from the hole. A loud moan accompanied his flight to the stairway. The men looked at each other in surprise.

"It must have been the birdshit sauce!" Scott laughed.

It took only eight days to reach the vault top. This time no pilot holes were drilled. The following evening, they made ready to go all the way to the safes.

Two hundred holes had been drilled in a perforated square measuring sixteen by twenty-four inches. At 2:10 they entered the vault. A crude copy of the Edson air pump had been built by the German machinist Steurer, and it was lowered into the hole.

Two large horse blankets were carefully placed on the floor to catch the doors, should they be blown free. Lumber and material was placed about the wall burglar alarm to prevent its being tripped.

Everything ready, Dunlap called for a book and pistol. Dunlap mounted the pistol to the book and placed it on top of the Dodd safe. He aimed it into the explosives, adding a pinch of DuPont's 75 / 10 / 15 mixture to the area just to be sure. A piece of twine was attached to the trigger as the vault rapidly emptied. Once again Dunlap was the last man free, and he climbed into the hall, trailing the string behind him.

Cummings went to the basement door and stood ready with a pistol in case the boy sleeping there might be awakened. Scott tugged Billy an "all clear?" After a long, five-minute wait, the go-ahead signal. Dunlap tugged the twine, and the resultant explosion rocked the hallway.

Cummings waited outside the basement door, pistol ready, but the boy heard what he took to be a falling object and rolled back to sleep.

Billy noted that a light came on at the Reed photography studio immediately after the explosion. Scott yanked the string again, asking if it were all clear. He waited to answer, eyes sweeping the street, expecting patrolmen to pour out of the station house. He signaled the men inside to hold their work. *This is the hardest part,* he thought. Remembering his studies at home he told himself, *In stillness and in staying quiet, there lies your strength.* Then he remembered his mother's *Why do the wicked prosper and the traitors lie at ease?*

Billy mumbled his favorite, *What use is money in the hands of a stupid man? Can he buy wisdom if he has no sense?*

There were no policemen. The Reed studio went dark once more. He gave the signal to continue.

It had been almost ten minutes since the explosion, and the men knelt at the hole waiting for footsteps racing the stairs. With Billy's go-ahead there was an audible hush of relief, for the Dodd's doors lay on the floor, the first reward ready to be claimed. There was a quick scrambling down the rope ladder leading into the vault. Dunlap began to putty the second safe, while Scott passed out the innards of the Dodd to Mason at the hole.

"I'm going to pay you back every cent I owe you, Jim. I promise. I'm going to do that the very first thing."

At seven in the morning, William Cross, the black porter, arrived at the bank for his usual morning cleanup. He went to the closet to pull out the tools of his trade when he noticed that the wall clock had stopped at 2:15. He made a face, opened the closet door and was buried in a torrent of loose plaster. Coughing, choking, unable to see, the porter staggered out, rubbing his sleeve across dust-filled eyes. When he was able to see, he wished he could not. Knowing he would somehow be blamed for this, he blinked and fumbled for the broom. Pulling it from the debris, he tried to sweep the area clear, but a huge pile of plaster oozed from his own closet. Even when he noticed large cracks in the ceiling near the vault, Cross was still sure he would be blamed, for it was obvious the plaster was coming from his repository. He gathered up several pounds of rubble, wandering in an ever-widening circle as he tried to think of a place to hide it. But there were several hundred pounds that must be disposed of and quickly. He filled a large wastebasket and continued to sweep and eye the ceiling. It was several long minutes before he began to wonder why all the cracks seemed to be springing out from the direction of the vault. Grasping at the hope that it might not be his fault after all, Cross dropped the broom, smelled the vault doors and flew for the bank's officers.

The cashier, Penfield, was the first on the scene. He immediately attempted to open the vault doors. Employees Lockwood and Mills arrived to assist him. Mills left the two tugging at the doors and went above to check for damages to the railroad offices, and the lodge on the third floor. He only needed to reach the hallway and the large hole in the flooring to report to bank officials weakly, "Gentlemen, we've been robbed."

A BOLD BURGLARY! the *Quincy Herald* announced the following morning. "One thing police and public may rest assured of—this is not the work of loafers about Quincy."

The *Quincy Whig* marveled, "The bank is located in the most prominent part of the city, only one block from police headquarters, and is passed every few minutes. How the parties escaped without being seen is a puzzler."

The *Herald* tried to talk to the Pinkerton agent sent out to assist Quincy Captain John McGraw, but found it "about as profitable to interrogate him as to cross-examine a cast-iron lamppost."

The first tune of the evening was a rousing rendition of "When Johnny Comes Marching Home," and the patrons assembled at the Fourteenth Street Armory were thrilled by the sixty-five musicians of Gilmore's 22nd Regimental Band.

The men in the audience, those who were veterans of the Great War, sat ramrod straight as the music stirred up fresh memories. It swept Dunlap to the chestnut forests of the Kenesaw Mountains. He could see the signal stations high on the peaks from which the rebels telegraphed General Sherman's every move. He could hear the bugles beckoning them into the thick foliage where the sound of axes and toppling trees promised a well-entrenched enemy. The roll of the drums was each man's invitation to come and die among the gleaming bayonets flickering in the trees. The sound rolled down into the valleys where they lay waiting. Then came the rain—three longs weeks of it—a reprieve from duty, a stay of execution. They promised him he would see Atlanta from the heights, but he never reached the heights. Somewhere between the valley and the peak, rebel marksmen found him, sending a Whitworth hexagonal bolt into one leg and then as he whistled up his courage, a second marksman drove a bullet through the other. He never did see Atlanta, trading the view for a small hospital cot in Nashville, Tennessee.

Listening to the music, Dunlap was amazed any of them had ever made it home, let alone marching, as the lyrics suggested. He rose as the music ended, applauding wildly with the others. Scott was two seats away, standing upright, hands crashing together, as the conductor bowed and struck up "The Erie Canal."

George Radford, the New York detective, elbowed his way to the empty seat beside Dunlap.

"You're late," Jim said irritably.

Radford ignored him. Sitting heavily, he scratched his long pointed nose. "You have something for me?"

Dunlap pulled the carpet bag from between his ankles and slid it across with his foot as Linda Knight sang out, "Fifteen miles on the Erie Canal!"

"How much?"

"A hundred and sixty-four thousand dollars. Your 20 percent." When he looked at the detective, he could see the shock on Radford's face. The large ears twitched in bewilderment. The man's mouth gaped open as the audience sang, "Fifteen miles on the Erie Canal!"

Dunlap smiled and looked away.

"The Quincy bank?"

"We took 820,000," Dunlap whispered, eyes on the musicians.

"God Almighty!" Radford choked.

"One hundred and twenty thousand was in cash and 700,000 in securities and bonds. You have twenty percent of each in that bag."

"God."

"A note should be arriving at Captain Irving's home any minute telling him what we've paid you and where it's from. Just to keep everyone honest."

"Sure."

"He also has a list of the bonds included. There are a few Treasury bonds, a thousand dollars apiece. Railroads bonds from the Quincy, Alton and St. Louis Railway. Some La Grange City Municipals, all of which should be easily disposed of."

Radford was sweating profusely, and he nodded absently.

"For that tidy sum I'm sure that me and my friends will be well protected from Pinkerton's?"

"Don't you worry none about Pinkerton's. We have ways of taking care of them."

"I hope that means we'll receive better care than that Bank of England forger . . . whatever-his-name. As I remember, Pinkerton's snatched him right out of your hands."

"You leave them to us. Don't you worry none."

"I hope you're right," Dunlap said sternly.

Radford placed a hand on the bag at his feet. "You just keep this coming, and you'll be fine. We were beginning to worry about you. Irving was giving you another week to come up with something, then we was going to have a little talk."

"You tell Irving that's the last of it for awhile. Maybe a year— maybe more." Dunlap stared coldly at the Bank Ring detective. "Don't push us," he warned. "I know for a fact no one has ever paid off with that kind of money—not Langdon Moore, not George White, nobody!" he hissed savagely.

Radford's cocky smile was forced. "I'll be in touch," he whispered.

The band slipped into a medley of Stephen Foster songs. Linda Knight was totally caught up in the music, her feet tapping the wooden floor, hands clapping in her lap in time with the baton. Jim had been trying to tell her for two days that he was about to embark on a long vacation, perhaps for the better part of a year. Each time he summoned the courage, she set those dark, sloe eyes on him and destroyed what little confidence he had. He faltered several times, and now there was little time left for explanation.

He wanted to spend the summer alone on the New England coast. The Quincy robbery had left him nicely fixed for a carefree vacation. Each member of the group had received forty thousand in cash, with the bonds as yet uncompromised for cash. A large amount of the securities would be held for bartering purposes in the event any of them were arrested, and the rest would be negotiated and divided equally.

As he looked at the excited young girl beside him, he wondered if he could manage the nerve to tell her he was leaving.

The discovery of oil in Pennsylvania in 1857 doomed the whaling industry, yet when Dunlap arrived in New Bedford, the wharf was lined with barrels of whale oil stacked higher than a man's head and stretching as far as the eye could see.

He ventured among the whalers bellied up for repairs. Beached at low tides then drawn over by pulleys attached to the mast, they resembled the very creatures they hunted. Seamen caulked exposed keel and hull with odd-shaped, two-headed hammers and chisels mending the heart of a livelihood already in its death throes. The sound was similar to that of the railroad workmen whose mauls rapped spike heads, clanging against the rails while bolts squeaked stubbornly into fishplates.

Dunlap visited the banks in each and every town, his practiced eye taking in the safe and vault, the alarms and cashiers' routines. Everything was recorded in a small notebook. When he tired of an area, he'd move on, determined to finish the year in Maine.

A telegram awaited him in Boston, urging him to return to New York at the earliest possible moment. It had been sent by Billy Connors.

"Edson knows we lost his pump at Elmira," Billy told him worriedly. "Don't ask me how, but he managed to get it back after Barry's trial. I guess you heard that Barry was given five years in Auburn. Edson also knows we used a copy of it at Quincy, and he wants his money!"

"Then let's pay him," Dunlap replied, already sorry he had come back for such a trivial matter.

"He's not being paid out of my share," Scott said firmly.

Dunlap greeted this with a long quiet assessment. Scott studied his nails, a soft felt hat atop his curly dark hair, a silk scarf at the collar, cloth-topped buttoned shoes—the perfect gentlemen.

"How much will he take, Billy?"

"We promised him ten thousand." Billy shrugged helplessly.

"I'll draw seven from the bank first thing in the morning," Dunlap decided. "I'll tell him keeping Barry quiet cost a lot of money. I'll tell him he's damn lucky Barry didn't talk or he'd be inside with him. He'll take seven thousand, you can be sure of it."

"I'd sure hate to lose his connections," Billy worried. "He already has a few he thinks we should look into."

"He mentioned one bank in Northampton that sounded good," Scott volunteered.

"We don't need it!" Jim disagreed. "We're pushing our luck with another one so soon after Quincy!"

"The Bank Ring detectives looked me up," Billy ventured. "A guy named Radford. He says he has a job he wants us to do."

"Tell him we don't run errands!"

Scott mused, "It could be a good thing . . ."

"We don't need it!"

"Speak for yourself," Scott said evenly. "I could use a few extra dollars if the situation was right. And I'd like to do a job in the summer for a change."

Dunlap was suddenly suspicious. He looked at Billy, who slid back into the cane-bottom chair on Scott's patio, removing himself from the discussion. "You're *not* on the fence again?" Dunlap asked, somewhat incredulous.

Scott eyed him coolly. "Sounds like you're losing your nerve, Jim."

"It sounds like you're losing your common sense!"

"I do believe you're afraid of being caught."

Dunlap steeled himself. Fists clenched, he rose and stared down at the taller man. "I'm not afraid of anything and you know it! You're acting like a lunatic, Scott! At the rate you spend your money we'll have to do four jobs a year to keep you and Mary in horses and silver service! You won't be content until Mary's a prison widow and we're all behind bars!"

Scott rose, extending his body to its full height, reminding Dunlap that he was some five to six inches taller and several pounds heavier. "You keep Mary out of it!"

"I'll take me out of it!" Jim spat as he hurried from the Scott residence on Washington Square.

Mary arrived just in time to see Jim Dunlap storming to Washington Avenue. "What on earth is bothering poor Mr. Dunlap?"

Billy Connors shrugged uncertainly, while Bob drew his wife close to his chest and said, "How can one ever fathom what's happening in the mind of a bachelor? Billy comes up with a wonderful opportunity for us, and Jim's upset that it's not his idea. It's just business, my love, you shouldn't worry your pretty head about it."

"Are you writing another play?" she asked excitedly.

"Sort of." Scott grinned. "Someone's offered me a great deal of money to help them with a new script. I offered Jim the chance to pick up a good deal of change remodeling the theatre, but he wants no part of it."

"Does that mean we can redecorate the library?" She snuggled up to him.

"By all means! That's a very good idea! Pick out anything you see that strikes your fancy."

She seemed somewhat hesitant. "It could cost a great deal of money."

He cupped her face in his hands. "You're not to worry yourself about money. That's the husband's responsibility. You're to go ahead and hire that fashionable Frenchman, Henri-what's-his-name, and begin immediately, if it pleases you."

"Oh, Robert!" she shrieked, hugging him tightly about the waist as he pressed his lips into her hair. "You are a darling!"

She rushed from the patio, leaving Scott beaming after her. The smile slowly left his lips, the shoulders sagged, then he slid heavily into the wicker chair, ignoring Billy's curious gaze.

"She's going to have to know sometime," Billy sighed.

"What shall I tell her?" Scott asked bleakly. "Do I begin at the beginning and tell her of my five years in prison? Do I tell her she's all I ever wanted in life and that everything else around her is a lie? How can I hurt her like that?"

"You can't hide it forever."

"I can deny her nothing, Billy. She has only to ask—and I begin to empty my pockets." He threw his arms out in frustration. "The one thing she wants more than anything in the world, I've denied her. She wants a child," he said painfully. "I can give her diamonds. Furniture! A beautiful home. I can spend fortunes distracting her from the one thing that doesn't cost a bloody cent—a baby. Others have only to look sidewise at their wives and they're suddenly with child! Me—I pray every day that she'll wake to find herself with one of those glorious symptoms of motherhood."

Billy tugged at jaw-length sideburns. "Have you mentioned this to Jim? It might help him understand . . ."

"No!" Scott insisted. "The very words marriage . . . babies . . . send him flying. I was certain Linda Knight would spirit him to the altar. Then he ups and dashes to the coast like a frightened deer."

"He's worried about Pinkerton's," Billy offered. "They've been called in at Quincy. Each morning he starts the day with the newspapers, certain they're on to us. Maybe he's afraid of leaving a missus behind if we're ever caught."

"Billy," Bob chided gently, "that's exactly what does you in! You cannot walk around looking over your shoulder at every shadow and see a Pinkerton agent! Jim should know better! The facade is all-important! Even Mary suspects nothing. She's seen the bank drawings and assumes Dunlap is simply arriving with more of his theatre projects. Isn't the facade what keeps the swells in clover? They steal everyone blind with both hands, but the facade is there. No one can prove anything against us! If the Pinkertons happen to find their way to our doors, we simply show the proper outrage and send them packing! That'll be the end of it, believe me."

"I dunno," Connors said wistfully. "I don't like having the Pinks around."

"They're just men, Billy." Scott grinned his boyish smile. "Mortal men with their noses in the air sniffing the breeze. Should they be dogs now, *then* we'd have cause to worry."

Billy rose with a shrug and adjusted the clothes about his portly frame. "What about this Radford? Do I tell him we're closed for the season?"

"No," Scott said carefully. "Let's see what he has to offer first."

"Even though Jim wants no part of it?"

"There's no harm in listening to a business proposition, is there?"

"I'll talk to him."

"You know, Billy," Scott sighed, rising to put his arm about the shorter man's shoulders, "just once I'd like to turn off a bank in the summer when the weather's tolerable. Just once I'd like to work without my fingers frozen to the bone. I wish Jim could see that side of it."

"I'll talk to him about it, but it won't do no good."

"I know." Scott sent Billy to the street with a slap to the back.

The chubby pipe waved his goodbye, his shoulders hunched in thought. A rift had been opened in the ring's leadership, and he now worried that his services might no longer be needed.

*   *   *

The summer ferry left Hyannis Port for Nantucket Island with Dunlap at the rail. Elbowed between the tourists admiring the Sound, he was deeply troubled by his argument with Scott. He was thoroughly convinced that what he had done was right, that Scott's weakness for money would jeopardize the ring's security. But he still felt remorse, for Scott was, without doubt, the finest partner he could have had.

For several weeks he walked the cobbled streets of the glacial island, brooding over Scott, the Bank Ring and Pinkerton's, wondering why he felt so choked by a sense of impending doom. He didn't know which to fear most, Scott's recklessness, the Bank Ring's dubious protection, or the ever more successful Pinkerton's. Before leaving the city, he'd met with George White and voiced his doubts. White had been in complete agreement, warning, "The Bank Ring may have outlived its usefulness." But there was no way they could be skirted, for failure to pay them their percentage was certain to lead directly to imprisonment. And it was becoming increasingly obvious that the reach of Pinkerton's extended far. Their track record of arrests prompted most banks to hire them immediately upon discovering their assets missing.

The ferry that brought James Dunlap to Nantucket Island also brought a harried Billy Connors four weeks later. The chubby bankie was beside himself with despair. They were seated in the elm-shaded square, the Pacific Bank at one end, the Rotch Market opposite, when Billy wailed, "We had a *good* team! The Scott-Dunlap Ring was the best ever conceived!"

"What ring?" Dunlap snorted. "It was just a few of us who did all right robbing banks. The whole idea of the Scott-Dunlap Ring was Bob's idea. I never wanted it to be a ring, or gang, or anything else! Just a bank now and then to keep us in smart tailoring and spending money."

"You have to talk to him, Jim! He's been meeting with George Mason about shutting off some bank in Des Moines, Iowa! It's one of Mason's ideas, and sometimes I think he's crazy! I don't want to work without you, Jim! But I don't know what to tell Bob."

"That's simple, Billy. You either tell him you're with or without him."

"I don't know," Billy cried in total confusion. "I don't need the money." He put his face in his hands and moaned, "We were such a good team! I don't understand what happened!"

"Things change."

"In five months he went through all his money! Maybe he owed more than the rest of us and didn't have that much to start with, but it's gone, Jim! He owes Ryan again, and you know Ryan, he's been good to us. He helped us with Edson and made contacts for us to have horses in Elmira and Quincy. I hate to speak out of turn, Jim, but I think Bob's gone crazy!"

"He's in love," Dunlap said gently. "He's in love with that girl and can't see anything else. He wants to give her everything, whether he can afford it or not. And she's so young—she can't see where it's coming from or what it's leading to."

"Maybe," Billy said excitedly, "maybe if she knew how he earned his money, she mightn't be so eager to spend it?"

Dunlap disagreed. "It would break Bob's heart if she were to find out what we did on those long trips away from home. She went to a convent school—there's no telling what she might do. No," he said sadly, "I wouldn't be the one to tell her. I may disagree with Bob on our methods, but I care for him more than my own brother, and I would never be a party to that—never."

"I don't know what to do!"

"I can't tell you what to do, Billy. If you decide to go to Iowa with Bob and George, I'll understand."

"We were such a good team. We had a few bad breaks, but we were going to be the first ones to turn off a Herring or Hall safe and collect the $1000 reward."

"We'll do it yet, Bill, you'll see." No one had ever broken a Hall or Herring safe, and the companies offered a standing reward to anyone who could. Hall even went so far as to offer to take their safe to a hill with a week's rations for those determined to try. On lonely nights chiseling in some hole, they relished the moment when Billy could be sent to claim the reward. As luck would have it, every time a bank was spotted with promise, it lacked either the Hall or Herring to make it a challenge.

One week after Billy's return to New York, Bob Scott, George Mason and Billy Connors left for Des Moines, Iowa, intent on turning off that city's treasury.

Following a splendid lunch at Boston's St. Charles Hotel, shared with Big Jim Burns, one of Boston's finest cracksmen and an unfortunate accomplice in the Elmira fiasco, Dunlap purchased a *Boston Herald*, took it to a bench overlooking the Charles and settled down to digest his meal. He lit a cigar as a long flat-bottomed barge drifted the shoreline. It was beautiful weather, unlike the fog that covered Nantucket one out of every four days. He read the day's events, working his way slowly through the paper until a small item caught his eye. "Arrest of the Quincy robber," was the caption. He read, "The supposed bank robber Scott arrived from Chicago via the C B & Q railroad, at ten o'clock yesterday morning, in company with detective McGraw and Simmons."

Dunlap read on quickly. "Scott, the supposed bank robber, has a wide reputation as one of the most adroit burglars and safe blowers in the United States."

Dunlap skipped ahead in dread. " . . . from Warsaw, Illinois . . . served a term in Joliet." There was no doubt it was Bob Scott all right. Dunlap felt faint. He closed the paper, uncertain what to do first. Mary would be terribly worried and upset. He was about to send a telegram to soothe her fears but thought better of it. He would go to Quincy and somehow decide what should be done after seeing Scott. He cursed his friend's stupidity as he hurried to the hotel to pack.

It was dark when Dunlap arrived in Quincy. Dressed in workman's clothes, carrying a wooden tool box fitted out with the implements of a modern tinsmith, he rented a carriage for a leisure tour of the Adams County bastille. Windows and exits were noted in the hope he could somehow secure a breakout. Back in his hotel room, the Quincy papers spread before him, Jim saw that a substantial case had been built against Scott. Several witnesses had already identified him and the papers boasted that the trial would be a mere formality. Pinkerton's was publicly thanked for their assistance, since the notorious Scott "was so adept at opening safes, that the safe hadn't been made that he could not open in less than half an hour." The papers described Scott as being heavily guarded and kept in irons, for the rumor had reached the press that his "gang" would attempt his freedom. The trial was set for Monday morning.

Jim Dunlap was at the courthouse early with the others vying for seats. The small room filled quickly, and he was forced to take up a position against the wall. Still dressed in tinsmith's coveralls, clean shaven to avoid recognition, he waited impatiently with the cramped spectators. The officers entered in clean, well-fitting uniforms. He wondered if any among them were from the Pinkerton office. Would he be able to recognize one if he saw one?

The noisy room grew silent as the sounds of rattling chains were heard in the distance. A buzz of excitement sprung up in the gallery as sightseers climbed onto chairs and benches for a better view. The clank of iron was drowned out by the noise of the crowd as the prisoner entered the courtroom.

Someone, somewhere, rapped for order.

The first view Dunlap had of the prisoner was in the dock. He was not prepared for Tom Reilly humbled in irons.

Reilly gazed bravely out at the spectators, wrists bound to his waist with heavy links that hung to a steel strap around the ankles. Tom scanned the crowd, holding Dunlap's startled eyes for a brief moment of recognition.

Dunlap sagged against the wall. He felt tremendous relief and a crushing sadness. He felt wretched seeing his old friend from Chicago in the dock for a crime he hadn't committed, guilty of little beyond bringing him and Scott together. It had been two years since he'd seen the man, and he felt terrible that Reilly had been caught in the net. But to know that Bob Scott was still free gave him a needed lift.

Tom's hand came up awkwardly, the face was bent to meet the bruised thumb as it itched the massive scar. For a moment, Jim wondered if Tom might not relish all the attention.

Dunlap slipped quietly past annoyed spectators, trying to create as little stir as possible. Once in the fresh air, he took a deep breath and felt his eyes grow moist. Deep in thought, fighting wildly veering emotions, he checked out of the hotel, stopping in Springfield to gather his clothes and discard the tinsmith's outfit. Once in New York he obtained a lawyer, suitable witnesses and alibis to establish Tom's innocence. Scarface Tom Reilly was later acquitted and sent Dunlap a one-word note from Chicago: "Thanks."

Salt marsh hay was in harvest when Dunlap returned to New England. The valuable crop was stacked high on poles, awaiting the freezing of the marshes so the wagons could haul it home. Gundlow barges filled with the crop poled the shoreline and inlets as workmen prepared for the long winter ahead.

Farmhouses bustled with late summer activity, and the farmhand whose only talent was stacking slippery hay came into his own. Oxen and horses patiently trod their treadmills, driving saws to cut the last of summer's logs. Summer barrels, stored beneath roofs to catch rainwater, were filled with winter necessities and rolled to the basement. Roofs and shutters were given a last nail, and the sound of hammers echoed through autumn leaves.

The last log drive of the season bullied its way down the Connecticut River. The coastal lights, dark from July to October when there were presumably no wrecks or need for warning lights, were turned on for navigational markers.

Dunlap found a small inn near Kittery and had all his possessions delivered there. Billy Connors arrived two weeks after the first snow.

"Name something that could go wrong, and you'd be right! I'm tellin' you, Jim, I never saw such luck! We worked on the vault for two weeks! Then the landlady got suspicious and went to the station house. The police turned up just after we went down over the roof. There was snow on the ground and we must have walked twenty miles! We left tracks a blind man could follow—footprints this deep!" he said, indicating the height of the table.

"We finally made the train depot in some little burg and hid in the woods till daylight. No food! No fire! Damn near froze to death! Then just as the train arrived, a dozen detectives came out of nowhere to watch the station. So, back we went into the woods! We didn't eat for three days—it was a real disaster."

Jim filled Billy's glass with bourbon and shoved it into the fleshy hand. Billy twirled it, raised it, set it back down before continuing, "I stole a damn carriage from a barn. I guess the farmer saw me; two hours later we had a posse breathing down our necks and we had to leave the carriage and take off on foot again. Two more days without food. I've never gone five days without some sort of food! Mason stole a loaf of fresh-baked bread, and a woman with nine kids chased us three miles before we finally lost 'em! I'm tellin' you, Jim, I don't know what in God's name I was doin' out there! I'm a city boy, you know that! I don't know anything about the woods!"

Dunlap held back the smile tugging at his lips. He stared into the fireplace, content with the warmth of his room, the snow-laden forest beyond the window, far away from the hazards of Des Moines. "But everyone made it out all right?"

"There was just the three of us." Billy downed his drink, vest open comfortably, sack coat hanging over the back of his chair. "Nobody but Mason and me would go along with Scott. Leary dropped out when he heard you wouldn't be goin'. Draper hisself changed his mind at the last minute. That's why it took us so long, there was only two to do the work, if you count one man on lookout. We couldn't get Big Jim Burns, Eddie Goodie or anybody."

"Big Jim's still in Boston."

Billy made a sour face. "Davey Cummings was off to Philadelphia somewhere." He inched the glass forward for another shot.

"Bob's already lookin' at another job, and we lost everything we had on the last one!"

"Damn tools!" Dunlap thought aloud, wishing there were some way to compact the bulky load necessary for each job. The list of tools seemed to grow endlessly. It included bellows, steel bits, dark lanterns, fuses, cartridge caps, sectional jimmies, tubes for inserting explosives, pistols, several boxes of powder, torches, waterproof fuses, a fur muff to deaden sound, spatula, putty, adjustable wrenches, bit stocks, five dozen steel wedges, mallets, chisels, files, bolts, nuts, blankets, gossamer, handcuffs, screw jack, screw brace, feed screw drill, augers, nails and screws.

"Did you take Edson's pump?" he asked hesitantly.

"Thank God we didn't lose that! It's checked into a hotel in Des Moines."

"Don't ever let that get away, whatever you do!"

"Bob's desperate. If something doesn't come up soon, he'll have to sell the house. He's sick over losing the tools." Billy looked to the frosted window as he said, "Bob wants me to tell you that he's going to sell the bonds we took at Quincy. He needs the money more than the protection they might offer."

"He'll have to split whatever he gets with the others—it's their money, too."

"He knows that."

Dunlap shrugged helplessly. "If he needs the money that badly— go ahead." Powerless to stop Scott's disruption of their plans, he snapped, "He'll be lucky to get $150,000 for $700,000 worth of securities. Split that five ways, deduct lawyer's fees and go-betweens, and he'll be lucky to realize thirty thousand. Even at that, it's risky. Pinkerton's might trace it back to us. What the hell's the matter with him? He takes a sum that could last a lifetime and runs through it in three months!"

"I don't know," Billy brooded.

"I talked with White before I left, and he has the same feeling I do. The Pinkertons are doing to banks what they did to train robberies. It's not as safe as it was last year, and next year won't be as safe as this. It's not what it was when we started. Even George is careful about which banks he turns off. He's reluctant to move again. Langdon Moore's laying low. They drove Mark Shinburn out of the country, and even now they're trying to extradite him. The banks are all going over to Pinkerton's! In another year, it won't be safe to rob a bank anywhere! Those that aren't broke will be Pinkerton protected!" Dunlap stared glumly into his empty glass. "We're on a downhill slide, Billy. I feel it in this ankle of mine. We're paying a fortune in protection, and they still can't protect us from the one enemy we have, Pinkerton's."

"Are you going to quit for good?"

"No, but I'll take it easy for a while. I'm still on the lookout for a nice safe bank somewhere. I'm not ready to change these clothes for prison garb. I may just sit out next year before I move again."

"Edson still thinks you're with us. He gave me another list of banks he thinks show promise. There's one in Covington, another in Connecticut, Northampton, and one in Pittston, Pennsylvania."

Dunlap nodded agreeably but refused comment.

"Did you hear that Linda Knight got married?"

"No," he said slowly, a twinge of regret welling up within.

"She waited for you, Jim. Then when she heard you were back in town and didn't try and see her . . . "

"She did the right thing."

"She married that fellow Barnhardt that deals three-card monte for the suckers at Coney Island. A Jew, I think."

Three-card monte was the same as the shell game, except that the player had to pick the ace of spades instead of the elusive pea.

"I'm happy for her," Dunlap offered unhappily.

"So," Billy stretched comfortably, "you think it'll be a year or longer."

"Yes."

"That sounds like retirement to me."

"It does, doesn't it?" Dunlap grinned.

When he tired of the room, Dunlap would walk the two miles to the local blacksmith shop and join the other idle men around the heat of the forge. Farmers, shopkeepers, lobstermen, sardine fishermen and sardine canners, tinsmiths, lumbermen and livestock tradesmen would offer tall tales and lament their professions as they waited out the winter. Irish, Dutch, German and Italian listened patiently to each other's complaints, and there were many. The lobstermen predicted one of the worst seasons ever. Eighteen seventy-three had seen eighty thousand tons taken from local waters, and the listeners agreed that the lobster was about fished out of the area. Hadn't canning operations already been moved to the British provinces, further proof the lobstermen's trade was at an end?

Tinsmiths had better prospects. The American Sardine Company at Port Monmouth would offer ample employment for their spring and fall catches. There was plenty of opportunity for an experienced tinsmith soldering lids on the cans to be shipped round the world. Not content that their future was somewhat insured, they lamented trivial things like their women washing good silver in soap and water, giving it a pewter look, when anyone with common sense knew silver should only be cleaned with soft leather and whiting.

The trains were always easy prey. "I took the train from Boston and we were sidetracked four times. Then they left us waiting for another train! I sometimes wonder how they keep us from being killed!" Of course, everyone present would nod profoundly in agreement.

"It's getting so," the blacksmith offered wisely as he lit his meerschaum from a straw ignited off the coals, "the most uncommon accident on trains is a safe journey." There was no disputing him.

"Habit makes an eel indifferent to skinning."

"Put a beggar on horseback and he'll ride to the devil."

"Nothing goes so slow as a boy on an errand."

"My wife and I agree on only one thing," the fisherman offered. "She wants to be boss and so do I."

"The most curious thing in the world," a farmer observed, "is a woman who's not curious."

"So tell me, Timothy, why did you waste your summer nights fencing that rocky piece of property of yours? There's no way on earth a single cow could survive on that ground, let alone a herd."

"Well, Luther, I thought the same thing myself. I was just fencing it to keep the poor bastards out!"

Dunlap seldom joined in but would laugh heartily at the end of each story or groan with the rest when new infamy was reported. He was content to listen to their tales and share the camaraderie. They complained and made fun of each other, but he could see each one was satisfied with his simple life and the place he'd selected to spend it. He was the only nomad among them and often thought he might mention that he had robbed several banks and was now in possession of large sums of money. He expected they would simply nod in unison and, after a moment's contemplation, turn the subject to the weather or the telegraph poles springing up everywhere, blighting the landscape.

By the spring of 1875, Dunlap could stand the solitude no longer. Thirteen months after the Quincy robbery, he packed his trunks, hired a teamster to take him to the station and left for the excitement of New York.

George White greeted him warmly above the stables, indicating a chair next to his littered desk. Before the conversation had even begun, White had Jim reading the recent *Herald* account of the robbing of the Long Island Savings Bank.

"Mr. H. S. Powell sold his liquor store at #43 Fulton Street to two men in the middle of March. Last evening Powell saw one of the men standing in front of his old saloon and asked for a hat he'd left behind. The man appeared flustered and offered to bring the hat around. Powell rathered that he would like it now, and the man suddenly fled down Fulton Street, much to Powell's bewilderment. In the rear of the saloon Powell found a hole in the floor leading to the cellar. He called police, who discovered the cellar led to another hole in the partition to #45 Fulton Street and from there into the basement of the bank. The new owners entered the vault through the floor and were at work on it when Powell came to reclaim his hat—" Dunlap dropped the paper. "Who was it?"

"Scott and Connors. Botched it badly, I'm afraid."

Dunlap glanced at the list of tools found on the site, relieved to see that Edson's pump was not among them. "He must be having a bad go of it."

"He's desperate," White explained, idly twisting the recently waxed end of his moustache. "He talked Georgie Mason into a job at Covington, Kentucky. From what I hear, they're already there."

"I haven't heard from Billy in over six months. I've no idea what they've been up to."

"Scott's practically bankrupted poor Billy. Even at that, he's lost his house."

"I didn't know that."

"Enough talk of Scott. It's all so depressing. What are your plans?"

"I thought I'd look around to see what was available."

White smiled. "Going back into business."

"I think it's about time," Dunlap laughed.

"You'll need tools. The German Steurer's been arrested. I'll give you the name of another man."

"Thank you. Would I be in your way if I went to Massachusetts for a job?"

"No." White lay back in his chair. "Go anywhere you like. It may be a long time before I move out of here and into a job."

"I just wanted to be sure."

* * *

Dunlap had his old room back at the Grand Central Hotel, a corner accommodation overlooking Fourth Avenue and Broadway. He was just finishing a large breakfast of chops and eggs, the morning paper in his lap, trying to recover from a night at Shang Draper's, when a familiar two-wheeled carriage drawn by two horses drew up in front. The horses were matched bays, though the small carriage needed only one, a typical extravagance of Scott's. Bob shrugged nervously, his tension discernible from the window. Then he summoned courage and disappeared into the hotel entry below.

Dunlap called for a pot of coffee and was seated at the window, his back to the door when the knock came.

"Come in!" he called, apparently engrossed in the paper before him. "Good morning, Bob!" he said cheerfully without turning.

"Morning, Jim."

"Been reading about you, Bob," he smiled, shoving a chair out with his foot. "Nothing in the paper today, but there was an item yesterday."

Scott threw his silk hat onto the unmade bed and took the chair offered.

"I've sent for more coffee," Dunlap mumbled as he pretended to read a last item from the news. "How's Mary?"

"Fine . . . she's just fine, Jim. Asks about you often."

"Asks about Mr. Dunlap, you mean. Does she still call me that?"

"I'm afraid so," Scott smiled.

Jim scaled the newspaper into an empty chair and inspected Scott closely. "You've lost weight. From what I read, things didn't go too well in Kentucky."

"I guess you heard it all already." Scott shifted his shoulders restlessly.

"Not too many secrets in this town. Have you had your breakfast?"

"Just coffee."

"I'm glad you came by. I was thinking of calling on you."

Scott seemed surprised. "Hell, I don't know what for! Is it about a job?"

"That's what I was thinkin'!"

"When you hear what's happened to me, you may change your mind!" Scott scoffed.

"I doubt it," Jim said easily.

"Did it say anything in the papers about the damage we done in Kentucky? We destroyed that place! Talk about blowing a safe! You know what I know about Hall safes—"

"It was a Hall?"

"An ugly Hall! Big! Ugly! Dared us to blow it open! Never saw a safe look so damned ugly in all my life! Just stared at me while I loaded the doors with two pounds of Hazard powder—"

"Two pounds!" Dunlap was almost out of his chair with disbelief.

"Biggest! Ugliest Hall I ever saw in my whole life! It knew what I was doing and it just *dared* me to try it. When that thing went off, it sounded like war had broken out in Kentucky. I never heard such an explosion in my whole life! We went outside after the noise because we knew we had woke up the whole damn city!! The lampposts were still shaking five minutes later. The ceiling came down around our ears! Jim, it was the damnedest thing!"

Scott saw the smile on Dunlap's face and relaxed visibly. "There was an Odd Fellows hall right above us and every night we had to take up a dozen seats and a mile of flooring to get inside. But we didn't have to put it back. When that thing blew, it all ended up in the vault!"

Dunlap couldn't contain himself any longer. He threw his head back and began to roar.

"I tried to signal Billy to ask if anybody'd heard anything, and the string was even gone. Blown right out the hole! Billy had to come to the window and when he did, I noticed that even the glass was gone!"

"You're making this up!"

"I swear it's God's truth, Jim. Billy and I was talking just like this," he laughed, sweeping his hand across the breakfast table. "I yelled to Georgie Mason, 'I told you it was too much powder!' But he couldn't hear me because he was buried under the plaster ceiling, and besides, none of us could hear each other for the damn ringing in our ears!"

The porter arrived with coffee, and it took a tremendous effort for Dunlap to rise from the chair and tip him.

"Billy's face is real close, Jim, and he's saying something, but I can't hear it for the life of me! Georgie's digging out from under the

ceiling, and finally I hear Billy yell, 'Let's get the hell out of here!'
Now you know Billy. I ain't never heard him swear before in my whole
life. Not with all that religious upbringing, but he swore that time! I
figure he's right, 'cause it was so damn late when we got to the safe
that the whole town must be awake by now! So we leave like wild
horses are between our legs!"

Dunlap was laughing so hard he could barely pour the coffee, spilling it on everything before Scott took it from him and completed the
service.

"I guess everybody made it away all right?" Dunlap asked through
his tears.

"Sure we made it!" Scott shouted in disgust. "And you want to
know why? Because nobody heard a damn thing! That's why! The
damage wasn't discovered for two days!"

"No!" Dunlap shouted skeptically.

"Yes!" Scott insisted. "Do you know what we left behind? *Four
hundred thousand* in *greenbacks* and a *million* and a *half* in *bonds*!
The figure was published the next day, and I looked for a railroad
trestle to hang myself from."

Dunlap bit his lip to control the laughter. "That's the worst story
I've ever heard!"

"That ugly Hall blew right open like a piece of crockery. I've left
behind enough tools in the last year to open a large factory."

Dunlap clutched the table for support. "I'm going to open a shop,
making tools for you to leave behind. I'll get rich!"

Scott was seized by the insanity of it and began to roar, too. "Banks
will pay me not to destroy their buildings!"

"You'll make a fortune!"

"Mason and I should go into destruction!"

"Let me know when you're going to work in the neighborhood—I
have some things I don't want broken. . . . "

"What goes up . . . must come down."

Dunlap tried to bring the coffee cup to his lips, but each time he
would start laughing again and the cup was hurriedly sent back to its
saucer.

"We were a good team," Scott choked.

"Damn good"

After eyes had been dried and coffee cups thoroughly inspected, Scott confessed, "I haven't done anything right since Quincy, since our last job together. Nobody will work with me anymore—even Billy won't touch me. Davey Cummings has been arrested and sentenced to seven years at Cherry Hill."

"I didn't know that." Dunlap sobered rapidly.

"I feel sick about all the trouble I've caused. Billy's last words to me were, 'When Dunlap's back with us, call on me.' I just can't seem to do anything right. I cashed the bonds from Quincy. I spent most of it—your share, my share, Davey's share—I lost the house that Mary loved. She knows nothing, of course. I told her I'd had several reversals at the stock market and that business had fallen off. I tried to recoup at the track and, instead, I lost another six thousand in a week. I'm afraid Mary's going to find out something soon. It's hard to tell someone you've been lying to her all these years and then expect her to believe you when you say you love her. How will she know one lie from the other?"

Dunlap offered the distraught Scott a cigar. Bob accepted it slowly, clipping the end with a gold cutter, then placing it between even, white teeth.

"I've the luck of a beggar without you, Jim. It's all bad luck without you beside me. I'm a weak person by nature, and I hope you won't feel badly toward me for it."

"How are you and Mary doing now?"

"We're fighting the horses for feed."

"Have your coffee," Dunlap said quietly, "then I'll take you to the bank. I have some money in my account that will tide you over for the next month or so."

"Then we're still friends?"

"I always thought so."

Scott covered his mouth with his hand, and the deep blue eyes grew moist. "I'll pay you back, Jim—everybody—every damn cent. I've learned my lesson."

"No," Dunlap whispered, "I don't think you have, Bob." Then he added, "But I guess it doesn't make any difference. You have your mistakes and I have mine. Just tell our friends the old Scott-Dunlap Ring is back in business."

Chapter Five

The old man with the silver imperial goatee decided during supper that he would turn off the Hall safe of Alexander Pate's bank. It was a simple decision based on the fact that he could think of no sane reason why he shouldn't. It seemed ripe for entry. The weather was perfect. Gale force winds would be driving the citizens indoors, whipping any telltale sounds far out into the country. He could not think of a single reason why he shouldn't rob the bank. Yes . . . there was one, but he brushed it quickly from his mind.

He had carried a few things with him, but he would need a few more that could be purchased that day in Watseka. He needed explosives and a few additional drill bits, nothing that couldn't be picked up in a few minutes' time.

The coffee was stirred as he pondered the single reason why he shouldn't enter the bank. He was far from his home in Chicago; there was no reason for this to be tied to him. Who could possibly suspect him of such a petty robbery? It was quite safe, he decided.

Should he do it alone? There were several very young toughs in Chicago who might be willing to join him. Still . . . there was the nagging notion he might just be able to do it alone. That in itself would be a tremendous accomplishment. A tremendous challenge.

He cut the skin on the baked potato into tiny squares and ate them with butter. The bread was dipped into the juice from his steak and disappeared between the silver whiskers. Operating without a lookout appeared to be the only problem. Yet, if he worked quietly, triggering the explosion from outside, he could act as his own lookout. It certainly was worthy of consideration. A string perhaps, tied to a pistol, outside with him where he could see the town when the explosives went off. It sounded simple enough. If it attracted attention, all he need do was walk away.

"Yes, why not?" he said aloud.

New York had nine watchtowers to protect it against fires, the highest and finest being the one at Spring and Varick streets. Equipped with a ten-thousand-pound bell, telescope and telegraph, it could sound an unholy clangor.

The meeting had just begun in Big Jim Burns' flat when the alarm blared through the room. The men adjourned to the windows to see a structure on Spring Street engulfed in flame.

"The biggest problem we have is leaving the island," Dunlap said to the window. "Turning off the bank then having to wait for a ferry could spell disaster. A telegram to Pinkerton's and they'll be waiting to greet us with handcuffs when the ferry docks. We need a ship that will take us to Nantucket and back. We need a skipper we can trust to wait for us on the island and take us back to New York. For that we give him a full share."

The Fire Insurance Patrol had already reached the site. Several fought the fire, while others dragged huge fourteen-by-twenty-foot oil-treated cloths inside to cover the goods. Formed by insurance companies in 1839 to protect insured goods, the patrol was often first to arrive on the scene.

"That's a long way by boat," Red Leary argued. "I ain't never been on anything except a short ferry ride."

"I don't like boats, either!" Shang Draper argued.

"I can't swim!" Big Jim cried.

"I can't swim, either!" Eddie Goodie whimpered, trying to see over the shoulders of the larger men. "But that don't worry me half as much as getting sick!"

"I don't like nothin' that's got boats in it!" Leary decided, as the Spring Street fire fighters arrived.

"Gee," Big Jim worried, "I never thought about being sick."

"There's no cause for concern," Scott said. "We'll get a good vessel that won't arouse suspicion. I can't swim and I'm not worried!" He turned to Billy Connors who sat silent at the table, ignoring the fire and the men fighting it. He looked pale when Scott asked, "Do you see me worried?"

The *Duguoin* listed at the foot of Murray Street on the North River, a colorless steam vessel with a lanky, toothless skipper grinning from the top of a warped boarding ramp.

Leary dropped the two large bags of tools. "*This* is it?"

"It's the best I could do," Connors piped weakly.

Scott took a deep breath, then announced, "A sturdy vessel to be sure!" Even in the dim light of dusk the missing paint and rusted bolt heads were obvious. The craft reeked of neglect. Scott thought Dunlap mad to rent this derelict for a full share.

"I thought it would be larger!" Draper cried. "Ain't the bigger ones better ridin'?"

The toothless Scots skipper waved them aboard, daring them to negotiate the ramp, while a wide-eyed deckhand chinned the ladder in amusement.

"Let's get aboard!" Dunlap urged. He led the reluctant group up the swaying, rotted gangplank, past the toothless captain to the deck. Draper was next. He set both feet on the deck and stomped the flooring before he'd release his grip on the rail.

Leary set both feet firmly on the vessel, cast a turned-up nose about, discovered the foul smell to be a hemp line just inches away from his face. "Phew!" he cursed, veering away from the odor.

Billy eased onto the deck, gripping the rails before deciding to give the ship his full weight.

Scott was halfway across the ramp when the breeze shifted and a black cloud of smoke engulfed him. He choked his way to the rail, and on touching it, discovered a fine layer of soot on his clothes and fingers.

Eddie Goodie waited until the wind shifted the black, noxious chimney smoke rearward, then raced the ramp and jumped aboard. Moments later the breeze changed directions, and they were lost to each other in the engulfing blackness.

"This is Captain McNaughten, the skipper," Dunlap stated in the darkness. "He'll be in charge."

Billy's voice shrilled, "Is this bucket guaranteed to get us to Nantucket?"

A laugh came out of the dark fog. "She'll ride well in any storm!"

"Let's avoid the storms at all cost," Dunlap muttered as the breeze blew them visible.

The captain indicated a stairwell leading below deck. Dunlap went first into the stifling interior. A hurricane lamp hung over a large food-stained and fish-scaled table. A half dozen dark bunks were recessed into the walls, their straw mattresses gray and foul smelling.

Cloth bags filled with tools were dropped into the dreary corners as they surveyed the cheerless quarters that would be their home for the next few days.

"They cleaned fish in here," Billy groaned.

"Not live ones!" Leary added.

"But recently!" Draper gagged.

They left the pier under cover of darkness, the moon conspiring to hide their departure. Too uneasy to sleep, they broke out the cards and took seats at the table. With each successive hand, the room grew warmer. Coats were shed, then shirts, until finally they played in their undershirts. With the heat came the smell.

"What cargo do you suppose he hauled?"

"Octopus dung!"

"You think so?"

"No question."

"You think this tub was ever a wreck?"

"It is now."

"I mean, they have to come from somewhere!"

"It's a prime candidate, that's for sure."

"I think he's burning that octopus dung in the boilers. Coal don't smell like that!"

Dunlap won several hands, and he rubbed Billy's birthmark for luck as the *Duguoin* headed into open water. The kerosene lamp over the table began to sway, but the men resolutely ignored the creaking and hammering of the steam engine. The heat continued to rise, and they sat gasping for air, the cards wilting in their moist hands. Slowly they began to rock in unison, swaying against the table and away, following the hurricane lamp's every move.

Dunlap brought a bottle of bourbon to the table. He took a long pull and passed the bottle to Scott. Scott drank, then sent it on to Leary. The *Duguoin* groaned over each swell, with each roll carrying them further from the table.

Eddie Goodie left the table to relieve himself in one of the buckets provided. He clutched the bulkhead as the *Duguoin* pitched, tossing him over the bucket, then drawing him away as he tried valiantly to direct his stream into the small container. He buttoned his pants and returned to the game, leaving the bucket barely damp and a tell-tale wetness on walls and floor.

Connors offered, "I have some food if anybody's hungry."

The men turned narrowed eyes upon him, and Billy quickly studied his hand. The hurricane lamp's course began to shift as it made a slow arc to the ceiling. It remained there, defying gravity, and the glass chimney set up a chattering that threatened to shatter it into a thousand fragments. Then the mysterious hold was released and it quieted, making a slow return trip to the opposite side of the room where it reached for the ceiling to begin its chattering complaint again.

The deckhand, his body covered with dark soot, ignored the ladder and dropped heavily next to them. Billy screamed in fright, and everyone bolted from the table. The hurricane lamp swung out to reveal white eye sockets and thin red lips set in an ebony face. "The captain says there's rough water ahead, but for you not to worry none."

Leary asked, "This isn't rough?"

"Aw, this ain't nothin'!"

Draper's mouth was tight and dry. "What's comin' up *is* somethin'?"

"If you want to sleep, there's them bunks over there."

"We saw them," Dunlap thanked him, returning to his seat.

The deckhand nodded at the men in undershirts, sweating profusely in the tremendous heat. He grinned and jigged up the ladder from sight.

"Imagine," Draper swore, trying to find his hand amid everyone's cards, "he does this for a living!"

Leary dropped back to his chair. He held a thick finger to Dunlap's face and snarled, "I ain't never goin' on a boat again, Jim Dunlap! And I ain't so sure that once this job is done I might not take my chance with the Pinkertons and take the train back to New York!"

Dunlap explained, "It's just a little rough weather!"

"Damn rough!" Leary shouted.

Thirty minutes later the *Duguoin* ceased its rolling from side to side and instead began to buck. The bow came out of the water, then fell into a deep trough that slammed up into the hull, raising the front of the ship steeply where it plummeted back into an angry sea. The near empty bourbon bottle pitched to the floor as the men searched the walls in panic. Scott flashed Jim a reassuring smile, but it died on the lips, turning sour as Scott's mouth went wide, and he began sucking for fresh air to stem mounting nausea.

Cards were held in trembling fingers. The lamp swung over their heads in a wild effort to dash itself against the ceiling. Shadows danced up and down the walls as the players gasped for the fresh air they so desperately needed.

The captain slid down the ladder in answer to their silent prayers. The toothless smile pulled the chin almost to the tip of the runny nose.

"How's the storm?" Dunlap asked uneasily.

"No cap'n worth his salt is scared of rough weather," he cackled. "Not with a lively vessel like the *Duguoin* beneath his feet." From the inner pocket of a soiled slicker came a fresh sardine. It went to the toothless mouth, where gums tore the body free. Scales spilled onto his chin and a suspicious looking green and red liquid fell to the floor.

"You boys had your supper?"

Leary was the first to leave the table. He tossed the chair aside, brushed past the startled skipper, slipped several times on the ladder rungs and groaned his way topside.

"Seasick," the captain observed, the broken sardine held limply by the head.

Eddie Goodie gave a strange "aaah" and took the ladder two rungs at a time. It launched a stampede. Draper, Burns, Scott and Dunlap bolted past the astonished skipper as they scrambled up the ladder. When the way was clear, Connors fled.

Dunlap reached the deck to find that there wasn't an empty spot at the rail, and he had to race forward into the sleet thrown over the bow before he secured a space near the wheelhouse.

Scott was revived by the cold, wet air, but the sounds of everyone around him feeding their supper to the sea drove him over that perilous edge, and he, too, retched at the rail.

The captain passed among them. One hand holding the sardine, the other lifted the men by the hair for close inspection. "Seasick," he observed. Captain McNaughten shook his head and negotiated the ladder to the wheelhouse, both hands at the handrail, sardine clenched between nose and chin.

As each one got control of the violence that churned his stomach, another would begin again. This prompted a second to join in until all seven followed suit. Stomach muscles aching, mouths sucking the wet night air, they fell back from the rail.

They hugged the bulkhead with their nails, the deck tossing beneath them. Relief was momentary. Leary rushed to the rail, then Connors. Soon they had abandoned the bulkhead and stood shoulder to shoulder, heads bent to the waves.

"I'm dyin'," Burns moaned.

"I can't make it."

"Let's stop the boat."

"I have to get off."

"Pray for me, Kate!"

"Oooh."

"Ooowhop!"

"Save me, God!"

A lantern appeared at the wheelhouse over their heads. McNaughten spilled the light down on his passengers and made an elaborate ritual of counting noses. "It's gonna get a little rough ahead!"

Seven chalk white faces dripping sea water and perspiration turned up to him in disbelief.

"Its goin' to get worse?" Connors cried.

The captain nodded. "You'd better get below, lads!"

"I have to get off!" Scott shouted deliriously. He rolled off the men until he had Dunlap's head between his hands. "I can't stay another minute!"

Dunlap called up to the wheelhouse, "How much further?"

"Another day!"

"Another day?" they groaned.

"I can't last another day!" Leary screamed against the wind.

"Just hang on!" the captain cheered them. "Think of the poor people who live on shore!"

"What did he say?" Scott asked Dunlap, sea water running from the end of his nose, his eyes wide and insane, his black hair plastered across his brow.

"He said, 'Pity the poor people on shore.'"

Scott searched Jim's face for a hint of understanding. Then he turned with a scream and attacked the ladder leading to the wheelhouse. "You're crazy! Get me off this thing! Right now!"

"Turn back!"

"Make for land, man!"

"Where's the nearest land?" Dunlap shouted above the storm.

The chin reached for the nose, deep in thought, and the captain pointed out into the darkness. "Greensport!"

"Make for it with all possible speed!" Dunlap begged. "I'll pay you well!"

Leary started another rush to the rail.

On the coast, twenty-foot cast-iron steam trumpets bellowed their warning to sea. They could be heard through the gray light as a large wooden wharf loomed out of the fog just several feet away from the handrail. Before a line could be secured, the passengers were throwing themselves over the side and leaping for the safety of the shore. Soaked to the skin, they lay on the wharf, its rough security against their cheeks. Leary began to cry like a child.

The deckhand stared at the seven men lying on the pier as he set the bags of tools beside them. Their clothes were laid over the bags; shirts, vests, hats and coats awaited their owners.

An early morning peddler's cart creaked out of the fog. An apparition dressed from head to toe in oilcloth rolled his wares to a halt as the men began to stir.

Dunlap had a handful of the peddler's wares thrust under his nose. "Fresh mussel, sir?"

The horror-stricken Dunlap sought the space between the wharf and the *Duguoin* to crank his empty stomach. The peddler watched the curious men in undershirts crawl to the wharf's edge and retch to the surf below.

The storm that struck the ill-fated *Duguoin* was of European origin. In Sicily it drove the Eagle steamship *Schiller* on the rocks, killing the two hundred aboard. In the English Channel, a hardy adventurer named Captain Boyton set off from the coast of France in an India rubber suit, intent on making the English coast with his invention, a sail tied to his foot. The captain was mid-channel when the storm struck. The crew of an attendant ship managed to lasso him and drag him to safety before he was swept out to sea.

Each man favored a different choice. Edson was for a bank in Northampton, Massachusetts. Connors was for the First National Bank of Rockville, Connecticut. Bob Scott was primed for the First National in Pittston, Pennsylvania. Dunlap didn't care as long as they didn't have to return to Nantucket.

William Edson insisted that either of the two Northampton banks was by far the better choice, with the First National in that city drawing a slight advantage over the older Northampton National. They agreed to check it out.

They arrived in Northampton on the late train. Dunlap picked the lock to the firm of Delano and Hammond, directly above the vault. A test hole was drilled beneath the firm's carpet to determine the protection above the vault. Satisfied with the results, the hole was puttied and the trio of Connors, Scott and Dunlap returned to New York.

"I don't like either one of the banks in Northampton," Dunlap confessed. "The old bank there requires four keys. We're right back where we were in Elmira. The new one, the First National, could take three weeks to make an entry, and I'm not convinced there's that much in there."

"I'm with Jim," Scott decided. "I think there's more money in the old Northampton National. But the question is, if we don't tunnel in, how do we get possession of the four keys?"

"We hold the cashier and officers hostage," Edson said brightly.

"No hostages!" Dunlap said quickly. "Something could go wrong. I'd rather take our time and tunnel in. I won't work with hostages!"

Edson frowned. It had been over a year since he'd last been paid for the use of the pump. It had been just a few weeks earlier that he realized Dunlap was no longer connected with the ring. Just when he discovered this, Dunlap was back again. They were a very confusing bunch to be sure.

"I've been called to a meeting with the old Northampton Bank officials next week," Edson told them. "Let's postpone it until then. Maybe when I see what it is they want, we will know how to pursue this. There may be an easier way into the vault."

A week later, they thought their luck had finally changed. Edson reported back, "It's a new vault door for the First National, but the old bank also wants to make some improvements! They want a new door and a Herring lock!"

"What kind of lock?" Dunlap asked eagerly.

"A key combination affair that would eliminate all four keys. There would be only one key to deal with, plus the combination. You can go in the front door!"

Scott hinted, "It would sure be nice if we had a copy of that key."

Edson snapped it up. "I'll see what I can do."

"And the cashier's routine," Scott added. "We know nothing about the cashier's habits."

Dunlap reminded them again, "I won't have any part in hostages."

"Nobody's said anything about hostages!" Scott sounded exasperated. "I'm simply saying we have no idea of the man's habits! We wouldn't want him walking in on us if we went in through the front door for a change, would we? Suppose Will here is able to get us a copy of the key and the combination to the safe. Won't we want to know the copper's schedule and the cashier's habits? I mean, if he checks that vault after supper, we'd damn well better know it!"

"I agree with Bob," Connors nodded. "I think we should make another reconnaissance. This time I'll keep an eye on the police, and you two can sit on the cashier's house all night, just to be sure."

Dunlap thought there was something wrong with their sudden shifting from tunneling to front-door entry. He was also beginning to dislike Edson immensely. The man was so obviously hungry for cash he might easily lead them to irons. Edson had already managed to convince Scott and Connors that this new idea was worthy of consideration. Dunlap didn't like it a bit. Reluctantly he replied, "I'll go back. But if everything's not perfect with the new vault doors and the cashier, we move on to Connecticut or Pennsylvania."

"Agreed!" they echoed.

Cashier Whittelsey left the old Northampton National Bank for the brisk two-thirds of a mile walk to his Elm Street home. He didn't notice the two men following some distance behind him. It was a beautiful late summer day, and his thoughts were obviously with the day's business and the renovations to be made by the Herring Safe Company. He entered his home, and the Irish maid took his coat, closing the door to their view.

The smell of the evening meals wafted down Elm Street as Scott and Dunlap took up refuge in the quince bushes at the rear of the Whittelsey home.

"I knew we should have eaten," Scott grumbled as he tried to shuck his coat in the tight confines, sharp twigs poking his side and neck.

"I was the one who said let's eat before we go, and I remember you distinctly saying you weren't hungry!"

"Well I'm hungry now. Grab that sleeve. I can't smell all that food and not be hungry!"

Dunlap drew his own coat free and wiped at the perspiration gathering on his brow. "I feel like an Indian, hiding here like this. This is stupid! You look like Pocahontas with those leaves on your head."

"Poco-who?"

"Pocahontas! The Indian lady that saved John Smith."

"What did she save him from?"

"The Indians."

"Didn't you say she was an Indian?"

"Yes."

"She's an Indian that saved him from the Indians?"

"That's right."

"I never read the Bible," Scott grunted as he tried to squirm into a position of minimal comfort. Scott's legs were into Dunlap's stomach and Jim backed deeper into the burrow, a branch snapping his hat off before he decided to fight back.

"Watch your feet!"

"There's something in my side."

"Move your damn feet!"

"I can't!"

Dunlap managed to make it to his belly, allowing Scott's legs to extend to their full length. "This is terrible!"

"Sshh," Scott whispered, sighing in momentary peace. "It's better than sitting up there on top of them cars riding the brakes." He pulled the imaginary whistle, "Whoo-whoo!"

Dunlap was resigned to a long night ahead. A smile lit his face. "There was this engineer who worked for the Rock Island when I was a fielder—"

"What's a fielder?"

"He's the fellow who pulls the pin disconnecting the cars. Risky business. You can always tell a fielder—they're the ones with two fingers on each hand. That was before the new couplings. In the old days you had to get right between them with the coupling pin and hope to God the hand got out in time. Nobody wanted to change the system to the new couplings because they were so damn expensive. Fingers were cheaper."

"You were lucky."

"I know. So this engineer was fired, and he applied for reinstatement. The superintendent said, 'You were dismissed because you twice let your train come into collision.' 'That's the very reason I want to be reinstated,' the engineer argued. Of course the superintendent didn't understand and asked the engineer, 'Why is that?' And this cheeky fellow replied, 'Sir, if I had any doubts before about the possibility of two trains passing each other on the same track, I am now entirely satisfied. I have tried it twice, sir, and it can't be done! I'm not likely to try it again, I assure you.' "

"So what happened?"

"He got his job back."

"I'll be damned!" Scott said in dismay.

Dunlap pulled up several pieces of summer grass and stuck a stalk between each tooth, leaving them hanging below his lip until he had a dozen fan shaped appendages hanging from his mouth.

"You've done a lot in your life, Jim, I envy you that. I've had more excitement with you than a dozen men."

"Like now?" Dunlap mouthed, the grass flopping about as he talked.

"Even now!" Scott laughed. "If I hadn't been so damn foolish with my money, I'd be living like a king!"

"That's what got you in trouble, living like a king."

"I guess so. I went home to Warsaw to see my mother and brother. I was dressed to the teeth. Mary looked sensational! I gave my mother a few hundred dollars, told her I made it on the stock market. She wasn't fooled, though. I'm the big disappointment of her life. I was in prison when most boys are beginning to apprentice. Hell, I was a veteran at sixteen! She's never forgotten that."

"My mother died two weeks before my eighth birthday. I've never forgotten that."

"Do you know what she said to Mary? She told her, 'When the time comes, when everything with Bob is finished, I want him back.' Isn't that an odd request?"

"What did Mary say?"

"What could she say? She said 'Of course,' though neither one of us knew what she was talking about."

Dunlap removed the grass and dropped it near the opening of the bushes. The heat had died down, but inside the quince protection, the air was humid and still. Collars were pulled open and vests removed.

Dunlap whispered, "It's been a long time since I lay in the woods like this."

"Where was that?"

"Gettysburg. Makes me feel old just thinking about it."

"I saw Lincoln. Did you ever see him?"

"No, but he was at a hospital I was at once. They said he came right by my bed. But it was after surgery, and I didn't get to see him. Would have liked to. The fellow across from me had just had his arm taken off at the shoulder and the doctor told Lincoln what a nice operation it had been. 'We learned so much because of the war,' he said to the president. Lincoln asked the doctor, 'But what about the soldiers?'

"He waved at us once when we were on the road. It happened so fast that not many knew who had passed. I told everyone it was the president and he was waving hello to me. Nobody believed me, so I told them, 'I'm from Illinois! Ain't I?' They still weren't convinced, but the sergeant later admitted Lincoln had gone by in the carriage and they were not sure he wasn't waving to me."

"I saw Grant. Saw him twice. I remember he was always smoking this meerschaum pipe. Both times he had this pipe. One of them curved ones about eight inches long that kind of sits on the chin. Nobody ever says anything about him smoking a pipe. They always mention him smoking cigars. But I saw him with the pipe and always wondered about that, why no one ever mentioned the pipe."

"You know they're having a sale of trotting stock at Crystal Lake? I hope we get back in time," Scott worried aloud.

The sun lingered on the horizon undecidedly. It challenged the lamps burning in the white clapboard residence of the cashier and his family, then reluctantly dropped from sight.

Scott lay a hand on Dunlap's arm, pointing to the far side of the property. A figure moved through the bushes, dropped to a crouch, then moved on to a new position.

"Who's that?"

"No friend of mine," Dunlap whispered.

The figure remained on his haunches for the better part of twenty minutes. Then the rear door of the Whittelsey home opened, and the kitchen girl came out. She shook a table cloth, folded it several times, then disappeared inside.

"What's he doing?"

"Nothing. Just like us."

Moments later the door opened again, and the servant girl walked out into the yard. She spun about aimlessly as she walked toward the rear of the property. Reaching the far brush she whispered, "Steve?"

The figure lying in wait went forward and took her hand. There was a brief but ardent embrace. The girl, with an eye to the house, led the boy directly to the area in front of the quince bushes.

"Are you sure it's all right, Kate?"

"Mr. Whittelsey's in bed smoking his pipe, and the missus has her needlework."

Steve stood six feet in height, and his appearance suggested he spent his early years lifting heavy barrels. Clad only in a thin shirt and overalls, the boy allowed himself to be pulled to the ground just eight or nine feet from the hidden bankies.

"Don't hurry me now!" Kate chided, rearranging her dress in the light from the house. She sat primly on the ground, her legs tucked neatly under. "Tell me what you've been doing all day."

"We found one of our oxen with a broken leg this morning, and Pa had to shoot it. He was so darned mad he made me move all these rocks we have at the north, 'cause he figgered she fell over 'em and broke her leg."

"How awful!"

"Sure was."

"No, Steve! I swear, you don't give a girl time to catch her breath!"

"You take mine away, Kate. I can't even breathe when I see you."

Scott looked over at Dunlap and rolled his eyes, his tongue hanging from the corner of his mouth. Jim placed a hand over his mouth to hold back a laugh.

"So you moved all them rocks?"

"Sure did."

"It must be easy, being as strong as you are."

"Heck, I can lift anything. I . . . I bet I could pick you up and run all the way to town and back and never be tired a bit!"

"Steve Guilford, I believe you can, too."

"I can . . . I can lift a horse damn near!"

"My. Now *don't*, Steve! You'll get stains on my dress, and what'll the missus say!"

"Sometimes, Kate, I swear you don't like me at all."

"Steve Guilford! That's the silliest thing I've ever heard!"

"Then you do?"

"Silly . . ."

In the silence that followed Steve's easing Kate back to the grass, a solitary mosquito winged in from a brackish pool of water some forty feet away. It buzzed the hidden men several times before flying off to signal its friends.

"Oh, Steve."

"Oh, Kate."

The squadron leader, a large gray-backed champion, skidded to a halt on Bob's cheek and boldly scouted a site.

"You'll tear my dress—let me do it."

The darkness made the mosquitos invisible. Yet when they flew between the light of the house and the bushes, Jim and Bob could see they numbered in the hundreds of thousands.

"I can't stand it when you do that, Steve!"

"Do what? This?"

"Oh, my God."

Scott pulled the blood-gorged leader from his cheek as a determined comrade flew a reckless mission to his nose.

"Shall I stop, Kate?"

"Steve . . ."

Scott followed Dunlap's lead by quietly pulling the jacket over his head. Undaunted, the insects reconnoitered the backs of the bankies' necks.

"Oh, Steve! I can't stand it when you do that!"

"I can't help it, Kate. . . . you make me feel like I'm crazy!"

"Oh, Steve . . ."

An exploratory squad commenced drilling test holes in the backs of Scott's hands, testing his endurance with casual disdain.

"Steve! Steve!"

A rear guard marched up the pant legs, halting momentarily as they sampled the ankle and calf.

"Steveeee!"

Scott's face felt bloated. Courageously he freed a hand and pointed in the direction of the unknowing couple just ahead of them. The insects selected the wrist and hand instead.

"Oooh . . ."

"Ooooh . . . my God . . ."

"Kiss me, Steve! Oh, Steve!"

"I could do this all night."

Dunlap groaned, sick at the lack of urgency on Steve's part.

Scott was beginning to thrash uncontrollably from the assault on his inner ear. The moaning of the girl and the surging of the boy hid their struggles.

"What time is it?"

"It's early, Kate."

"No. I must get indoors before the missus needs me."

"We've still got time. . . . it's early."

"No, maybe tomorrow, Steve. You're the dearest boy."

The boy left in the direction of Springfield upon the closing of the door, and the quince bushes came alive with flight of the mosquito-mauled pair.

Billy Connors was across from the bank on Elm Street. He was not prepared for the two figures who staggered into the street light. Hair askew, collars open, eyes swollen shut, lips and cheeks puffed to twice their normal size. He staggered back and exclaimed, "Good God Almighty!"

"My God!" Mary exclaimed. "What happened to you?"

Bob tried to pull her in close, but she remained at arm's length, eyes wide with horror as she studied the distorted features.

"We were scouting a location for a theatre," Dunlap said quickly. "And these mosquitos—they came from nowhere!"

"Oh, you poor dears!"

"Ugly beasts!" Scott offered as Mary buried her head against his chest.

"At least scorpions commit suicide when they're done. If mosquitos would do the same, I'd think better of them," Dunlap mumbled.

"Why didn't you run, Mr. Dunlap?"

"Well . . ." He forced a grin that pulled the skin painfully tight across his cheeks. "We did run! We ran fast, too."

"I don't think that was the problem," Scott said over her head. "The problem was we didn't start soon enough."

Mary pushed herself away from Scott. "You're like children, I swear! Perhaps I should go with you from now on, instead of staying here all by myself! Maybe you won't come home looking so ragged."

"That's a good point, dear, but unfortunately . . ."

"You're not leaving again?"

"Well," Bob stumbled.

"Now?" She asked painfully.

She had gained a few pounds, Dunlap thought. Her cheeks were a little fuller, but the face had the same guilelessness. She was incapable of hiding the slightest disappointment. Her ample bosom trembled noticeably as she asked hesitantly, "So soon?"

"I didn't want to!" Scott pleaded. "But business has been dreadful, you know that."

"Couldn't you leave him home with me just this once, Mr. Dunlap?"

"Well, I . . ."

"That's a good idea, dear. How about it, Jim? How about you going to Pennsylvania without me?"

Dunlap hated this game of Scott's. He gritted his teeth and said firmly, "I think you had better go."

"I hate being away from home so much. Just this once?"

"I would think it best for your financial condition if you went with me."

"Oh, please, Mr. Dunlap! Just this one time!"

"I don't think that would be wise."

"You see, dear! What choice do I have!"

Her tears were muffled against her husband's chest.

Dunlap shook his fist at Scott for putting him through his charade. Bob shrugged helplessly in reply.

"I thought you would be working in Boston!" she cried.

"Boston isn't quite ready," Scott soothed. "We may have to go to Pennsylvania and then back to Boston."

"How long this time?"

"A few weeks—maybe a month."

"That's what you said the last time!"

"I'm sorry, dear."

"As soon as we're back, Bob will take you for a nice trip somewhere," Jim explained.

"Where?" she pouted.

"Philadelphia? The Fair?" Scott suggested.

"That isn't until next *year*!"

Dunlap sagged with fatigue. He went to the door and called, "I'll see you at the station tomorrow at eight. Good day, Mary. Good day, Robert."

"Remodeling?" Dunlap asked the clerk of the Wellsborough Bank, for tools and workmen lay idle about the open vault.

The young man shook his head gravely. "Repairs, sir."

"A new safe? Vault?"

"A fire, perhaps?" Scott inquired.

"It is my misfortune to admit, a robbery."

"Robbery?" they asked in unison.

"Several hundred thousand, I'm afraid."

"When?"

"How?"

"Some soundrels tore off the top of the vault and plundered the safe during the dead of night." The clerk spoke in a shamed whisper. "Is something wrong?"

"My friend's not feeling well," Dunlap smiled as he propped the weakened Scott against the oak counter. "This robbery . . . was it very recently?"

"Four days ago."

"Four days?" Dunlap locked the smile on his face, assisting the taller, heavier Scott to the street. "Have a nice day," he bade the clerk.

"Somebody beat us to it!" he told Billy.

"George Mason!" Scott recovered angrily. "He knew I had spotted this bank for myself!"

"At least he's had better luck than we've been having," Dunlap added morosely.

Rockville, Connecticut, prided itself on its Methodist church. The ring prized the church for other reasons. Directly beneath it were two banks, the First National and the Rockville National. A difficult choice to be sure, but several factories had been spotted in the few dozen miles between Hartford and Rockville, and the ring had reason to believe the First National was the recipient of local industry dollars.

The congregation sang the great Robert Lowry hymn "Shall we gather at the river," while three men waited in the darkness.

"The beautiful, the beautiful river," Billy sang softly along with the voices inside. "Gather with the saints at the river, that flows by the throne of God."

Scott accompanied Billy on his Matthias Hohner ten-note harmonica, while Dunlap cursed the lateness of the assembly and itched to get on with it.

The church was silent, and Scott sent the harmonica to an inside pocket, while Dunlap tapped peaked fingers together impatiently. Billy Connors sat quietly in the darkness.

"We have a good chance here," Dunlap murmured.

Billy intoned, "Speed does not win the race, nor strength the battle. Bread does not belong to the wise, nor wealth to the intelligent, nor success to the skillfull. Time and chance govern all."

"A chorus of 'Gather at the river' and Billy's quotin'."

"How did a preacher's son ever get to be a bankie, Bill?" Dunlap asked jokingly.

Connors answered, "Can the Nubian change his skin, or the leopard its spots? And you? Can you do good, you who are schooled in evil?"

"Let me guess!" Scott demanded. "Was that that Pocahontas you were telling me about, Jim?"

"I don't think so," Dunlap worried. "I think it was John Smith. He said that when he realized they were going to cut off his head."

Billy ignored them. "To be patient shows great understanding, quick temper is the height of folly."

"Let me try again!" Scott begged. "Aaahhh . . . Boss Tweed, 1872."

"That's it!" Dunlap whispered excitedly.

Billy shook his head and sighed wearily, "Why hast thou made me thy butt and why have I become thy target?"

"Because thou art such a big target, Billy!" Bob teased, slapping Billy's abundant behind.

Suddenly the doors across the way opened and lamplight spilled

onto the street below. The patrons filled the stairs and moved off noisily into the darkness.

"Thank God it's over!" Dunlap whispered as the last of the congregation filed from the church.

Wagon and carriages were driven off, and inside lamps were extin-
guished. A lone figure locked the doors securely and made his way
awkwardly down the stairs. They gave the man ten minutes' grace to
remember a forgotten item, and when he failed to return, Scott asked,
"You ready, old man?"

Dunlap rubbed his aching leg and nodded. He crossed the street
quickly, under Scott's watchful eye. Billy went for the wagon and
tools while Scott watched Dunlap at the head of the stairs, picks and
fingers working feverishly to open the church door.

Dunlap lined up the tumblers and sprung the lock. He stepped
quickly inside, breathing heavily as he waited for the first of the tools
to arrive.

Everything unloaded, the wagon was driven to a distant alley and
secured behind a print shop.

Glazed cloth was draped over the windows and secured with awls
and tacks, allowing them to light a kerosene lamp.

"Put something in front of the keyhole!" Dunlap warned. A piece
of black gossamer was placed on a chair a foot from the keyhole. This
would allow an attentive watchman to stick a pencil in the slot to
make sure the door was not locked from the inside, while preventing
light from leaking through the opening. It was a common mistake of
most burglars, locking the door from the inside and leaving a telltale
key in the lock, only to have an alert guard trip them up.

Each plank was drilled for a mounting screw, with careful note tak-
en to countersink the heads so they would be smooth beneath the carpet. Then a small ball of putty was tinted to match the wood color.
Satisfied the screws could not be seen, they removed the planking
once again and entered the hole.

Billy handled the reins as the three weary men rode toward Tolland, a few miles east of Rockville.

"Six bricks," Scott groaned, "all that work and all we got up was six
bricks."

"Will we be in the vault by the weekend?" Billy asked.

Dunlap pitched about the front seat, his head drooping on his chest. "I hope so. By tomorrow we should have another course free, and then we'll know what's underneath."

Dunlap pulled the blanket up to his chin and settled as comfortably as possible on the hard wooden seat. The hat was drawn down over his eyes, and he snored in rhythm with the creaking wagon.

Scott nudged Billy. "That man can sleep anywhere."

"He told me it was his army training."

"I can't sleep if Mary's not beside me. When I sleep without her, I wake up in a sweat. It's like a nightmare."

"It's best when the fire's burned down and the room's chilly."

"I've been having nightmares lately. I'm in jail and Mary's not with me. I can't sleep. When I wake up, my bedclothes are soaked clear through."

"I had a terrible dream last night," Dunlap said, staring into the hole made by the removal of the brick.

"What's that?" Scott asked.

"This bank's been here a long time. Supposed the brick's been plastered over and we don't know it. We could pull out one of these next bricks and be stuck with a hole over the safe. Then what do we do?"

"We don't know how many bricks there are! We have to keep going just to find out!"

"But think about it a minute. Billy has a pretty good eye, much better than mine. He thought there was five feet between the top of the vault and the church floor. We already know three feet of it is air space. Maybe there isn't a piece of iron in the whole damn thing!"

"So we work carefully!"

"I just hope all the hammering doesn't knock something loose inside."

Scott lay on his side at the hole, while Dunlap eased the brick back and forth. "I was just thinking what a shame it was that Georgie Mason beat us to the Wellsborough money. I could have used that."

"The paper said 275,000."

"Damn shame."

"I'm getting so that I hate Pennsylvania."

"You told me Gettysburg and the surrounding area was the prettiest country you'd ever seen."

"I'll clarify that. I hate Pittsburgh! It's the dirtiest, ugliest city in America. It's the only place in the world where you can hang out your boots at night and have them black enough in the morning to last you the year."

"Dirtier than Mulberry Street?"

"The Mulberry tenements look like the Elysian fields compared to Pittsburgh."

"What?"

"I felt it give."

"Easy!"

Six hours after he began, Dunlap wiggled the brick carefully from the hole and set it off to one side. Both men peered down into the vacancy.

"Cripes!" Scott exclaimed when he saw the gray plaster beneath. "There isn't any iron in it at all!"

Dunlap pressed a finger against the plaster. It bowed easily away, permitting him to see that it hung loose from the surrounding bricks. "Stop breathing!" he cautioned, "the whole damn thing could fall any minute!"

"The plaster's so old it's just hanging there!"

"We'll never clear away the rest of the brick by morning!"

"Can we risk waiting two days for the weekend?"

"I doubt it. We'll go a day early. Tomorrow night we'll do it. It doesn't give us as much time to get away, but the whole damn thing could collapse during banking hours tomorrow!"

"Thank God at least we won't be drilling iron plate for a week. I think I'd rather be routed from the job then have to set up all that bracing."

"Signal Billy. Tell him we're closing up shop for the night."

Plans were to smash in the ceiling and be on the early morning train from Hartford, arriving in New Haven before the robbery was discovered. Additional time could be bought by wedging the doors to the vault, which might enable them to be far away before the blacksmith forced the doors. Billy also planned an alternate escape route. A fast team of horses had been arranged for in Hartford, should they be required to leave Connecticut in a hurry. Extra mounts were ready in Middletown, should the train be avoided altogether. With his usual thoroughness, Billy Connors had taken every precaution. Steamship tickets waited in Boston. Rail and horses provided alternate escapes. All that was needed was to wait for the long banking day to draw to a close, and a chance to work undetected for a few hours on the Briggs and Huntington box within.

At five that evening Mr. Kite, the cashier, locked the bank and went off to supper. Billy showed his watch to Scott and Dunlap. It read two minutes after the hour. "Right on time," he smiled. "One hour to go. One hour away from the safe."

Scott passed a hand through his rumpled, dark hair. He shrugged nervously. "I saw an electric clock in Pittsburgh this summer. It never needs to be wound."

"Electric?"

"Electric. And there are others in Cincinnati and Washington, I was told. You can look at any of them and they all have the exact same time."

"How do they know that?" Billy scoffed. "By the time you go from Pittsburgh to Cincinnati, who can remember what time it was when you left?"

"They know."

"I don't know about electric," Billy mumbled warily, "I hear its kick is worse than a horse."

Scott continued undaunted. "The man said that pretty soon everything's going to be electric, even streetcars. New York's going to be one of the first cities with electric streetcars right in the middle of town."

Dunlap looked at Billy suspiciously before asking Scott, "Where they going to put that electric?"

"*I* don't know where they're going to put it!" Scott bristled, "but the man says that's what they're gonna have!"

"You can't sit on electric!" Billy guffawed.

"Billy's right," Dunlap decided. "Electric can kill you. It has to have wires! If an ice cart or something ran over them, psssst!"

"Well, vaults have electric clocks, don't they?" Scott said testily.

"But they have wires!" Jim grinned victoriously. "You ever stop to think what New York would be like with all them wires running down the street? They'd need a couple dozen fellows at every corner just to keep them from getting tangled!"

"The telegraph poles have wires!" Scott fumed.

"How they going to run the wires from poles to streetcars?"

"Maybe they'll be on spools!"

"You know how much wire they'd need to get to Central Park from any of the ferries? Them spools would have to be as big as a building!"

"I didn't say I understood it!" Scott hissed. "I just said they *was going* to have electric cars! I didn't say *how* they was going to have them! The fellow didn't *tell* me how it was going to be done! He just said it *was* gonna be done!"

"I believe it," a man replied.

They seemed startled by the voice of the stranger drawn to their loud argument. "I believe it," he repeated.

"This is a private argument!" Scott snapped, turning the man away.

Billy found himself looking around to see who else they might have attracted.

"Bob," Jim said unperturbed, "sometimes I think you'll believe most anything."

Scott stared stubbornly out at the bank and Methodist church. "I admit I don't know everything. But I never expected my two best friends to make sport of me."

Dunlap brought out a small silver flask and passed it to Scott as a peace offering. He slipped Billy a wink as Scott ignored the overture. "Y'know, Bob . . . I remember when I was in the army, and I asked this sergeant how they made them cannons we used. Fierce brutes they were, too. I couldn't understand for the life of me how they could make them so's they wouldn't blow up. So I asked the sergeant and he says, 'Jim, they just take this long holé and pour iron all around it.' You know for years I accepted the fact that cannons were made that way."

Scott's anger crumpled, and he snatched the flask and downed a healthy swig of cherry brandy. "That's dumb. You remember that morning in Elmira when Red Leary bet Big Jim Burns he couldn't hit that squirrel at the top of the tree?"

Connors continued excitedly, "Big Jim shot him right off the branch!"

Together they repeated Leary's scornful response. "Hell, that was a waste of gunpowder. The fall alone was enough to kill him!"

"I remember once telling Red that my grandfather died when he was eighty-three," Connors laughed. "Red said, 'That's nothing, if mine had lived he'd be a hundred and six!'"

Huddled together in the darkness, the laughter dying in their throats as they finished off the cherry brandy, Dunlap asked, "What time is it, Billy?"

Billy rotated the watch several times. "6:15."

"Has he ever been this late before?"

"No . . . 6:10 was the latest."

The bank was dark, the gas jet unlit. Scott cursed worriedly, "Damn! Where is he?"

Billy giggled, "Maybe Mrs. Kite burned his supper!"

A full October moon joined their vigil. The night air cooled rapidly, leaves rustled in the empty street, Dutch families served suppers, tantalizing the waiting men with the odor of beef and kidney pie and fresh baked bread.

"What time *is* it?"

"Seven o'clock."

"He's never been this late!"

"Damn him to hell!"

"We could have been through the ceiling by now!"

"There's still plenty of time," Connors sighed, mentally recalculating their probable departure time.

"Damn!" Dunlap fired out to the dark, empty bank.

Cashier Kite didn't leave home until a few minutes before eight, having entertained a visitor with eleven hundred dollars in scrip that had been brought to Kite's house for safekeeping. Reluctant to leave the parcel in the house, the cashier returned it to the bank. It was a few minutes after eight when he arrived. There was still plenty of time, he reasoned—the watchman wouldn't be making his rounds before nine, and as long as the gas jet was lit by that hour, his duty would have been performed.

He did not realize he created a minor sensation among those who watched the building. He entered the bank, locking the door securely behind him. A match was struck and the gas jet ignited against the wall. It was the second time in a year that he'd had occasion to enter the vault after closing time. The bag of scrip was taken to the combination, the numbers set, and the huge doors wheezed open. Kneeling by the safe, Kite found the light poor and so struck another match. The door opened easily, and the bag was left inside. Kite locked the Briggs and Huntington securely, the single gas lamp throwing a long shadow as he went to secure the vault. But the ceiling of the vault caught the light in a curious way. A large bubble bellied out over the safe—how long it had been there, he couldn't recall. He stood for a long time with the vault doors in his hand, puzzled by the peculiar pucker. Since the plaster belly of the ceiling was well above his head, he went to the closet and returned with a mop. He had to raise the mop end high in order to feel it hit solidly against the masonry protection above. Easing the mop away, restoring the plaster to its drunken shape, he made a mental note to himself to inform Mr. Talcott, the bank's president, of this decay first thing in the morning. Satisfied there was nothing irregular afoot, he was about to close the vault when, without warning, the bubble burst and the plaster crashed about the safe.

When the dust cleared, he could see the missing brick and a rather large hole above that. Reacting swiftly, still not sure what it might mean, he opened the safe.

"What in God's name is taking him so long?" Dunlap cried.

"I'll take a stroll by the bank," Billy offered.

The moment Connors saw the cashier on his knees at the safe, the plaster debris around him on the floor, his heart sank.

Kite, suddenly realizing everything he was doing could easily be seen from the street, chose that moment to rush for the windows and draw the drapes. He narrowly avoided seeing the portly little man duck from view.

From their position across the street, Scott and Dunlap saw the drapes drawn across the window as Billy rolled hurriedly in their direction.

"He's found the hole!"

"No!"

"He's taking everything out of the safe!"

"God, no!"

"What have I done to deserve this!" Scott cried to the autumn moon.

"Let's get the hell outta here!"

Mr. Kite gathered the town's savings and, without thought to his being robbed, made his way to Sheriff Paulk's office. Together they went to the bank president's home and repeated the cashier's story. Mr. Durfee, the bank teller, was summoned, and the four men made arrangements to transfer the town's assets to the Rockville National Bank just next door.

This done, an investigation of the Methodist church was made. It revealed nothing, and further exploration was set aside until morning.

By tapping from inside the vault during daylight hours, they located the area of the hole. The pews were removed, the carpet lifted, the beeswax and puttied screw heads uncovered, the tunnel discovered. Sheriff Paulk observed that it was the finest bit of carpentry he'd ever seen.

Inside the hole were found two leather valises, two pair of coveralls, two working jackets, two pair of new woolen stockings, an auger with patent handle, four auger bits and one gimlet bit, a twelve-inch back saw, a small iron wrench, cold chisels, bars and chisels both crooked and straight, two dozen tiny wedges, a jack screw, an oildrop, glazed cloth, a sectional jimmy, attachments to the jimmy for prying and pushing, carpet tacks, awls, screws, putty, beeswax, explosives and a single putty knife. They found every tool owned by the men with one exception, the Edson pump.

A Pinkerton detective spent several days with the tools, inspecting them carefully for identifying marks or a hint to the manufacturers. The coveralls were of medium and large sizes. Cuffs had not been rolled on the legs, so he reasoned that one man was a full six feet in height, while the other was in the five-foot-six-inch range.

The awls he traced to Tolland, the thumbtacks to Rockville. The explosives he found were sold in New York City, while the oilcloths had been purchased in nearby Middletown. The agent began a methodical canvassing of Rockville's rooming houses, boarding homes, and hotels, searching for tenants who might have bolted the night of the attempted robbery. When this proved fruitless, the agent expanded his search to Middletown and Tolland.

Both banks announced the following day that changes were being made to add to the town's security. New safes, burglar- and fire-proof, would be installed in both banks, as well as a new iron vault for the First National Bank of Rockville. By week's end the small Connecticut town was swarming with salesmen. Thousands of dollars of enterprise had been created, but the ring profited from none of it.

Chapter Six

The old man with the silver imperial goatee worked quietly at the side door to Pate's Bank. A thin chisel sprung the lock, and two bags of tools were hurried inside. A tin can, its side removed, was placed over the gas flame. To anyone passing it would appear that the lamp was burning, but the metal shade reflected the light to the front of the store and left the safe in darkness.

Several crates were moved in line with the safe, further insuring total privacy from prying eyes. The drill was set up and the outer door drilled. He was breathing heavily when he finished and was forced to rest for several precious minutes before resuming.

Sacks of flour were carried from the dry goods section and placed around the door of the safe. A dozen trips were necessary before the box was properly enclosed. Each trip required a respite of several more precious minutes.

His heart worked rapidly, triphammering loudly within his chest, threatening to explode with excitement. It was more than he could take, and he slid down on the pile feeling faint and near exhaustion. He wondered if he hadn't been foolish in attempting this by himself. An old man's vanity, he reasoned, had led him to

*death's door. He closed his eyes to quiet the ache within, to restore
the strength to his arms and legs.*

*Satisfied that the dangerous excitement had been quelled, he
charged the safe with powder and set the pistol. Certain it was
properly locked into place, he attached a string and ran it to the
side door. A heavy carpet from the floor was carefully laid over
the safe and flour barricade.*

*The side door was opened cautiously before he ventured out-
side, spooling off the string as he walked a considerable distance
away. He rested against a tree as the new snowstorm threw a few
flakes between him and the Pate building. The heartbeat began
again, wildly thumping, pumping furiously as he gathered up
slack in the spool. He closed his eyes, counted ten, then gave it a
yank.*

The sole custodian of Pittston, Pennsylvania, finances was the
night watchman of the Pennsylvania Coal Company on South Main
Street. Each evening he made his rounds, casually checking a low,
tin-roofed, one-story structure called the First National Bank of Pittston. Every sixty-nine to seventy-three minutes, he would appear, peer
inside at the gaslit banking room, spill his lantern into the corners,
shake the door gently so as not to trip the telegraph alarm, but hard
enough to determine the entrance was secure. He had little cause for
concern. Inside the vault were three Marvin spherical safes, the latest
in burglar-proof containers. Their round, chrome iron bodies, Marvin
insisted, "were impossible to open." Installed on a slightly raised
platform in April of 1871, their keg-shaped double doors turned away
all challengers.

The watchman lowered the lantern and moved confidently back to
the mill, his big woolen coat pulled up against the November wind. In
the distance he heard several shots and a small explosion, lingering
enthusiasts celebrating the Pennsylvania gubernatorial election. The
polls had closed several hours ago and the incumbent, Governor Hart-
ranft, was successfully driving off the challenge of Cyrus Pershing,
the personal choice of the state's railroad and coal interest.

The wind was frosty, and the watchman hurried the last fifty rods to the warmth of the mill, wishing the voters would cease their festivities and turn in for the evening.

"All right," Billy whispered to the three men on the tin roof of Pittston's bank.

"All right," Big Jim Burns repeated.

Scott and Dunlap scraped the putty free of the hole cut several nights earlier. Color-matched to the roofing, it had withstood a driving afternoon and evening rain. The tin section was removed and passed to Burns, who eased it down to Connors. One course of brick had already been removed, all that was required now was to punch an entrance hole through the last course into the vault below.

The moisture on the tin roof and the pitch rearward made working almost impossible, as the night conspired to freeze the dampness into a sheet of ice. The simple act of raising a hand sent them on a gentle slide backward, and Big Jim was allotted the task of grabbing arms and legs as they slid by his perch alongside the chimney. It was a twelve-foot drop to hard ground if anyone was unlucky enough to disappear over the edge.

"I don't know why I agreed to come here!" Burns lamented, a wad of the new substance called chewing gum working energetically between horse-sized teeth. "With your luck, we'll all end up like White."

"What happened to White?" Dunlap asked, pulling himself back to the hole after an unsuccessful attempt to drive the first brick into the vault.

"We didn't get back to New York," Scott explained. "We came straight here from Connecticut. Had to take a job at the Pittston Paper Mill for a week while we scouted this job! I've still got the blisters to prove it!"

Dunlap angrily cut Scott off. "What happened to White?"

"Pink's arrested him. They nabbed him for $400,000 he took from Barre, Vermont, last month. He thinks they have him dead to rights."

"George was going to lay off for a while!" Dunlap moaned into the hole. "Shinburn and now White."

"You remember the Greek named Leslie?"

"Sure. I worked with him on a job in Waterford with White."

"He's dead. Some say Red Leary killed him for paying too much attention to Kate."

Dunlap insisted, "Red wouldn't do that!"

Scott disagreed. "Yes he would. You know how he feels about Kate. I wouldn't want to cross him.

"Shot Leslie in the head and dumped his body. The coppers say they have no leads, but they know dead to rights Red Leary did it."

"Damn! George White! Who would have thought it." Dunlap drove the mallet viciously against the brick, striking it twice before he'd slid from his target. Scott and Burns grabbed him and helped him back to the hole.

When Billy signaled the watchman's return, the men went flat to the roof, clouds of steam betraying their position in the moonlight. The heavy boots were heard stamping the mud free on the wooden boardwalk. Dunlap closed his eyes and rested, both gloved hands locked firmly to the edge of the tin hole. The creaking lantern accompanied the footsteps to the edge of the platform. The heavy thumping was replaced by the slurp of mud giving way to weighty boots as he inspected the side of the bank.

Dunlap opened his eyes to find that Scott's face was not just a few inches away. He glanced over his shoulder to see his partner sliding silently past Burns, whose attention seemed to be on the street. Scott reached for Burn's foot, but his hand fell short. Dunlap swung a leg in Bob's direction, extending himself as far from the hole as possible. Bob locked a hand on Jim's ankle as the footsteps splashed back to the boardwalk. The added weight, the sharp edge of the sheared tin, cut into the gloves, drawing them both toward the steep edge. Bob's legs stuck straight out into the night, the watchman somewhere below. The look in Scott's eyes told Jim he could hang on no longer. The footsteps were moving away from the bank when Jim Burns turned to signal the danger was passed. He saw Scott dangling from the waist into the air. A quick belly crawl, the chimney between his legs, and he had Scott by the armpits and drawn back to the roof. Safe at the hole, they hung on the edge of the opening and fogged a billowing cloud of warm, panting breath.

Big Jim gasped, "You had to take a job outside."

Dunlap tapped his temple. "Planning."

Seventy-one minutes later, when the watchman returned, they were inside the hole. A speaking tube was rigged between Burns in the hole and Connors parading between the bank and the Stove and Tin Shop. A rope ladder had been secured to the chimney for a quick departure.

Scott asked Connors for the signal to blow the first safe.

"All clear."

Dunlap tugged the string to the pistol, and the explosion blew the blanket high into the air. Instantly Dunlap was at the rope ladder into the smoke-filled vault. One of the doors was blown clear across the room, but the other half, the one providing access to the safe deposit boxes inside, remained twisted but in place. Unable to remove the boxes without the door completely open, Dunlap puttied the hinges for a second charge. A paper funnel was rolled, and the few first ounces of Curtis powder had oozed into the opening when there was a tremendous flash, rendering the paper funnel into microscopic pieces. Dunlap ran around the room, moaning as he raced the vault's narrow confines, his hands tucked under his armpits.

"There's a fire in the safe!" Burns called down.

Dunlap dropped to his knees and counted his fingers as Scott cried, "Don't let the money burn!"

"What the hell am I supposed to do?" he screamed back.

"Water!" Burns suggested. "Pour water in the safe!"

"Where in the hell am I supposed to get water? You want I should piss on it?"

"Do *something*, for God's sake!"

Dunlap gathered a small amount of powder and leaned carefully aside as a second funnel slipped a few grains inside the hole. The accompanying flash told him there was indeed a fire in one of the boxes. He hurriedly gathered all the blankets and wrapped the smoldering safe in an effort to stifle the air supply.

The next explosion had ripped the safe deposits from the safe and scattered them around the room. The bottom of the Marvin was littered with charred bills and securities.

"Oh, God!" Scott moaned as he crawled back to Dunlap and thrust the burned prize under his nose. "Look at this!"

"What is it?"

"It's the goddamn money! *That's* what it is!"

"Damn! Gather up everything! We'll decide what's salvageable later!"

Dunlap staggered to the brace, intent on finishing the hole into the second safe, when Burns shouted, "The bit's busted!"

Scott ventured. "It must have been hit by the door of the safe!"

"Damn!" Dunlap cursed, kicking the brace with his foot, prompting Scott to add his own well-measured kick.

"What'll we do?" Scott cried.

Dunlap kicked the brace again. "Move this thing! I'll blow the safe without it!"

"That'll take forever!"

"I don't care *how* long it takes! No damn safe's turning me away!"

As soon as the men were clear, he attacked the spindle, swinging like a madman, until it snapped free and rolled around the room. The door seams and lock were thoroughly powdered, the Edson pump drawing a full sixteen ounces into the tight seams. The revolver set, Dunlap ordered them out of the vault. Cowering behind the first safe, completely hidden in several blankets, he shouted impatiently for Billy's permission to blow the safe. The speaking tube replied "Go ahead."

The explosion bounced him off the walls. He crawled from beneath the blankets, lost his bearings and fell heavily onto his side. He managed to get his feet under him, and, when the smoke cleared, he saw the first plate was badly dented and several dozen spot welds had snapped, but otherwise the safe was intact.

"Powder!" he shrieked, his attention locked to the safe, one hand held to the hole for the sack of Curtis powder.

Big Jim scampered down the hole to assist him. "This could take all night," he said worriedly.

"Shut up!" Dunlap shouted, dark hair flying, eyes wide with hate for the Marvin Company and all their workmen. His face was covered with black soot so that only the wild flashing eyes could be seen. He worked feverishly, puttying the door edges, while Scott climbed back to the roof.

"Tell Billy I want an all clear!" Dunlap demanded.

Huddled in his blanket, the string to the pistol disappearing beneath it, Dunlap fired the weapon before Billy had a chance to finish the words.

Before the smoke cleared, Burns and Scott swung down the ladder to find Dunlap reeling drunkenly at the damaged safe, which sat three feet away from its original position.

"It broke two bolts is all," Dunlap cursed. "This damn thing is incredible! There's still another bolt holding the plate in place!"

Billy Connors paced nervously as Scott asked permission for the sixth explosion. Knowing they still hadn't opened the second safe, he experienced a sinking sensation. He gave the street a careful glance, then gave his permission. Almost immediately a roar whipped out into the wind and was blown down Main Street. Again, he searched the doorway of the Coal Company, the windows of the Stove and Tin Shop, the Fenn Hardware, just two doors away. It all seemed miraculously quiet.

He had no way of knowing what was going on inside. He heard incoherent screaming and shouting that resembled Dunlap's voice garbling up the speaking tube. He didn't know that the safe had been blown free of its moorings and that Dunlap was chasing it around the vault, powder and putty at the ready.

"Once again, Billy?"

Connors checked his watch, still ten minutes before the watchman's rounds. "Go ahead, quietly."

Number seven roared up out of the hole, was captured by the chilly November wind and flung across town.

Billy saw the door open to the Coal Company, the watchman silhouetted against the light inside as he pulled on his heavy coat and gathered the lamp.

"The watchman's on his way. Take a break in there."

Burns appeared at the hole. He gathered the rope ladder and drew it up on the tin roof, then vanished into the vault.

Dunlap's clothes were in tatters as he sat in the corner breathing heavily. "You know what I'd like more than anything right now—an ear of hot corn with melted butter, sprinkled liberally with salt."

Scott looked at Burns, and the big Irishman only shrugged.

Dunlap stared blankly at the badly dented Marvin safe. "Who makes these bastards anyways? Where do they *get* these ideas?"

Scott offered softly, "I bet grabbing a cashier and having him do all the work sounds pretty good right now."

"I don't know," Dunlap mumbled in confusion. His body ached from the tossing about. The Marvin seemed to be laughing at him.

"When we get back to New York, Jim, I think we'll take Edson's advice on the Northampton job. If the safe's ready and the lock's been changed, I think grabbing the cashier is the best solution. I can't go through another night like this." Scott allowed his head to fall back against the wall. "We're going to be lucky if we don't kill ourselves."

"I wonder whose idea it was to make them round like that?"

"All clear," the speaking tube declared.

Dunlap had to be helped to his feet. He staggered to the safe, took the putty and stabbed it slowly into the cracks.

Billy felt enormous relief when the watchman closed the coal company door and left them to their work. He danced in a small circle to restore circulation, wondering if the second safe had finally been opened. A few minutes later he gave permission for number eight.

"How much do you think we have?" Dunlap asked as he puttied the partially open doors, wedged solidly against each other.

"Not enough to put a spalpeen to shame," Burns retorted. "Three or four hundred in greenbacks, twenty thousand or so in bonds and securities."

Billy relayed permission for number nine. Ten minutes later, he fretted an "all clear" for number ten.

A few moments later, Billy heard Scott's troubled voice. "Do you think the city can take one more, Billy?"

"I don't know. A light just went on at the Stove and Tin Shop. You'd better hold up for a minute or two."

Robert H. Green, the sleepy resident of 32 North Main Street, had heard three distinct explosions, and, as he peered from his window, he was pulling on a shirt.

"Go back to sleep," Billy crooned. "It's only your imagination, Mister. Sounded like a victory firecracker didn't it?"

Green left the window and reappeared seconds later with his jacket.

"We need one more, Billy."

Billy's heart was racing as he replied, "Be ready to clear out. It looks like we may have a visitor."

"God, no!" someone called into the tube.

Lights were going on all over the Green's house, then Green himself stepped out of the doorway.

"Get out!" Billy whispered into the tube.

There was a mad scramble for the tin roof. Burns emerged first, then Scott. They pulled the dazed and battered Dunlap up onto the slippery roof, where his feet immediately went out from under him and he slid past the rope ladder, only to be caught between the chimney and the dark space at the building's rear. Billy was waiting at the bottom of the ladder, holding the swaying cords, as Dunlap, weakened by the fumes, shocked by the chill night air, tried to negotiate the braided rungs. Billy caught his arm and held him erect on solid ground as Scott clambered over the roof edge.

Green came around the corner just as the three turned into the alley. Burns was still on the roof and, after a moment's hesitation, leaped out into the night. He hit heavily near the surprised Green, who started back, then turned and gave chase. A waiting wagon was whipped into action and Green watched the four pull quickly away.

Near the Susquehanna River, close to the Western pier of Depot Bridge, the tools aboard the wagon were thrown over the side as they approached the toll bridge.

The Daily Record of the *Times* described the ring as "Knights of the revolver and jimmy, who evidently understood their profession, for what they did accomplish was done in a masterly manner."

Green was awarded one hundred dollars and a new Smith and Wesson revolver for his efforts, and safe companies rallied at the town in hopes of a sale.

Among the bank's curious was Frederick Gueist, a Herring Company employee. Gueist found the discarded tools of great interest, but his attention centered on the vacuum pump. He examined it several times, then remarked, "If I didn't know better, I would swear this was one of our pumps."

The young man nearby caught the salesman's words and asked, "What makes you think so?"

"We had two just like this."

"This couldn't be one of them?"

"What would it be doing here in a burglary?"

"I don't know. I was just cruious."

"I'm sorry. I didn't mean to be rude. Please forgive me. Frederick Gueist, with the Herring Safe Company."

The young man accepted the hand and smiled, "Robert Pinkerton."

"I don't like it at all!"

"If we pick our people carefully . . . "

"Suppose someone panics? There are seven people in that house! Any one of them could make a run for it or start screaming! What if one of the children acts up? Then what?"

"Ssshh," Scott begged, a finger to his lips.

Dunlap sought refuge in his brandy glass as Billy paced nervously in front of the fire.

"I don't want Mary to hear us."

Connors said to the fire on the grate, "With the right people we can eliminate that risk. I think both of you are right. We've never done a job like this. I take that back—Jim did one very much like it in Waterford with George White."

"It was exactly like this."

"All right—exactly like this, that's why he's so hesitant to try another."

Connors turned from the fire and spoke directly to both men, his voice quiet and sure. "We didn't do too well at Pittston. They lost five hundred in cash, we got less than three hundred because of fire and damage. They lost sixty thousand in securities, we got less than thirty thousand after damages. Six thousand went to the Bank Ring, and the rest we won't be paid for until we can negotiate them back. So we're still broke. The safe we left with the doors jammed was opened by a blacksmith in five minutes and contained seven hundred thousand in securities. It was just within our reach . . . but escaped us. We're having a run of bad luck, to be sure. Now Edson's offering us Northampton. We have a new safe and vault. The combination to the safe we have." From his vest pocket came a key. "The key to the vault, we have. Edson was good enough to make this for us, at considerable risk. We have the key that unlocks the combination to the bank vault, but that's all it does. It frees the spindle so that the combination may be set. What we have is one-half of a very complex puzzle. We have one half—cashier Whittelsey has the other. All we need is the cashier's knowledge of the combination, and the money's ours. We know everything about the job; we've been there twice. Edson thinks there's several million inside. He's personally seen at least a million. Anything over a million makes it one of the biggest burglaries of its kind. No one to my knowledge has ever taken over a million. We stand a chance to be the first. There are risks, yes. But there were risks at Pittston. God knows the other method hasn't worked too well for us lately. Maybe this will put an end to our run of bad luck. I don't know—personally I'd hate to see us pass this by. It's an hour's work once we have the right numbers. Myself, I'm for Northampton."

"I think there's too much at stake to pass it by," Scott submitted. "I think this could end our hopping about the country, digging into vaults, selling safes for other people. I think Edson's right, Jim. There's a fortune in Northampton. We could be rich beyond our wildest dreams. If Edson hadn't laid so much groundwork on this, I'd be the first to say no, but as it is, we'd be fools to pass it by."

Dunlap downed the cherry brandy, knowing both men waited for his reply. "I've always been against this," he said softly. "We've turned down other banks for the very same reason. Someone could be hurt. The money? If it's the largest bank robbery, as you think it might be, they'll never rest till they catch us. You both feel this is right for us. I tell you, *nothing's* right about it. Nothing good will come of it."

"I told you after Covington that I would never venture out without you again." Scott said. "I won't go back on my word, Jim, you know me better, but I'm a desperate man, Jim. We've realized nothing from Pittston yet, and I'm all for doing anything that will convince you to join us. I'll even stay with the hostages to insure their safety."

Dunlap eased into the chair and closed his eyes. After several minutes of silence he asked, "When did Edson think it should be done?"

Connors broke into a wide grin. "Right after the holidays—New Year's Eve, if possible."

Scott's voice trembled with relief. "There won't be any mistakes, Jim, I promise."

"The mistake has just been made, I fear."

"You're going to be proven wrong, Jim. Mark my words!"

"For the first time there'll be witnesses who can identify us. We've never risked that before."

"We'll have masks, Jim!" Connors said eagerly, moving to Dunlap's chair. "We'll do what White did in Waterford—call everyone by number!"

"It'll be dark, too!" Scott added. "That'll be in our favor!"

"And we won't load the revolvers, if that will make you feel better."

Scott suddenly made a face. "Someone will have to tell Mary we're leaving again."

Dunlap groaned.

"Well you know how she is, Jim! She's going to be terribly upset! She's like a little girl during the holidays, you know that! How can I tell her?"

Mary was singing "Long, Long Ago" at the piano when the three sheepishly left the bedroom. Dunlap went immediately to the mantle and examined the garlands of spruce and evergreen on the marble.

"So what has Mary Scott been doing with herself?" Connors began.

"Oh! Bob took me to Central Park yesterday! Miss Tebbins' angel looked so forlorn with the fountains off! Then we went to Lord and Taylor's!"

"She likes to ride the elevator," Bob explained, making signals with his eyes for Jim to get on with it.

Dunlap circled the dining table, fingering the Dresden china before he said, "Mary, I'm afraid I'll have to take Bob away for another week."

"Not *now!*" she cried, genuinely hurt. "Not over the holidays! Christmas is just a week away! Oh, Mr. Dunlap, you can't take him from me now!"

"After Christmas," Billy explained.

"Perhaps we could delay this?" Scott wondered aloud.

This forced Jim to grimace and say, "No, we need you, Bob."

Scott frowned. "You're sure?"

Jim seethed with anger, cursing Scott silently for making this more difficult than need be. "I think you had better be there."

Scott flung his arms wide. "You see, darling, I have nothing to say in the matter!"

"Sometimes I hate this work of yours! I've been alone for over a month! Now you're telling me you're leaving me again!"

"Just for a few days, dear. Isn't that right, Billy?"

"Just a few days."

"See, darling?" Scott kissed her cheek as she stared at Dunlap accusingly. "Jim promised me this would be the last trip for a long time. Didn't you, Jim?"

"The last one," Dunlap repeated.

"Now, what's for supper? I'm starved!"

"How can you think of food when you've just broken my heart?" she cried bitterly.

Scott took her in his arms and held her tight. "Don't be so hard on them, dear Mary. You know how bad business has been. We can thank Jim that we still have a roof over our heads."

"I just can't bear it when you leave me alone."

"I know, dear—I feel the same way, too."

Supper was taken under a pall of silence. Afterward, as the men entered the parlor, Mary took Jim's arm and separated him from the rest. She led him quickly into the sewing room and closed the door.

"Mr. Dunlap," she faltered, "you know I have deep respect for you as a friend of Bob's. I also know that you do not care a whit for me."

He started to protest, but she placed a soft damp hand against his mouth.

"I love Bob Scott. I always will. Yet I feel you resent what I mean to him. Please, don't interrupt me. Let me speak." She took a deep breath and assembled the necessary courage. "It is therefore very important to me that we agree on certain matters. We both care for him, in different ways, of course—you as a business manager and I as his wife. Why you resent me, I don't truly know. Perhaps it's because he married without your permission, I don't know. But I do love him and I want to make him a good wife. Therefore, I would propose some sort of truce between us, for his sake. I will stay out of your affairs and you will stay out of mine. I will say nothing disparaging about you, and you in turn will not make fun of me or ridicule me with those snide asides to Billy. I'd like to be friends with you, Mr. Dunlap. Lord knows I've tried everything within my power, but you remain cold to me. Don't deny it, Mr. Dunlap, I can feel it. You seldom speak when you're with us, and, when you do, it's usually something under your breath. I am willing to ignore the past and meet you on some neutral ground, under whatever conditions you impose. Just so long as we end this rivalry."

It had been almost three years since the marriage, and, as he digested her words, Dunlap realized he had thought her a child and treated her accordingly. That this had not gone unnoticed taught him how wrong he'd been. Barely out of her teens, Mary was a strong-willed young lady, with more spunk than he thought possible. "I behaved very badly, I'm afraid."

"The past has little meaning for me, Mr. Dunlap. I'm from hardy Dutch stock. My parents worked hard to provide me with a good education at the Moravian Seminary. I am a worthy opponent, I assure you."

Her determination caused him to smile. "I have no doubt of that."

She began to waver, the eyes welling with sadness. "I don't have need of an enemy, Mr. Dunlap. It's a friend I'm needing."

He could never resist a weeping woman. He took her hands and told her gently, "If you can find a way to forgive a fool, you'll have that friend. I swear it."

Complications arose in Northampton, forcing a three week delay. Mary was delighted that their New Year's Eve journey had been postponed, and nothing would do but that the three of them celebrate their good fortune.

They began the evening touring the glittering night palaces of Broadway. From there, they moved to the Bowery beer gardens and their elaborate frescoed ceilings and merry music. All New York appeared to have had the same idea, and patrons roamed the three thousand barrooms, past shady gamblers with tiny folding tables working the curbside, trying to entice the unwary into a quick shell game or three-card monte. Boys with hoops racketed through the curious crowd.

Ornately carved wooden figures crowded the tobacco shops and storefronts, forcing the pedestrians into the streets where winter's muddy slush sucked at the finest leather footwear. Gay saloons spilled ribald music to the street, as pink-tighted prostitutes languished in the doorways, dark eyes searching for potential customers. Men staggered about, drinking openly from long black gin bottles as they ducked from one dram shop to another, jostling the crowd in drunken celebration.

Dunlap finally announced, "This is no place for a lady!"

"Oh, Mr. Dunlap," Mary pleaded in disappointment. "Please stay! I want to see it all!"

"Jim's right!" Scott agreed. "This is the worst sort of place for a lady!"

Locked safely between them, her arms tight through theirs, she cried, "Oh, please, Robert! Please! You *must* let me see it!"

Scott looked across to Dunlap and shrugged, then laughed aloud. "You see, Jim, I could never refuse her anything! If you insist, my dear, see it you shall."

Passing a wooden clansman standing solemnly before a tobacco shop, Scott threw his arm about the statue and struck a pose that sent Mary and Jim into convulsions. Then as the crowd began to force them from the spot, Scott ducked quickly to peek beneath the kilt.

"Robert!" Mary shrieked in amusement and shock.

He winked at Dunlap as he gathered her arm, "Just curiosity, my dear."

"And what did you see?" Dunlap choked.

"Wood!" Scott grinned. "Just wood!"

A heavily enameled Chinese, complete with queue and lustrous smile, drew low bows from the appreciative trio.

Dunlap left the group to waltz a wooden squaw about on her wheels, to the Scotts' delight. Then Mary clapped her hand over her mouth as several scantily clad young girls giggled their way through the crowd and entered a concert saloon to a roar of approval.

Two brawlers flew from a saloon and cleared a wide path of spectators. Mary drew the sleeves tight to her cheeks in excitement as the fighters squared off. It was a one-sided match, ending when the smaller of the two sent a resounding blow to the larger man's ear, tumbling him unconscious into the gutter. The winner spat on both hands, hitched up his pants and returned to his drink, leaving the groggy loser to clutch a ragpicker for support. The trio started a deserved applause for the loser that continued well after they moved off.

Mary's silk shawl was suddenly whipped from her shoulders. The thief raced off through the crowd with the winded Scott and Dunlap on his heels. Moments later, Scott returned with the shawl, then Dunlap joined them, breathing heavily and nursing his gloved hand. Mary held the two gasping men upright as they fought the frosty night for air.

"See!" she crowed, "I'm perfectly safe!"

A whistle sounded in the harbor, and other ships took up the call. "Midnight!" Scott shouted, as the horns began sounding and church bells tolled the last few seconds of the old year. Fire lookouts sounded, drawing sirens to respond. Patrons poured from the pleasure palaces drunkenly firing revolvers into the air. Mary held fingers to ears as she blinked at the assault on her eardrums.

"Happy New Year, darling!" Scott shouted.

The pair embraced as Bob kissed her about the cheeks and eyes.

"Happy New Year," Dunlap smiled.

Mary twisted free of her husband, kissing Dunlap's cheeks as she cried, "Happy New Year, Mr. Dunlap! Happy New Year!"

Scott pumped his hand. "Happy New Year, Jim!"

Dunlap held her at arm's length and shouted above the tumult, "Dear Mary, let's start the New Year right. You can begin right now by calling me Jim, not Mr. Dunlap, but Jim."

Mary looked quickly at Bob, who nodded. "All right!" she cried gaily, "Happy New Year, Jim!"

"Happy New Year, Mary!" he announced, drawing her close. Scott joined the embrace as fireworks went off in the street, causing frightened horses to bolt. The dram houses, saloons and beer gardens emptied into the streets as pandemonium seized the Bowery.

The roar of the New Year swept over the heads of the happy trio. Arms clasped tight around each other, they stood in awe of the deafening greeting.

"I propose," Scott cried passionately, "that from this moment on, we may always be together like this."

"You have my word on that," Dunlap vowed.

"Together!" Mary cheered. "Always!"

On January 25, 1876, the Northampton National Bank was relieved of $1,250,000. Eight masked men, identifying themselves by number only, forced the cashier, Whittelsey, to provide them with the combination to the vault.

The *Hampshire Gazette* proclaimed it "The Greatest Burglary on Record", and it launched the largest manhunt ever seen on the eastern seaboard. As clues dwindled, the reward climbed. Newspapers as far away as Chicago published accounts. When no arrests were made, it moved from most dailies' front pages to the rear columns for more pressing news throughout the nation.

The Indian Affairs scandal led the readers right into President Grant's office. Indian Affairs agents and the secretary of the interior were charged with stealing from the Indians and the government—charges so desperate that Red Dog and Red Cloud of the Sioux nation came east to plead their cause. Ten counts of fraud were quickly whitewashed, leaving the red nation in despair. A Sioux warrior named Sitting Bull retaliated in the only manner he thought possible. Leading a large force and outnumbering the calvary of General Custer by two to one, he destroyed the object of his frustration. The Little Big Horn Massacre drove Northampton out of everyone's minds.

Boss Tweed was arrested and housed in the same Ludlow Street Jail from which he'd first escaped. Rutherford B. Hayes defeated Samuel Tilden in a bitterly contested presidential election that saw many delegates charged with bribery and corruption. The reading public now had the Congressional Ring to deal with. For those too confused by the many parties involved in the Congressional Ring, there was the American ambassador to England to consider. The charge against him was easy to follow—a simple matter of swindling. The man was merely thrown out of England for fraud.

One year after the robbery, not a single newspaper in the nation carried any mention of the Northampton burglary. On February 13, 1877, one year and nineteen days later, Bob Scott and Jim Dunlap ventured from their New York quarters and boarded a train for Philadelphia. There they purchased two tickets south to Richmond, Virginia. They had just settled in the car when a half dozen men confronted them.

"James Dunlap? Bob Scott?"

Dunlap said quickly, "I think you have the wrong men."

Scott smiled, "I think you've made a mistake."

"There's no mistake," another stated coolly. "My name is Robert Pinkerton and these are agents Benjamin Franklin and Tom Gallagher. You're under arrest for the robbery of the Northampton Bank."

Chapter Seven

The old man with the silver imperial goatee pulled the string and was rewarded with a muffled roar that rose up into the night, shaking loose a flurry of snowflakes from the blackness as it flew away like frightened doves. He turned about several times, spinning in all directions as he watched for lamps being lit, shades lifted or curtains parted. He alone seemed to know what transpired. He and the dark tree were rewarded with a few gentle, cooling flakes that kissed his face and told him all was well.

Inside Pate's Bank he found the outer doors hanging free and sighed in relief. The inner door was yet to be drilled, and he set up the feed screw drill after tumbling the flour sacks away. The enormous effort required to clear a path for the brace sapped his strength and left him clutching the brace and wheezing for breath. Throwing his weight into the drill, he was forced to pause every few minutes to rest his weary arms and give his tripping heart a brief respite.

He was just forty minutes into the morning of Saturday, March 24, when the drill broke·through the last obstacle between him and the money. He slid to the floor in exhaustion, breath straining through his chest, perspiration soaking and chilling his de-

pleted body. His head rolled back as he fought for air. The orange flame of the gas lamp flickered, taunting him with its virility, urging him to close his eyes and sleep. He could not rest— to close his eyes embraced disaster. He weaved drunkenly around the room in search of the powder, discovering it under one of the heavy flour bags. Rolling a paper funnel took enormous effort. Holding it steady while a black stream of Hazard ffffg powder oozed into the door required herculean steadiness. He could barely keep his eyes open as he moved in a dream, struggling with the sacks, grunting with the exertion of rolling them back against the safe. The pistol danced before his eyes, and he couldn't remember if it had been loaded. His mouth hung slack as he worked to clamp the pistol securely in front of the Hall safe. He almost fell unrolling the string to the side door. Once outside, he clutched the tree and begged the night for assistance.

"Mr. Davis, what do you do for a living?"

"I'm an engineer, sir."

"Is this your floor plan of the home of cashier John Whittelsey?"

"It is, sir."

"Did you measure the distance between the cashier's home and the Northampton National Bank?"

"I did."

"And would you please tell the court that distance?"

"Two hundred and thirty and a half rods."

"Approximately two-thirds of a mile."

"That is correct, sir."

"Thank you, Mr. Davis. I have no further questions, Your Honor."

District Attorney Field took his seat as defense counsel Sweetser announced, "I have no questions, Your Honor."

"Will the witness John Whittelsey please take the stand!"

"Oh oh," Scott said under his breath to Dunlap, though he showed a brilliant smile to the jury.

An old man arriving late squeezed into a seat being held for him. He squinted at the surroundings, then leaned into Scott and asked, "Where are the prisoners?"

Scott grinned and touched his chest. "Here's one of 'em."

The old man blinked in surprise.

"It was a little after midnight when I woke," Whittelsey began. "I was startled from a sound sleep to find two men in my room. They were dressed in masks with eye- and mouth-holes . . ."

"What about their clothes, sir?"

"They were wearing long linen dusters. One handcuffed me while the other handcuffed my wife."

"Is that all you saw? Two men?"

"No. Three others came in a moment later and two more shortly after that."

"So there were seven altogether?"

"Yes, that's correct."

"Now, Mr. Whittelsey, do you recognize the two men who handcuffed you and your wife?"

"I do."

"Are they in this court?"

"They are, sir."

"Would you please point them out for the court."

"The tall man, there, Robert Scott. And the shorter man, James Dunlap."

Both prisoners made a great show of the fact that there was some mistake being made.

"Would you please tell the court exactly what happened after you and your wife were handcuffed by Scott and Dunlap?"

"I had other guests—Mr. and Mrs. Cutler, my niece, Miss White . . . and Miss Benton was with us. She was very ill and was staying with us at the time—and of course, the servant girl, Kate Nugent. The men brought them to our bedroom. I remember thinking there was a man for each of us, and I thought that quite odd."

"Seven masked men brought seven occupants of the house together for the first time. That was the first time you were able to see your captors?"

"Exactly."

"What happened next, Mr. Whittelsey?"

"Six of the occupants were taken to another room and I was ordered to dress. The tallest one, Scott, helped me into my clothes, as it was very difficult to dress with my hands handcuffed. Then they led me into the hall where both Scott and Dunlap took turns guarding me."

"Now, Mr. Whittelsey, up until that moment, did you have any idea what the men were there for?"

"No, not really. It wasn't until Scott said something about the bank, there in the hall, that I suddenly realized their intentions."

"What did you tell them?"

"I said it was foolish for them to attempt to get into the safe or the vault, as the locks were of the finest Herring make and impregnable."

"How did they respond?"

"Scott said, 'We know more about locks than you do, so shut up!' I also was made to understand that I was to accompany them to the bank vault and open it for them."

"Did they threaten you in any way?"

"Scott said, 'If you don't open the locks it will get very hot for you.' Then they took me downstairs and demanded the bank keys. Dunlap took a key from his own pocket and asked me if it was a key to the bank door. I told them it was."

"Was it actually a key to the bank?"

"No, sir."

"Then you lied to the robbers? You risked your life in order to protect your trust and possibly purchase a little time in order that some sort of help might arrive?"

"Yes, sir."

"What happened next?"

"That same key was fitted to the front door of my home and proved to be the door key. Scott became very angry and accused me of lying to them. I began to feel ill—began to worry about my wife . . . my niece. It was all I could do to stand. Mr. Dunlap asked me if I was feeling all right. He said, 'Would you like a little brandy?' I said no, I would be all right. Then Scott got down to business and asked me for the combination to the locks."

"Who did?"

"Scott."

"Mr. Whittelsey, may I hold you at this point in time and have you tell the court the actual number of locks involved at the bank?"

"Well, there's a lock on the vault door. Inside the door, there's a second door. After opening these two doors, one has access to the safe. The safe is also provided with a lock, and once the safe is open, a locked strongbox within the safe remains to be opened."

"Then we are talking of four locks in number, plus the lock on the building itself?"

"Yes, sir."

"Stout defenses against the average burglar."

Whittelsey nodded.

"Then it was Scott who asked for the combination to the door of the vault?"

"Yes. I gave him a fraudulent number, which he wrote down. Then he asked for the combination to the inner door. I told him it wasn't locked, and he didn't believe me. He became very angry. He asked for the combination to the safe. When I hesitated, he struck me in the chest with the pencil and ordered me to repeat the numbers I'd given him. I tried to remember them, but he was quick to catch me in the lie. I just couldn't remember what I'd told them! Another man in the hall grabbed me and began to punch and choke me. He said, 'It's no use to lie!'"

"At this point, Mr. Whittelsey, where was Scott and where was Dunlap?"

"Dunlap was in front of me with his pistol while the man choked and punched me. Scott was at my side."

"Then what did you do?"

"I gave in . . . gave them the correct combination. Scott wrote the figures and asked me to repeat them until he was satisfied they were correct. Then they brought me back upstairs and blindfolded me. Dunlap said, 'Bind this man close, so he can't get away.'"

"Now, Mr. Whittelsey, how much time had elapsed from the time they entered your room to the time you were brought back and blindfolded?"

"Hours—maybe four hours."

"So Scott and Dunlap were with you for a considerable period of time?"

"Quite a while, yes."

"Even though they were masked, you were able to recognize certain mannerisms that would allow you to identify them at a later date?"

"That is absolutely true."

"There is no doubt?"

"No doubt whatsoever."

Scott allowed his gaze to fall on Mary seated in the front row. She held a handkerchief in her hands as she stared numbly at the witness. The lace was knotted and rolled into a tight little ball as her hands nervously kneaded it limp and useless.

"Who was the first to leave the house?"

"Scott and Dunlap. They left sometime after four in the morning. The last two left about six."

"You finally managed to free yourself?"

"Yes, somewhere between six and seven. I hurried straight to the bank and arrived by seven. I remember the time almost to the minute. At first we didn't think anything had been touched—the vault looked like it had not been tampered with. So our hopes were high that the robbers had been thwarted. However, when we went to open the vault, the spindle fell off and we knew someone had knocked the combination from its mount. Now there was no way for the vault to be opened except through the efforts of a professional locksmith."

"How long did that take?"

"Until the following morning. The lock had to be sent to a shop and some sort of fitting added. It was almost dawn before we opened the vault."

"And what did you see?"

"Calamity . . . the safe wide open . . . the strongbox barren . . . all the bank's funds gone."

"Would you please tell the court the total amount of loss?"

"Well over a million dollars—$1,250,000 is the closest estimate we have."

"As the bank's cashier, you were thoroughly familiar with the workings of the vault and safe. Yet you said, 'I thought they had been thwarted.' What led you to believe that?"

"I gave them the combination to the vault only! A key and other combinations were necessary to get inside the safe. They hadn't asked for those! I reasoned they would be turned aside once they reached the vault!"

"Then you naturally assumed the robbers would be unable to reach the safe or open the strongbox unless they had the key to the vault?"

"That is correct."

"You had no reason to think they had access to these other valuable necessities?"

"Of course not!"

"But this proved false, is that not so?"

"Yes. Then during the investigation, I remembered that shortly before the robbery, we had had trouble with the key and found it necessary to have it filed."

"Who made this correction?"

"An employee of the Herring Safe Company, one William Edson."

"Then for a short period of time, the key was in the possession of this William Edson, a trusted employee of the Herring Safe Company?"

"Yes."

"Now, Mr. Whittelsey, do you have any hesitation in repeating your statement to this court that the men with you in your home were Robert Scott and James Dunlap?"

"No hesitation whatsoever."

"Even though they were masked?"

"No doubt at all. I can remember their size and shape and their voices. Their voices impressed me more than anything else."

"Did they call each other by name? Did they, at any time, use the names of Bob or Jim, Scott or Dunlap?"

"No, sir. They were clever enough to use numbers. Scott, the taller one, was number one and, I suspect, their leader."

"Have you had occasion to hear Scott speak?"

"Yes. I visited the jail and I heard Scott ask Robert Pinkerton, 'Have you seen my wife lately?'"

"Was there another occasion?"

"I heard Scott tell Pinkerton, 'I would like the money that was found on me.'"

"What about James Dunlap?"

"At the same time I heard Dunlap say, 'Will you see about my trunk and have it left in Mrs. Scott's care?' Then on another visit to the jail I heard him say, 'How is Connors's case coming along?'"

"There is no doubt in your mind that these are the two men we see here in court?"

"No doubt whatsoever."

The rain began early in the afternoon. The day grew dark and the gas lamps about the walls had to be lit for the remainder of the testimony. When court adjourned for the day, the prisoners were led past Mary, who sat dazed and alone in the front row. She avoided her husband's eyes, preferring to contemplate her hands.

At the rear of the courthouse, deputies shackled them in leg irons and an elaborate system of handcuffs and iron links that restricted them to a noisy shuffle.

Awaiting the carriages, the rain spilling over leaf-filled gutters, Dunlap whispered, "You wanted to be number one."

Sheriff Longley barked over his shoulder, "No talking, boys!" Then he stepped outside in the downpour to hurry their transportation back to the Northampton Jail.

Scott mumbled, "Did you see her crying, Jim? Did you see how I've hurt her?"

Dunlap nodded. "Mr. Wright," he asked the deputy holding him firmly by the elbow, "who are all those people in there? The place was packed!"

"Pinkerton agents, other bank people."

"I meant the ladies! Eighty percent of them were ladies!"

Wright grinned, readying an umbrella for the trip to the carriage. "You boys are real celebrities! When word got out that a couple of young men like yourselves were responsible for the largest bank robbery in the country, well the ladies just had to see how handsome you really were. Hell, I hear you practically emptied that girl's school, Smith College!"

"Well I'll be!" Dunlap laughed.

"They've been writing notes to the sheriff to give you boys. But the sheriff is holding them for after the trial."

"You hear that, Bob? We're getting fan mail, too!"

"It's just beginning," Wright chuckled. "You just wait a while. You boys are gonna be real attractions, you'll see."

Deputy Potter looked at Scott suspiciously. "Where's my umbrella?"

"Hell, Henry," Scott cursed, "we don't steal umbrellas!"

"Where in the hell's that umbrella?"

"You lost it, Henry," Wright sighed in annoyance.

"Damn! Who finds all those umbrellas, anyways?"

The vehicle was drawn up, and armed guards stepped out with rifles ready. Dunlap had deputies Wright and Munyan to assist him in walking the short distance to the carriage, a sturdy brougham with the body slung low between the massive wheels.

Scott ventured out into the rain without the protection of Potter's missing umbrella. "You get an umbrella tomorrow, Mr. Potter, or I won't be going with you."

"I'll have one, Bob, that's God's truth."

Wet riflemen squeezed in beside Scott as the carriage was driven into the crowd. He saw Mary through the rifle barrels, the blond curls wet and limp, the eyes vacant, the sagging shoulders warning him she had been mortally wounded.

"Do you swear to tell the truth, the whole truth, so help you God?"

"I do."

"You may be seated."

"Would you please tell the court your name?"

"William Edson."

"Are you currently employed, Mr. Edson?"

"No, sir."

"Will you tell the court your former occupation?"

"I was a salesman for the Herring Safe Company. I left their employ in January last."

"That's a very specialized field, to be sure. In what city do you reside, Mr. Edson?"

"New York. I've been there since 1871."

"Have you had occasion to visit Northampton before this trial?"

"Yes, I came here to install a lock and do some work on behalf of my employer, the Herring Company."

"At the Northampton National Bank?"

"Yes. I supervised all repairs and installations."

"Mr. Edson, do you recall the cashier, John Whittelsey?"

"Of course."

"Do you remember at one point, several months ago, when Mr. Whittelsey complained about the key not fitting properly in the vault?"

"Yes, I do."

"Would you tell us about it, please?"

"Mr. Whittelsey's complaint was that the key was not fitting the vault. I, in turn, took the key on the pretext of filing it and made wax copies."

"Wax copies? Wax copies from which other keys could be made?"

"Yes, sir."

Dunlap leaned to Scott and whispered sadly, "He's going to peach."

"What was done with the keys made from these wax impressions?"

"I gave them to Bob Scott and Jim Dunlap."

Scott sagged visibly while Dunlap remained outwardly composed. The court buzzed with excitement, and Judge Bacon rapped for order.

"Then you know the defendants?"

"Yes, sir. I've known them since September of 1873."

"Would you tell us about that, please?"

"I first met them at the home of William Connors, on Houston Street in New York City, in September of 1873."

"Did you see them many times that fall?"

"Four or five."

"For what reason, Mr. Edson?"

"To discuss a bank robbery in Elmira."

"Objection!"

"On what grounds, Mr. Sweetser?"

"I object to a reference to a robbery in Elmira. That has nothing to do with the case at hand. We are dealing with the robbery of the Northampton Bank, Your Honor!"

"Mr. Fields?"

"Your Honor, the court will be shown that a conspiracy was entered into by these three men, Scott, Dunlap and William Edson, to rob various banks throughout these United States. The prosecution will prove that this unholy alliance resulted in the robbery of the Northampton Bank."

"Objection overruled."

"Exception, Your Honor."

"The exception is noted, Mr. Sweetser. Mr. Field, you may proceed."

"Thank you, Your Honor. Mr. Edson, will you please tell this court your part in the Northampton robbery?"

"My job was to keep them advised of the bank's situation. I made the copy of the key and even gave them a working model to practice with."

Dunlap heard Scott suck in his breath as it became apparent Edson was not only going to tell all he knew about Northampton, but that he might peach on Quincy and the other robberies as well.

Across the room, bank president Warriner sat intently listening to Edson's betrayal. Next to the bank officer sat Robert Pinkerton, watching Dunlap dispassionately. They were both young men—Dunlap just thirty-two, and his nemesis in his late twenties. They made silent conversation with their eyes.

So that's how you did it.

That's how we did it.

You leaned on him, and he cracked under pressure.

That he did, Jim.

He was the ace in the hole.

That's right.

I never trusted Edson.

You shouldn't have. I've seen dozens like him.

You've got us proper, I fear.

I think so, Jim, I do think so.

What else do you know about me?

Everything, Jim, I know everything.

I knew the rules. . . .

That you did.

We played the game fairly.

You did that.

I have no ill will about this.

Thank you.

You did what you had to do.

That I did.

"The bastard!" Scott hissed. "Why doesn't Sweetser do something to shut him up?"

"I don't know," Dunlap said helplessly. He knew Bob Pinkerton had left little to chance and there was no hope for them. Only Scott seemed to think there was still a chance.

"I told Bob Scott and Jim Dunlap that they had better settle with the bank very soon," Edson continued, "as the situation was becoming extremely warm. Dunlap wanted to know what they would give to have the securities back. I thought maybe $100,000 or $150,000. Scott wanted more. Jim wanted freedom from prosecution for all involved."

Dunlap looked at Pinkerton and silently asked, *Why did you wait so long? You must have been onto us for a long time.*

Edson answered, "Robert Pinkerton took me to his office. I told him everything. I saw there was no hope for a peaceful end to it. He had known about me for some time, months actually. Bob and Jim he had been onto for five months. Pinkerton wanted the securities in his possession before the arrest was made."

"Do you know where the securities might be at this time?"

"No. They were hidden here in town right after the robbery. Then Jim came back one night and took them back to New York. I have no idea where they are now."

Pinkerton smiled the barest hint of a smile. *Your ace in the hole, Jim.*

And a good one, you'll have to admit, Bob.

On cross-examination defense attorney Sweetser took Edson back to Elmira. The Herring employee freely admitted his efforts in the bungled robbery. It became apparent that the attorney was attempting to show the court that Edson was, in truth, the ringleader, even to supplying a pump found at the site of the Pittston burglary.

Dunlap then realized that it had been the pump, tied to Herring, with a Herring employee figuring so prominently in the Northampton robbery that had done them all in.

Was it the vacuum pump? he asked Pinkerton.

The detective closed his eyes slowly in affirmation.

Dunlap sighed and slid low in his seat.

"He's a damn fool!" Scott whispered.

"So were we."

"What does he hope to gain by prattling on so?"

"Just one unimportant little item, his freedom."

"I'll get that bugger!" Scott hissed.

"But not before he gets us, I'm afraid."

Dunlap closed his eyes. Seven months they had been languishing in the Northampton Jail awaiting trial. Now he dreaded the prospect for their future. When he opened his eyes, Pinkerton was listening to Edson. Jim turned to the audience. He saw Mary, her eyes red with tears. He wanted to tell her it would not get better. Best she go home and await the inevitable decision.

Court ended for the day. Edson left the stand, carefully avoiding the defendants eyes. Dunlap was aware the man never once looked at them, though he'd mentioned their names several hundred times.

As they passed the evidence table, Scott saw a picture of Mary lying amid the exhibits. That it would be used as evidence so incensed him that he snatched it. The guard grabbed his arm. Pinkerton dashed forward and demanded the picture be returned to the table. Scott shouted "You can go to hell!" The photo disappeared into Scott's mouth as the guards wrestled him to free it. It was retrieved, but not before it was torn and wrinkled.

"Damn you!" Scott cried on the verge of tears. "If we were alone!" he warned Pinkerton, before he was subdued and carried from the courtroom.

"He's upset," Jim offered.

"I understand," Pinkerton said softly.

"It's been a bad day."

Pinkerton nodded.

"It was the pump, wasn't it?"

"Yes, it was."

"I thought so. . . ." The guards took him by the arms. He saw Mary standing forlornly against the rail, witness to her husband's dismay. Jim knew he should say something of comfort, but he allowed the tugging of the guards to spare him an awkward moment.

"Now, Mrs. Whittelsey, can you identify the two men who were in your house?" Assistant District Attorney Gillett asked.

"Yes. Definitely. It was Mr. Scott and Mr. Dunlap. I can tell by their size, voice and peculiarity of manner. Scott's nervous habit of shrugging and his broad shoulders are unmistakable. I noticed the same shrug and nervous manner at the indictment at Town Hall. Dunlap's voice is just like that of my attendant that night, and his manner is like his, quiet and self-possessed. I stroked his hand as I begged him not to hurt my husband. He assured me no harm would come to him, provided he did as he was told. A gentlemanly manner that impressed me very much."

A parade of prosecution witnesses followed. Men swore under oath to having seen either Scott or Dunlap loafing suspiciously about the town. But most were in error.

Two Pinkerton detectives, Gallagher and Benjamin Franklin, detailed the duo's arrest in Philadelphia and the tracking of Edson to various meetings with Scott, Dunlap and Connors.

Defense attorney Sweetser succeeded in having Billy Connors' name struck from the trial. But then he quit the defense in a verbal battle with Judge Bacon that saw the defense of Scott and Dunlap falling to the ill-equipped Northampton attorneys the Bond brothers.

Dunlap learned that Billy Connors had been arrested in New York. Billy managed to stall extradition to Massachusetts. Then one night he walked to freedom from the Ludlow Street Jail, assisted by the well-paid members of the detective's Bank Ring.

Three days after the trial began, closing arguments were filed and Judge Bacon charged the jury. At ten o'clock on the morning of July 12, 1877, the jury left the room. They took less than two hours to reach a verdict. At 11:50 the foreman, Joshua Crosby of Williamsburg, entered the courtroom and read the verdict. "The jury agrees upon a verdict of guilty for the robbery of the Northampton Bank." There had been three ballots taken. The first, seven for conviction and five for acquittal. After a heated discussion of just a few minutes, a second ballot was voted with eleven for conviction and one for acquittal.

Immediately a trial date was set for Monday on the charge of "breaking and entering of cashier Whittelsey's home and stealing his gold watch."

As the sheriff scoured the countryside searching for jurors to be impaneled for the second trial, word reached the press that the notorious bankies Scott and Dunlap had been convicted. Citizens and bank employees from Quincy, Elmira, Pittston, Covington, Rockville and Louisville, Kentucky, arrived to see the men that had created havoc with their vaults. Edson's testimony opened fresh wounds. It linked the two with a half dozen unsolved bank burglaries and created an overnight sensation.

No one could have predicted the reaction of the ladies of the eastern seaboard. Artists' sketches had the two handsome men sitting in the dock, poised and aloof to their predicament. The more timid ladies wrote notes, while the bolder of the species set out for Northampton itself.

The first day of the second trial found the banking community turned away from the courtroom by hundreds of eager women pushing and shoving their way inside, leaving the bewildered bankers outside with the press. Only two newsmen managed to find a seat; the others had to content themselves with secondhand reports.

James Dunlap's brother, Andrew, hearing of his brother's plight, mortgaged his home and provided the men with a Springfield attorney named Leonard to assist in the defense.

Leonard exhausted the supply of jurymen, and Sheriff Longley was sent out again to dig up an unbiased jury. It took several days before the twelve were seated. Meanwhile, a rumor had circulated among the women that the men were willing to part with a lock of their hair for the paltry sum of twenty-five cents. They beseiged the Northampton Jail.

"I guess it's all right," Longley sighed. His desk was littered with envelopes, the guards adding hourly to the pile. A small table was set up in the barbershop, and Scott was the first to part with several precious locks. Then Dunlap took his turn. These were placed in an envelope and a signature attached for posterity.

"It doesn't take a fool to see we have more customers than hair," Dunlap said.

"You're right," Scott agreed. "I don't intend on baring my scalp for a few coins."

A work detail was led back into the cell block—several dark-haired men among them. Scott eased over to Deputy Potter and remarked, "Unsightly looking bunch, Mr. Potter."

Henry Potter looked at the prisoners, then at the table set up next to the barber chair. "Of course it wouldn't be right, Bob, if *all* that money didn't see its way back to men who look so unsightly, now would it?"

"You're absolutely right, Mr. Potter!" Scott smiled. "I would think a nickel for each lock taken and a nickel for the jailers might be an even split."

"Sounds fair to me," Potter reasoned.

"Of course we won't pay for redheads or those other unlikely types," Dunlap added quickly.

The prisoners were lined up with the barber's chair, and Dunlap circled around it, gathering each precious lock and hurrying it to the table where Scott placed it in an envelope and signed either his or Dunlap's name, depending on the color of the hair.

By week's end they had gathered enough hair to make a good-sized parlor rug, and still the requests poured in. When the supply of prisoners was exhausted, they reluctantly closed up shop.

Defense attorney Leonard impressed them with the importance of being acquitted of the second charge—this in turn would lead to a reversal of the first conviction and might secure their freedom still.

The two prepared an extensive list of witnesses in New York who were prepared to swear they were in that city on the day of the robbery. They even decided Dunlap had been ill and unable to travel during the period in question.

But Edson, his memory sharpened, repeated his testimony, freely adding that he assisted Scott and Dunlap in stealing three million dollars in three short years. The gallery swooned with admiration for the two daring young men on trial.

Scott remained cool, conscious of his fans watching his every move, but from the corner of his mouth he asked Dunlap, "Where did he get *those* figures?"

"I don't remember no three million."

"It's a nice figure, though."

With seats at a premium, women of all ages and persuasions were at the courtroom before dawn. The irate bankers, for the most part never did get to see the two desperadoes who caused them such grief and undermined their standing in the community.

The trial itself was a replay of the first. The same witnesses took the stand and pointed the same accusing finger at the two seasoned defendants. The prosecution introduced only two new witnesses. The first, Joseph Payne, described as a handwriting expert, took the stand to testify that the signature "Rufus" on various notes negotiating the return of the Northampton securities were all those of the same man, James Dunlap.

"You can't do that!" Scott cried out in the trial's only outburst. Before the stunned attorneys could speak, Scott turned to Dunlap and insisted, "They can't do that!"

Defense attorney Leonard, the Springfield lawyer, didn't know if it was legal or not, as he had never heard of such a thing. When Scott finally asked him, "Can they do that?" Leonard only shrugged.

Then Robert Pinkerton took the stand. He testified to being a detective for ten years and summarized the circumstances that led him to James Dunlap's room at the Grand Central Hotel. It was there, he testified, that Dunlap's trunk was found, complete with burglar tools, wax for key impressions and the other incriminating articles now on display. He also listed the other thirteen Pinkerton men who had worked on the case at one time or another and pointed out that the agency's compensation was not contingent on the outcome of the trial.

The defense began its case with Mary's music teacher, who swore both Scott and Dunlap were at the Scott home during the period in question. He also remembered Scott as having a full beard at the time, which was directly at odds with reports that the Northampton burglars were clean-shaven.

The owner of a New York dog and bird bazaar confirmed that Scott had a full beard during the winter of '75 and '76. He remembered it distinctly, he said, for that was when Bob Scott bought a dog for Mary.

Mary's sister, Amelia Wood, took the stand. She told the court that Bob had sprained his ankle right after New Year's of 1876 and was unable to walk for several months, hardly making him a fit person to rob the bank at Northampton on January 25, as charged. She testified to being with both men on the days of the twenty-fifth and twenty-sixth, remembering it quite vividly, as Dunlap was ill with consumption on the dates in question.

A New York history professor named Naevius, whose name he demanded be pronounced the same as the Naevius spoken of in the Second Epistle of Horace, took the stand. At this point prosecuting attorney Gillet calmly informed the professor that "epistle" was being mispronounced. It was not "epistel" but "epistle." This so unnerved the professor that his testimony concerning the existence of Scott's limp and his worries about whether the poor man would ever walk again was shadowed by his shaky beginning.

"You took history lessons from that man?" Dunlap whispered to Scott.

Scott reluctantly agreed he had tried to improve himself.

"Good God." Dunlap whistled quietly in disbelief.

A piano teacher followed who swore to the same events. Then Silas Packard, a business college manager, arrived late, to swear that the signatures of "Rufus" and those of Dunlap were not the same hand, as Payne had testified. On cross-examination, Packard admitted, however, that there were numerous similarities.

As closing arguments approached on Friday, the emotions of the women in court reached hysteria level. Due to long lines for the morning and afternoon sessions, those finding seats in the morning refused to leave during the lunch recess. Box lunches were opened, and the case of the handsome defendants pursued with vigor. Throughout the hot noon recess, the women defended their seats.

As the weekend drew near, Judge Bacon decided the women were overdoing things and ordered the courtroom cleared during the noon recess. When the doors were thrown open after lunch, the hysterical crowd thundered back into the tiny room, leaving battered males outside cursing the "weaker" sex and loudly denouncing "women's rights." Only two men managed to make the Saturday afternoon gallery.

After twelve days in court, the jury retired. Three hours later they announced their verdict, guilty. The defense filed for an exception and a new trial. The matter was moved to the Supreme Court. Meanwhile, Hampshire County debated the means of paying the five thousand dollars incurred in the first two trials and moaned publicly at the thought of additional monies for a new trial.

Their convictions secured, Scott and Dunlap were allowed to see what the outside world thought of their adventures. The *New York Sun*, in an article entitled GIGANTIC BANK ROBBERIES, summed up their escapades as "will never be equaled." Others whose reporters had been unable to gain admittance quoted the *Sun's* reverence for the two bankies, forgetting the fact that the *Sun* had once pushed for a statue to Boss Tweed with the same energy.

Harper's Weekly said, "Seldom has there occurred in our country a bolder or more successful bank robbery than the recent one at Northampton."

A Worcester, Massachusetts, bank president was quoted in the weekly as saying, "I'm sick of this rascally world. Don't want to see or do business with anybody. I'd rather be a farmer, living on a crossroad four miles from the sight of everybody, with a barrel of cider and two hogs, than to have anything to do with banks, money or men."

At Christmas, the prisoners received the news that the Supreme Court had dismissed their motion for a new trial. Four days later, Scott and Dunlap stood coolly before the stern old Berkshire judge who wrote out the sentence. It was passed to a clerk who read it silently, then repeated it for the prisoners and their attorneys and fans.

"Twenty years at hard labor in the Massachusetts State Prison, and one day's solitary confinement for each prisoner."

A wail of indignation went up from the gallery. Several women burst into tears, two fainted. Mary Scott trembled and went white as she sagged into Andrew Dunlap's arms.

The prisoners were taken to the east side of the courthouse, into the jury room where the deputies waited with shackles. Dunlap was heavily chained, then his wrist was locked to Deputy Potter's. Scott stood weakly against the wall, as the links were locked and Deputy Wright joined to his right hand.

Dunlap had spent ten months in preparing for this eventuality. But Bob Scott had remained skeptical, convinced he would never see the inside of prison. The shock drained him completely.

The elm trees were barren, their branches cushioned in snow. A soft powder covered the courtyard as the prisoners emerged. The sky was white and joined the ground on the horizon, making it impossible to tell where one began and the other left off.

"There's something I have to know," Potter asked. "Why didn't you rob the First National instead?"

Dunlap said softly, "Well, Henry, you have to know a little about safes to understand. The First National just had rubber padding installed on its safe. The pump we normally used wouldn't have worked because it was impossible to create a vacuum with the door rubber-sealed. So we had to turn to the ol' Northampton National."

"But Edson said you drilled two holes over the vault to see how thick the material above might be."

"That's true, we did."

"You drilled two holes?" Potter persisted.

"Yep."

"Well I'll be damned if *we* can find them!"

"They're there, Henry, in the ceiling right above the safe. They're filled with putty so you'll have to know where to look."

The carriage drew into position, and Dunlap turned to Scott, who stood transfixed, eyes moist, while mist billowed from his mouth in the icy air.

"Hey," Jim said gently, nudging Scott back to reality.

Scott stared vacantly at his partner.

"It'll be all right," Dunlap said. "We'll be together."

A young boy ducked under the arms of deputies holding the silent crowd back from the yard. He skidded to a stop before the trussed prisoners, looking undecidedly from Scott to Dunlap.

Dunlap managed a smile. "Hello, boy, what's your name?"

"George, sir," the boy panted, pulling the cap away. "George Dragon, sir."

"George goes to the Bridge Street School," Potter explained. "He's the lad who found your hiding place and tools."

Dunlap extended his hand as far as it would reach. "Pleased to meet you, George."

"You're not sore at me?"

"Why no, boy," he grinned as the boy took his hand hesitantly. "You did what you had to do. I'm sure your paw's real proud of you now, ain't he?"

"Yes, sir."

"Move on, George!" Sheriff Longley barked. The boy ducked the sheriff's boot and raced back to his schoolmates, the treasured hand offered for inspection'.

The crowd was so thick the horses had to be led slowly through it. "Move aside now!" the deputies threatened.

Dunlap thought there were twice as many as usual, possibly in response to the consistent rumor that the "gang" would break them out.

The silent crowd parted in an orderly fashion until from somewhere a woman shrieked. Someone else moaned. A sob ran through the gathering, passing from woman to woman until they began to resist the rifles advancing in front of the horses. The animals pranced nervously at the pressing, wailing mass that surrounded the carriage.

The deputies resisted the outflung arms and dragged the horses forward a step at a time, certain that at any moment the men's companions would materialize to keep their comrades out of prison.

One young lady threw herself against the wagon and dropped a note onto Scott's lap. "I pray for you every night!" she cried. Deputies pried her hands free of Scott's coat as he stared straight ahead at Sheriff Longley.

A hand snaked into Dunlap's window and a pretty young miss of twenty jerked his face around and mashed his lips with her own. His hat was knocked to the floor as Potter shouted, "Stand clear, miss!"

Paper missiles flew through the open windows, peppering the carriage floor.

"I'll wait for you, dear Jim!"

"I ain't never seen anything like it!" Potter said in amazement.

"You're in the wrong business, Henry."

Hands snatched at Dunlap's silk tie. Suddenly it became a life or death struggle when the knot refused to give. Potter came to Dunlap's aid and, with his one free hand, yanked it loose. Dunlap's hat was whisked out the window in the grasp of a slender white hand. His collar was next to go. Tugged free of the shirt, it slipped away in a sea of fingers, flailing wildly for a memento.

"Get this damn thing moving!" Sheriff Longley shouted.

The horses picked up speed as the crowd thinned. Several dozen die-hard young boys from the Bridge Street School ran beside the prisoners.

As the high, vaulted windows of the Northampton Jail came into view, it was plain to see that a second crowd waited at the gates. Deputies rushed forward to clear a path from Union Street to the enclosure. Slowing the horses allowed women and children to board the carriage easily and reach inside for a last opportunity to touch the prisoners. The gates were finally secured against the crowd, and when the prisoners emerged from the carriage, they shouted and waved their goodbyes.

They were marched to the two holding cells nearest the jailer's office. They knew it would be the last time the journey would be made. The handcuffs and irons were removed and the heavy doors locked. Bob Pinkerton stood nearby, watching with mild interest. He moved forward, stopping momentarily at Scott's cell. The prisoner sat heavily on the cot, staring blankly down the row of iron bars.

Pinkerton moved past to Dunlap. Jim had a cigarette in his mouth and struck a match to the end of it. He waved the flame away as Pinkerton leaned against the entry. A Harvard pocket cigarette roller lay on his cot as Dunlap examined the burnt match.

"You know, Mr. Pinkerton, the man who invented this thing lived just a few miles down the road in Springfield. His name was Wood, the same as Mary's maiden name. Alonzo B. Wood. It's just a splinter with a little phosphorus and brimstone, chalk and glue—amazing, isn't it?"

"It is indeed."

Dunlap dropped the match into a tin container. He passed the cigarette to Scott, finally nudging the man for his attention. Scott looked at the extended offering. Slowly he shook his head in refusal. The cigarette was withdrawn through the bars.

"It's all over, Jim. You and Bob have to realize that. In a few days Warden Chamberlain will be here to take you boys to Charlestown Prison. Your only hope is in getting the sentence reduced, and the only way that can be done is to help the bank recover its money. I can promise you there'll be no parole as long as the money's out there with your friends. I'd like to help you. But I can't if you won't talk to me."

"I'll talk to you," Dunlap decided. "But only in Bob's presence. I won't talk about the money, not yet. Not until Bob and I have had a chance to discuss things. The money's the only hope we have . . . We have to be darn sure before we act."

"I understand."

"But I'll tell you anything else you want to know. I'm not looking forward to serving twenty."

Pinkerton went to the sheriff's office, and in a moment the two returned with tin cups of hot coffee and writing tablets. Scott sat just a few inches away in the other cell, oblivious to the meeting.

"First," Dunlap sighed, "the money was hidden in the school-house, but not in the attic where the Dragon boy found our cigars and chicken bones. That was where we waited before leaving for the cashier's home. The money was hidden in the room itself, in a platform beneath the blackboard. It's a sort of step the smaller children stand on to reach the blackboard—about five feet long."

Sheriff Longley shook his head. "We went over every inch of that room. That's damn near impossible!"

Dunlap continued, smiling wryly, "The step faces the cemetery. If you look real close, Sheriff, you'll find the nail heads were cut with a chisel so the boards could be removed and put back at will. We replaced the nails with screws and covered them with putty. If you don't know what you're lookin' for, you'll never find them."

The sheriff still wasn't sure it was possible. "What will we find there?"

"The keys to the bank . . . a few tools. The money's no longer there."

"Are you telling me the money was there all the time we were searching for you boys?"

Dunlap nodded agreeably.

Longley told Pinkerton, "We went through that schoolhouse with a magnifying glass after the hideout in the attic was discovered!"

"You need a better glass," Pinkerton said sarcastically.

"I'll be damned!"

"When did you put the money in the schoolhouse?" Pinkerton asked.

"The night of the robbery. The same night. We didn't want to get caught with it on us, so we left it there for about a month. Then I came back and took it with me to New York."

"When exactly was it taken north?" Pinkerton persisted.

Dunlap rubbed his eyes wearily. " . . . I can't remember for sure. . . . About four weeks later . . . sometime near the end of February . . . I came from Amherst at night. . . . The snow was coming down real hard . . . "

"There was a bad snowstorm on the night of February 27," the sheriff said brightly.

"That sounds about right. I left the horse some hundred rods from the schoolhouse and came the rest of the way on foot. I didn't want to be seen carrying too much baggage, so I made two trips.

Longley halted everything momentarily as he sent Potter and Munyan off to search the school platform under the blackboard.

Pinkerton sipped his coffee thoughtfully. "Will you tell me the details of the robbery?"

From the adjoining cell Scott said flatly, "No names. We won't tell you any of the names of those that were with us."

"I know who they were," Pinkerton said. "Red Leary, Shang Draper, Big Jim Burns, Eddie Goodie and, of course, Billy Connors."

Dunlap was surprised Pinkerton did indeed know the names of those in attendance, though Joe Howard had not been mentioned. "I'm not saying. You can think what you want."

"All right."

Dunlap took the cigarette roller and passed the first one to Scott. "We left New York together. Bob and I separated in New Haven. Bob came by way of Springfield—"

"We took the steamboat to New Haven," Scott told the men in Dunlap's cell, turning his body slightly as he talked. "I had a sleigh because the *Herald* said there was two feet of snow on the ground down here."

"And?"

"There wasn't an ounce of the white stuff. I had to send the sleigh back and rent an old wagon to make the rest of the journey."

"How did you get here?"

"The old Connecticut River road."

"What about you, Jim?"

"I took the canal road from Westfield. I arrived first, about half past eight."

"Those witnesses of yours", Bob snapped, "the ones who said they saw us on Elm Street near Whittelsey's house, were lying!"

"You mean Mantor and Crafts?" Longley asked.

"They lied!" Scott repeated. "We were never there!"

Dunlap added, "And Mrs. Whittelsey was mistaken when she said we spent the night of the robbery under her quince bushes."

"And that man Sexton? The one who swore Billy Connors was at the hotel in Springfield? He was lying, too. It was Jim who was there, not Billy!" Scott snorted.

Pinkerton asked carefully, "What about Edson's testimony?"

Dunlap sighed and withdrew the cigarette from the roller. He examined the twisted ends. "Edson was telling the truth."

Scott cursed, "Damn the man!"

"Everything he said?" Pinkerton asked, somewhat surprised.

"Everything," Dunlap stated calmly, closing his eyes and leaning against the iron bars. "As well as he understood it, he told the truth."

"You were hoping he would lie to save himself? Then your attorney might be able to trip him up?" Pinkerton asked.

"Sort of . . . "

"Did you pay Edson twelve hundred in cash? What he claimed was his share of the cash inside the safe?"

"We took twelve thousand in cash which we divided equally. Edson was given twelve hundred after expenses, yes."

Pinkerton's pencil paused above the paper. "There are still a few details that need explaining. It appears some United States Coupon Bonds were sold."

"We needed the money!" Scott stormed. "It had been four months after the robbery, and we still hadn't negotiated the securities! I needed cash!"

Pinkerton looked at Dunlap for a long moment. He was beginning to see Scott's situation and how Dunlap fared within it. "The greatest robbery in the world netted you twelve thousand dollars in cash."

"That's it," Dunlap grinned.

"What else did you dispose of?"

"A guy named Thackery had $25,000 in Union Pacific Railroad Bonds he wanted back." Dunlap sipped the coffee as he waited for Pinkerton's pencil to catch up. "He contacted us in New York, and we sold them back for $8,000 in cash."

"In the year since the robbery," Scott explained angrily, "the value of those bonds had risen over two thousand dollars. He made out all right, he did."

"What else has been disposed of?"

"We took out a loan for another $8,000, and we used the best of the railroad bonds to secure it."

The pencil was set aside, the coffee cup raised as Pinkerton eyed Dunlap suspiciously. "How did Thackery contact you to make the deal for the return of his bonds?"

Dunlap smiled. "I don't have to tell you how it is, Mr. Pinkerton. These bank people don't give a damn about anybody. Not you! Not me! They don't give a damn what happens to the little man or what he's lost as long as *they* don't end up losing themselves. They were willing to negotiate the whole thing months ago! We wouldn't be here now if we could have agreed on the price! We all know that! Robbery takes place on both sides of the teller's cage, Mr. Pinkerton."

"What about Thackery? How did the transaction take place?"

"It wouldn't be in our best interests to talk about that. Let us just say Thackery sent out word that he was willing to pay instead of pressing charges. We made a small business transaction is all."

"Anything else sold or lost?"

"No."

"Didn't your attorney advise you that the best deal you could make would be to surrender the bonds?" Pinkerton asked.

"Yes," Dunlap admitted.

"Couldn't you see the case was hopeless?"

"I hate that word!" Scott shouted.

"Well, Bob," Pinkerton said evenly, "what's a better one? You've just been sentenced to twenty years in prison. You don't have the money or securities in your hands. You're going to spend the best years of your life behind bars! And hard years they'll be, too! And you don't find it hopeless?"

"No!" Scott insisted.

"I don't understand you!" Pinkerton turned to Dunlap. "I don't understand, Jim. Why didn't you take the $150,000 offered by Detective Gladstone? Why did you risk trial?"

Dunlap stared at his hands until Scott slapped a palm into the iron bars. "Jim *wanted* to take the offer! It was my fault! I guess the whole reason behind us being here is my fault. I thought they might go as high as $200,000 and still give us our freedom. Jim said I was being a fool. I was wrong—he was right. He didn't want to do this job. We've never dealt with a cashier's family before. I got us into this."

Scott pressed his face to the bars in anguish. "If it's any consola tion, Jim, before these men I want to apologize for all the trouble I've caused you. As God is my judge, I wouldn't have had this happen to you for the world."

Turning to the sheriff and Robert Pinkerton, Scott confessed, "This is my fault! If there's something that can be done for Jim, Mr. Pinkerton and Mr. Longley, I wish you would do it!"

"Don't worry about that," Dunlap whispered.

"I'll make it up to you somehow," Scott said softly.

"What about the rest of the money?" Longley asked.

"I think that is something Jim and I will have to discuss. It's the only card we have left. It would be a shame if we used it foolishly."

Dunlap nodded silently. "If the money was returned, could you guarantee us a reduced sentence?"

Pinkerton closed the book. The pencil was replaced in an inside pocket. "It's too late for deals, Jim. I can only promise this. As long as the money remains in your hands, there'll be no talk of parole. Your cooperation in seeing it returned to its rightful place will look good on your record—that's all I can say. The bank president, Edwards, will fight your parole tooth and nail if you try and get it without returning the money. There's no room left for discussion. The sentence has been passed. The amount of time to be spent in prison is really up to the two of you." He took a small white card from his vest and set it on Dunlap's bunk. "Write or wire me when you've decided what you want to do."

"What about Jim?" Scott asked. "I'm willing to take the blame for the whole thing!"

Pinkerton looked from Scott to Dunlap. "What about it, Jim? You're a couple of years older than Scott. Did he tie you up and drag you down here to rob that bank, or did you begin to wonder if it couldn't be done?"

Pinkerton went to the cell entrance and hung for a moment on the open door. "We've spent a year on the arrest and trial. I think I know both of you pretty well. Bob, you needed the money. That's all it ever was to you. But, Jim," Pinkerton shook his head sadly, "you can't live without the excitement. In a sense, Jim, you're more dangerous than Scott. All Bob needs is a healthy income and he's content. But you, Jim—could you ever be happy doing anything else?"

"We've made a right good mess of it, I'm afraid," Scott whispered into the night. It seemed they'd been here longer than the year since their arrest.

"Aye," Jim sighed. "That we did."

Deputy Potter stoked the pot-bellied stove across the room, then cursed his fingers as he kicked the metal door shut with his foot. Settling into the chair, he gave the prisoners a careful scanning before he settled his newspaper into position.

"Twenty years," Scott trembled, drawing the blanket about his chin.

"Maybe . . . " Jim whispered.

Scott rose quickly on one elbow. "What are you thinking? Good God, man! Do you have some plan?"

"No," Jim said softly. "But the money's hidden, and we're the only ones who know where it is."

"Billy knows."

"He's the only other one." Jim said gently, "we have a lot of friends out there."

"Of course!" Scott exclaimed. "Billy Connors won't let 'em take us without a fight!"

"We've got Red Leary in our corner . . . and Shang Draper . . . Big Jim Burns. . . . There's a lot of money hidden out there. The boys will think twice before kissing their shares goodbye."

"Red Leary alone can put together a dozen men!" Scott said excitedly.

"Sheriff Longley won't be easily fooled," Dunlap said quietly. "But Mr. Bridgeman told me today that it's the custom for the Charlestown guards to come here and accept the prisoners. Bridgeman says they usually send three or four."

"Billy and Red won't have any trouble at all with just three or four guards! A few of the boys . . . well armed to show they mean business. Hell, Jim, I was a fool not to think of it myself!"

"Goodnight, boys!" Potter called out in annoyance.

"Sorry, Mr. Potter," they chorused.

"No talking now."

Several minutes later, Dunlap swung his feet to the floor and called softly, "I can't sleep, Mr. Potter. Is it all right if I smoke?"

The deputy eyed him suspiciously across the newspaper. Then he bobbed his head, "Go ahead, Jim."

Dunlap was on the edge of the cot, the blanket around his shoulders as he huddled over the rolling of the cigarette. "Can I borrow a match, Mr. Potter?" he whispered.

Potter dropped the newspaper to the table and let his boots fall heavily to the floor. He groaned from the chair, moving through the lamplight as he searched his pockets for a match. The tiny box was placed on the crossbar where Dunlap could reach it. The deputy stretched to the ceiling as Dunlap struck the match and held it to the twisted end of the paper.

"You ever know anyone to get twenty at Charlestown, Mr. Potter?"

"Not twenty, Jim," Potter yawned, "not twenty."

The matches were placed on the crossbar and the deputy gathered them in, tucking them deep inside the heavy wool jacket.

"What's it like there do you suppose, Mr. Potter?"

"You won't like it, Jim. It's a bad place—maybe the worst I've ever heard of."

Jim thought for a moment, then chuckled. "Do you suppose Mr. Longley would let us spend it here in Northampton?"

Potter grinned ruefully. "I don't think that would be possible, Jim."

"I've been here so long," Dunlap smiled, "it's starting to feel like home."

"Been a year next week, I think."

Dunlap shook the chill from his body and pulled the woolen blanket tight around his shoulders. "I hate the thought of being taken out there again in irons. It's hard to have all those people staring. Do you suppose there'll be a crowd when we leave here?"

"I'm sure there will."

"No way we can do it quietlike? In the dead of night, or something?"

"I'm afraid not." Potter said. "You boys are the first real celebrities we've had since Lincoln came through here more than ten years ago. No. I think there'll be a real large turnout. Besides, there's no night trains to Boston."

"I just hate to have everyone see us in chains and all. I never minded the handcuffs, but the chains . . . "

Potter shrugged. "Those are the rules."

"How much longer will we be here, do you think?"

"The sheriff wired Charlestown right after the sentencing. It can't be tomorrow, that's for sure. Maybe the day after."

Dunlap cupped his hands around the heat from his cigarette. "I'm going to miss you boys, Mr. Potter. You've been real good to us, and we appreciate it."

"You and Bob have done good time here. There isn't a guard or deputy here who doesn't wish you boys well."

"Well . . . we thank you, both Bob and I."

"You'd better get some rest now, Jim. You're gonna need it."

"I'll try, Mr. Potter."

The deputy turned from the cell and was headed for the warmth of the stove when Dunlap asked, "Mr. Potter? Do you suppose Bob's family in Illinois knows about the sentencing?"

"It was in all the papers," Potter called over his shoulder. "I'm sure of it. Wires went off to New York and Chicago right after the trial. I'm sure the whole world knows what's happened by now."

Dunlap shrugged resignedly. "Thank you, Mr. Potter. Good night."

"Good night, Jim," Potter mumbled before the fire.

Dunlap snuffed the butt into the metal can, then rolled to his cot. He pulled the covers around his ears against the cold night air.

Scott shifted slightly, then whispered, "So, Red Leary and Billy Connors should know by tonight what's happened to us."

"There may even be an account in the papers of how they plan on moving us to Charlestown. They'll need at least a day to put together some men."

"They should be in town by the time the guards arrive here from Charlestown."

"They should be . . . " Dunlap sighed wearily.

Scott smiled contentedly, burrowing into a ball against the night and closing his eyes to dream of their escape.

*   *   *

Two days later Warden Chamberlain and four deputies arrived by
train to take custody of the prisoners. The Northampton jailers
grouped around the two tiny cells. Dunlap passed a gold watch and
chain to the sheriff. "Mr. Longley, I want you to have this. It's the
only watch I've ever had that kept the correct time."

"Thank you, Jim."

"Mr. Bridgeman?" Scott brought forth a small item wrapped in
newspapers. "You been very kind to us for the past year, and I wanted you to have this."

"Thank you, Bob," the turnkey mumbled as he rolled the gift about
in his hands.

"There are others here for the other jailers," Dunlap informed the
gathering. "You have behaved very kindly toward us, and we won't
ever forget you."

"Well!" Scott announced bravely after an embarrassed silence.
"Let's get on with it!"

Fifty pounds of iron chain and shackles were dropped to the floor.
The Charlestown deputy joined Dunlap's feet together with a short
link. A second chain circled his waist. A third joined the wrists tightly together. A fourth went about the neck and locked at the waist. A
fifth section joined feet to waist, and then the wrists were tight against
the coat. Hats were placed on their heads as they shuffled to the heavily armed carriages.

They boarded the train at the Bridge Street crossing, unable to
wave to the silent crowd watching from a wide circle drawn up by the
Northampton deputies. The familiar faces of the courtroom blew
frosty kisses that went unanswered. After a long, punishing delay, the
train pulled them mercifully from sight.

At every city along the line, large crowds gathered for a glimpse of
the desperadoes. Changing trains at Springfield, they found several
thousand.

As they shuffled between trains, Dunlap looked anxiously about at
the faces, convinced Billy Connors and Red Leary would not stand idly
by and let them be carted off to prison for twenty years. Scott shuffled
slower than usual, giving whoever might be waiting ample time to exe-

cute whatever plan they had. Even as the crowd followed them to the Boston train, Jim's eyes and ears were keened for a tell-tale sign of the escape attempt. He was shown his seat and sat lightly, feet beneath him, ready to bolt for the door.

The signal given, the train began to crawl out of the Springfield station. *They're waiting until we're away from the crowds,* he told himself. *It would have been foolish to plan an armed intervention with so many people present.*

Boston, Dunlap thought quickly, gathering his courage. Connors and Big Jim Burns would wait for a crowded city where escape was easier before making their move. When he had Scott's attention, he mouthed the word, "Boston." Scott nodded imperceptibly.

The train reached snow-whipped Boston and unloaded the prisoners to a small, curious crowd. "Happy New Year!" a woman cried.

"New Year?" Dunlap asked the guard. "This is New Year's Day!"

"Shut up!" the man warned.

They were into the sleighs before they realized no move had been made on their behalf. Scott's eyes began to water as he realized they'd been betrayed. When the realization that hope was gone seized Dunlap, he too felt the embarrassing wetness creeping into his eyes. Big Jim Burns, Billy Connors, Red Leary—all had deserted them. At Charlestown Prison, the massive doors closed ominously behind them.

The guardroom was cold, cement and unfriendly. The snow from their shoes melted into little puddles at their feet.

"Remove the chains!" someone barked.

The uniformed guards, wearing coats agains the chill, dropped the links to the floor with a melancholy ring that rattled off the walls.

The warden took the clipboard offered. "Names?" he asked brusquely.

"Robert Scott," he said rubbing his wrists. "Robert C. Scott."

"Residence?"

"New York."

"Age?"

"Twenty-eight."

"Name?"

"James Dunlap. New York City. Thirty-three years of age, September 2."

A deputy with a heavy oak cane took a signal from the warden and addressed them. "The state allows a commutation of five days a month to each prisoner for good behavior." He walked back and forth before them, the cane clicking aginst the cold stone flooring.

"If you behave well, and there's no reason to believe you won't, you'll be able to gain sixty days each year. Good behavior will shorten your sentence from twenty years to seventeen years and sixty-three days. Bad behavior will cost you the friendship of the guards. For we do not take kindly to troublemakers. We do not take kindly to any breaking of the rules. We do not take kindly to insolence. We do not take kindly to repeat offenders. Do you understand?"

The cane came down hard in the man's palm, letting both men know there was more than oak involved in the crooked cane.

"Yes, sir," they mumbled.

"Speak up!" he shouted.

"YES, SIR!"

The warden rose from the edge of the desk. He gave each man a close inspection. Then he turned in disgust, ordering, "Deputy Clark will read you the rules of the prison." He left by an outside door that sent a frigid wind whipping about the quarters.

Clark set the cane on the desk and retrieved a well-worn sheet thumb-tacked to a piece of thin pine. "Rule number one," he read stiffly. "At the first striking of the gong in the morning, each convict will turn out, wash and dress, make his bed neatly, put his room in order, prepare his dishes and make ready to march from his cell."

Clark signaled to the deputies, who moved in close. "At the sliding of the bar, you will open your door without slamming, step out of your cell and march in an orderly fashion down the corridor."

One of the guards tapped Dunlap's coat. "Take it off."

"Rule number two! The shops!"

"You, too," the guard whispered to Scott.

"Each convict is to be prompt in taking his proper place in his division. He is to march the lock step, with head inclined toward the officer in charge, body erect, the left hand by the side of the leg, the right hand resting on the shoulder of the man directly in front of him."

Dunlap pulled the coat loose and held it over his arms. Scott watched Dunlap and followed suit.

"The file leader is to march with folded arms."

"The pants," the guard informed them quietly.

"At meals! Each convict will take the first dish the hand is put upon. He will be careful not to drop or spill his food in the corridors."

Dunlap hopped about on one foot as he pulled his pants free.

"Remove the articles from your trousers!" Clark snapped, before returning to the rule sheet. "Rule number three! On entering your room, each convict will place the food and drink on the table. The door will then be closed without slamming. The prisoner will stand with one hand clasping the bar of his door until a satisfactory count is made by the officer in charge."

Clark indicated the desk, and both men deposited their valuables next to the lead-weighted cane.

"Rule number four! Each convict is to be clean in person, keeping his room in order, and not spitting on the floor or corridors."

"At the striking of the second gong, all convicts will retire at once. From that moment, silence is to be observed until the striking of the first gong the following morning."

Dunlap watched as another guard gathered up their valuables and placed them in tiny cloth bags.

"Shirts."

"Rule number five! In the chapel, each convict will take the seat assigned him, with arms folded on his chest, face inclined toward the chaplain. All attention will be on the service. Any unnecessary noise, shuffling of feet or spitting on the floor is forbidden."

"Take it all off!" someone hissed behind them, obviously enjoying this much more than his comrades.

"Number six! Any convict who wishes to see the warden or have an interview with the chaplain will make his desire known to his officer. The convict's name will be placed in the letterbox of the official he wishes to see."

Both men stood barefooted on the stone flooring, their possessions gathered in their arms.

"Rule number seven! Each prisoner has the right to send a communication in writing addressed to His Excellency, the Governor, and to deposit in the commissioner's locked letterbox such a document addressed to the commissioner or any member of the board."

Dunlap began to shiver noticeably, and Scott dropped one shoe as Clark bawled, "Rule number eight!"

The pine board was lowered as Clark waited to see if Scott would pick up the shoe. When Scott remained at attention, leaving the offender lying before him, Clark said wearily, "Pick it up, you dunce."

The rule sheet came slowly back in place. "Each officer in charge of convicts will keep a weekly record which shall show the conduct and industry in labor of each convict under his charge. It will also include the amount of labor performed."

Someone opened the door and a blast of iced air stung their naked bodies. A guard laughed at their discomfort, but neither man was eager to turn and look for the culprit.

"This same weekly record will be returned to the warden every Saturday night."

For some reason the door remained open, and Dunlap risked a sidelong glance to see one of the guards standing there with a heavy woolen coat, obviously amused at their inconvenience.

"Rule number nine! Each convict whose record of conduct and labor is perfect for three months shall be entitled to receive one visit and to write one letter. Close that Goddamn door!"

The freezing blast eased with the clicking of the lock, though the room seemed colder by thirty degrees.

"Are there any questions?"

Scott was shivering so hard he feared his voice and replied by shaking his head no.

"No, sir."

"Rules for the workshop!" Clark continued, turning to the sheet beneath. "First! Upon reaching the workshop, convicts will take the place assigned them by the officer in charge and will not leave the same without his permission."

Dunlap held his clothes for a little warmth, hugging them to his chest only to have someone else come in through the outside door.

"Second! Convicts will labor diligently from bell to bell, performing such work as is given them by the superintendent or officer."

The force of the gale almost knocked Dunlap from his feet, and he staggered, juggling his possessions.

"Third! No talking will be allowed. No convict will communicate with another without permission of the officer in charge of the shop, nor hold any conversation with any person from outside the prison without permission of the warden or deputy."

Clark lowered the board momentarily and stared at the two shivering men. "Fourth!" he announced, raising the board until it met his eyes. "When a convict desires to communicate with an officer, he will raise his right hand and remain in that position until permission is given him to leave his place."

The board was dropped. Clark's eyes narrowed. "Is this clearly understood?"

"Yes, sir."

"I don't want you coming to me for breaking one of these Goddamn rules and saying you didn't understand. Do you understand what I've been saying or am I talking myself hoarse for a couple of dunces?"

"I understand, sir."

"I understand . . . sir."

"Goddamn, I hope so."

The board was handed off, the cane came back to Clark's hand. He moved between the two men until toes were almost touching. The cane tip swung slowly from one to the other, just grazing their noses, forcing them to stand erect and give its weighted end a clear path.

"Receiving and writing letters, seeing friends, using library books, having gas in your room, receiving fruit and extra food on holiday's are *Privileges!*" he shrieked. "Not rights! Any or all may be forfeited by persistent violation of any of those Goddamn rules! Do you understand?"

"Yes, sir."

Clark moved away. They could hear the cane clicking behind them as he inspected their naked bodies. Dunlap felt the cold tip of the cane on his shoulder.

"Where did you get that scar, boy?"

"Gettysburg . . . sir."

The cane went to the ankle and tapped painfully against each old wound. "And these?"

"Kenesaw Mountain, sir."

"Got us a Goddamn hero here!" Clark laughed, encouraging the other guards to do likewise.

Clark turned suddenly from the room, calling "Happy New Year" over his shoulder. A guard ordered them into the "lock step." They shuffled their clothes quickly and marched off to the barber shop. There, all their hair was removed with a dull pair of clippers and prison showers of ice water followed. Hurriedly dressed in prison denim, they were led to the isolation cell and their first night in Charlestown. The bolting of the door to the dark hole was a sound neither would ever forget. It rumbled about the corridors with ill-omened finality. It was January 1, 1878, the start of their new life.

The following morning they were led to their assignments in the cutting room of the shoe factory. Deputy Owen warned them, "Make no friends here. There's not a man among them who won't run to the warden with news that will better his own condition. They'll do you no good, this lot."

The cutting room required them to remain on their feet from sunrise until late evening. They closed out each day by gaslight, cutting shaft patterns for leather boots from thick, foul-smelling hides. They soon found their lives were regulated by the seasons. Days and weeks meant nothing. Life was warmth and cold, winter and summer.

Ten months later, as the first snows were on their way into the courtyard, they were summoned to the warden's office. Robert Pinkerton awaited them with news. "The release of the securities is now out of your hands. Red Leary's run to Europe. We have reason to believe that he and Billy Connors have taken the loot from wherever it was hidden, and they're spending like drunken cowboys. By the time they're done, there'll be nothing *left* for you to return."

Dunlap asked, "Will you guarantee us a pardon if we help you get it back?"

"You know I can't do that," Pinkerton frowned. "Talk Leary into returning the money and securities and I'll see your sentence is lightened. That is the best I can offer, but I personally guarantee that much."

Scott began coughing into a damp, soiled cloth he kept tucked into his sleeve. "That's a damn flimsy promise."

"What are you doing about Leary?"

"We're trying to catch him in Europe." Pinkerton shrugged, skeptically. "He knows we're onto him, and he keeps moving pretty fast, and spending just as fast, I'm afraid. I'm worried there'll be nothing left to bargain with once he's caught."

"We'll have to talk it over," Dunlap told the detective, not altogether certain Red Leary would leave Kate and run off to Europe alone.

Scott was certain it was a Pinkerton trick to make them believe the securities were in jeopardy, and with them, their freedom. Through the winter and into the spring they debated the logic of Red Leary having the securities, when only Billy Connors and themselves knew their hiding place. Their primary concern was that Pinkerton might be trying to panic them into revealing the location of the Northampton swag. That summer they decided to trust one other person.

Every three months Mary came to the prison for a one-day visit. She brought fresh fruit the men devoured as soon as it had been inspected. There had never been any remonstrations or bitterness on her part, and Dunlap began to realize what a rare woman Mary was.

He broached the tricky subject on her next visit. "Mary, Pinkerton told us there's a chance we can win an early release if we can come up with the securities. Our problem is that we can't be sure they're where we left them. We need someone we can trust to find out if the stocks and bonds are still where we hid them."

"Jim's right," Scott pleaded. "I won't last another year in here. We think Pinkerton may be lying to us, but we can't be sure! Would you see if the bonds are safe?"

Jim said helplessly, "There's no one else we can trust."

Mary shook the basket free of debris before replying, "On one condition. If the bonds are there, I must be allowed to go to the Pinkerton office and tell them they can have them."

Scott shrugged that away. "That's no good, dear Mary. Pinkerton will then have the bonds, and where are we? No, we must make the arrangement with Pinkerton ourselves. We have to have some sort of guarantee that we'll be released."

"Bob's right," Jim agreed.

Mary's pale blue eyes misted. "But you must promise to do so immediately!"

"Yes, of course." Scott smiled warmly and clutched her hands. He brought the fingers to his mouth and began to kiss them.

Dunlap eased himself from the bench and kissed her forehead, the blonde curls smelling fresh and soft against his lips. "Thank you, dear Mary," he whispered before wandering away and leaving them alone.

It was a long three months between visits. There was a chill in the air as they emptied the basket and inspected the goods like children at Christmas. A few apples were tucked away inside their shirts for a later feast. Tomatoes were halved, salted and downed immediately.

"I did exactly as you told me," she said. "I made sure I wasn't followed and I went to the belfry of the old Astoria Church—but the money was gone, just as Mr. Pinkerton said."

Dunlap slammed a fist into the table. "Then he was right! Connors told Red Leary where it was hidden, and they've made off with it!"

Scott sat stunned. Mary took his face between her soft hands and pleaded, "Oh, Robert, cooperate with Mr. Pinkerton! What have your friends done to ease your or Jim's suffering?"

"How can I return money I don't have?" Scott asked numbly. "How in God's name can I negotiate something that is no longer mine?"

"Jim!" she begged. "What possible good can come of this? We'll be old before we're able to sit and enjoy a simple meal together! Look at Robert, Jim! He's aged ten years since the day he arrived! I fear for both your lives! I fear for your health in this terrible place! Please! Please! Tell them what it is they need to know!"

She began to cry, tugging Dunlap's light shirt in desperation. "Let's end this once and for all! Please!"

"I'm afraid it's out of our hands now," Dunlap said gently.

"There must be *something* we can do!" she cried. "Tell them the truth! Tell them the money is no longer in your hands, but you will do whatever is in your power to correct the wrong! Please do something!"

"I don't know," Scott mumbled, crushed by the sudden turn of events.

"Please!" she pleaded, the tears racing her cheeks. "I love you both! I've asked nothing of you! I just can't bear to think of you spending another year, nay, another month in this horrible place! I fear for all of us!"

Mary gathered Bob in her arms, and they rocked gently in the fading light of the afternoon. Soon Scott's shoulders began to shake, and Jim drifted to the far side of the yard, leaving them what little privacy they had. Then the guard arrived to send them back to their respective worlds.

On Fast Day the prisoners were allowed in the yard for one full hour. The men were free to talk and mingle as they wished. Gus Raymond, a fellow cutter from the boot shop, led Scott and Dunlap to a far corner of the yard where a white-bearded inmate waited.

"Bob Scott, Jim Dunlap. This is Langdon Moore." Having completed his duty, Raymond left the three men alone.

Dunlap didn't know what to say to the legendary bank robber. Then he offered, "It looks like they have us all now."

"Appears that way," Moore shrugged, smiling easily.

"Word has it Eddie Goodie caught fifteen years," Scott offered.

Moore nodded. "You worked with Big Jim Burns . . . well, he went to England to escape Pinkerton's. Mark Shinburn's been arrested in Belgium. George White's in Vermont."

"Jimmy Hope's in San Quentin."

"Ned Lyon's in Connecticut."

"The bank people must feel pretty safe now," Moore grinned.

"Mr. Moore," Dunlap began, "we heard you just arrived and we bow to your expertise. We are in need of advice."

Scott summarized their situation, taking the old bankie from the Northampton robbery to the storage of the loot in the belfry of the old Astoria Church. He told him of the conversation with Pinkerton and the news that Red Leary might be in Europe spending their money.

Moore shook his head. "You shouldn't have waited until you were in court. You brought too many people into the case. Once that trial was held . . . " he scratched the white beard uncertainly. "I always made my settlement before trial and conviction. That's what you should have done."

"But we didn't!" Scott said ruefully. "The question is, what do we do now?"

"The bank people can't pardon you out, it's too late for that. But they can surely keep you here. The stuff is of no value to you now you're inside. The unfortunate thing is, the parties who now control it can betray you for the reward. That will be paid to whoever holds the securities in their hands at the time of recovery. If they were in your hands, I would say hold out a little longer. But . . . as someone else has them, I don't see that you are taking any risk in helping Pinkerton get them back. That is, of course, upon condition that the bank people promise to use their influence with the governor and the prison council to pardon you or reduce your sentence considerably."

"I see."

"How long have you been here now?"

"Two years," Dunlap groaned.

"And the money was taken when?"

"January . . . 1876."

"Then the bank people must be skeptical about ever seeing it again," Moore reasoned aloud. "It's been four years since the robbery. The time might just be ripe to strike a splendid bargain."

Scott asked worriedly, "Can we believe their promises?"

"I firmly believe," the old man smiled, "pledges given by honest men to crooks should be held as sacred as those given honest men."

"Thank you, sir," Dunlap smiled. "We'll take your advice."

"You can answer me something," Moore questioned them. "I was piping the Quincy bank back in '74. You and Georgie Mason beat me to it. How much was inside?"

"Almost 900,000," Scott grinned.

"Damn," Moore said easily. "I knew it was worth plenty."

"You know Georgie Mason? The wild man?"

"Of course," Moore smiled. "Georgie put me here by peaching on me. Yes, I know Georgie Mason."

* * *

The following day, a note was sent through the warden's office to Oscar Edwards, president of the Northampton National Bank. It read, "Will take whatever steps necessary to return the securities, for your promise to use whatever powers you have with the governor in executing a speedy pardon." The note was signed, "Bob Scott and Jim Dunlap."

Edwards forwarded the letter to Pinkerton, who saw to it that it reached Kate Leary and Billy Connors' wife. But weeks went by without an answer.

A second letter, urging their friends to speed the money to the bank, also met with silence.

It was Pinkerton who took the next step. "We'll arrest Shang Draper, Red Leary and Billy Connors at the first opportunity. They'll be told the two of you will testify against them if the securities are not returned. Is that agreed?"

"Agreed," they decided.

Shang Draper was picked up immediately and transported to the Northampton Jail. Arrest warrants were issued for Connors and Leary, circulated to the New York police and Pinkerton branch offices. But it was to be another year before either was caught.

In February of 1881, Pinkerton trailed a Butch McCarty to a hotel on the outskirts of Brooklyn. Pinkerton agents were stationed in a stone yard near Twenty-fourth Street and Fourth Avenue. A sleigh approached with two men inside. An agent grabbed the reins, and Bob Pinkerton leaped into the carriage, thrust a large horse pistol under Leary's nose and announced, "Throw up your hands, John, or suffer the consequences!"

"I guess you have me, Bob," Leary surrendered.

Leary reached the Northampton Jail just as Billy Connors was arrested in Philadelphia. Within a few days the three men were under the watchful eye of Northampton's Sheriff Longley.

Informed of their arrest, Scott wrote a letter to Leary. "As you and our friends have not seen fit to help either Jim or me in prison, we see no recourse but to urge you to turn over the wanted material at the earliest possible moment. For three years we have been here without any word from you. It is now put upon us to urge you to give up the securi-ties, or we shall be forced to return to Northampton and testify against you, guaranteeing you the same twenty-year sentence that befell us. It is simply a matter of delivering the securities, or we shall arrive in Northampton and down you." It was signed, "Bob Scott and Jim Dun-lap."

Leary and Connors at once came to terms with the bank and the Pinkerton agency. A Brooklyn lawyer handed over the securities in three installments, returning over a million dollars in mildewed stocks. A grand jury dismissed the charges against the three, and they retired to Cooney's Nonotuck house to celebrate. They carried the party to the Florence Hotel and set up champagne for all that en-tered. By 6:30 the next morning, they were on the canal road back to New York and freedom.

Five years after the great Northampton robbery the case was officially closed, leaving two men in Charlestown to pay for their crime.

Chapter Eight

The old man with the silver imperial goatee felt the rough bark against his cheek and opened his eyes. The night was dark. A few errant snowflakes floated before his eyes. He woke with a start and dug the gold watch free. Ten minutes after one. He had dozed for no more than seven or eight minutes. "Thank God," he mumbled as he noticed the string in his hand. He rolled the slack back on the roll until he felt there was nothing between him and the trigger of the .38 pistol. He shook his head clear and gave Wellington a careful survey. Satisfied there was no one about, he tightened the string and heard the rewarding explosion.

Wellington, Illinois, slept through the second explosion, even though its savings were in jeopardy. When the old man entered the dry goods store and bank, he found the second set of doors wide open. He slid to his knees before the safe. The pale eyes swam with tears of thanksgiving. It was his for the taking. His reward for remembering his craft.

It had been twenty-five years since the great Northampton burglary, and he hadn't forgotten any of it. Seeing the safe exposed was a great healing for his spirits. That was more important than the money itself. He wasn't certain he could have gone much *longer without it. It was question and answer all in one. It was salvation itself.*

Tears ran down his cheeks as he took the cash and placed it in several Munn envelopes, those with wires inside for quick opening. Each was addressed to his landlady in Chicago. Over two thousand dollars was sealed in five Munn containers. A cigar box with Alexander Pate's initials beckoned, and he gathered it and placed it in the valise. A leather pouch with fifteen dollars in gold coins was also dropped into the grip. Sixty dollars in revenue stamps was added, along with a check for one hundred and twenty dollars on Hamilton and Cunningham's Bank in Watseka. He took it all, though he wasn't completely sure of what use some of it was. It rightfully belonged to him and, as spoils, belonged in his grip.

It was after two when he tossed the grip on the rented wagon and rode toward the Watseka station.

The long winter that followed the release of Connors, Leary and Draper saw no change in the prisoners' confinement. Word reached them that the case had finally been settled with their cooperation and that their help would be given its "proper weight."

Mary Scott's Chrismas visit was a bleak affair. Her husband coughed continually and left for the latrine several times during her visit.

"He looks terrible," she told Dunlap.

"He's not been too well," Dunlap agreed, though he avoided telling her Scott had collapsed several times in the Waring Hat shop where they now labored. "The food's been very poor lately. It could be just a bad cold."

"But he's been coughing like that for almost a year now! Isn't there a doctor? Isn't there someone who could see to his condition?"

"We have an infirmary," Jim explained, though he avoided mentioning it was common practice for the guards to leave the windows open to discourage malingering. He avoided mentioning that Scott dreaded the place, as did most inmates.

"I'll remind him to see the doctor again," he smiled.

"He looks terrible—his spirits seem so low."

"We've been waiting news of our sentence. Nine months now and there's been no word! I don't understand it! Bob's worried the bank will go back on their promise to help us!"

"They couldn't do that!" Mary cried. "Without your help they would have lost everything!"

Dunlap managed a smile. "I'm sure these things take time. . . And you, dear Mary, how are you doing?"

"I have a pension at a very nice boarding house run by Mrs McGroarty." She smiled bravely. "She's a lovely woman, really. teach a few piano lessons. . . . " Then she added brightly, "I've been thinking of opening a millinery shop, just until Bob's set free."

"That's a wonderful idea! If you need any money," he whispered "you know where to find it."

She blushed slightly. "The truth is, Jim . . . I've used a great portion of your savings already. I'm ashamed to admit that your account has been severely depleted."

"No matter," he chuckled. "It's of no use to me here. Use any portion of it you wish. Use it all!"

She rummaged in her purse and passed him the most cherished item of all. "Ten-cent tobacco papers!" he cried in surprise. "You dear girl!"

Scott emerged from the latrine. He held the door unsteadily, the ever-present cloth pressed to his lips.

"Oh dear," she whimpered in anguish.

"He truly has me worried. That tremendous fire that used to burn within him seems quenched. He's always been quick to argue . . now. . . . He desperately needs reassurance that everything's going to be all right. It can't come from me, dear Mary, for I am in no position to learn of news from the outside. But if you were to tell him there was a great deal of hope for a speedy release, it might do wonders for his health."

They turned to watch Scott approach. The broad shoulders were no longer squared, the head hung listlessly against his sunken chest The muscle tone had vanished from his sturdy frame, and he looked a man pushing ninety.

Dunlap rose to assist Scott to the bench. "Mary was just saying she's heard from Oscar Edwards, the bank president! The governor's been told to secure a quick release for the prisoners Scott and Dunlap!"

Scott's blue eyes were gray, the skin white as a china plate. "Is it true?" he asked Mary in wonder.

When Mary could not force the words to complete the lie, Dunlap said, "Of course! There's probably reams of paperwork and signatures needed! Isn't that right, Mary?"

She nodded slowly, then more rapidly.

"Things like this take time!" Dunlap insisted.

"Dear Robert," she managed, "please give it time."

"Bob's always been short on patience," Dunlap scoffed. "It's always been hurry, hurry, hurry with him."

"Just a little longer," she pleaded.

Bob began to cough into the rag while they waited, patiently. The hacking weakened him. "Please tell them to hurry," he whispered.

Eight weeks later, Bob Scott collapsed in the hat shop, and this time no amount of attention would revive him. Jim Dunlap and a black stitcher named Pierre Alexis were given permission to hurry the stricken man to the infirmary. It was several days before Dunlap was granted a visit. He found his friend wrapped in blankets against a bitter gale blowing in through the open windows.

He was about to close them when the guard warned, "You'll leave those open if you know what's good for you!"

"My friend is very sick!"

"Not as sick as you'll be if I have to repeat my order!"

Dunlap relinquished his hold on the window and angrily bent to the bundled figure. "How you feeling?"

The eyes fluttered open in the blankets. "Hello, Jim . . . have they come for us yet?"

"Not yet." He smiled reassuringly. "Any day now. You'll have to hurry and get well before they allow us out of here. They've been telling the people what good care we receive and how well we're fed. We don't want to prove them liars now, do we?"

"How are things in the shop?"

"There was a strike in the cutting room last week," Dunlap whispered, dropping his voice so the guard couldn't hear. "All the windows were broken in protest of conditions, and someone ran through the machine shop and smashed a lot of the equipment. The hat shop and blacksmith shop suffered the same punishment. The situation's a bad one; the men are on the point of rebellion."

Scott smiled in satisfaction. "How are the hogs doing?"

Warden Chamberlain's pet project was five hundred hogs that were raised on prison fare. Most everyone knew the food was better suited to the animals, since they ate the better part of it.

"They're getting fatter than we are," Dunlap laughed.

"Love to butcher one. . . . Love to have one of those thick ham steaks right now. . . . "

A cane was inserted between their faces. "Time's up!" the guard barked.

"I have to go. I'll be back first chance I can. Is there anything you want?"

"Heat . . . " Scott coughed.

Outside the room he could still hear the coughing until it grew too weak to carry down the hall.

The prison was at explosion point. The warden no longer dared enter the yard without a pistol in his pocket. Word was passed from shop to shop, "Refuse the food," "Don't eat the swill," "Take only the bread." The evening meal was completely boycotted and was sent to the warden's hogs. The morning breakfast received the same treatment. A riot broke out in the wood shop. Inmates attacked the milling machines and smashed the windows. Encouraged by their actions, other shops followed suit, venting their anger on the machinery and buildings, smashing anything that belonged to the system and everything within sight. At the Sunday service, the warden was openly booed as he took the pulpit, and several hundred men began stamping their feet, drowning his words.

The rebellion festered in the shops. Hides were ruined with sharp knives, and chisels gashed wood stock until it was unusable. The prisoners fought back in the only way they knew against the poor food, long hours and brutal treatment by the guards.

A fire was set in the Waring Hat shop and all the guards turned out to fight it. But the flames did their duty—shop, building and goods inside were totally destroyed.

A new warden named Earle was appointed, and the rebellion simmered on the back burners while Earle made sweeping changes. Gradually he won enough confidence and the upheaval ended and the shops were put back in order.

Scott spent the revolt in the infirmary. When the new warden allowed Dunlap to visit, Bob told him, "I'm going over the wall, Jim. I can't take it here any longer."

"Good idea!" Dunlap agreed enthusiastically. "Get your strength back, and we'll make the break."

"I can't wait, Jim."

"You have to have your strength, man! How far would we get with you in this condition? I'll get in touch with Billy and have him meet us with some fast horses. I wish I'd thought of going over the wall!"

"Now you know why it was always the Scott-Dunlap Ring."

"How could I forget you were the brains of the group."

A thin index finger snaked out from the blankets, trembling in the direction of the newly closed windows. "We can get over the walls easily from here."

"I think you're right."

"What month is this?"

"April."

"What year?"

"1882."

Scott blinked in confusion. "It hasn't been five years yet?"

"Not till January 1. Five years New Year's Day."

"Fifteen to go. . . . We're not even halfway there. . . . "

"Old Moore says the first five are the hardest."

"More than fifteen to go. . . . "

"Unless you get strong enough so we can go over the wall."

A tear slipped from Scott's eye and ran down the almost transparent skin. "I don't want to die in here, Jim."

"You won't," Dunlap promised, choking back his own feelings.

"Time's up, Dunlap!"

* * *

"Consumption," the prison doctor said with finality. "Fresh
air . . . good food . . . a proper diet and plenty of rest and he
might have made it."

Dunlap petitioned the new warden for permission to spend his
nights at Scott's side. Warden Earle agreed, provided Dunlap was at
his shop post first thing each morning.

It was obvious to Jim that Scott had lost the will to live, and no ruse
of momentary freedom would alter the fact that he was dying. A letter
was sent Mary in New York, urging her to come with all possible
haste. It suggested that Scott's mother in Warsaw, Illinois, be con-
tacted, if she wished to see her son alive.

Mary Scott arrived, and Warden Earle allowed her to spend from
nine to six each day with the dying man.

Scott's mother arrived a few days later and made arrangements for
a shroud and casket.

Mary told Dunlap, "He doesn't want to die in here. Help me, Jim."

"Perhaps," Chaplain Barnes suggested, "the governor might allow
a pardon for a dying man. It's been known to happen."

"It could never get through the governor's office in time," Dunlap
stated flatly. "These things take months."

"I can get it through!" Mary announced with fierce determination.
"I'll sit on the steps of his home if need be!"

"Ask the Governor for permission to move Scott to my home in the
meantime," the chaplain urged her.

"Where will I find this man?" she stormed, "this governor?"

"We had 'em fooled, Jim . . . "

"Aye, Bob, that we did."

"We were a good team."

"The best. Even Pinkerton himself said that."

"He did?"

"He said the Scott-Dunlap Ring was the very best. Who can argue
with such an authority!"

" . . . he would know, all right. . . . "

"He's a square fellow, that one."

" . . .my mother . . . where's my mother?"

"She left last week. Went back to Warsaw."

"Oh . . . "

"She'll see you next visiting day."

Scott nodded agreeably. Then he lolled off to sleep for a few minutes before something snatched him back. His eyes went wide until he saw Dunlap's face, then he visibly relaxed. "We almost made it."

"Almost made it," Dunlap answered uncertainly.

"How did we get to the gate?" Scott wondered.

"The gate?" Jim looked to the doctor, who indicated Scott might be delirious. "Oh, that was easy!"

"They wouldn't have caught us if I'd remembered to bring my shoes."

"It was my fault. I should have remembered them."

" . . . how did we get out?"

"I bribed a guard."

"Which one?"

"Ah . . . one of the new ones. You don't know him."

"I had those oysters you brought me . . . and a big thick steak . . . and they took 'em from me."

"I'll get them back, Bob. You just rest now."

Later he asked, "Is Mary back yet?"

"Not yet. She's due at any moment."

"Tell me when she returns."

"She'll have a big surprise, you'll see."

"The pardon?"

"I think so!"

Scott sighed with relief. "You were right, Jim—dear God, you were always right."

"I wish I had been, Bob. That I do. You know, there was a detective here last week. He wanted to know if we robbed the Uxbridge bank in '72."

Scott smiled, his eyes closed, head buried deep in the new pillow the chaplain had provided.

"I told him there happened to be a few banks robbed that we had nothing to do with."

"If we robbed all the banks they said . . . we would have been too busy ever to spend the money. . . . What happened to all the money?"

"I guess we spent it."

"I guess we did."

"So, do you know what I said to this detective?"

"What detective?"

"The one from the Uxbridge bank! I asked this fellow how much was missing from Uxbridge. 'Fourteen thousand!' says he. 'Fourteen thousand?' says I, very angry. 'Why, sir!' I says. 'We don't turn off no fourteen-thousand-dollar piggy banks!'"

Scott's face lit up brightly. He rolled his eyes to the ceiling in silent laughter.

"Course I didn't tell him about Pittston, where we burned all that damn money and would have been glad to get fourteen thousand."

Scott clutched his chest in agony.

"Sorry, Bob, I didn't think it would hurt you to laugh."

Later, Bob asked, "Where's Mary?"

"Any minute now, Bob. She's with the governor hurrying that pardon along. It's finally come through."

Scott's breath came in whimpers, and he forced himself to smile painfully. "I won't die in here."

"Hell, Bob, you and Mary'll be in the park in no time. A good trotter in harness, everybody looking at the dashing couple, wondering who they are to afford such a fine livery and animal. You just wait and see—hang on just a while longer, Bob."

"I'm trying, Jim. . . . I'm really trying."

It was dark before Mary returned. Scott lay open-mouthed on the cot, his thin, veined hand in Dunlap's. The chaplain and doctor rose when she entered the corridor, flying past the other patients, skirts and petticoats rustling, blonde hair disheveled. She shook her head in disappointment, bitterly repeating the governor's words, "You will hear from me soon."

Dunlap shook his head. He took her shawl and offered up his chair. He left her with her pink cheek pressed against the back of Bob's hand. Closing the doors, he stepped out into the entry hall. A guard looked up from his newspaper. Dunlap trembled, "May I smoke, Mr. Chaney?"

"Go ahead, Jim."

"Thank you, sir." He lit a butt harbored in his shirt pocket, the hand unsteady, the smoke catching in his throat.

Near midnight, Dunlap heard the chaplain intoning his litany of death. The door opened, and Mary stumbled into the entry hall, the doctor at her elbow.

Her voice trembled. "He's dead, Jim . . . he's just thirty-two years old . . . and he's dead."

The words stunned him. He'd spent several months preparing for this possibility, but the words struck him with surprising impact. It was just as though it were all a complete surprise. "I'm truly sorry. . . ."

The perpetual little girl pout was missing from her lips. Her mouth was hard. "He made me promise to do whatever was in my power to help you, Jim. And I'll help you, though God help me for saying this, I wish it were you in there instead of him."

"So do I," he offered.

She pulled the shawl tight around her shoulders, seeking comfort and solace in its rough warmth. "He said it was all his fault. . . .I should work for your pardon." She touched the stray blonde hairs, absently tucking them into position. "I'll wire his mother. . . . He wanted to be buried in Warsaw, near his home. She should be told he's on his way. She gets his body, and I get you, Jim. Is that a fair trade for a young widow?"

"I'm sorry, Mary. Don't worry about me, I'll be all right."

They were interrupted by footsteps. A guard arrived, puffing heavily. He doffed his cap and presented Mary with an envelope.

"What is this?" she asked, leaving it unopened in her palm.

"Permission to move the prisoner Scott to the chaplain's home, ma'am."

Her head bobbed silently. The tears she so carefully contained spilled over as Dunlap folded her against his chest.

"Are we too late, Jim?" the guard asked, casting a quick glance down the corridor where the chaplain's voice hummed about the cot.

"We're too late, Mr. Willis, but thank you."

"I'm terribly sorry, ma'am."

Dunlap was at the window in the hat shop when the carriage rolled into the yard. The plain pine coffin bounced in protest against the hurried exit. Mary sat firmly erect near the driver as the gates were swung open.

Deputy Erskine came to Dunlap's side, and the two watched as the wagon went through the gates and the heavy doors were walked shut behind it.

"Might that be Bob Scott?"

"Yes, sir. What day is this, sir?"

"April 26, Jim."

"Thank you, sir."

The guard turned his attention to the sky, twisting his neck past the stitching machine as he leaned in close to the windlow. "It's spring, Jim, can you feel it in the air?"

Dunlap looked up at a sky he had not seen in weeks. "I can't feel a thing, sir. . . ."

On December 29, 1892, ten years, eight months and four days after the death of Robert Scott, the new warden, Lovering, stopped in the corridor outside a small cell.

"Jim, your pardon's come."

Dunlap stared at the man in disbelief, then took a deep breath and bowed his head. "Well, I'm glad it's come at last," he whispered.

He had served all but one year of his sentence; the dream of an early release vanished years before. It was, without doubt, the severest sentence offered any of the bankies. Big Jim Burns got three years. Langdon Moore, only six. George White served seven; and none of these men had aided the bank in seeing that the money was returned.

He was led into the rotunda of the warden's office, where a large group of people surprised him. His entrance caused a stir among the newsmen present. Dunlap was not prepared for this. He ran his fingers through his graying hair and swallowed nervously, his eyes

ixed to the floor. Fifteen years of training wouldn't allow him to look
anyone in the eye. To do so in the shop or corridors was punishable by
days of solitary confinement.

A plump Mary Scott Rowlands, since remarried to a St. Louis businessman and hotel keeper for almost nine years, staged the event
carefully. Newsmen were kept to one side while she went forward and
stood between the warden and Jim.

"Does he know, warden?" a newsman shouted, as the press corps
elbowed for advantage.

"Yes, I told him myself," Lovering said. "I've been expecting this,
so it was no real surprise for me. Jim was real close to being pardoned
last year."

"Was it a surprise, Jim?" someone asked.

"What's your feeling at this moment, Mr. Dunlap?" another asked.

Dunlap could only stare at the floor and shrug, completely unpre-
pared for all the attention.

"About a fortnight ago," the warden said proudly, "a feeling that
Dunlap would be pardoned came over me. I went to him and said,
Jim, I don't want to raise your hopes again for fear of disappointment, but I've got a feeling you're going to get out before the first of
the year and I want you to look respectable when you go.' As you can
see, he's a rather large man and cannot wear the usual prison dis-
charge suit. 'So run over to the tailor's and have a new suit made for
you. Then if your pardon comes suddenly, you'll be all ready, and if it
don't, your time will be up in a year, and I guess the moths won't eat
it.'"

When the warden had finished, Mary led a small applause that
caught Dunlap off guard. He wasn't sure whether they were clapping
for the warden or him.

"How about a statement, Mr. Dunlap?" several cried.

"Say something, Jim," Mary urged.

Dunlap lifted his eyes for only an instant. "Thank you."

"What do you say to a woman who worked so hard for your release,
Mr. Dunlap?"

The man was right, Dunlap thought. Each year for the past three
years, Mary had led the fight to have him paroled, but each attempt
had ended in failure. Mary tugged his arm, prompting him to speak.

He cleared his throat. "I am too overcome . . . to give proper ex
pression of my gratitude . . . for your efforts on my behalf." He fel
silent, and Mary nudged him again. With his attention glued to an oal
peg in the floor, he said, "It is true my time was nearly up, but it i
nonetheless welcome to me." He fumbled in his pocket for a handker
chief; the peg swam in his vision. He refolded the cloth as everyon
waited. He was too ashamed to blow his nose. He wiped at his eyes a
he tried to collect his thoughts.

Several times he tried to speak, but words eluded him. Finall
Mary took his arm and turned him to face her. To her he said softly
"I am glad . . . that you find so much satisfaction in knowing tha
your efforts were not extended in vain." He wiped at his eyes. "To thi
dear woman, I owe much . . . and I will try and repay . . . as fa
as possible . . . the obligation."

He began to weep openly, unable to go on. He extended his hand t
the newsmen in appreciation. He took Mary's hand and kissed it a
someone slid a chair to this legs, and he collapsed in unashamed hap
piness.

Mary bent to one knee, taking great care to see that the newsme
were able to see what was to transpire. She took something out of he
purse and held it ceremoniously between her fingers. "Mr. Dunlap,"
she said softly, as the newsmen pressed closer, "my mission has bee
fulfilled. If it had been fifty years instead of fifteen, I would hav
worked with as much energy. I had about given up hope, but I mean
to be true to the promise I made my dying husband."

Taking his right hand gently in hers, she placed a thin gold rin
with a cameo setting on his finger. "My husband wanted you to hav
this, his ring, on your day of freedom." Then she broke down in tear
as the *New York World* reporter jotted furiously.

Two nights later, New Year's Eve, the *New York Times* sent a re
porter to 123 Fifth Avenue to get a statement from the recentl
released bank robber James Dunlap. He rang the bell and had it an
swered by a woman he described as, "a plump little woman, below th
average height, blonde hair with large expressive eyes, and a good
natured, rather attractive face."

"Where might I find Mr. Dunlap?"

"I do not think you'll be able to find Mr. Dunlap tonight," she said with a twinkle in her bright eyes. "He is stowed away where he will have some quiet."

The reporter realized he was speaking with Mary Scott Rowlands and began to take notes.

"He has heart disease," she said slowly, allowing him time to record her words. "He wants to be in a place where he can have absolute rest. Tonight he is in such a place. During the fifteen years he was in prison, he has only talked with one person. All he would like me to tell you is that he feels deeply grateful to all who interested themselves in securing his pardon."

"Has he any plans for the future?"

"I think not," she smiled. "Today is the first day in his new life. He told me it seemed like a dream to him. He's like Rip Van Winkle after his long sleep." She began to laugh as she waited for the pencil to stop. "Why, in Boston, he stared at the big buildings like a child! So you can imagine how he regarded the great changes made in the appearance of things in New York since 1877."

"What about money, Mrs. Rowlands? Has he any means?"

"He was a soldier in the late war, and has a considerable sum in the form of pension money due him. The matter of money need not trouble him; as long as we have a good home here, he is welcome to share it until he can get back on his feet again."

"Did you ever receive any assistance from Tom Draper, Billy Connors or Red Leary?"

The good-natured smile faded. "No! They did not do a single thing in aiding me to secure Mr. Dunlap's pardon! On the contrary, I think they tried to keep him in prison! Leary is dead now some six years, hit on the head with a brick, the foolish man. And I've heard that both Connors and Draper have money."

"Is Dunlap likely to resume friendly relations with these men?"

"No!" she cried indignantly. "He does not want to know them! In prison for nearly sixteen years, he's had a chance to find out who his friends were. Draper and Connors were not among them!"

"Could you tell me, who helped you secure the pardon?"

"General Sherman, for one. He was one of Mr. Dunlap's command-

ing officers. He knew that Mr. Dunlap had been wounded twice an
was quite sympathetic. Ex-Governor Long of Massachusetts wa
another. Robert Pinkerton . . . the former sheriff of Northampton
Mr. Longley. A bank president from St. Louis . . . and there wa
Mr. Dunlap's good behavior trimming his sentence."

"Mrs. Rowlands, what about the promise made your late husban
and Mr. Dunlap by the Northampton Bank authorities?"

"A promise was made to my husband," she bristled, "and Mr. Dun
lap—an implied promise—that they would be released if the mone
was returned. And that was why all the money was returned! Afte
that, Mr. Oscar Edwards, president of the Northampton Bank, too
no interest in the prisoners. I worked alone on the case because
made a promise to my dying husband. And for that reason, I knev
that Mr. Dunlap, who had never been a criminal, was a victim o
Leary and the others. I am glad this thing is over, because it bee
a great strain on me. I will sleep easier tonight than I have for a lon
time."

Dunlap was at the upstairs window when he heard the door close
After the reporter left, he dropped a cigarette butt to the snow below
He opened and closed the window several times, waving the room fre
of smoke with a newspaper. Then he closed the window and raced th
footsteps to his bed. When the door opened, he was lying on the bed
one hand across his eyes and breathing deeply. She entered an
tucked the covers to his chin. He waited till she was gone before h
dropped the hand from his face.

Dunlap slipped from the covers and sat by the window overlookin
Fifth Avenue. Another cigarette was lit, the window opened, admit
ting a few stray snowflakes. He caught them in his hand, destroyin
them with his warmth. Below him, sleighs jangled up the street, an
he marveled at the world before him.

It took Dunlap several weeks to convince Mary he would be bette
suited to a small pension in New York and out of her home. Mar
fought him with every conceivable argument, but Dunlap persiste
and moved into a tiny apartment. Within the week he visited th
Pinkerton office and left a note for Bob Pinkerton, thanking him fo
all the effort on his behalf.

Three days later he was awakened in his new quarters by the sound of keys jingling in the hall. The door opened, and Mary was admitted by the housekeeper. She was in a great state of excitement. She threw herself on the foot of the bed as Dunlap struggled to open his eyes.

"Jim!" she exclaimed, trying to catch her breath. "The most *marvelous* idea!"

"What time is it, Mary?"

"There's a man, a Mr. Green, he wants to promote your stage career!"

"What?" he asked, looking at her out of one eye.

"Your stage career, Mr. Dunlap!"

"What stage, Mary?"

"Mr. Green has the most marvelous idea! You will play yourself in a drama about the Northampton burglary! Isn't that marvelous?"

"A stage play?" he asked, the quilt tugged tight against his chest.

"Of course I told him that Bob had left a manuscript with all the actual events recalled. But I insisted whoever plays Bob will have to be tall . . . and very handsome."

"What time is it?" he asked in bewilderment.

She bounded from the bed and threw open the drapes, flinging her arms wide to embrace the sunlight. "James Dunlap! the King of the Bank Robbers, starring in *The Great Northampton Bank Robbery!*"

"I don't know, Mary," he said, squinting at the intolerable light assaulting his eyes and the words attacking his senses. "I don't know about this."

She rushed back to the bed and hugged him excitedly. "Oh, Jim! It will be perfect! Mr. Green thinks that, of course, I should play Bob's wife!"

"Of course."

"Mr. Green knows some fine actors to play Mr. and Mrs. Whittelsey, the cashier and his wife."

"I don't know about a play, Mary."

"Oh, Mr. Dunlap! You'll be perfect in the part! You would need a little coaching from me, of course. Voice. Projection."

"Voice?"

"Of course, I'll help you all I can! I told Mr. Green that what is important here is that it be simply not a display. It should have . . . stature! Tragedy! It should be about the evil in men! We'll need an especially fine actor to play the villain, William Edson. And there should be a lesson to be learned from Billy Connors, Red Leary and Tom Draper. We should show these men who abandon their comrades after introducing them to a life of crime. We are the tragic victims, Jim!"

"We are?"

"The play will end with me weeping while you and Bob are being led away by Sheriff Longley. Betrayed by your friends and comrades! Left to your fate by this unholy alliance!"

"Maybe we should think about this awhile—"

"Do you think it would be better if I was shown leading the fight for your freedom? Alone? Abandoned?"

"Either way," he shrugged helplessly.

Slowly and dramatically she sank from the bed to the carpet, her hands clutching her ample bosom, one hand extended imploringly. He followed her hand, gazing intently into the dark corner above the wash basin. Then just as suddenly, she bounded to her feet and shouted, "Won't it be marvelous, Jim?"

Jim was thunderstruck.

"You'll have to work very closely with the playwright. The lines should be exactly as they happened. I'll probably write my own, since I alone know what I went through. I will of course assist you in the correct selection of wardrobe." She held the hem of her blue dress against the light from the window.

He suddenly realized the enormity of it. "But, Mary, you know I've never acted before!"

"You'll be wonderful!" she said into his mirror, her fingers chasing errant strands into position atop her head.

"Have an experienced actor play my part!" Dunlap cried. "We were wearing masks anyways, so who will know the difference?"

"The masks!" she shrieked in horror. "We can't hide your face from a paying audience! They must be able to see your face!"

"But I was masked! Otherwise, Whittelsey would have recognized us!"

"Jim," she chided him gently, "the audience will be paying to see us. We can't hide our faces now, can we?"

"But that's the way it happened, Mary!"

"Then we will simply take poetic liberties. It's done all the time."

"This troubles me, Mary."

"Nonsense!" she laughed, gathering her things. "Stage fright is a common phobia. You don't see me worried, do you? Hurry and dress now, dear Jim. We have a very important appointment with Mr. Green."

Mary's announcement to the press made them overnight celebrities. Dunlap found there was nowhere he could hide. Her vision of fame took control of them. Most of the eastern papers were critical of his plans, laying the blame for the whole scheme with Dunlap. One paper even denounced the playwright as a "dentist from Madison Avenue." One of the Massachusetts papers noted: "Since the first attempt failed in Northampton, Dunlap might have better luck with the second." It guaranteed its reading public that the attempt to put the robbery "on the boards" was certainly safer.

Bank officials across the nation began to worry that an enthralled audience might learn how easily the Northampton Bank had been robbed. An angry protest sped to the governor of Massachusetts. Oscar Edwards from Northampton joined other banking officers in demanding that Dunlap not be allowed to demonstrate just how easily a bank might be robbed.

A hand-delivered letter from Governor Russel's office made it clear that Dunlap's parole was in jeopardy, should he continue with this folly. Much to Mary's disappointment, but Dunlap's relief, the acting career of the King of the Bank Robbers was over.

But Mary was undaunted. Not a few weeks later she decided a restaurant fronted by the King of the Bank Robbers might draw considerable business. Unable to dissuade her, Dunlap borrowed $2,000 from William and Robert Pinkerton and slipped away to Chicago, his intent, to open a saloon. Within a short time, he proved better bankie than businessman, and the saloon at 219 Wabash foundered, then went under. Having lost Pinkertons' money, Mary hot on his heels again, he borrowed train fare from Robert Pinkerton and headed for Portland, Maine. It would be the first of many flights to avoid Mary's protection.

Chapter Nine

The old man with the silver imperial goatee examined his pocket watch: 7:45. The train sounded its whistle, and the first imperceptible nudge of the wheels was felt along the cars. Outside the window, the Watseka, Illinois, firemen were pulling on their new rubber coats and aluminum helmets as the train gathered speed. The fire company's new mockingbird whistle sounded, and the train blew its reply.

He was just ninety-four miles from home on the Chicago and Eastern Illinois line. By nightfall he would be in his apartment on Wabash Avenue, to sleep as he had not slept in years.

He had selected a seat next to an elderly woman, in case the train should be boarded by detectives. She was well dressed, gray-haired and could easily pass for his wife.

"I have grandchildren in Chicago," she offered.

He nodded, smiling attentively, though he was still in a great state of excitement and found it difficult to completely relax. The smell of the Hazard powder was still in his nose, as intoxicating to his senses as a beautiful woman's expensive perfume. He closed his eyes in the swaying coach, savoring the delightful aroma.

"Are you retired?" the woman asked, nudging him back to reality.

"I beg your pardon?" he smiled. "My thoughts were elsewhere."

"Are you retired?"

He took the watch from his vest, eight o'clock, the cashier, Webster, would just now be inserting the key to the Pate Bank. He snapped the case shut. "I was retired."

"Then this is a business trip?"

He grinned and stroked the silver beard and moustache. "It didn't start out that way, but as fortune would have it, I made a small transaction which has greatly benefited my spirit as well as my pocket."

"How nice." She smiled sweetly.

"Yes . . . isn't it," he laughed.

A Parmalee hansom took him to his quarters at 1152 Wabash Avenue. He tipped the driver as a harsh March wind blew in off the lake. His body ached as he followed the driver up the steps to the Follansbee Flats. The man waited patiently with the luggage as he rang for the landlady, Mrs. Devine. When she failed to answer, he withdrew his keys and examined several before selecting one for the door.

"Put them in the hall," he told the driver.

The man departed, leaving him to carry his own grip to Apartment 21. He would gather his clothing in the morning. It was only six P.M., but it had been a long night, and he longed for nothing more than his own bed and a good night's rest.

He sat the grip on the floor outside his door as he tried to find his key. The door opened before the key had been fully inserted. Three man sat patiently waiting, while a fourth held the door for him. He recognized three of them immediately and slid the grip from view with his foot.

Mrs. Devine stepped into the lamplight and said nervously, "I told them you were at Billy Boyle's Chophouse."

He looked beyond the men and saw the burglary tools from his closet spilled about the floor.

"Hello, Jim," one of them said rather grimly.

"Sergeant O'Keefe!" he recovered, trying to show pleased astonishment as he closed the door against the valise in the hall. "What a nice surprise!"

"Is it now?" O'Keefe asked, motioning Mrs. Devine to leave. "You know Detectives Murtaugh, Culhane and Connick?"

"Of course!" he said expansively, as he shrugged from his coat trying to ignore the worried looks of the departing housekeeper "Don't they always pay me a visit everytime somebody robs a post office or grocery store!" he smiled.

Culhane saw Mrs. Devine out and returned to the room with the grip.

"Would you mind telling us where you've been?"

Dunlap saw Culhane and Connick bending at the valise. They removed the shirts stored above the prize. "I took a trip . . . went up to Warsaw . . . I have a friend buried there." He had been surprised to find two stones marking Scott's grave at the Wythe Congregational Cemetery. One was a small military marker that read, "Robert C. Scott. 'H' Company, 13th U.S. Infantry. Born May 29, 1849 Died Apr. 25, 1882." Then there were the words, "Gone but not forgotten." The other had been a simple four-foot obelisk.

"I'm sorry," Dunlap explained, tugging nervously at the silver beard. "What did you say?"

The cigar box was removed, the gold initials sparkling as the box was passed to O'Keefe. "These wouldn't be your initials on the box would they, Jim?"

O'Keefe had asked him a question, but Dunlap was unable to think clearly. The room was oppressively hot, and he was still preoccupied with the snow-capped obelisk in Warsaw. He couldn't admit eighteen years had passed since that horrible night in the infirmary. That his life had continued still amazed him.

O'Keefe had his arm, shaking him back to the stifling room. Jim saw the leather pouch juggled in Connick's hand, the drill bits in Murtaugh's palm. There was still cement from the Hall safe clinging to the flutes.

"These are not your initials, Jim."

He gulped nervously, wishing he could send them away, to return when his brain was rested and he could match wits with them. They had him at a distinct disadvantage. He had been up all night, forty-eight hours since the old gray head last touched a pillow.

"Tell the truth, Jim."

"No . . . they're not mine."

O'Keefe shook his head sadly. He tucked the damaging box under his arm as he produced a pair of chrome handcuffs.

"I guess it's the toils," Dunlap whispered.

"Can we do this peaceably, Jim?"

Dunlap nodded weakly. "I guess there's enough here to send me over the road several times."

Culhane chuckled as he restored everything to the valise and snapped it shut. "We've got everything we need."

Dunlap eyed the metal closing about his wrists. "It's all up with me, I guess—hard luck."

The men gathered the evidence and went out the door, leaving Dunlap to follow with O'Keefe. The slim detective paused at the door and asked, "Why did you risk it all for such a paltry sum?"

Dunlap searched the halls for an answer. "I don't know. . . ."

"It'll go hard on you."

"I know."

"You won't tell my why?"

Dunlap could only shrug.

He was led downstairs and helped into a carriage bound for the Harrison Street station. O'Keefe helped him with his hat after they were seated.

"I went to visit Bob Scott's grave," he said aloud for no particular reason.

O'Keefe watched him closely.

"I went because I was tired of being alone. I needed someone to talk to—someone I thought would understand."

"But you have friends."

"No . . . they're all gone except me. It's no good to be the last. . . . Jimmy Hope . . . Paper Collar Joe's in London . . . a millionaire, I hear tell . . . Tom O'Brien killed Kid Waddell in Paris. . . . Tom's on Devil's Island. . . . I wanted Bob to know he was the lucky one. . . . I guess that's when I first thought about doing it."

"But you took your tools with you, Jim," O'Keefe said gently. "That sounds to me like you had already decided."

Dunlap looked at O'Keefe in surprise. "I guess I had," he said slowly, giving it the full weight of his tired brain.

"What would Bob Scott have said if he could see you now?"

"He would say, 'You've made a mess of it.'"

O'Keefe was silent for several minutes. Then he leaned in close and whispered, "I don't think he'd say that at all."

"You don't?"

"No." O'Keefe slid down in the seat, smiling at Dunlap as he said, "You only made one mistake, Jim, you left no clues! Hell, that's the trademark of only one man I know of!"

Dunlap looked bewildered. "It is?"

"Clean as a toothbrush! I knew immediately only one man could have done that job!"

Dunlap began to shake his head.

"You're just too damn good, Jim! And that's God's truth!"

Dunlap felt tears rising. He sniffed audibly and turned away to the street. "Thank you, Mr. O'Keefe . . . thank you very much."

On November 17, 1900, an Illinois jury sentenced the man described by the *Chicago Times Herald* as the "King of the Robbers" to twenty years at Joliet Prison for his confessed guilt in the Pate Bank burglary. The press crowed that the public had seen the last of James Dunlap.

Yet, three years and one month later, Robert Pinkerton went to the aid of his stricken nemesis and secured a parole for Jim Dunlap.

On December 7, 1903, the inner door to the yard at Joliet opened and prisoner number 4082 advanced into a cold, wintery day.

The young guard watched him feeling with his cane as he crossed the large open area to the outside gate. He found it difficult to believe that this ancient man in the ill-fitting suit was the notoriuos "King of the Robbers." But he had to admit the man was well liked by every one, including the guards themselves.

He waited patiently as the prisoner, almost totally blind now some said, tapped his way slowly across the yard. A badly damaged heart and loss of vision had prompted Pinkerton to pull a few strings. This seemed sensible to the young guard. There was no use in keeping a crippled man in prison, much less a blind one—though he found it hard to believe that this old man approaching could even open a box of dry goods without seriously damaging the contents, much less a safe.

There was also talk that prisoner 4082 would not last out the new year. But he was a new guard, not privy to the gossip of the upper echelon.

Dunlap presented his pass, and the guard read it extra slowly. It was taken to the log book, where the time and permit number were entered.

"It's a big day for you, Mr. Dunlap."

"Yes, sir."

"We won't be seeing you again, I hope."

"Oh no, sir."

The guard passed the permit back to Dunlap. When the man didn't see the hand extended before him, the guard placed it directly in his palm. "Oh, thank you," the former prisoner whispered, tucking the paper into a pocket in his baggy coat.

The guard opened the door in the large gate, and Dunlap sent his cane against it to find the opening. The guard shook his head and took the frail elbow to assist him over the metal threshold.

Dunlap stopped on the other side, took several small steps and turned back toward the guard. "Is the press here?"

The guard looked out on the empty street, amused that Dunlap would think himself worthy of a press reception. "No," he chuckled, "there's no press here."

"Thank God," Dunlap sighed. He waved the cane toward the street. "Is there anyone here for me?"

"Not that I can see. Can you find your way to the station?"

"I think so."

"Goodbye, Mr. Dunlap. I hope we won't ever see you again, and good luck."

"Goodbye, sir. Thank you for all your help."

The guard pulled the heavy door closed and locked it securely, thinking that the rumor had been right—the man wouldn't last the year.

Dunlap heard the door close and felt a shudder chase up his spine. He sighed loudly, inhaled the fresh air and sent the cane before him tapping and swinging a clear path to whereever the station might be. He'd gone less than a block, eyes bent to the ground, when a voice stopped him. "Hello, Jim."

Her hair was totally gray and a few pounds had been added over the

years, but there was no mistaking that sweet smile. "Mary?" he questioned in disbelief.

She came into his arms and began to weep. She held him tight,
forcing him to join her, and he wept openly. She repeatedly petted the
thin, gaunt frame beneath the ill-fitting coat. "I didn't think you'd
recognize me," she told him.

He hugged her tightly, saying "Mary, Mary," against her hair.

"I didn't think you would be able to see me. They said you were almost completely blind!"

Against her neck he whispered, "Then we won't disappoint them,
will we?"

She pulled back and looked at him closely. She wiped his cheek
with her soft finger, and he caught it and drew it to his mouth, kissing
its length. "You're a fraud!" she whimpered.

"Sshh," he pleaded. "Take my arm now and lead me off as you
might your crippled father. Not too fast, now," he smiled, "just slow
and easy. We wouldn't want them to see my miraculous recovery,
would we?"

"You!" she choked, shaking her hair, beginning to cry anew.
"Shall we go home, Jim?"

"Yes, please," he sobbed.

James Dunlap outlived his friends and enemies.
He died October 4, 1928, at an old soldiers' home
in Virginia, just one month after his eighty-fourth
birthday.